ALSO BY JENNIFER GILMORE

*Golden Country*

# SOMETHING ★ RED

A NOVEL

## JENNIFER GILMORE

SCRIBNER

New York   London   Toronto   Sydney

SCRIBNER
A Division of Simon & Schuster, Inc.
1230 Avenue of the Americas
New York, NY 10020

First Scribner hardcover edition March 2010

SCRIBNER and design are registered trademarks of The Gale Group, Inc.,
used under license by Simon & Schuster, Inc., the publisher of this work.

For information about special discounts for bulk purchases,
please contact Simon & Schuster Special Sales at 1-866-506-1949
or business@simonandschuster.com.

The Simon & Schuster Speakers Bureau can bring authors to your live event.
For more information or to book an event contact the Simon & Schuster Speakers Bureau
at 1-866-248-3049 or visit our website at www.simonspeakers.com.

Manufactured in the United States of America

10  9  8  7  6  5  4  3  2

Library of Congress Control Number: 2009040482

ISBN 978-1-4165-7170-4
ISBN 978-1-4165-7594-8 (ebook)

*For my parents, the Washingtonians*

As for you, fellow independent thinker of the Western Bloc, if you have something sensible to say, don't wait. Shout it out loud right this minute. In twenty years, give or take a spring, your grandchildren will be lying in sandboxes all over the world, their ears to the ground, listening for signals from long ago.

—Grace Paley, "Faith in the Afternoon"

# SOMETHING RED

# CHAPTER 1

# Not Everyone Carried Marbles

**August 25, 1979**

It was hot as hell and Sharon Goldstein knew everyone had to be positively sweltering out back. Her mother was especially intolerant of humidity and boastful that Los Angeles, the paradise that she and her husband had been wrested away from to come here, to *Washington,* did not make its inhabitants bear such humiliating conditions. (What about earthquakes, Nana? Vanessa had said yesterday, but Helen had waved her away.) It was only six o'clock and already the cicadas were screaming.

As Sharon made her way around the kitchen, she pictured each one piling paper-thin sheets of prosciutto (well, not her father, whose newly kosher regime she refused to acknowledge) on melon wedges, and spreading runny Brie on the baguette she'd baked yesterday. Imagining her family eating in the yard bordered by the lit tiki lights pleased her. More, she had to admit, than actually sitting there with them.

The neighborhood sounds of skateboards scraping asphalt and kids playing kick-the-can drifted in through the open doors, and she could see the Farrell girls across the street waving their thin arms in the air so the gnats would go to the highest point, far away from their tanned, freckled faces. As Sharon diced cucumbers and apples for her gazpacho—what made hers special was a garnish of peeled green apples and long slivers of tender basil—she wondered if her idea of an outdoor dinner had been misguided.

"To see Ben off!" she'd told Dennis last month. They'd been lying in bed watching President Carter talk about the energy crisis, and she'd opened her night-table drawer, taken out an emery board, and begun to saw at her nails. *The erosion of our confidence in the future is threatening to destroy the social and the political fabric of America,* Carter had said, and

Sharon had turned to her husband. "Let's have a family dinner for Ben," she'd said. "We'll have your parents and mine, and we'll eat in the backyard. The night before he goes."

"Shh," Dennis said. "I'm *listening* to this."

Sharon hadn't been able to focus on the speech, perhaps because her son's impending departure had caused alarm, or was it a symptom of the general malaise of the country that the president was speaking about? Apathy was not like her; once Sharon had been a woman who had cared about politics deeply. Too deeply, perhaps, and this had led her to flee conservative Los Angeles, her parents' Los Angeles, the one with her father's balding B-movie cronies chewing cigars on the back deck and discussing the HUAC hearings. I don't give one goddamn who goes down, they'd said. Communists? Just ask me. They'd spit names up at the sky, toward the fuzzy line of the San Gabriels. *That* Los Angeles. Sharon had come east to George Washington University, even though Helen said no one smart went to GW, *ever*, and at the end of her junior year Sharon had found herself sitting at a Student Nonviolent Coordinating Committee meeting planning the Freedom Riders' trip from Washington to New Orleans, to register voters and fight Jim Crow in each city along the way.

By summer, Sharon and her roommate, Louise Stein, decided they wanted to accompany the hundreds of other kids, black and white, all ready to sit together at luncheonettes across the South. The Klan was rumored to be waiting in Birmingham to beat Riders, but Sharon and Louise ignored these reports, believing that being together and doing what was right would somehow arm them against terrible violence.

The night before they were to get on that Trailways bus to Mississippi, however, Sharon's father forbade it. Don't you so much as set foot on that bus, he'd phoned to tell her. And Sharon had listened. The next day, she stood at the door gathering her robe at her throat and watched Louise go out into the foggy Georgetown morning alone. She returned not a week later, after a night in jail in Jackson, Mississippi. Sharon had been nearly feral with envy as she'd run her hands along the white insides of Louise's wrists, where the handcuffs had been locked too tight, the blue-black bruises flowering where the metal had pinched her skin.

But Sharon had listened to her father, and instead of fighting for civil rights, she'd dated two doctors, a lawyer, and one potter before settling on Dennis, marrying, and having children.

The night of Carter's speech, though, she thought instead of Benjamin throwing his jockstraps and Merriweather Post concert T-shirts into a green duffel bag and heading north.

"Don't you think a dinner will be nice, D?" Sharon had asked.

*Our people are losing faith,* Carter had said. The phrase had momentarily stopped her menu planning—an elegant barbecue, steak and grilled corn and cold soup and some kind of a summer cobbler. She looked up at the screen and wondered if the president had just read her mind. Lost faith. She had thought then of her father, finding God as if He were a shiny penny he'd come upon along a crowded city street.

It was 1979; only a decade and a half previously, Sharon had been pregnant with Vanessa when Louise had come to D.C. to march for jobs and freedom. As they'd entered the Mall, she handed Sharon a fistful of marbles. So horses will slip and fall and the pigs will be crushed, Louise hissed. Things could get violent, she'd said. Dennis had looked askance as he held Ben high, so he could see just how many people were standing against inequality, and Sharon remembered fingering the marbles, the feel of them pinging against one another along her hips when she moved. They'd given her a sense of reckless power, but she did not let them fall. Sharon was no revolutionary, she knew that now, but she had tried and she had cared profoundly, and she had been so furious at her father that she had fled for the East Coast, but in the end she had not defied him. Yet, she had thought that glorious day, it was not every girl who could say she carried marbles.

Now her faith in the power to make changes in the world felt like a fluid that had been drained from her.

"Okay!" Dennis said. "Please, Sharon." His hand hovered over her wrist to stop her from filing her nails, and Sharon settled back and decided right then: gazpacho.

Now Sharon opened the fridge and lifted the large serving bowl, hugging it to her chest. As she headed out back, she thought that though the outdoor dinner may have been a flawed idea, she had known it would be perfect to have the family sitting together in the backyard, all along the large communal table, the scuffed wood illuminated by lit candles and flickering torches, before Ben became a dot on the horizon and left them all behind.

Benjamin absentmindedly carved at the wooden table with his steak knife until he saw his mother emerge from the porch with a colossal glass bowl of red soup, the screen door slapping behind her. She carried it with the same beaming pride with which she brought out her impeccably browned turkey at Thanksgiving and her tender brisket at Passover, with an air that made it impossible—and unnecessary—to compliment her.

"Borscht!" Tatiana, Dennis's mother, threw her delicate white hands up in delight.

Sharon nudged in between Ben and her father to place the bowl on the table. "Gazpacho," she said. She swished her long hair to one side. "Andalusian gazpacho."

"Well, it looks delicious," Tatti said, nearly wicked, like Natasha on *Bullwinkle,* her Russian accent so intense it always sounded bogus to Ben. She seemed to him to be the very embodiment of Russia; when she rose from her seat, he'd half expect her ass to leave an imprint of a hammer and sickle.

Sharon looked for a moment at the bowl, then shot up and sprinted back into the house, the porch door smacking again behind her.

"From And*alusia,*" Helen said, leaning into Vanessa. "Fancy-pants." She giggled, poking her granddaughter in the side with two of the pearly daggers she called fingernails.

Vanessa bristled, holding her stomach.

Sharon returned with a small bowl of cubed apple, and sliding in next to Benjamin, she began ladling out the deep red soup.

"Here, Dad," she said, sprinkling the tiny cubes of apple and cucumber on the smooth surface, then a few strands of basil.

"Looks lovely, sweetheart," Herbert said.

"It sure does," Dennis's father, Sigmund, said. "You won't be eating this well in college, that's for sure, Ben."

Everyone laughed except Vanessa, who looked around the yard as if she were waiting for someone to pop out of the hedges that separated their property from that of Mrs. Krandle, a thick-ankled woman who lived alone and once caught an eight-year-old Vanessa picking her lilies of the valley. She'd stomped over to the house to complain. I'm sure she'll turn into a fine young woman, Mrs. Krandle had said, but right now, she's stealing and I can't say that bodes well for the future. Soon after, her bushes went up, which, Dennis pointed out, didn't bother him one bit, even if he was opposed on principle to folks being portioned off from one another. When they'd moved in, almost twelve years ago now, Sharon had wanted a fence. Dennis had argued against it first for the expense, and then against the concept altogether. We as people should not be closed off from each other, he'd argued. But now that the hedges were there, the privacy was appreciated.

"You'll have plenty of bagels to eat, that's for sure," Vanessa said, taking the bowl from her mother in both hands. The hedges had concealed much over the years: her sunbathing, Ben squirming around on the hammock with some cheerleader or lacrosse player, two bodies caught in a net, and the parties her parents used to have when she and Ben were young and had to come downstairs to say good night to the red-faced, slurring guests. This summer Vanessa was grateful that her awkward first embraces had been obscured. "How much oil is in here, Mom?" she asked, looking into the bowl.

"Hardly any," Sharon said. "It's mostly just vegetables." Vanessa had started a diet in early July, and at first her constant questions about nutrition had cheered Sharon, a champion of any kind of interest in vitamins, minerals, and general nourishment. She believed in the power of wheat germ; she had been thinking for years about how to extract nutrients from one food, say, sardines, and placing them in an altogether different food, say, her famous scones, to see if the nutritional benefits could be transferred. She wondered now if Vanessa's attention to food had not become a bit obsessive. She had lost a good deal of weight, which looked lovely, as if she were hatching from the egg of her adolescence, her features now fully formed, cheekbones high, eyes pronounced in their wide sockets, the muscles in her arms and legs long and defined. But Sharon wanted it to stop now with Vanessa fixed right here in her emergent state of about-to-be-womanhood.

"Now come on," Sigmund said, leaning over his soup. "I'd say Brandeis has a lot to offer besides bagels."

"That's true," Vanessa said. "They probably have chopped liver and kugel too."

"Where does she get this?" Herbert shook his head.

Sharon sent Dennis a sharp look.

"You really shouldn't talk that way," Herbert said to Vanessa, who also looked over at her father for support.

"It's a school with a very strong history," Sigmund said. "Benjamin is going somewhere with a history of protest. This is extremely important."

Avoiding his wife's and his daughter's pointed looks, Dennis put down his spoon. "Thanks, Dad. We're aware." He willed his father not to start up tonight, to stay silent about the Bolsheviks, Joe Hill, and all the dead labor icons, the shit conditions of the workers, the way the corporate pigs were draining them for every goddamn penny. He knew. He knew: the workers' bodies were not machines; they were giving out! Just like John Henry hammering down the railway spikes; industry will beat you or it will *beat* you. Dennis knew this, but tonight was not the night.

Dennis looked at his father, his home, framed by the hydrangea and the azalea bushes, behind him. Dennis was unable to shake his father's look of disappointment the first time he and Tatiana had come here, when they'd just purchased the place. He'd driven his parents from the train station, Sigmund turning in the passenger seat and clicking his tongue as he watched the District recede in their wake as they headed up Sixteenth Street, toward Military Road, toward the suburbs. His mother had sat up straight in the back, her lime green beauty case in her lap. Didn't his father realize Washington was nothing like Manhattan? Here, there were the rich neighborhoods, hardly urban hubs, on the streets above Dupont, and Foxhill and Georgetown Park—unaffordable all, Dennis worked for the *government*—and then there was ghetto, and it was black ghetto, not a bunch of Jewish socialists buying chickens and herring and potatoes like his old neighborhood on the Lower East Side. He remembered taking the stairs two at a time, racing his sister up to the third floor and into that railroad apartment. Outside the closed windows of the flat, shut against the cold and then the dust and the stink, Orchard Street screamed. It hollered with rage and it shit and it breathed its halitosis breath and it urinated on its own stones. It would have been one thing if there'd been no choice, but his father had decided to live where the *workers* lived. They could have gone west into the Village or to Stuyvesant Town like so many of their neighbors had. But not Sigmund Goldstein.

His father seemed oblivious to the way cities had changed. The public pool on Pitt Street turned overnight from Jewish and Italian girls in red lipstick and white bathing suits cutting into protuberant thighs to the lithe bodies of the Puerto Rican and Dominican women. Dennis didn't even know who sat on those lounge chairs now. The Cantonese? Sigmund's friends had gone, but he wouldn't move, insisting he wanted no more—nor less—than what anyone else had.

"Absolutely," Sharon said. "Brandeis has a history to be proud of." She was relieved Ben had not chosen one of those schools so far south, with their emphasis on fraternities and sports.

"The spell of revolution is powerful." Sigmund wiped his mouth with a napkin. "Right, Tatiana?"

"Well, yes, I suppose it is in this family, isn't it?" she said.

Sharon nodded and Dennis bent his head and resumed eating.

"Hmmm," Dennis said. "You didn't seem to think that during Vietnam."

"That's simply not true," Sigmund said. "You know I was as against the war as you were. Our methods of protest were different, absolutely. But what I'm saying here has nothing to do with Vietnam. Nothing at all. Clearly you don't understand."

Dennis nodded. "Well, to my generation, Vietnam defined us. But while we were rioting in the streets, your friends were inside, writing about it. It is a lot more relevant than the Bolsheviks, that's for sure."

"Every movement can be traced back to the Bolsheviks," Sigmund said. "You cannot turn your back on history."

"Well, I think I have a better understanding of Vietnam. And let me tell you something. You can't turn away from the future either, Dad. It's going to happen again. Because we're giving the Soviets their Vietnam now, aren't we? This is what will happen if—or I should say when—there's an invasion in Afghanistan. The country will be ripped to bits. And it will never end! You know we've authorized funding for arming the mujahideen there, don't you?"

"Of course this doesn't *surprise* me." Sigmund scratched his throat. "Because they are anti-communists. It doesn't surprise me at all."

"Well, it's true," Dennis said. "And I'm telling you, it will be just the same as Vietnam."

"Dennis," Sigmund said, leaning toward his son, "why is it always this way? We are on the same side."

Vanessa groaned. "Enough about politics!" As a child she'd wondered if little kids growing up in other cities were also stuck listening only to discussions about affairs of state or if her unfortunate proximity to the White House was to blame for the constancy of these arguments.

"It's gonna be a problem," Dennis said. "There's going to be a big problem is all I have to say. Carter's going to do something really, really stupid."

"Let's not forget," Herbert said to Ben, returning to the original conversation, "that Brandeis is a Jewish institution. This is important. This is what makes it special."

Sharon closed her eyes. She didn't know what had happened; one day not so long ago she woke up to find her parents no longer ate oysters, and Friday evenings they went to shul instead of the Brown Derby. They were full-fledged Jews now, and tonight her father wore a colorfully embroidered yarmulke pinned to the few strands of hair he had left. It reminded her of her father's fanatical nationalism, the way he'd go nuts when they watched the Olympics together. Goddamn Reds! he'd scream, hitting the television when the Soviets were skating. He cried every time the national anthem played and an American stood with a hand over his chest.

"Yes," Sigmund said. "That historical aspect is interesting as well. But it is not in fact a Jewish institution, Herb. It's not a synagogue; it's a university."

Herbert shrugged. "Well, I'll tell you this, it sure as hell wasn't built by the gentiles."

Sharon hated it when her father spoke this way: of us and of them, especially since he had spent a large part of her youth trying so goddamn hard to be *them*. There had been a brief period when he'd gone by a different name—Thomas. Herbert Thomas, but then, when it had come to legally changing the entire family's name, he had let it go. Sharon wondered, as she had many times before, exactly why Dennis was so angry at his father. Because Sigmund was so, well, cool. What would it have been like to have had him as a father? She knew Sigmund would have let her go on the Freedom Ride. He would have given her his blessing, and she would have gone down South and seen the disenfranchisement and the segregation and the sadness and the poverty firsthand. She would have had bruises of her own. Sharon looked around the table. Perhaps she wouldn't even be here, she thought. Maybe she'd be a lesbian, as Louise turned out to be.

"Ummm, can I talk here?" Benjamin said. "Because I'm the one leaving tomorrow, right?"

"Yes, Ben," all the adults murmured.

"Of course, darling," Sharon said, touching his wrist.

"We know!" Vanessa said. "Ben's going!" She set her spoon down loudly on the table. It seemed as if there had been talk of little else all month. Everyone deferred to Ben—the college boy!—and her mother must have cooked what he'd wanted for dinner each night for the entire fucking summer. Go already, she thought, just go! But she hadn't yet processed what it would mean to have him actually leave. Because Ben was in nearly every memory she held. So many late nights they had met in this backyard and lain back on the soft grass, letting the night sky shift and twist for hours over their drunken heads. They'd make sure their mother was sound asleep before they tiptoed up the stairs—avoiding the creaking ones—together.

"She's upset," Sharon said.

"I am not!" Vanessa said. "I am not upset, okay?"

Ben looked down at his soup, quiet for a moment, slightly panicked to think of arriving on campus to find that Grandpa Herbert had been correct, and he'd be greeted by several men in long black cloaks, white threads at their waists, and twirls of hair emerging from tall black hats. Or worse, a long line of reform rabbis would pat him on the shoulder—What a good little bar mitzvah boy! they'd tell him—and encourage him to join Hillel, date only girls with lifetime memberships to Hadassah, and exchange some of his bar mitzvah loot for Israeli bonds.

He hadn't thought of it much at all until last spring, when his friends got wind of his decision to go to Brandeis in the fall.

"Brandeis?" His friend and teammate Nick Papadopoulos, left forward to Ben's right, and who was heading to Notre Dame, was most incredulous. And Jon Ratner, the goalie, who got into Columbia, the lucky shit, said, "They don't even have a football team. And the soccer, is it even Division Three?"

"I don't know," Ben said. But he did know. Brandeis was hardly known for its excellence in sports. It was just that his priorities had changed, overnight it seemed, and what he'd valued so much until this point seemed saved for high school, completed. After that day something "Jewish" appeared in Ben's locker each week: a jar of gefilte fish, the large ovals nesting in a gelatinous mass; a box of matzo, *Go Brandeis Bagels!* written across the label in blue pen; a massive jar of Manischewitz beet borscht that crashed to the floor and splattered along the hallway and all over Ben's new Levi's when he opened the locker door.

"It's a radical place to be," Ben had told his friends that day, and he told his family the same thing now. "The Ten Most Wanted on the FBI list of 1970 all went to Brandeis. Abbie Hoffman, the Yippies, they were all there."

"Yes, they were," Dennis said, pointing his spoon at his father. "Radicals come in every generation, Ben."

"Oh my goodness, we forgot a toast!" Sharon wobbled up from the bench and lifted her glass. "To Benjamin!" she said, leaning awkwardly over the table. "At the beginning of this brand-new adventure!" Sharon choked on the last word.

"Hear, hear," Dennis said, standing, also raising his glass, in part to save his wife from tears. "Ben, may this next chapter of your life be fulfilling and fruitful. We wish you the sweetest happiness and success."

Sharon waited as Dennis clinked glasses with Ben.

"Wait, wait!" Tatti said after all the glasses were lowered, because they had not clinked in every conceivable combination, and she had not yet touched stemware with her son's.

*"Pust' sbudutsya vse tvoi mechty!"* she said. May all your dreams come true.

*"Vashee zda-ró-vye,"* Dennis said to the table. To your health.

"What?" Sharon said. "Tell us!" She disliked it when Dennis and his mother spoke in Russian together. While Dennis's Russian was useful for his work, and while she understood that it was a gift passed from mother to son, she envied it.

"Don't worry. It was just one of Tatti's many toasts." Sigmund laughed.

"In the old days, every first toast was to Stalin." Tatti shook her head. "Well, at least when we thought the neighbors were listening. But not now."

"I'm not worried," Sharon said, sniffing toward Sigmund. "Though I can't say I've learned the entire collection of them." Sharon sat back. She had sat through countless long and sentimental Russian toasts: to the dead, to the newlyweds, to the soldiers who had died in the war, to those who were still fighting. But she had never heard one to Stalin. "When did you?" She smiled at her father-in-law, thin and wiry in the blue jeans he'd taken to wearing, right around when he'd started getting into disco music, odd choices both, as she had always seen him as a man steeped in the past. Sharon wondered now, if she were to shake Sigmund, would his bones break and only those ridiculous dungarees, perfectly creased and thick with Tatti's starch, keep the rest of him intact?

"I manage in Russian," Sigmund said. "After all these years."

"Oh, go ahead, have some wine." Helen reached over Vanessa for the bottle of Chianti on the table. "It's a special occasion tonight."

Vanessa covered the top of her glass. "I don't drink anymore, Nana."

"Since when?" Helen's ash blond hair, sprayed high, was now

wilting like a dying bouquet, and beads of sweat trickled down her brown, spotted chest into the deep opening of her blouse. "You don't eat and you don't drink. What else is there?" Helen said, turning to Sharon.

"I don't think I want to know," Sharon said, laughing, but she had also begun to wonder about her daughter, who seemed to be reducing herself to only the most necessary elements.

"I'm not interested in living numb," Vanessa said. It might have been Jason's lingo, but there was truth in it. And truth was what she was after now. Which was why she had stopped doing the empty, false activities her friends seemed to favor and that she too had once fallen prey to—drinking at country-club bonfires, smoking pot at Rachel's beach house—stuff that led them on an endless search for comfort, for male attention, for beauty. It made them live life unaware of the larger machinery that kept them all *down*. When she'd met Jason this past June, she'd felt able to cut loose from what she only now realized had been an isolating experience with her friends.

"My lord, sweetie, you're young! Have some fun while you still can!" Helen said. "Right, Herb? Tell the poor girl to have some fun. Do you dance, honey?"

"Sure," he said. "Have a good time. Whatever you want, sweetheart." He smiled at Vanessa.

"Yeah, Nana." Vanessa smirked. "I *dance*." In a way, though, her grandmother was not wrong. She had stripped herself of frivolity and had begun to go to shows this summer at Fort Reno and d.c. space, entering a world where kids thrashed to hard music and whipped themselves fiercely into one another. And while she couldn't say she felt a natural connection to this world, it was new, and it felt important; the music itself was essential. It seemed to be making a case for art in general, that it was not stupid or tertiary or unnecessary, and it brought her away from her girlfriends and their beach houses and crocheted bikinis and their transistors blasting ELO and Styx.

"Oh my God, the meat!" Sharon said, standing suddenly and beginning to stack everyone's soup bowls, Vanessa's half-filled bowl on top.

"Let me help you," Sigmund said, rising.

"It's okay, Grandpa." Vanessa stood to help her mother clear. Even though Tatti had waited on him for nearly forty years, Sigmund had recently become acquainted with women's liberation. It was a logical extension of workers' rights, and he seemed amazed—and a little ashamed—that he had not thought of this sooner. Now he often made huge efforts to help, getting up from the dining room table at holiday meals and clattering his own dinner plate and flatware toward the kitchen.

Tatiana rose as well. "Not tonight, my dear. Just sit."

Helen lit a cigarette.

"Mom!" Sharon said, climbing over the bench with the enormous serving bowl. "We're eating, for Christ sake!"

"Go on then," Helen said, pointing her Winston, mashed between two brown fingers, at the door. "You won't notice if you're not here, now, will you?"

Dennis looked over at his mother-in-law and shook his head as she threw her head back, cackling with laughter.

"Oh, Dennis, relax. What are you going to do, *report* me? To your *friends*."

"Yes," Dennis said, bracing himself.

"Your friends in Moscow?" Helen squinted at Dennis, then at Tatti. "Huh?"

"I'm from St. Petersburg," Tatti said, laughing, the deep red hair at her hairline darkening, wet with sweat. "My brother is the only person I know in Moscow, I'm afraid."

"Yes," Dennis said again, getting up awkwardly off the bench. He thought of his uncle Misha in a badly cut boiled-wool coat, the collar rimmed with fur, the Kremlin rising behind him as they made their way through Red Square. Red for beauty, Misha had told him. Not for communism, he'd said, wagging his finger. Misha was his mother's only living relation, yet only Dennis had met him, when he was on business in the Soviet Union. The old ladies, hair tied in kerchiefs, bending over their wares, always threw out their bright scarves and polished their babushkas when he stepped up to their carts with Misha. "I believe I will have to report you," Dennis said. Helen had been accusing him of being a spy since Vanessa's birth, which he'd missed. He'd been on a business trip to Moscow, traveling for the Department of Agriculture, and Vanessa had been two weeks early! The Cold War had heated and cooled for sixteen years since then, but no matter its temperature, Helen was convinced her son-in-law was not really an undersecretary at Agriculture, but an agent in some complicated espionage ring. "I need to make a call to my superior," he said, "right after I get us another bottle of wine."

Sigmund shook his head. "This gets more and more ridiculous every time I hear it."

"Oh, lighten up, Sigmund," Helen said. "It's just a game I play with your son. Games are good! They don't hurt anyone, now, do they?" She exhaled up into the sky, but the smoke lingered, heavy above the table.

"You really shouldn't," Herbert said across the table to Helen. "It bothers her."

Vanessa wished she could have a cigarette with her grandmother, the way they did behind her house in Beverly Hills, Helen's housecoat pulled tight around her, balled-up tissues and matches bulging from her pockets, as they blew smoke toward the mountains and talked about Helen's past—as a *singer,* in a *nightclub,* before I married that son-of-a-bitch grandfather of yours. Helen had taught Vanessa how to blow smoke rings, and she had spent an entire visit jutting out and popping her bottom jaw just so, and then watching the smoke rings rise up and cross one another—which always reminded her of the rings of the Olympics her mother so freakishly adored—before they disappeared. Cigarettes, Vanessa found, were not something that she had to forgo.

Helen shrugged. "Everything bothers her. All I can say is, we gotta live how we gotta live, right, Dennis?"

"As long as everyone is happy," Dennis said, picking up the empty bottle and turning toward the porch.

After the steak—which Sharon had marinated in ginger and soy, and a touch of cream for sweetness, even though she knew Vanessa, who had a few weeks back announced she was a vegetarian, would not touch it—and the corn and the salad were finished, Sharon brought out the cobbler she'd made with blackberries and raspberries from the Haley farm. Dennis opened another bottle of wine, though he wasn't sure if anyone but he and Helen, whom he had never seen refuse a drink of any kind, would partake.

He filled Ben's empty glass.

"College boy," he said. Ben, I hardly knew ya, he wanted to say, thumping him on the back. But it was true; how he had raised a kid whose thigh muscles bulged from the speed and coordination that enabled him to start varsity soccer as a freshman still confounded him. Ben had *lettered*. Dennis had felt as if he were living in some teen movie about high school when Ben had come home with that big *W,* for

"Wildcats," and handed it to Sharon to sew on the back of his jacket. Only now did Dennis realize he had been waiting for the moment that Benjamin would come home with a passion that was not of the body.

Because that was another thing about Ben. Ben and his *body*. Sometimes if Dennis arrived home unexpectedly, he would be greeted by the sound of his son schtupping in the bedroom down the hall. Always some different little tart. If it weren't so off-putting, it would be admirable, Dennis supposed, but it *was* off-putting, terribly so. He tried not to think of the girls. Just last week, Dennis had been unable to sleep and had gone downstairs to the basement, his little spot beneath the house where he did his own brand of yoga. It was also where he stored his living-room-banned artwork from the painting and sculpture classes he'd taken at the Corcoran when the kids were young. As he'd slipped into the sleeping bag he kept rolled behind the couch for just this purpose, his bare legs were met by something cold and wet. He stuck his hand inside and was besieged by the sharp, tinny smell of what he realized, as he brought his fingers to his nose, was semen.

He wouldn't miss being confronted by Ben's semen, that's for sure, Dennis thought, clinking glasses with his son. But he missed the young Benjamin, the one he'd carried around in that little sack strapped to his chest, the Benjamin he'd buckled into swings at Candy Cane City and pushed high in the air to his exhilarated delight, the preverbal Ben, his hot breath on his cheek as he lay in bed with him on Sunday mornings while Sharon baked popovers downstairs. That Ben—the one bobbing to Peter, Paul and Mary, pretending he had a hammer, and a bell, and a *song! to! sing!,* going at the bongo drums and the xylophone, gifts from a friend at the State Department—he'd been gone for quite a while now.

"Oh, Ben," Dennis said. "We're really going to miss you."

Everyone watched Ben take a sip, and then they saw him smile over the rim of his glass as three blushing young women, followed by Jon Ratner, made their way up the side path to the back of the house.

And that, Sharon thought, stacking the plates in the dishwasher, was that. The torches had been extinguished, the gray twilight had darkened to night, and everyone had moved inside. Her father was talking to Tatiana in the living room about how Brandeis was giving Russian Jews asylum, which was really nice, he was saying, didn't she agree?

Ben was gone for the night. He'd gotten up to greet the girls, his back turned to her, his arms wide, and Sharon had seen the girls' faces—such tan, small-featured, young faces—their eyes shut tight, lips quivering into smiles, their chins hooked over his shoulder. "Hey, Mr. and Mrs. G," Jon had said. "Looks like I missed a good dinner."

"Ben," Sharon had nervously said, just before he shook free of the girls' embrace.

"Let him go," Helen said. "It's his last night home, darling, just let him."

Sharon sighed and sat up straight. "Are you going out, Ben?" she asked stiffly.

He turned back to face the table. "Yeah. Just for a bit, okay?"

"There's a party over at Papadopoulos's," Jon said by way of explanation.

Sharon nodded quickly and, looking down at the table, ran her finger over the scratches in the wood. "Sure."

"Of course!" Dennis grandly stood up. "Have fun, gang."

Vanessa cringed. *Gang.*

"Thanks." Ben went to kiss his grandparents good-bye. And then his mother. "Dinner was totally great." He waved at Vanessa. "See ya, pal," he said, to which she rolled her eyes and flipped him the bird.

"Bright and early." Dennis leaned lightly on Helen's shoulder for support as he climbed off the bench.

"Yes," Sharon said. "We need to get an early start for Boston."

They all watched Benjamin lope down the hill, following Jon and the girls into an old magenta Pinto. Then they sped off, the tailpipe dragging down the empty street.

Vanessa was swinging out back in the hammock, watching her mother through the window as she cleaned up in the kitchen, when she heard the singing of Jason's tires halt as he stopped at the driveway, the sound of metal hitting brick as he leaned his bike carelessly against the walkway, then his muffled footfalls on the lawn. She could see his blond hair bobbing as he made his way out back, and she didn't get up, but waited, watching him scan the yard for her in the glow of the kitchen light.

Not until he turned to leave and tiptoe away did she call out, "Hey, there."

Jason put his hand to his forehead, as if to shield his eyes from the sun. "Hey. Where are you?"

"Here." Vanessa sat up and felt the thick, looped rope—handmade by the Amish or something, her mother had said when she bought it at the Torpedo Factory in Virginia—gripping her in all the wrong places. "Back here in the hammock."

"Can I sit?" he asked, coming closer and closer until he peered over her.

"I'm getting up." She placed her hands down to rise, and her fingers got caught awkwardly in the netting. She struggled to swing her feet to the ground.

Jason pulled her up and hugged her to him, and she felt the dampness along his spine, and at that place below his shoulders where it seemed he should have wings, and at the back of his neck. His sweat smelled of french fries and evergreens. "Want to go for a ride?" he asked.

Vanessa thought of her grandparents and her parents sitting in the living room, drinking coffee and agonizing over Ben's departure. "Sure," she said, heading toward the garage for the blue Schwinn she'd had since she was a kid. She and Heather and Bee and Jessica used to tie red, white, and blue streamers to the handlebars every Fourth of July and ride through the neighborhood, ringing their bells.

This is what I've always wanted to feel, Vanessa thought as soon as she was sailing down beneath the trees of Thornapple Street behind Jason, heading toward Rock Creek Park. She could feel the moist air at her neck and shoulders as her hair flew out behind her. I am changing, she thought as she watched Jason rise in his seat and pitch his body forward, leaning on the handlebars. She wriggled her fingers, as if to feel if they were still her own. Everything will be different, she thought.

"Vanessa?" Sharon called out back, wiping her hands on her apron. She flipped on the porch lights and bugs swarmed toward it, a swirling galactic spiral in the unremitting glow of the outdoor light. She squinted out into the dark. "You out there, Vanessa?" she called, but Vanessa was way too far from the house to hear, and she was light as air, and she was flying.

# CHAPTER 2

# Food Matters

When Ben left for school, Sharon was in despair, and Marlene Edelstein, Sharon's business partner, was the first to encourage her to get help. Marlene, who had married an attorney and lived off Chevy Chase Circle, had a far more state-of-the-art kitchen than the Goldsteins' or even the kitchen at the Food Matters offices, and more often than not they'd try out new recipes there. The day Marlene gave her the LEAP! business card they were testing braised tofu in curry sauce, sesame broccoli, and also their traditional scones, to which they were adding walnuts, orange zest, currants, and cranberries in different combinations. The tofu they'd perfected, but Sharon was not totally convinced it should become a signature dish.

Actually she had become unsure about soy in general. Hadn't the government convinced them, after all, that corn had been such a great thing after the war? There'd been so much goddamn corn in this country they hadn't known what to do with it, and so the campaigns for corn syrup and cornmeal and corn oil and corn chips, promoted as these healthy alternatives to wheat, had begun. Mickey Mantle was on television every two minutes proclaiming Karo syrup gave him energy (*and tastes great!*). Well, that had certainly paved the way for fattening Americans, hadn't it?

Sharon had picked up the *Post* just days after they'd returned from dropping Ben off at Brandeis, and buried on page 12 was an article about the negative aspects of corn. It was all a conspiracy! The country was probably just shit out of corn. She had folded down the paper with her index finger and peered over it to glare at Dennis.

"What do you make of this?" She'd thrust the article at him. "Now they're telling us corn is bad."

"Hmmm," Dennis said after taking the paper and quickly looking over the piece; too quickly if you asked Sharon. "Maybe they've found that it's just not healthy for us. It's a tiny piece, Sharon."

Sharon's eyes had followed his hands as they returned the mug to the table. They'd bought the large mugs at the Torpedo Factory several years ago. An image of the kids drinking cocoa from these mugs, she and Dennis their morning coffee, had made Sharon run back to the potter's space to purchase four of them when they'd already been halfway to the car. The cups were chipped now, and one of them no longer had a handle, but still they were everyone's favorite mugs, just as she'd known they would be. She shook her head. "Does there have to be something rotting in this country for anything to be done about it?"

"Or maybe it's just damage control for now not having enough corn *left*." Dennis sat back in his chair and folded his arms. "Who can you trust?"

"Ummm, the government? Can't we trust the fucking government?"

Dennis snorted. "I think we both know better than that, Sharon."

He took a swig of coffee, and Sharon continued to watch him for clues. All she knew was that somewhere in the heartland of this country soy had to be growing from the Mississippi River to the horizon in absurd quantities. Perhaps Dennis and his Agriculture cronies were in on it, starting to perpetrate the use of soy because they knew that soy futures were dropping and the government would soon be left with barrels of the stuff, rotting in some silo next to the corn and the winter wheat.

"There is always too little or too much, isn't there?"

Dennis nodded.

"All I'm saying is we're being tricked into buying what there is too much of and somehow we no longer want what there's not enough of. How is that?" She thought of the year the Soviets purchased enough wheat and corn and soy to make it look as if the feared global food shortage had begun in earnest. There had been panic—even the price of rice at the grocery store rose dramatically. That was 1973; Sharon remembered because Ben had his sixth-grade science fair—Dennis had been away—and he and Jon Ratner had created a lung from a bell jar and a balloon to demonstrate how scuba worked, a stark contrast to the other kids' drab papier-mâché volcanoes and prosaic shoe-box dioramas. For weeks she'd watched Benjamin slap around the house in flippers, cutting out photos of sharks and dreaming of becoming a deep-sea diver.

As her father-in-law would say, What are you eating your heart out for, Sharon? That's capitalism for you.

How could they—and who *was* they anyway, the government?—play around so much with what we, as a country, eat, what we, as individuals, put in our *bodies* when her son had his dreams to fulfill?

We are being tricked, Sharon thought as she poured chopped walnuts into Marlene's gleaming white KitchenAid. "Do you think we can inject the braised tofu with minerals and vitamins the way farmers shoot meat through with hormones?" she asked Marlene, who was pulling the dish from the oven. A rush of curry filled the room.

"Farmers inject live animals though, don't they?" Marlene closed the oven door and pushed her straight black hair from her face with her free hand.

"Oh," Sharon said.

Marlene absentmindedly jotted something down on the recipe card. "Well, maybe we could grow our *own* soy."

"No," Marlene said. "We couldn't. We're caterers, not farmers."

Sharon nodded. But she would have liked her own chickens. Fresh eggs for the baked goods would be divine. She'd recently been reading cookbooks that championed fresh, seasonal ingredients from local farms and markets, and this would be about as close to home as you could get.

Sharon peered into the mixer, watching the nuts get lost as they were churned into the folds of the scone ingredients. She imagined her tears, falling silently now, bringing her own story into her baking, as in a fairy tale. Would the scones go hard from grief, or would suffering make them as light as air?

Since Benjamin had gone, Sharon found herself crying often, which she was not usually prone to, and she had also become terrified of her changed and sullen daughter. They'd had dinner alone together for the first time in quite a while this past September. Vanessa no longer ate meat, though Sharon wasn't sure if this was related to her newfound interest in hard-rock concerts or not, and so Sharon had made brown rice and tempura-style eggplant, which she'd rolled in wheat germ, combined with the panko bread crumbs she'd gotten at the new Asian specialty store by the health club. She'd even offered Vanessa a glass of wine. This was when Vanessa had looked at her mother's Chablis as if it were the reason for the atomic bomb and explained—*for the fiftieth time*—that drugs and alcohol were just another way for the government to keep the people down. And she'd told her about PMA, a positive mental attitude, which, if it had any effect on her daughter whatsoever, was fine with her. She had liked the sound of it: positive mental attitude.

Sharon had said it over and over to herself as she watched her daughter scrape the fried coating from the eggplant and take a few bites of the naked vegetable. Sharon guessed she'd been about Vanessa's age when she'd stopped believing in government. That's just when the HUAC had come to town, when her father and Dick Yates of Republic, the studio where her father produced westerns for most of the blacklist, smoked cigars on the back deck and laughed at the shit-faced communists who clearly no longer wanted to work in this town. Sharon hated westerns! They seemed even less real than other films. But how, at sixteen, does one convey, I am not my father? She'd been so busy trying not to be her mother, she had not known then she would want to escape him as well.

What about sex? she had wanted to ask Vanessa. And she had wanted to reach across the table then and grab her daughter by the collar, or just hold her tight enough to ask her, What on earth is happening to you? But she did neither of those things.

"That has wheat germ in it," Sharon had said instead. "For strength!" She balled her right hand into a fist and shook it, she knew, not with power of protest as she'd intended, but with the wan wave of apathy.

"I don't do fried," Vanessa had said.

Sharon noted this for the future, not mentioning that fried was once all Vanessa would eat: french fries, fried cheese, fish sticks, and heavily breaded chicken tenders. Sharon had tried to make these as healthily as possible when she cooked, but there was no stopping Dennis's taking Vanessa to McDonald's just as soon as she'd won a soccer game or received an A anywhere on a report card, even in handwriting. How could Vanessa not learn that food was reward, that it was tied to love? And with all her new dietary restrictions, where was her daughter getting that love now?

Sharon turned the mixer off, went over to the sink, and leaned into the faucet. She could not control her weeping.

"What is it, Sharon?" Marlene asked, rubbing Sharon's back in soft, round circles, just as Sharon had when her children were sick. She was ashamed to admit, she loved them best when they were ill, their resistance down.

"I feel like everything's just gone," Sharon told Marlene. She was experiencing a sort of hopelessness that seemed momentarily worse to her than the depression she'd felt after Vanessa was born. It was a time when women were making such variegated *choices,* and she had thought she'd gone crazy. They'd had to get a nanny to come in while Dennis was at work. All she could remember about it was the dreadful sensation that she had lost touch with the earth, with the actual ground of this planet, with her home and the people in her home, and that she floated, wholly untethered, unsure as to what her role in the world now was and how she would ever get back down to realize it.

She'd not experienced that with Ben or she mightn't have had another child. She was two weeks early with Vanessa, which was why Dennis hadn't been there, despite her warnings that he was cutting it pretty damn close, and in the few days before she'd gone into labor Sharon started having terrible dreams of Ben falling off railings and tumbling down stairs. She'd wake with the profound wish that she not have another child and she'd rush to Ben's brand-new big-boy bed, panicked by the impending transformation of her family. Never would it be the three of them snuggled in bed together against the cold, the three of them marching on the Mall, Ben secure against Dennis's chest. Nor would it be just the two of them, she waiting for Ben across the room as he slowly made his way to her, one delicious little-boy step at a time. Now they would always be at least three, she'd thought, not realizing that one day, as today, it would be only she and a grown Vanessa. Sharon had wondered lately if Vanessa had sensed even in the womb that her presence had been feared.

"Ben's just the first in the line of it. Dennis has also all but disappeared," Sharon said. She thought of reaching out to her husband in the middle of the night and the way he had turned away from her, even in sleep. "And I'm scared stiff of my own daughter." Sharon wiped her nose with the back of her hand. "I dread talking to her, that I'll either make her angry or, even worse, find out what's actually going on in that head of hers."

"Look," Marlene said. "This is all normal. We're at that age."

"Don't," Sharon said, straightening. "Just don't." She shook her head and cleared her throat.

"You know what helped me when Gus and Lindsey left home?"

Sharon interrupted, "Vanessa is still here, for two more years. What kind of a mother does that make me?" She thought of her daughter, locked in the den bathroom after dinner. She knew what she was doing in there. Sharon had known women in college who all herded to the bathroom together to vomit up those butter-cream cakes and sugary fruit pies they served at afternoon teas. They were dieting, they told the group, as they laughingly returned, falling back onto the couch, their full skirts flying above their knees until they rocked back up to seated and indulged in more pastries. They were slim as pencils, these girls, each with a waist cinched tight. Was this a silly phase Vanessa was going through, or some kind of obsessive neurotic behavior, something of more concern?

"Irregardless," Marlene said. "Remember what a mess I was last year? Don't laugh, but I started getting more involved in synagogue, like when they were kids. At Sinai, off the park."

"I know, we used to belong, when the kids were young." Sharon shook her head.

Marlene nodded.

"Does Frank go with you?" Sharon went over to the mixer and examined the contents of the bowl again. She leaned on the counter—marble, she thought with envy, even in her distraught state—and looked at her friend. Marlene might have a fabulous kitchen, and those Bvlgari earrings Frank brought her from Italy, but she had put on weight. Marlene's face was pudgy now; her whole body had acquired an extra layer since they'd started this business together five years ago. Marlene might be getting fat, but she seemed happier than ever, thought Sharon, imagining Marlene frying up a mushroom omelet and bringing it to bed with champagne after she and Frank had made love.

"He comes to services with me sometimes," Marlene said. "But it's more my thing. He started going when his mother died. He said kaddish and so on, but it was really more for her."

"Yeah, well, it's not for me anymore," Sharon said. "That's over." Dennis had gotten to her in the end. Before they'd had children, Sharon and Dennis had decided to give them the tools to make an educated choice. One must know one's past to diverge from it, they'd agreed. But once the kids had showed up, bright and shiny and yet somehow unexpected, Dennis fought Sharon at every turn. Hebrew school was prosaic; bar mitzvahs were gauche. He refused to help carpool; he wouldn't assist with any planning; and on Yom Kippur he made a point of eating bacon cheeseburgers.

Marlene shrugged and looked at her, mouth cocked exaggeratedly to the side, her eyes large. "But maybe it *is* for you is what I'm saying.

Maybe it's perfect for you. Life got so busy, maybe we just forgot. I know I did." Marlene brought her left hand over her heart.

"Not me. I didn't forget. Dennis drove it out of me."

How many Passovers had she cooked matzo-ball soup and made her own gefilte fish and forced them all to sit there and go through the Haggadah, in which she herself was not the least bit competent? It hadn't seemed natural. She thought of her father, showered and shaved, his white hair still beaded with water beneath his yarmulke, his navy tie, his prayer book—the one he'd had when he was a boy on Hester Street—held tight to his side. But where had that prayer book been for all these years?

"So you think you know what you need." Marlene turned her palms skyward and shrugged. "Who am I to say? But you need something. Or you will go mad, I can tell, Sharon, I know you."

"How does a drink sound then?" Sharon headed over to Marlene's fridge, where there was always an open bottle of California Chardonnay.

"See what I'm saying?" Marlene glanced at her watch. "It's not even two o'clock. Look." She went around her kitchen counter and over to the sitting area, flipped down her desk, and began to sift through a box filled with business cards. When she found what she'd been looking for, she brought it over to Sharon.

"Emma Osher, from the health club, married to Morty? From the drug lobby? She passed this on to me when I was going through the same thing." Marlene handed the blue card to Sharon, who took it and held it with the tips of her fingers and thumb. It said, *LEAP!: An invitation for you to leap from here to exactly where you want to be.*

"Oh, I know Morty, sure." Sharon nodded. "I think he used to lobby for DDT, the creep. What is it?" She shook her hair out of her face.

"It's this program that started in California." Marlene looked down and brushed the front of her apron, shaking off invisible walnut dust. "It's supposed to be just wonderful. I thought of going, but like I told you, synagogue was what I needed."

Sharon turned the card over to the other side, a blank indigo. "Thanks. Really." She stuffed the card in the back pocket of her jeans, her old ones, not the new, trendy ones she'd bought at Neiman's a few weeks previously. Calvin Klein. It was not like her to buy expensive designers, but the salesgirl had said they made Sharon's ass look incredibly perky, and she had been stupid enough to believe her.

Sharon went back to the counter, twisted off her wedding rings, and placed them in the teacup Marlene always had set out for her. She poured half the scone mixture onto the floured counter, cocking her head this way and that as she absentmindedly worked the dough into a perfect circle.

"This is the walnut-cranberry batch," she said to Marlene, throwing flour on the patty of dough. Sharon thought of sugarplums. They could add sugarplums! She remembered seeing *The Nutcracker,* at the Pantages, a Weissman Christmas Eve tradition, one celebrated yearly before her parents denied they had so much as acknowledged Christmas. She'd wanted to be a fragile ballerina in a sparkly pink tutu and pink slippers, and so her mother had sent her to the finest ballet school in Los Angeles. There, Mistress Fonseca proclaimed her a flat-footed klutz who should give it up now. Helen declared the mistress an idiot communist and took Sharon to several other, lesser dance studios, where Sharon still maintained her flatfeet, weak ankles, and general lack of grace.

She slapped the dough and began to roll it out. They could call them the Dance of the Sugarplum Fairy Scones, and they could make them a little smaller and serve them at next year's holiday brunches, Sharon thought. They would be lovely; so delicate. Next year: would Carter make it to the next term? And since she was trying out this seasonal cooking, this wouldn't work, as sugarplums were only really available in July and August. But then why were they always such a Christmas treat? Where had that come from? Some sugarplum lobby in the UK with a barn full of frozen sugarplums, to be sure.

"Okay," Marlene said. "Got it."

Sharon let the idea of sugarplum-fairy scones fade as she rolled out the dough and then sliced it into triangles.

"The next will be the walnuts, currants, and the orange zest. I got organic oranges since we're using the zest."

"Sounds good," Marlene said. She went over to the counter by the sink, where all the variations of the recipes of the day were spread out on lime green index cards, and leaned in, looking for the scone recipe.

"Be sure to mark the organic part."

"I got it, Sharon."

Sharon laid the scones on the cookie sheet and brushed them with egg wash. When each one glistened, she went over to the second preheated oven. As she opened the door, she felt that rush of hot air she always loved, even in the dead of summer.

★   ★   ★

Sharon had found the midnight blue LEAP! card when changing purses, and she'd taken it out of her jeans pocket and thrown it facedown into her night-table drawer. Each day she'd gone for the lint brush or a pen, that blank blue square was next to her diaphragm, dusty with cornstarch, nestled in its case. Then one unbearably quiet morning at the end of October, after Dennis had left for the airport, she'd impulsively called and heard about this journey to self-fulfillment and enhancing one's life in order to live in important and meaningful ways. This had spoken to Sharon; she'd gone to her first LEAP! training two evenings later, while Dennis was still in Moscow.

Now, nearly three months later, Sharon lay in bed, trying to use some of her new LEAP! tools to transform her negative energy about preparing for tomorrow's party into a positive force for success. She and Marlene had decided on the menu ages ago—a far more traditional one than Sharon would have preferred—and now it was just a matter of precise execution.

It was a new year, a brand-new decade. Yet Sharon couldn't stop thinking about the past, daydreaming about the Olympics, the winter ones coming up: slalom trails lined with evergreens, athletes unrecognizable through their padded jackets and hats and gloves but for the identifying flags sewn to their backs and at their hearts. She thought of shining rinks, skaters' blades winking in the camera lights, the ice dancers' diaphanous costumes swirling as they glided and turned. During the last games, in Innsbruck, she and Ben had sat propped against this headboard, two happy birds on a sturdy branch watching Dorothy Hamill spin to gold. But this year, she thought, as she did about so many things, he was gone.

Sharon had always been drawn more to the Winter Games, probably because skating had been an anomaly in Los Angeles when she was growing up. There had been a single indoor rink in Culver City, not terribly far from their bungalow on Franklin Avenue, but Sharon's weekly skating classes, begun when the ballet had failed, always seemed to correspond with the height of rush hour. She remembered being on the 10 for hours as Helen smoked and futzed with the radio until she found a station that played something big band enough to accommodate her singing.

Dennis also loved to skate; it was one of the few physical activities his Russian mother approbated, and when the kids were young, they'd drive downtown, parking at his office, and go skating on the Mall. Sharon, who'd had her own white leather skates in her youth, found the rentals were always either too big or too small, the leather too stiff or too soft, and this deflated her experience. Looking back on it now, she should have said, I will not be a perfectionist; I will simply accept this moment for what it offers. But Sharon had not yet begun her training. The kids, though, their teeny ankles caving in as they grabbed for her and Dennis's hands so urgently, made her discomfort manageable, and she fought through the imperfection, looking up from their sweet smallness out to the grandness of the city, the exalted buildings before them. Dennis would always swoop in from behind and scoop up one of the children— Vanessa usually—and hold her high in the air as he skated swiftly around the rink. Sharon's stomach would practically skid on the ice due to fear, but the kids' delighted squeals were as close to flawless as she could find.

Sharon had encouraged Vanessa to take skating lessons—Look how much you loved it when we skated with Daddy! she'd told her—but she'd had no interest and Sharon hadn't pressed it; she had her own negative associations with being pushed. For her very first lesson—when the dancing had not worked out—Sharon's mother had dressed her in full skating regalia: shining white leather skates, a pink leotard with a lighter pink gauze skirt, opaque white stockings. She'd pulled Sharon's hair in a bun so tight her cheekbones popped to the surface of her face. "Like a sugarplum fairy you look!" Helen had told her daughter. "Just lovely. Now stand up straight and show 'em what you got!"

Sharon was surprised how much the thought of her son in a different room in another city, watching the skating and hockey next to someone else, upset her. She was distraught to think that Ben and she would never again shuffle their legs beneath the covers, anxious as the skiers flew out of the gates and over the mountain. Because there would be girlfriends, real ones, not those fast girls he brought around from high school, but those who would deepen him, and one of these women would become a wife. Then there would be permanence. There would be children. And yet wasn't this something a mother was supposed to long for?

Sharon wanted to continue the tradition of watching the Games as she had with her father. She remembered being barely eighteen and the dust motes in the living room rising in the huge shafts of light— brilliant, golden light; the light of the West; *her* West—streaming in from the glass doors that led out to the garden. That was the year Tenley Albright, an American figure skater, won gold. A great American story, her father had said, pride spilling over as this girl arched her back and lifted her graceful hands skyward. Watching her twirl, Sharon had felt her own appalling lack of grace.

But it was the Soviets who swept the medals that year. It was 1956, just before she'd moved East, and they'd watched the Soviets participate for the first time; it was as if she were watching the very moment they achieved world domination.

"Come on already!" Herbert got up from the couch and banged the television until waves of static threatened to overtake the screen. "Bums!" He looked at his daughter and threw up his hands.

This was not just an ice hockey game. She began to believe the Russians would steal everything: the secrets to the atomic bomb, yes, but also famous paintings, keys to towns and cities; they would be able to open every home, take anything they liked, her mother's stuffed jewelry boxes, her father's gleaming set of Olympic coins. The Russians came with a mission to succeed and they had seized their medals, as if their athletes' bones had been kept from sport for so long they could no longer contain their strength.

"Let's *go*!" her father would scream. But his concern—she soon understood it was also scorn—was not directed at the Soviet Union. It was the Americans, she realized, who were losing everything.

The Russians! It had always been the Russians. March 29, 1951, the day Ethel and Julius Rosenberg got the death penalty, was a day of celebration in the Weissman home.

Herbert hung his American flag out in the front yard when he heard the news. "They got what they asked for," Herbert said. "Those provincial Jews, so ungrateful to this country. That has given them everything!"

Helen smoked her Winstons and drank coffee at the kitchen table in her blue nylon bathrobe that zipped up the front. "Enough, Herb," she said when he came inside. She pointed her cigarette at Sharon and her older brother, Michael. "They don't need to know this stuff yet."

"I think they should know," Herbert said. "Those two shoulda gone back to Russia is what they shoulda done, they love it there so much. Let's send them there COD. You couldn't get me back there for a million bucks."

Helen stubbed out her cigarette. Her mouth was caked with the coral lipstick that also filled in the fine lines that intersected at her lips. "Come on, scootch," she said to her kids. "Time to get ready for school."

"Ahh, who cares, Helen," Herb said. "Let 'em burn."

Two years later when the Rosenbergs were killed, Sharon was fifteen. That night they'd grilled hot dogs and hamburgers out back, and the adults all milled about, cigarettes sagging with condensation from their highballs, talking about the Rosenbergs' guilt. They were guilty as hell, *he* was for sure, but so was that little commie bitch who typed out the information. They didn't give a damn about their country, that's for sure, or their children. Hm-*hmmm,* they assured one another. Just like Hoover said. Really, it was the crime of the century.

Sharon's brother, Michael, found the newspaper clippings, and the siblings stole into their father's closet with a flashlight and sat beneath his suits, his smell of Old Spice and shoe polish, as they read the news of the Rosenbergs' executions. All the reporters claimed they were guilty. So did J. Edgar Hoover. And President Eisenhower said the punishment was appropriate to the crime.

But what Sharon could not shake was the image of dowdy Ethel Rosenberg refusing to die. They had to zap her twice, the papers said, and Sharon wondered what it would be like to live through an electrical surge that had wiped her husband out in seconds. Ethel was an immigrant from her parents' old neighborhood, a place they rarely spoke of but to curse it, a street filled with the stink of horse manure, cold-water flats shut away from the world's light, chickens squawking, bleeding in the street. How could they have grown up under such grueling conditions when she lived beneath this white, white desert light, under bougainvillea-scented skies, along streets so wide they were always better suited for cars than horses?

That night Sharon dreamed it had been she, not Ethel, who was strapped to that chair. Only in the dream she was an X-ray of herself with white bones and organs shot through with forked lightning, her body a house for a tremendous electrical storm. Upon waking, her armpits damp, sweat pooled in the caves beneath her eyes, Sharon couldn't understand how her father could encourage such violence. And how could this country—*her* country—have sanctioned it?

Now Sharon heard Dennis pull up in the drive and roused herself to greet him.

"Hello," she said from the top of the stairway as he left his briefcase on the landing, something she had tried for years to discourage.

"The embargo's on," Dennis said, stomping up the stairs. "We're fucked."

Sharon breathed in and out, trying to be mindful and maintain her tenuous state of relaxation.

"Oh, shit, D, I'm so sorry." She followed him into the bedroom. Dennis had cautioned that a grain embargo with the Soviets could be coming, despite his warnings of the cost to the United States, to those poor farmers. Sharon pictured them leaning over their hoes—as if any farmer still used such agrarian implements—and weeping. People will be ruined here; and the Russians, they'll starve. That's what he'd told her night after night since the Soviets had invaded Afghanistan last month. "No warning?"

"Nope," he said, sitting on his side of the bed, near the crammed bookshelves, and kicking off his Hush Puppies. "Security, security." He laughed. "We wouldn't want the Soviets to find out and then buy up all the grain before it happens. Then they wouldn't really suffer, now, would they?"

Sharon could not measure his sarcasm. "That does make sense, I suppose. If we are trying to keep the grain from them, I mean."

"Hmm." He placed his hands behind his head and lay back. "I was so depressed I left early. Announcing it so late on a Friday afternoon, too."

Even in his most tense moments, Dennis had a relaxed, fleshy quality that Sharon still found so sexually appealing. It had been there from the first night she'd met him, at a mobilization meeting; he'd approached her without apprehension even though she had come with a date. She had always thought Dennis would be the only one—even when the married couples they knew were opening up their relationships. Maybe she was square, but she had never felt jealous of those women who took off for the Continent with Carole King records and a year's supply of birth control pills. It just wasn't her.

Sharon studied her husband before going to the dresser, her sympathy quickly shifting to anxiety about how Dennis's unhappy situation would soon make them all miserable.

"Should we go out tonight and celebrate the world's demise?" Dennis asked.

"I'd love to but I can't." Sharon looked at him in the mirror as she dabbed her nape with Joy; Dennis almost always brought her a little bottle from the duty-free. "Marlene and I have to get ready for the Epstein party tomorrow night. Actually"—Sharon looked at her watch—"I'm running late, I was supposed to be at the office by four."

Dennis looked at her blankly.

"The *Epsteins,* Dennis, on Kalorama. I've told you." She stopped herself. I am me, she thought. I am myself, and I am calm. She took out a folded pair of jeans, shook them open, and stepped into them. "He's Mondale's advance man. Marsha hired us months ago."

"Oh, right."

Sharon stopped herself from chastising Dennis for forgetting. I will complete my mission and I will let Dennis complete his. Sometimes our journeys cannot be the same, but I, she reasoned, zipping up her pants, remain in control of all that I can be.

She turned away from the mirror. "Well, I'm off."

"Say hi to Marlene," Dennis said as she headed toward the stairs.

She looked at her inventory in the deep freeze in the basement, which still stank of Dennis's stale sweat from his morning sun salutations and jump roping, which he insisted on practicing in the nude. Though they had decided when the kids were little that nakedness was to be encouraged so the children would not fear their differences and at the same time could have a look at what they would most likely grow into, Sharon had had her doubts. It was her damn 1950s upbringing, but despite her discomfort, she had strutted around the house, her nipples freezing and erect, her bum flailing in the breeze, just to have the body seem natural. A lot of good it had done; Benjamin was a little too comfortable with being naked, and Vanessa, poor breakable Vanessa, seemed to hate her body. Sharon could just look at her and see it, and yet what could she do now? Strip down and sit next to her daughter and tell her, It's okay to feel vulnerable. One day, I promise, you will be you.

As she went to the freezer, she wondered if all this nudity had been the right thing. The thought of Vanessa coming upon Dennis jumping rope in the nude, his penis flapping, buttocks shaking; should this be an image to carry with her into adulthood? Did her son really need to see the thick thatch of her own pubic hair? Sharon heaved open the old freezer to count her trays of anchovy puffs and cheese sticks and crab cakes, and after lifting cartons of ice cream and pastry dough, shifting several plastic containers of various pestos and sauces, she saw that the canapés she needed for tomorrow were all in place. She breathed out.

I have made the right choices, thought Sharon as she let the heavy door fall. I am exactly the woman I was meant to be.

# CHAPTER 3

# Winter: Unbreakable Chain

**January 4, 1980**

When President Carter announced the embargo, Dennis did not initially think about the American farmers who would be wrecked, or of the disastrous effects on trade, or the implications of using food to swing politics. What he first thought of was his mother, her hips knocking the linoleum kitchen table as she mixed egg whites and sugar in a porcelain bowl for her tiny meringues, her long, bony fingers, knuckles white, gripping the metal eggbeater. He watched her sprinkle in dried cherries—because, she'd say, wrapping the cookies up in wax paper and sealing them tight in Christmas tins to send to her brother in Moscow, Americans love their cherries—from high above the bowl. She rubbed the tips of her fingers together as if casting a spell.

Since the Soviet invasion of Afghanistan at Christmas—which he had also known was imminent—Dennis had been aware that an embargo would be forthcoming. No way in hell could U.S. troops be sent in. Vietnam had just ended, for goodness' sake. The draft was kaput. But now the threat was nuclear. Why not let food do the work of weapons?

Still, the announcement had shocked him. He hated to be so selfish in the face of global starvation, but he couldn't help himself; what after all would become of *him*? His trips to the Soviet Union would be canceled; even the diplomats were being sent home. The consequences to trade would be disastrous, the effects global; devastated farmers were probably hanging themselves deep in the Midwest just as Dennis was leaving the office for home, but for a moment all he felt was a preemptive ache for Moscow—Stalin's skyscrapers, spiked spires illuminated by ruby stars, the twirled-candy tops of cathedrals, green borscht in the Ilyinka, and blini and caviar in the Garden Ring, near the Ministry of Agriculture, where Dennis took most of his meetings. He knew now where to get everything he needed in Moscow, and after a few potentially dangerous slipups, Dennis could now pace himself when socializing with the thick-necked men from Exportkhleb who bought U.S. grain. He knew how much vodka to drink and how quickly, and the way to tell real vodka from the crap (if it tasted like diesel, most likely it was. And as Viktor Uspensky, his counterpart in Moscow, had told him, it was probably Polish).

Food as a weapon. Perhaps this was what had made him think of his mother, her borscht practically nuclear, each dense little kreplach as dangerous as a grenade. And those meringues were no good either; they were misshapen, and often burnt and hard. His older sister used to pelt them off the fire escape at the Italians passing beneath. Once, Dennis had taken one from the tin and had bitten into a piece of paper, as if his mother had just thrown the recipe card or the top of the flour sack in with the batch.

Carter had said an unbreakable chain of events would be needed for the embargo to be successful. But who could know what was to come? If anyone had told Dennis that Bobby Kennedy would be shot, and in some kitchen, he would have laughed at him. And as brutal as the war had been, who could even have imagined such a travesty as My Lai taking place? No one could have conceived of it. Nor could Dennis have predicted most of the events in his own life, its smallness pasted over the life of the world. As well as he thought he'd known his children, he could never have foretold Benjamin's obsession with sports, and then how he'd just ditch that training the moment he'd set foot on a college campus. And perhaps Dennis had been warned that girls fall out of love with their fathers, that he would one day wake up and that love would suddenly be as unavailable as this wheat and corn sitting on trains, the Russians waiting, iron fists hovering over black communist checkbooks, but Dennis had never believed that would be *his* daughter. And so he could not have determined that one day, as sudden as a car wreck, he and Vanessa would face each other at the kitchen table as strangers.

He'd left work early thinking that Rock Creek Park would be clear, but still he got stuck in traffic. What would it be for him then, he'd thought, a temporary transfer from the Soviet Union to the North Korea or Japan desk? Or worse, staying in Washington generating more paper until the embargo was finished. The wooden gristmill along

Beach Drive still turned, even though it no longer provided power, just as it had all those times he'd walked along the path leading to the falls with Vanessa high on his shoulders, his hands wrapped tightly around her tiny ankles.

How long before he might travel again? Carter never listened; this was his big problem. He was single-handedly paving the way for the Republicans again. Though Dennis loved to go to the Soviet Union, and also, frankly, to leave Washington, something about Dennis's trips was disquieting. He was selling grain in the very country his mother had fled, the same country his father's parents thought they'd run back to as soon as the Bolsheviks had taken over. Leaving the ministry building and the arguments over prices and terms, he'd pull his coat tight and wonder, if the Soviets bought up everything and drove up the price of grain, with food in such shortage, how would the United States get wheat to those poor drought-wrecked countries in Africa? He'd walk out into the freezing street, and his mother would appear to him then, a tall woman with black eyes, deep red hair, skin lit from within, somehow superimposed over the Kremlin, her stoic face hanging above Borovitsky Hill, hovering over the Moskva River, far in the distance. Often Dennis felt sliced open by the memory of his mother's face, or her hands, always beating eggs or shaking a phonograph needle onto a recording, her fingers trilling the air in agreement with his father as he read aloud about the unions from the *Forward,* her hands reaching to touch his face. In Moscow, though, he saw her high-boned face in the sky.

On his way to and from the Ministry of Agriculture, Dennis would fantasize about what it might have been like to grow up a little Russian boy. What if his grandparents had returned, if all the streets below Grand Street, where he had spent his childhood, had been empty of all the Jewish socialists, nowhere on the East Side to buy so much as a pickle or a crust of black bread?

Dennis finally pulled his little red Beetle into the drive behind Sharon's blue Volvo. He slammed the car door and, looking up at the house, a Colonial, when his style was more modern, in a suburb so close to the city, no one could really call it *suburbia.* Suburbia was down the Pike in Columbia, Maryland, where every new aluminum-sided house came equipped with its own mini-pond, a real swan gliding on the smooth surface. Ticky tacky, ticky tacky, he'd think, the Pete Seeger song an obsessive loop spinning in his head, no matter how he tried to turn his focus to the Seeger he saw strumming his guitar at the Mall singing

"We Shall Overcome." That was the day they had all stood up for civil rights, and he had held his son high above the crowd and spun him around so Ben could witness the protest. *We shall overcome some day ayayay.* Sharon had run off with her college roommate to egg on the police, but he had still felt the magnitude of all those people marching together to right an injustice, singing as one; he had felt it so deeply. He had thought then that the world would be brought closer together, not blown apart.

When they'd bought the house on Thornapple Street, the wooden floors had purple pineapples on them, hundreds stamped across the entire first level, and when the carpenters came to strip the floors, Vanessa had screamed and cried.

"Van," Dennis had said, kneeling down to put his arm around her, "beneath these silly things are beautiful floors! You'll see."

"But the pineapples are beautiful too!" she'd sniffled.

She is the (pine)apple of my eye! he'd chuckled to himself—he really had—as he'd watched the tropical fruits disappear beneath the stripping machine. No matter how Vanessa had changed, her face now thin and drawn, her jaw always set forward in anger, rarely at night did he walk in the front door and not remember those purple pineapples, erased before their eyes.

Dennis often wondered what the previous owners might have felt about his obliteration of their handiwork. Would they find a way to punish him? He believed in ghosts. His college roommate Len Ford had bought a weekend house in a tiny town in Virginia, in Skatesville, not long after graduation, and the house was haunted. A reporter from the *Washington Post* had written a piece about the strange occurrences in the old place—slammed doors, split fences, shaking china cups on windless days. For some unfathomable reason the ghost was called Gloria, a friendly spirit who didn't instill fear but merely appeared to make her presence known.

Should he have left those pineapples, if only because his daughter had loved them? It would have been impossible; Sharon had despised them. Erasing them had been a condition of purchasing the house. And besides, back then Vanessa adored anything pink; everything purple! And anything Barbie too, though dolls were *verboten*. Sharon was entirely against dolls of any kind for Vanessa, as well as nail polish and makeup (though for Ben, she thought this was all to be encouraged). And while his wife's rules seemed to stem from all her consciousness-raising sessions and reading *Ms.* magazine, Dennis agreed with her because he wanted to keep his daughter from growing up too soon.

Sharon's mother, Helen, painted Vanessa's toes pink and her eyelids blue, but her worst offense was the purchase of a terrible Barbie head, this giant blank face for little girls to slather with makeup. Helen kept it in her closet in Los Angeles and would proudly bring out the decapitated head nestled on a pink plastic platter as if she were serving up this hideous head for one of her insufferable Shabbos dinners. The way that woman blatantly defied certain non-negotiable household rules was only one of the reasons Dennis couldn't bear to visit. Now there was all this business with the Friday candles, Helen leaning over the flames with some schmata on her head, and Herbert chanting this over the bread, that over the wine, a prayer at every goddamn meal. It was worse than the old Jews in his old neighborhood, and it was bullshit. Those bald, shriveled men wandering the streets looking for the ninth or tenth man for minyan. The streets were so crowded, but still there were never enough men for services.

For a four-day visit to the in-laws in goddamn Beverly Hills, Dennis usually brought two joints, just enough to get through it. One evening, when the kids were maybe six and eight, it was pouring rain and they'd all been stuck inside, which meant Dennis hadn't been able to do his usual sneak-out-back-and-light-up before dinner. Instead, he used the guest bathroom, inhaling deeply, then holding his face up to the vent, blowing out, and feeling very much *himself* now, in this uptight version of Southern California, so contrary to every image he held of hippies running barefoot from bed to bed in the canyons. He'd waved the smoke around and wetted his finger to tap the joint out, then spilled his Old Spice around the sink.

This was when Vanessa tapped on the door. "Hi, Daddy," she said.

Dennis looked around the small, sterile room in a panic, and then, because he could think of nothing better to do, he slid his back against the door. "Hi, sweetie," he said from the bathroom. He held the door closed with his foot while frantically pushing smoke toward the vent with both hands cupped together.

"What's that smell?" Vanessa said.

She'd said it so loud!

Dennis opened the door suddenly. Then, willing himself calm, he said in a screaming whisper, "It must be the maid!"

He could hear Sharon coming out from the kitchen, her leather sandals slapping the marble corridor until they stopped at the bedroom. Dennis stood frozen in a stare with his daughter in her green corduroy jumper, a *V* sewn with a quilted yellow fabric on the front, her hair in two perky pigtails at each side of her head. What, he wondered, did she see when she looked back at him?

"Everything okay? You guys ready for dinner?" Sharon asked from the hallway.

Benjamin was in the living room talking sports with Herbert. Baseball. It was always baseball with Herbert, and all Dennis knew about baseball was that Herbert had actually gained enthusiasm for the Dodgers since the team had moved to Los Angeles, and that this probably had to do with Koufax. Dennis was sure Herbert fell in love with the Dodgers the day Koufax wouldn't pitch on Yom Kippur.

Dennis was high—very fucking stoned actually—Len had gotten the stuff from some crazy West Virginian with GOP connections, and it was unusually strong. Dennis's heart raced with paranoia. He imagined his father-in-law's long, droopy face, his slavering mouth, a skullcap pinned to the few wisps of hair he smoothed down with pomade, assessing the situation. Looking at Vanessa, Dennis wondered what she might do. Then he felt something outrageously sinister. Perhaps, Dennis thought, his daughter was Helen's secret agent sent to discredit him altogether.

They could both hear Sharon humming in the hall, detained perhaps by some stain on the wall, or a speck of dust on one of the hanging Chagall posters, framed in ornate gold.

"Everything's fine, Mommy," Vanessa said, meeting Dennis's eyes.

He let out the breath he hadn't known he'd been holding and smiled meekly at his daughter, who turned and went to grab her mother's hand before Sharon crossed the threshold. And soon Dennis heard them making their way toward the living room.

Where had *that* Vanessa gone? When did the little girl in pigtails he'd placed inside a blossoming cherry tree to photograph, pink blossoms bursting behind her, the photo he still kept on his desk at the office, become an enigma to him, her thoughts and feelings blurred? Yet her physicality seemed to be moving into clearer focus, her baby fat erased, her body terribly slim, the features emerging abruptly from her face and the lovely bones below her neck.

"Hello?" Dennis called up the stairs now, his hands on the banister. "Sharon? Vanessa?"

"I'm here." Sharon came into view. "Here I am." She was rubbing in lotion, but it looked as if she were wringing her hands.

Dennis placed his briefcase on the landing. "Did you hear?"

"Please don't leave that there." Sharon pointed to the landing. "I almost broke my neck on it the other day. And then Vanessa thinks it's fine to leave all her stuff there." Dennis watched Sharon's mouth tense, and then, as if she thought better of it, she heaved a sigh and relaxed her shoulders a little. "What?"

"The embargo's on." Dennis picked up his briefcase and headed upstairs, his head down. "Carter just announced it." He understood that the Soviets could have bought up enough grain to feel none of the embargo's effects had they known in advance—and perhaps they had despite Carter's claim that the Soviet harvest had fallen by 48 million tons—but still the lack of warning was humiliating.

"Shit," Sharon said. "I'm sorry, D."

But she'd been *thinking positively!* again, Dennis knew it. God, the feel-good bullshit she brought into this house with that self-empowerment program. More than the religion, which he supposed was steeped in the past, and more than the women's groups, which was, he had to admit, a long time coming, this more recent grasp at outside help seemed truly suspect. Why can't you see *me*? she'd screamed last night when he'd shut off one of her paths-to-transformation tapes. Her face was so close to his he'd had to look away, which of course gave Sharon all the ammunition she'd needed.

Maybe she was *gone* and that's why he couldn't see her. Maybe she was a ghost, like Gloria, only hardly as benign. He missed that girl he'd taken to Skatesville eighteen years ago. Len had lent him the place, and it was the first night he and Sharon had made love in earnest. Afterward, Sharon had gone downstairs to the refrigerator in only her underwear—white, cotton, with a little bow below her belly button—and Dennis had followed several minutes later to see her leaning into the refrigerator, her panties riding up a bit to reveal two cheeks smiling up at him. He had almost gone to grab her by her hips from behind, then she turned toward him, the light from the fridge illuminating her lovely body. Dennis had wrapped his arms around her and she had fervently kissed him back, the taste of the onion dip she'd just eaten still strong on her tongue. Then the dishes started rattling madly in the cupboards and they'd split apart, Dennis holding Sharon by the shoulders, explaining exactly who Gloria was and that she meant them no harm.

He did not want to see her or hear any more of that cult crap, this constant *me me me.* It was the start of a brand-new decade! We were not going to think as much about ourselves as we had been. The thought of history—its constant change and the way it undid the present— exhausted him utterly. He thought of his father's ardent belief that socialism would provide utopia. Also bullshit. Utopia, schmutopia, Dennis thought as he headed into the bedroom. He loosened his tie, kicked off his shoes, and lay back on the bed, looking at the ceiling. All that grain just sitting there, silo after silo of it, he thought, grain elevators churning to a slow halt. Clearly Carter had not been thinking about the economics of all this, because there was going to have to be some kind of a bailout to the farmers and exporters. This year's harvests had been bin-bursting. The farmers had, after all, been told to plant fencerow to fencerow. Now the prices were dropping so fast and the developing world would soon swoop in, more than happy to purchase cheap U.S. grain. Carter had been a peanut farmer, for goodness' sake! What a disaster.

Of course he'd be jostled from the Russian desk. Only in the U.S. government was it a plus to have as little experience as possible; no one was to get too comfortable with one culture, with one country's politics, its people. With its secrets. They would be happy to know he was no expert on Asia; Dennis saw himself getting off a plane in Tokyo and being met by the bright lights of foreign letters and polite round faces.

Dennis watched his wife in the mirror of her vanity. Her eyes were large and brown, and looking into them now, he saw the girl across the room at a potluck to mobilize the vote in the South. *One man, one vote!* they were chanting that night when Sharon had shown up in a miniskirt and a turtleneck sweater with a med student, who later talked incessantly about preventing venereal disease. Dennis would have to have been blind not to have noticed the two of them.

"Why'd you leave early?" she asked him through the mirror.

"Out of embarrassment," he told the reflection.

He hadn't wanted to see his colleagues. Food as a weapon, he'd thought, nodding at Glinda, his secretary, as he slinked out of his office toward the elevator. Glinda. How many times had he imagined his heavy Jamaican secretary arriving to work in a pink bubble with a glittering wand to grant all his wishes? Now he remembered hearing his mother on the other side of the bedroom wall on the nights she sought to punish him for some misdeed by sending him to bed with no dinner. She'd hovered, her palms, he knew, flat against the door. The prospect of his not eating hurt her far more than him. Dennis could sense her bones then, her hips, her knees, her cheeks, pressed against the wooden door, and he would turn the dial of his transistor so the zap and fizz of the radio would reassure her. Denny, she'd say. Okay, my darling?

"Come on," Sharon said. "That's ridiculous."

"What are *you* doing home?" he asked.

Sharon sighed. "Marlene had some fund-raising something or other at the temple all day tomorrow, so we're prepping for tomorrow's dinner party this afternoon."

Dennis was silent.

"The Epstein party, remember?" Then she smiled at Dennis.

Dennis evaluated the authenticity of the smile. Was it truthful or was that the Essential Training speaking? "I do."

"I came home to do an inventory on the canapés in the deep freeze." Her reflection dabbed its neck with perfume.

He smiled now—in earnest—to think of his wife's famous crab cakes, made infamous at an embassy party in 1975. After three flutes of champagne, Andrew Steigman's wife had declaimed that she would not be returning to Gabon with her ambassador of a husband, but would stay here in Maryland and have Sharon Goldstein make these Maryland crab cakes for her every day.

"They do not have these in West Africa!" She'd held up the crab cake, her eyes filling with tears. "They don't even have green apples." She'd sighed, kicking the floor with the toe of her golden sandal.

Dennis had not told Sharon about the compliment, and now he thought this could have been because it might have meant yet another step toward her independence. He loved it now, but back then it had felt as if she were running off with a group of furious women who were throwing out their laundry detergent, refusing to have babies, and stepping away from the "confines" of marriage. They were having loads of sex and Dennis had missed out being on the receiving end of that, though he had managed to get stuck with the rest of women's lib. He hadn't realized the girl eating onion dip with her finger out of the refrigerator in the dark could become so autonomous, and perhaps this was why Sharon would find out how popular her crab cakes were from three diplomats' wives who called her the next day, each wanting her to cater a private party.

Sharon placed the perfume back on her vanity and watched him through the mirror. She looked terrific, still that freckled California girl with the long nose and light brown hair streaked with gold he'd seen stuffing herself with cheese puffs as her date droned on and on: gonorrhea, syphilis, it was really quite bizarre. No wonder she'd given Dennis her number when he'd caught her as she'd gone for her coat in the bedroom.

For their first date they'd gone paddle boating in the Tidal Basin one spring afternoon. The cherry blossoms had exploded around them. Those cherry trees were in bloom for only one goddamn week, sometimes less; the city waited each year to trumpet their blossoming to the nation, and he had somehow caught them in that moment of pure bursting, but he hadn't appreciated his good fortune. I want to fight for peace, Sharon had said, her little muscles tensing with each push. And equality. He'd looked at her tanned, bare feet, and despite all he knew by then, he had nodded encouragingly at Sharon, in a manner he hoped would seem supportive.

Because by that time Dennis had stopped even thinking he might go into politics. He was already twenty-five and politics felt wrong and false and theatrical. It was the people who surrounded the politicians who effected change. He'd already conceded that it was most beneficial to work from within.

D.C. is a remarkable city, Dennis thought now. He still loved to parade visiting friends up the steps of the Lincoln Memorial and turn them around to the perfect mirror of the Reflecting Pool. This is where we marched, he'd always tell them. For freedom. For as long as he'd lived here, he'd been showing off the exact line of that president's unfaltering gaze that reached all the way to the Capitol. He brought them to the Smithsonian, the zoo, the National Gallery. All free! he'd say. He especially loved to tell his father, This is everyone's city. It's why his mother must have been so encouraging that he stay here. They have the best museums, she'd said, such a clean city, she'd said. But did he really believe this when he'd dragged his parents across the Mall, into and out of the Smithsonian and the National Gallery? Because Washington wasn't really that kind of a place at all. What kind of a city didn't even have representation in the Senate? A city that was not real.

"You might want to wait a bit before leaving," Dennis said to Sharon as he sat up. "I hit a lot of traffic, even this early."

Sharon opened and closed bureau drawers. "Did you take the park?"

"Yeah," Dennis said.

"Well, I'm going the opposite direction anyway."

"As you wish." Dennis clasped his hands behind his head and closed his eyes.

When he drove out West with Len after graduation, endless fields of wheat had stretched all the way to the horizon. Had that image started him on his career path? The fields had bent and swayed in the breeze, the impression of a moving hand swept over rich velvet, and the shadows of birds and planes were cast over those golden blankets. Where had they been driving? Kansas? Iowa? Had they driven near the Mississippi? He remembered a river town, a grain elevator, barges tied up for the night. This image had always seemed far more American than the Washington Monument, the Jefferson Memorial, that twirl of a building he sometimes went out of the way to drive by on his commute to work. Looking up inside the Capitol, he still felt as he first had, that he was inside one of those Fabergé eggs his mother cried over as she cut photos from a glossy magazine article about the Bolsheviks closing down the house, the czar's family executed, the children's bones still not recovered. Those last jeweled bastions of imperialism that Stalin couldn't get rid of fast enough.

Capitalism at its most absurd, Dennis thought now, remembering his mother hiding those magazine photos in her bedside table. Sometimes when his father was out, Tatti would remove the pages she'd torn from *National Geographic* and spread them on the kitchen table.

"So beautiful," she'd say as she ran her hands over the pictures, leaving a new layer of fingerprints on the shiny pages.

The Coronation Egg, his mother's favorite, was so striking and bright and shining. He'd once had a replica hanging in a glass cabinet in the living room; it was enameled in gold, with guilloche sunbursts just beneath the golden surface, the trellis of the egg marked by stones set in the faces of imperial eagles. And inside, the plush purple velvet felt as palpable now in his imagination as it had been in the photograph. It housed in its folds a diamond-studded carriage. Just like one the czar rode in, Tatti had said. Nicholas, when he was crowned in Moscow. For his czarina.

Dennis's father hated everything about those eggs.

"It's imperialism, right there, it's the very essence of it," he'd said, the one time he'd come home from some rally for one disenfranchised worker or another and caught his wife admiring the pictures. "The waste. The excess! It's positively criminal."

"Oh, come on." Tatti had tilted her head to the left to admire the photo. "They're just so beautiful. Can't you see them only as beautiful? They are as beautiful as Russia! We should never have let them go."

"We?"

"It was bad for Russia to send them away. In this, Stalin was wrong," Tatti had said.

"In this?" Sigmund had said in disbelief. "In the Fabergés and a few other things, my dear."

Socialism hadn't saved anyone, had it? People were still hungry and poor and cruel and stupid. It hadn't changed a thing. What did his father think now that Malcolm Forbes had purchased that egg last year for over $2 million and that it was now on display in the Forbes lobby, the very embodiment of capitalism?

"In this Stalin was wrong," his father had muttered. "Look, Tatiana," he had said. "You must know by now that you cannot make an omelet without breaking a few eggs."

Two days after graduation Dennis and Len headed to California. West, this figment of Dennis's imagination, the beguiling place at the other end of this country that, when he thought of it now, must have been very much like his father's idea of utopia. Like the idyll his mother had anticipated when stepping off the boat, holding her little suitcase handle with two hands. He had always imagined her entry into the island of Manhattan a bit like Dorothy's wide-eyed advent into Oz.

Dennis too had said no to capitalism. That had been over twenty years ago, but even now he could see the flat black roads outside Houston, distinctly still, the waves of heat rising up from the asphalt and blurring the fields and oil rigs in the distance, those silos so stark and clear against the horizon. Dennis had no idea that Len would go on to break his heart by succumbing to his Republican DNA. He'd actually joined the CIA; he'd become a Republican because that was who he was, by *blood,* and Dennis had remained friends with him because Lenny had Skatesville and Dennis loved Skatesville, because he worked for the government and he couldn't afford a country house of his own. Even his Soviet colleagues had their dachas where they could schtupp their mistresses in the snow and plant beets and onions and breathe fresh air.

The CIA: Dennis would never shake his childhood perception, how he'd watched them come for the shopkeepers and engineers and the rabbis. His neighborhood was filthy with communists, as Hoover had said, and the CIA came around daily, pretending to need their trousers pressed or their hair cut. Stupid officers thinking they would go unnoticed. Or had it been the FBI? They had once seemed to Dennis to be one and the same institution. And to his father, who parted the curtains to watch the strange men with their mustaches. They are trying to walk along our streets as one of us, he'd said, letting the curtain fall. Tools of the ruling class! That's what his father called them. Ethel Rosenberg's mother lived just around the corner, and Dennis had seen Ethel's children playing in the street when the Rosenbergs were taken in for questioning. Only questioning, the neighbors all told one another. She was brought in just after her husband, and she'd left those boys, half wild, with her mother, who had barely minded them at all. There was a line even then, straight and clean as a razor cut, bisecting his neighborhood, and the longer those children were at Mrs. Greenglass's house, the more tense the neighborhood became. Those who supported the communists stood staunchly on one side, and those who did not stood self-righteously on the other. But the communists, in the end, did not help the Rosenbergs. They did not claim them and the Party had let them burn.

That's what Sigmund said. Let me be clear: the Communist Party killed the Rosenbergs, Sigmund said, it was not the U.S. government.

But before any of that went down, before the communists did nothing to help free them, did nothing until the end when it was obvious that Party sentiment had turned in favor of the couple and that they could now be useful to their martyred cause, before they were strapped in that chair—ol' sparky, they all called it—before they went, one at a time, before all that, Dennis woke up and those boys were gone. The lawyer took them away because Mrs. Greenglass couldn't care for them, so barbaric were they. But that was a lie, Sigmund told Tatiana. Dennis had heard him say it. That old bitch is siding with the son, he'd said. Dennis remembered because his father rarely cursed. He was not a drinker, and he was not a cigar smoker; he was not a crass man in any way. That old bitch, he'd said, sided with the son, who would, in the end, do his sister Ethel in.

But what would have happened had the Rosenbergs not been caught? Dennis had wondered that then. Over the years, he'd think of it often: what would the Rosenbergs be slipping to the Soviets now, he'd think, when the sand at Los Alamos had already burned to radioactive glass, when the Soviets had gotten what they'd needed, when the Bomb had already been dropped. He imagined the two of them up late at night writing complex equations on tracing paper and handing them off. But to whom? And what would be on those slips of paper now? Thermonuclear stuff? Disarmament info? Or perhaps they would just have stopped, the Rosenbergs. Perhaps they would have grown out of their radicalism, and they would have raised their children and fed them properly and moved to the suburbs like so many other radicals Dennis's father had once called friends. But they are frozen as they were in all their anti-American glory. They cannot pass gently through history.

How could Len have become one of those men trolling the street asking little kids questions when they got let out of school? That's what they do, watch outside the candy store to ask kids questions. What a creepy job, being in the CIA. Sometimes, it seemed to Dennis, it served the wrong people. While at Columbia, as he and Len haunted jazz clubs and ate ethnic food and went to civil rights meetings and *meant* it, all of it, had serving the wrong people been Len's intention? He'd been Sissy Ford's son, for Christ sake. Dennis remembered Len following Sissy into the dorm like a dog that first day of school. God, Sissy Ford; Dennis hadn't thought of that woman in years. He would go on to meet a thousand versions of Sissy—so many Washington wives with blond hair done up like Jackie Kennedy's, frosted lipstick, tweed skirt and jacket, lots of long, heavy necklaces, cigarette like an afterthought, dangling between long fingers. The look changed only slightly over the decades. But this Sissy Ford was to Dennis the first and only one of her kind, and she had disarmed him with her aloof, ironic, and direct looks and her old Connecticut Yankee accent. When she'd asked Dennis his *baahkground,* he'd told her he was Russian. Well, he'd said, my mother and grandparents were. And she had patted his hand and told him, That's okay, darling, some of our best and brightest have not been here for long.

Dennis got to San Francisco too late, in the summer of 1956; the Beats had already run their course, gone commercial. Dennis saw himself at twenty-two, walking down Haight Street, beneath the western sky. He even walked differently then; there had been jazz in his step. The neighborhood was still so quiet; the Victorian houses stood straight on their hills and the paint had not begun to peel from the wooden paneling. People were still washed; men's hair didn't fall below their ears. No one begged for money or dope, but people of all colors were dancing together. The sensation was still of standing on the lip of a world about to change. Or maybe he'd come too early; he left before Jack Kennedy was shot, before the hippies and the activists came in full force, and it pained him years later to watch the happy newsreels of the summer of '67, everyone fucking for peace and running naked in the streets. He was in the suburbs with two kids, about to turn thirty that summer; he had missed out on everything, and history was going down without him. Yet, watching the circus on the Haight, Dennis had a nagging feeling that he would never have been one of those shirtless men with long hair, smoking grass and inviting drifters and their dogs into his apartment, shacking up with a new woman each week on a soiled mattress on the floor. He was shocked to find himself nodding at the bumper sticker he'd seen on the back of a Mercedes speeding around Chevy Chase Circle: *You think cops are bad? When something goes wrong, try calling a hippie.*

What had going West been like for his in-laws? The Weissmans hated every inch of the Lower East Side and its immigrants, its crooked carts of herring and potatoes, the women in stiff, ugly wigs, their long, black skirts skimming the dirty, manure-filled streets. It was disgusting, Helen said. Anyone who could leave and stayed was a moron, she'd say, pointing her Winston at Dennis. Sorry, Dennis, she'd say, taking a long drag, but it's the goddamn truth.

They'd left for Los Angeles, where Herbert had some distant relative who worked in Hollywood, a few years before Sharon was born. The story was, Helen sang for their train fare, and Dennis imagined them on the train, heading from one ocean to the other, their hands in their laps, eyes trained on the moving landscape. The way they told it— over and over—from the moment they touched Los Angeles earth, it was only sunshine and happiness for them. It was clean and big and open, and the people were civilized. Ci-vi-lized, Helen would say. And money, Herbert would chime in, never missing the opportunity. Let's not forget about the big old bundles of California cash.

"Maybe you can get me a new job tomorrow night?" Dennis said to Sharon, propping himself up on his elbows and watching his wife gather herself together in different parts of the room. "This one's about to get very pissy."

"Stop it," Sharon said. "You'll never leave."

"Oh, you bet I would," he said, but even as he said it, he hadn't meant it. Had he given up when he joined the civil service? Absolutely not! It was an elite agency. There were only 750 of them, and not all were GS-14s and climbing, as he was. But Dennis had always hated that hierarchical grading system the government had to rank its workers. "Absolutely," he said.

Sharon rolled her eyes. "I gotta go. Duty calls. Or more," she said as she walked out of the room, "Marsha Epstein does."

Dennis watched Sharon leave their bedroom and head downstairs. He thought of tomorrow; he saw a map of the world and wondered where he would be told to fit inside it. One day, he thought, he might not fit inside. He thought of his mother, Dorothy, outside her world, looking at the brand-new skyline. When Dennis finally got up and went to pull the curtains back from the window, Sharon's Volvo was speeding up the block.

# CHAPTER 4

# Russian Doll

## January 5, 1980

Vanessa was born two weeks early, and instead of her father, who was tucked away in Moscow, Nana Helen had appeared in the delivery room. The story of her father's absence at her birth was told to Vanessa so many times—according to Sharon, the moment Vanessa was crowning, Nana Helen grabbed Sharon's hand and, instead of words of encouragement, loudly whispered in her ear, "How could you have married a spy?"—that she would swear up and down that she remembered the actual moment her father finally arrived home.

For her; he had come back for her, a tall man in an army green parka, with a fur-trimmed hood, and he leaned in and rubbed her nose with his in an Eskimo hello. He'd brought her a Russian doll, a real babushka. Vanessa was sure she remembered the swish of the nylon parka shell as her father came toward her, though she was born in late May. More likely she'd stolen the memory from the photograph on her father's bureau of him in this very outfit, the tips of jagged, snowcapped mountains behind him.

One of Vanessa's childhood rituals was unscrewing the doll, then opening the next and the next, then lining them all up on her bureau until the very last one, too tiny to be painted but for two black dots for eyes, lying on its side.

Now, perched over the den toilet, Vanessa Goldstein thought of that doll, its bucket shape cut in half at the stomach, a face drawn intricately by thin shavings of jewel-colored wood. Looking at them in a descending line, she would wonder if all these pieces together constituted one doll, or if they were really twelve different ones, with separate selves and souls.

Vanessa stayed in the bathroom so as to avoid her mother, who had stormed up from the basement in a rage. "I'm going to the *bathroom,* Mom," she said through the door, though it was a lie.

"Where are all my crab cakes, Vanessa?" Sharon banged on the door. "They were all here yesterday. I need them for my event tonight."

Vanessa heard her mother cursing beneath her breath as she went back into the kitchen. Vanessa flushed the toilet, splashed her face with the cold water, and leaned into the mirror. Her face was blotched red, and tiny blood vessels, barely visible hairline stars and signs, a galaxy beneath the surface of her cheeks, seemed to break open just below her eyes.

Vanessa wanted a cigarette and to sit at her window seat, blowing smoke out of the screen and into the backyard. For ten years she had hovered like a spirit, unseen above her mother's parties: *This paella is divine, Sharon.* Everyone seemed to have one line they screamed over and over, all night long: *Impeach the fucker, is what I say!* She could see the torches now, burning in the backyard on the evenings Roberta Flack floated up from the stereo, the adults growing more and more loose and wild, their laughs heartier. Their political arguments—who believed more *sincerely* in the importance of banning discriminatory housing in the South, or the *absolute* relevance of the formation of the Environmental Protection Agency, who was the most adamant about getting the soldiers *home. Right. Now*—always grew more fierce as the night faded into the blue-gray of early morning.

Vanessa wouldn't be able to smoke in the house now, she thought, as she sprayed Binaca in her mouth, then shot two short blasts into the air. Besides, it was freezing outside. I am a cowboy! she thought, holding the small bottle up into the air like a smoking gun in one of her grandfather's old movies. Bang bang.

She walked out of the bathroom and down the stairs. "Well, the crab cakes are not in the bathroom, Mom," she said coolly. "Are you sure you didn't take them to the office kitchen already?"

Sharon stood in the doorway, the mustard-, brown-, and orange-striped wallpaper of the kitchen to her back. "Don't you do that, Vanessa," she said, wagging her finger. "I'm sure I did not." Her pinkie moved a stray hair from her face in a manner that suggested she had been handling meat and had not yet washed her hands. "You're being very unfair to me, Vanessa. I had everything carefully planned, and now we'll have to find another appetizer. I don't have time for this." Sharon closed her eyes and breathed slowly in and out, in and out.

Last year, there could have been Vanessa's brother and all his soccer friends to blame for the missing food, those teeming almost-man bodies that wanted only to eat, play with a ball, and fuck. And it wasn't until Ben left that she could really have used his help; September was when this unbreakable cycle had begun in earnest. Up until then, it had only been occasional, too much of her mother's quiche and beet salad this night, a day of hot water with lemon as compensation, the next an empty day after school filled with cheese and apples and crackers and frozen blintzes she'd sauté with sticks of butter and slather with sour cream.

Vanessa watched her mother breathing, clearly summoning strength from elsewhere, running over her Essential Training: I must take action; I must not avoid; I must *transform*. Her mother used to say these mantras aloud, as if they were an argument she was having with herself. Then, when she realized it was not about *conflict,* but *breaking through,* she took to muttering her anchors nearly soundlessly under her breath, like the Orthodox women Vanessa saw on the Metro, bowing their heads and touching their well-worn prayer books with the tips of their fingers.

Her father found LEAP! to be anti-intellectual, anti-political, anti-theoretical, anti–everything we stand for in this family, he'd say when Sharon got up from dinner to take a fellow Leaper's call. At best, he said, it's a clever pyramid scheme. Her father with his gloom-and-doom global-starvation stuff. Far as Vanessa could tell, we were stopping the shipment of grain; it wasn't as if we'd dropped a *bomb*. All anyone at school wanted to discuss was the hostages in Iran. Today was day sixty-two, and there were bets on how long those diplomats could possibly be held. Each night Vanessa went to sleep imagining the release of prisoners destroyed by torture; their return to Washington, violence in their hearts. She pictured official-looking men—like her father's friend Len—unlocking their handcuffs, their bent heads rising, eyes as full of hate as Manson's.

Vanessa felt a little sorry for her mother, who was so clearly forced to turn to this random group of strangers to feel better, to these freaks who would call during dinner, wanting more and more of her time. Vanessa understood it a little. Some kids at shows Vanessa had been going to with Jason were big on PMA. A positive mental attitude, or not letting shit get you down.

"I don't know what you're talking about," Vanessa said to her mother now, knowing full well that she had taken the puffs from the freezer and shoved them into her mouth frozen, two and three at a time. That's what she did while she was waiting for the crab cakes to heat up in the oven.

"Please, Vanessa, you have to stop this!" Her mother reached for her wrist, her short nails grazing the tender inside.

Vanessa pulled her hand away sharply, not sure if her mother meant to comfort or punish. Vanessa walked into the living room: off-white sofa, off-white pillows, stark white blinds, ivory walls, but once it had been filled with worn, red Oriental carpets, Russian jewelry boxes and nutcrackers, Fabergé egg reproductions that sat with other schlocky miniatures in a tiny wood-and-glass cabinet, a chandelier Sharon had bought at a flea market in Paris, and Vanessa's grandmother's *Sheriff of Sundown* movie poster, *the only decent western Herbert ever made.*

The austere room seemed whitewashed, defying a past, but it had always made Vanessa think of blood, most likely due to what had happened there when she was a kid.

When they'd settled into the house, Sharon threw a tea for the neighborhood women. Ben was already in kindergarten, but Vanessa was still home, and her mother had let her shove her little hands into the bowl of ground meat to squish together the Swedish meatballs. Her mother set her wedding rings on the counter as she too dug her hands into the mixture, grabbing Vanessa's pinkie beneath the meat. And she remembered the crooked pink hairline spine of the shrimp, placed on silver trays with the deep red clotted cocktail sauce in a bowl at the center that her mother had set out for their new neighbors. Of course, there had been the broiled pineapple so she could scream with dismay—*once there were purple pineapples on these gorgeous wood floors, if you can believe it!*

Just before the guests turned up, Sharon was always at her best. Waiting suited her, and today was no different; she was relaxed and ready to win strangers' hearts.

Until a neighbor showed up with her Great Dane.

"Oooh," Vanessa squealed from inside the hallway.

Sharon straightened.

"Hi. I'm Elaine Rudwick," the woman said.

Vanessa tried to run and pet the dog, but her mother blocked her from leaving, and the dog and its master from entering, in one sure gesture.

"Hi, Elaine, so nice to see you, but there sure are a lot of kids here."

"It's okay." Elaine smiled at Vanessa. "Natasha is very friendly."

Sharon let Vanessa pet the dog, her fingers straight and tense along Natasha's broad nose.

"I know," Elaine said to Sharon, her shoulders dropping in a show of just how much this knowledge weighed on her. "I'm so terribly sorry to spring her on you, Sharon, but she just hates to be left behind. Looks really are deceiving with these guys, they're just big ol' babies. Is it okay?"

Vanessa and her mother could not see the women who had already arrived behind Elaine, crossing their arms and shooting one another knowing glances.

"I suppose it's okay, but you will keep her tight on that leash, right?"

"Absolutely," Elaine said, holding up the thick leather lead and smiling.

Children raced through the downstairs as their mothers tried to control them, attempting also to eat, drink, and have conversations of their own. Vanessa heard the same talk she'd always heard. "I just can't do it all," Mary Farrell, who had given up teaching when she had her first child, said. "I mean, I've read Betty Friedan and I've got the same problems my mother did. Only *she* got to take Valium."

"God, I would love some Valium," Ella Larson said, getting up wearily to get her son to stop hitting Mary's daughter.

Vanessa turned from this just in time to see five-year-old Trudy Macintyre, whose long blond hair Vanessa already knew enough to envy, holding a meatball up to the Great Dane's nose. Natasha was fixated, drool streaming from both sides of her great jowls, and just as the girl brought it back toward her own mouth, the dog lunged for it. She got the meatball, and part of Trudy Macintyre's face, in her enormous mouth. Blood poured down stunned Trudy's cheeks.

"It's her eye!" one woman screamed, and several mothers dropped to the floor, patting the carpet to see if the eyeball, large and hazel when it had been in the girl's socket, had rolled near them.

"She was going for the meatball!" Elaine said more than once to the room, though no one was listening. Then she looked directly at Vanessa. "Children should never tease dogs with food. She just wanted the meatball, it's only natural!"

Vanessa nodded slowly. "Okay," she said.

The dog's ears slammed back as a distraught Elaine took her from the house.

"That dog should be shot," one woman said before Elaine had closed the door behind her.

★ ★ ★

Eventually Sharon, who had gone with Mrs. Macintyre and Trudy, called from Sibley Hospital to let the waiting party know that the injury was not to the eye itself, but merely the right-hand corner of the eye*lid*. Trudy's sight would remain intact, but still, Sharon wept as she tried to clean up the awful mess.

"It's like Myra Hindley was here," Vanessa's father said upon walking into the house and scanning the living room.

"That's not funny, Dennis," Sharon said. She was still scrubbing the tiny bloody handprints from the freshly-painted-just-moved-in walls that made it look as if Trudy had been trying to escape.

"I know. I know. How terrible." He put his briefcase down and loosened his tie. "What can I do? Should I go talk to the dog owner?"

Sharon shook her head, talking at the wall as she scrubbed. "I already have. It was an accident."

"But it happened here. They can sue us."

"I don't think they will. They wouldn't!" Again Vanessa's mother began to cry. "It's just such a terrible way to move to a new neighborhood!"

Vanessa couldn't see her father's face as her mother went to hug him, the scrub brush, now bloodied, sticking out from behind her father's head as she leaned in.

No one sued the Goldsteins. The dog was not put down, as many of the women had suggested, and Elaine—not the Goldsteins—was the one vilified. Those who had witnessed her crime walked with hands placed firmly on their children's shoulders to the other side of the street whenever Elaine walked by with the dog. As Trudy grew up, five houses down from the Goldsteins', her perfect face, fringed by nearly white bangs, was informed by a jagged scar along the right side of her eye and cheek. Vanessa feared her, the same way she feared a friend of her father's who had been stabbed. They had gone to visit him at home after he'd been robbed and knifed on Capitol Hill, and Vanessa had refused to go inside. Instead she sat waiting on the front stoop, imagining the knife coming out of this man's side, a wound oozing pus and blood. There was something terrifying about seeing someone's insides, the effect of one man undone by another. Ben had made fun of her, but then he too had held back until Sharon put her hands on his shoulders and pushed him inside the house. Later, she brought

Vanessa a paper plate of red peppers and carrots and onion dip, and she set it down between them on the stoop and put her arm around her. When you're ready, we'll go in, she had said, and Vanessa had leaned into her chest.

After the dog incident, the living room that had just been redone from the previous owners to display the eclectic household riches went stark white. Replacing it were the neutral colored paintings purchased at the Torpedo Factory, where artists' studios were opened to the public each weekend. Dennis harrumphed that Sharon was so willing to shell out money for these amateur works, artists validated only by the amount of rent they paid for a place to paint, while his paintings were warping downstairs, stacked in the moldy basement.

"I could rent a space here and sell to the public too," Dennis had said to Sharon upon leaving a potter's space, fat brown mugs with swirled handles (Sharon would end up buying several), heavy magenta and black plates, and large mustard-colored bowls lining the walls on lopsided wooden shelves.

"They're very discriminating about who they rent to, hon," Sharon had said. "There's a board and a committee and all kinds of applications."

"These are crafts, Sharon, not art." Dennis squeezed Vanessa's hand. "Daddy's an artist too, you know," he told her.

"He is," Sharon said, nodding her head affirmatively. "Absolutely."

As her mother agreed with him so readily, Vanessa knew instantly that what her father had just said was not true.

Several hours after Vanessa's confrontation with her mother, after Sharon had sped off in a fury to her catering event, after her father had listened over and over to his recording of Carter's grain embargo announcement—who records *Carter?*—her mother called and demanded she get over to the Epsteins and help out, *now*. There was no getting out of it, and as Vanessa came downstairs, she paused, looking again out onto the living room. Only last year Ben would have been here, feeling up some freshman on the couch before their parents got home. Vanessa forgot for a moment how she'd been disgusted by the parade of girls her brother brought in, each one so comfortable with her body and what she was about to let him do to it, and she longed to feel less alone in this house, less inflicted upon by their parents. Last year, Ben could have gone and helped their mother at her party, which everyone would have preferred. Vanessa positively dreaded the prospect of an evening serving her mother's uptight food at some political event. Not only would the people be hateful, but Vanessa wasn't good at balancing a lot of trays and smiling as she picked up used glasses and crumpled napkins. And she didn't like to be around so much meat and sour cream.

She remembered the night of the dinner in August, before Ben left for school, how he had come back from hanging out with his friends and had drunkenly wandered out back, where Vanessa swung alone in the hammock, thinking of her ride along Rock Creek Park, a ravine waiting to swallow her and Jason up were they to tip and fall. Ben had climbed onto the hammock with her and lay on his back, and he smelled like a mix of beer and sickeningly sweet Love's Baby Soft, and Vanessa had curled onto her side and watched his lashes touch down to the skin below his eyes and then rise up again. They'd made fun of their mother's jars of wheat germ and the way she'd slipped while carrying a sack of bagels for some ladies' brunch. They laughed at her wobbly ankles and her obliviousness to stones and fallen branches that had always made her stumble as if she were having a seizure. Vanessa did not bring up how she had recently begun to wonder what would happen when her mother got older, her bones more fragile, bird's bones, hollow and delicate despite all that obsessive attention to nutrition. They'd ridiculed their father's T-shirts and folk-music posters, his beat-up car that made him believe he was still a sixties radical, which they weren't sure he had ever been anyway. Vanessa had cupped Ben's shoulder with her hand, and he had stretched out his arms and placed his hands out in front of him, the leaves of the trees blocked by his splayed fingers.

Wait for me, Vanessa had thought as she'd watched her brother throw his final duffel into the backseat of their mother's car. Her parents drove him away, and she stood alone with her four grandparents.

"There he goes," Tatti had said, sniffling. "Off to see the world."

"Oh, please," Helen had said. "The poor kid's going to Massachusetts."

Vanessa felt absolutely wicked for having eaten her mother's party food. Would her mother be consoled or mortified to know she hadn't enjoyed it? That her jaw actually hurt now from chewing through the frozen pastry dough and the sharp cheese sticks?

"I'm going to help Mom," Vanessa screamed up the stairs to her father, both hands on the banister. "I'm taking the car, okay?" She heard her mother's tightly wound demand. *Now*, Vanessa, right this minute, do you hear me? and she'd felt a pang of regret that Jason had taught her to drive stick, weeks and weeks of jerking the car down these suburban streets and still she hadn't completely mastered it. "Okay?"

"Sure, just leave me stranded here." Dennis dipped his head into view, then turned back to his bedroom.

"Me too," Vanessa said softly, grabbing the car keys from the bowl in the kitchen, pulling on her grandfather's old, heavy black coat from the front-hall closet, and heading out the door.

After stalling twice while backing out of the driveway, Vanessa zoomed up the block, opened a window, and lit up a Camel—finally. She lost interest in controlling the music and just clicked the radio on: *Once I had a love and it was a gas. Soon turned out had a heart of glass.* The song was so many layers, fused to form this perfect whole. Blondie's bubblegum voice was somehow also edgy, the lyrics savage, drums driving hard behind her. Vanessa drove in the direction of Dupont Circle, along Connecticut Avenue, thinking of breathtaking Blondie, enviably blond, beautiful, and strong.

Taking a long drag on her cigarette, Vanessa remembered teaching Bee and Heather and Jessica how to blow smoke rings, the way Nana Helen had taught her. It was before she'd met Jason, when it had been the four of them, climbing out her bedroom window and sliding down the drainpipe, quick as cats, and running to the playground. They'd pull cans of beer from the plastic rings of two six-packs and lie back on the spinning roundabout at Candy Cane City while one of the girls— usually Bee jumped off first—pushed them in circles. While it spun, they tried to stand as the platform rotated faster and faster beneath their feet. They'd raise their hands and scream out, then lie down again on the cold steel, and smoke until their throats hurt. This was before Vanessa had sworn off beer and pot, off anything fun but music.

Vanessa passed Bradley Boulevard and resisted the urge to turn right, toward Jason's house. The invincible Debbie Harry, who surely never had one moment of self-doubt, continued; how did she manage to *sound* blond? Vanessa guided the Beetle around Chevy Chase Circle, the last mark of Maryland before it became the District. These circles are modeled after London, her father would inform them as they chugged around toward it. Well, jolly fucking fabulous, Vanessa thought now in a mock British accent. She pictured London, Big Ben rising behind the kids in pink Mohawks, safety pins in their noses, that she saw on postcards all over Georgetown.

She'd barely had her license two months, but now she was free of her parents and Ben shuttling her around. Her brother had been so obnoxious when he was the only one who could drive. Vanessa would stand at the top of the stairs, all hope and shimmer in her Gunne Sax shirt with sparkly threads, and jeans, with Bee and Heather and Jessica, each in a version of the same, waiting for Ben to take them anywhere.

"Maybe next time, girls." Ben would wink, slamming the screen door shut and leaving the four of them stranded at home—what a *dick*—to read the best parts of *Forever* out loud in Vanessa's room again, or to walk over to their friend Ed Brady's on Primrose to listen to the sound track to *Grease*. Ed's father was a senior partner at Arent Fox, and their enormous, expensively decorated house—beginning with the unforgettable zebra-skin rug in the foyer—became famous when it was used as the setting for a party scene in *All the President's Men*. The five of them would smoke pot in Ed's massive bedroom and parade around his bedroom singing, *Look at me, I'm Sandra Dee, lousy with virginity!* Later, they'd all hold hands in a line, count to three, and jump into the heated backyard pool.

Then one night Ed took peyote when they weren't there and he never came back from his trip. His father found him under the hedges by the pool and put him in Psychiatric Institute, on Wisconsin Avenue. Vanessa and her friends hadn't seen him since, and instead they hung out in far less glorious friends' homes, soon moving on to the bonfires at Chevy Chase Country Club or the Georgetown bars that Ben frequented, places that were known for not carding. Then Vanessa met Jason, and she'd thought she could leave all the shining stupidity of boring suburbia behind.

They met the night the Tellers played the high school talent show. She and Bee and Jessica had come to watch Heather perform "Both Sides Now," the only song she knew on the guitar, which she played over and over whenever the four of them were together. Vanessa loved Joni Mitchell, but more the deep, saddened, abandoned Joni Mitchell, not this sweet folksinger who seemed to fly in on a unicorn and dress her songs in lace and fairy romance. The girls all stood and cheered Heather in her peasant skirt, her strawberry-blond hair held back by a roach clip dangling with a yellow feather.

As Heather walked off the stage, strangling her guitar by its neck, the Tellers rose up from below the stage playing hard, and Jessica and Bee looked on in disbelief.

"Yikes," Jessica said. "What shit!"

But Vanessa liked it. This was not—thank god!—Heather and her tentative fingerpicking. Nor was it her family's protest music, her father after work setting his briefcase on the landing, shucking his suit as if he were shedding a skin, and putting on his woven Guatemalan shirt and leather sandals. He'd play "If I Had a Hammer" on the record player over and over and over. Vanessa and Ben would dance around the room screaming, *I'd sing it in the evenin'. All over this land!* as her father balanced his drink on his knee and tapped his thigh. Sharon, holding a glass of wine, would sway from side to side next to him on the couch. Remember, D? she'd say, closing her eyes and waving her arms. The darkest it got was Dylan or Pete Seeger, a glass of whiskey sipped as Sharon banged around in the kitchen fixing dinner. Her father would sing alone, *And the boys go into business, And marry and raise a family, And they all get put in boxes, little boxes, all the same.* "Ticky tacky, ticky tacky," he'd arbitrarily say throughout the night.

Ben had his own music too; he'd blasted "Only the Good Die Young" from his bedroom for the past two years. She could hear him singing after dinner, *You mighta heard I run with a dangerous crowd . . .* and then his accompanying *yeah*s, as if Billy Joel had provided some kind of rebel anthem. Dennis would have to come up and tell him, "Ben, come on, enough. Not so loud," and Vanessa knew this pleased her brother, who was *not gonna turn my music down, man.* Her brother was ridiculous, yet there was something so lovely about lying on the floor with Ben and listening to "Piano Man" over and over. She'd first heard the song at camp, and the time Ben had played it for her had both ignited her memory of summer campfires—the stillness of the lake the campers learned to canoe on by day, the shadows of the evergreens rising along more distant shores—and seized her heart with what she did not yet know she would always search for in music: brokenness. The visceral feel of ruin. In all its many guises.

Grandpa Sigmund was also an avid music connoisseur, as was Tatti, who worked at a music company as a receptionist three mornings a week when Dennis was little and who, he said, was always trying to get her brother Misha permission to come to the States. Such a beautiful player! she'd still tell them all, shaking her head. Such beautiful music.

Sigmund had tried, and failed spectacularly, to teach Ben and Vanessa about Mahler and Handel and all the Puccini they could bear, but several years back he had also become quite obsessed with disco, which he had little more success in passing on to his grandchildren. Vanessa still had the compilation her grandfather had given her, K-Tel's *Disco Rocket*—a selection that actually contained more hits from 1976 than actual disco—stashed away somewhere in a closed box in her closet filled with pet rocks and Rubik's Cubes and the platform sandals her mother said she couldn't have because she'd break her ankles in them. She had pitched such a fit over them that Sharon had thrown up her hands and relented. And then, of course—*of course!*—Vanessa had sprained her goddamned ankle simply walking off a curb in front of the house because her ankles were exactly as weak as her mother claimed, and by the time her ankle had healed, the sandals—tan leather with the sweetest little yellow and red flowers you'd ever seen painted along the sides—were too small. Too small!

Listening to the Tellers allowed Vanessa to momentarily become a different girl from the one who wanted pretty sandals and Barbies and painted nails. After the set was over, Vanessa went up to the stage to wait for Heather, and freckled Jason McFinley in two-tone creepers and blue jeans, dyed green and cuffed at the ankles, was there waiting for his friend George, the drummer, to finish up.

"Hey," Jason said to Vanessa.

"Hey," she said. "That was great!"

Jason shrugged. "It was okay, I guess."

Vanessa was silent.

"You ever go to the Atlantis over in Takoma? They play *good* music there," Jason said.

As Heather stood with her guitar and her flush of performer's pride, Vanessa felt suddenly embarrassed by her friend's earnest playing. Vanessa shook her head.

"We're going out to Randall Park. Just me and George"—Jason nodded toward the stage—"and Flaherty."

Flaherty! For months Vanessa had watched Sean Flaherty Jr. loping through the hallway, his skateboard held as tight to his side as her father held his briefcase. Rumor had it Sean's father was a Republican in the Department of Energy, waiting for Carter to be *taken down*, but this hadn't quelled his mystery.

"It's cool if you want to come with us," Jason said. "We're just going to hang out."

Vanessa tried on an indifferent face. "Sure," she said, trying not to smile. "I guess so." She turned to Heather. "I'll see you guys later, okay?" Why hadn't she invited Heather along? She had rarely done anything without one of those girls, and as her friend stormed off, Vanessa felt suddenly relieved from the burden of them.

They all got in Sean Flaherty's pickup, he and George in the front, and Jason and Vanessa in the truck bed with Sean's skateboard.

Ah, skateboards. Yet another slice of youth culture that, despite its gender-neutral quality, had always been verboten. Period, Vanessa's father had said. It's a death wish.

The Goldstein house was perched at the bottom of a long, smooth-hilled street, and day after day she watched kids skateboard down the perfect curve of it: on their feet, on their stomachs, two together, sitting upright and sometimes three and four boys laid out flat on top of one another, the toes of their sneakers dragging and popping up behind them. Vanessa was dying to skateboard, *dying* to, but Timmy Farrell had broken his collarbone four times, and Dennis had said it was parental negligence on the part of Mary Farrell that she let him keep up with it. Someone should call the friggin' police, he'd said, and it was true Vanessa had seen Timmy supine in the backseat of his mother's wood-paneled station wagon on the way to the hospital at least four times. I find out you so much as put one toe on a skateboard and you'll be in the house all summer. Ride your bike, Van, you love your bike. See the world.

But Vanessa's blue Schwinn was decidedly *not* a skateboard, and Ben, content with four square and his kick-the-can-playing friends, always the team player, was of little help in the matter. Then he left the street for the field sports that would consume him, leaving Vanessa perched on the lawn, grabbing her shins, as she watched kids zoom down the hill with unfettered joy, then run back up again, all afternoon and into the evening, until the fireflies started blinking and their mothers called them all home.

They headed out of the school parking lot and Sean sounded his horn, which beeped out "Stand by Your Man." How *ironic*. No one so much as tossed back a beer, a stark contrast to her friends, who tipped their heads beneath the keg taps at bonfires or on the porches of out-of-town parents. Once, when her father was traveling on business, her mother, who had a late-night event, had come home unexpectedly early. Everyone made it out, except poor Richie Gonzales, who had been too fucked-up to run and had instead thrown up on himself in the closet where Vanessa had hid him. He'd had to sit in his own puke for hours, until Vanessa was sure her mother was asleep and he could sneak out. Though Ed, in PI, had been a cautionary tale, some of Vanessa's peers took LSD and peyote and smoked pot on the way to school and during lunch. Some would skip school altogether and go to Great Falls and trip all day in the woods, where, rumor had it, senators disposed of any kind of evidence that would impinge on their re-election, even, it was said, *bodies*.

As they drove farther into Maryland, Vanessa imagined these guys raised in the dirty living rooms of broken homes, single mothers screaming and throwing bottles at their criminal boyfriends. That's what had made them *them*. It's what necessitated their disenfranchisement, Vanessa thought as Sean played Elvis, loud. When they hit Macarthur Boulevard the truck lurched forward and Jason caught Vanessa in his arms. It was almost summer, and the sky was a deep indigo and they lay back and looked up at the sky as the truck headed out Greensborough Road, where there were no lights, toward Randall Park, which was not really a park at all, but a wide-open field beneath the radio towers of Bethesda, dotted by radio lines and receivers. There, the three of them—Jason, Vanessa, and George— lay in the grass and listened to the Specials: 2 Tone, manic, anarchic fusion. Vanessa giggled, and she and Jason nodded their heads to the ska beat as they watched Sean skate on the rails, until they all decided to go home.

The summer of 1979. Vanessa worked as a camp counselor at Evergreen Hill in Potomac, and after her day of schlepping seven-year-olds—the girls in her cabin were the Squirrels—from the pool to the arts-and-crafts tent to the drama area, Jason picked her up, and despite the astronomical price of gas and the time one had to wait to get it, they would drive either to Fort Reno, where bands played free each Monday all summer long, or into the District, down to the Watergate and along the Potomac. Behind her was Maryland; Virginia was just across the river. And before them was the whole beckoning city. She did not know what had happened before she arrived—Jason had told her countless stories of the destruction of the punk radio station WGTB, the Cramps at Hall of Nations, the Ramones at the Palladium in NYC on New Year's—but that summer Vanessa experienced d.c. space on E Street, July Fourth at Madam's Organ, *Road to Ruin*, and Bad Brains for herself.

The music was inescapably close. It was the opposite of Capital Centre, where Vanessa and her brother had seen David Bowie, a pinprick of moving light, a swath of flesh and gold and glitter. Before she'd gone to local shows, the stadium had been the only place she'd ever seen music played live. Someone passed out these homemade flyers with a photo of Carter, his fist in the air, say, some cartoon speech bubble condemning Madam's Organ emanating from his mouth, and next thing you knew, you were there, listening to the Insect Surfers and the Slickee Boys. You never knew who was playing until someone put down a piece of tape and said, Don't cross this line. Here is the stage; here are the people. Everything was so close and everyone was reacting, either running in or getting thrown back. What would it have been like to see Bowie here? It would have been outrageous, Ziggy Stardust parading so unimaginably close, unable to hide behind an alien alter ego, singing so strangely and deeply about all kinds of love.

Shirtless boys slammed into one another, bodies so thin and lanky she could see their blue hearts beating through their chests. There was no way to be separate. This was real protest music, Vanessa thought, remembering her father looking menacingly into his drink, so furious, but Pete Seeger singing "Little Boxes" had sounded so sweet. It did something, and it did it so close to your face. You needed to be straight to understand that. You needed to say no to everything but music. To have purpose. This was what Jason told her, and she believed it now, the way she believed what her grandfather said: No one needs to wait for permission for anything. Vanessa felt those first shows from the back of her throat to the tips of her fingers—the music was here and living in her now, ruining her. For the first time Vanessa believed that D.C. wasn't simply a generic place for bureaucracy, administrative buildings, and schools and stone monuments; it felt for once that this town had room for more than *government*.

Sex was not part of a punk education—a lot of the new bands were swearing off it, just as they were drugs—but Vanessa did have sex with Jason. It was July 3. She remembered the date as she'd thought to wait until the Fourth, Independence Day. Because that's what she'd thought it would be like; it would be throwing your hat into the ring of adulthood. Womanhood. She brought Jason deep into the woods of Evergreen Hill, after her campers had all gone home, and the sex was neither here nor there, she'd thought, as they sneaked out from the forest and into the parking lot, then out onto River Road toward downtown. There was no pain, or fear or blood, as Bee had lectured them all that there would be, merely the disappointment that it had ended before it seemed to truly have begun, and the mad itch of mosquito bites up and down the backs of her arms and thighs.

After, they met Sean and several of their friends, boys who wore black ska hats and skateboarded or wore suspenders without shirts and skateboarded or wore oxford shirts with the sleeves ripped off and skateboarded, downtown. That night they saw the Teen Idles and Bad Brains, and Vanessa stood way in the back watching, alone. She was not one of the boys whipping himself into a frenzy, charging behind the band as they played. Don't hurt yourselves now, someone said into the mike. Ian Ian! His songs were loud and short and fast, but that was all Vanessa got. She was not one of those girls who wanted to play, either. People were going nuts. Later, when Bad Brains came on, H.R., the lead singer, was wild, and he pinned several kids to the floor, screaming into their faces, spit flying. His voice warbled, it screeched and it howled while belting out lyrics about social ills, and free societies, all so rapidly she could hardly make out the words. Vanessa had never seen anything quite like the violence of him; the musical attack was relentless. Yet it also sounded as if it had come from the heart, that it had been cut from it, like with the jagged top of an old tin can.

There had been no pain or fear or blood, it was true, but there had been something else, sadness perhaps. She leaned against the dirty wall and thought of Jason—who was now jumping up and down in front with Sean—rocking on top of her, and it felt as if everything were ending, not beginning. She thought she'd feel the way some of her mother's friends did who came by over the years and tapped out cigarettes, chatting about their birth control pills and their ex-husbands and their brand-new *lovers* when they thought Vanessa had not been listening. They had felt so freed by sex, it seemed to her now. But she had felt awkward and crushed and unsure, more childish than before they'd begun.

"Was that okay?" Jason had asked when they were brushing off dirt and slipping back into their underwear.

Vanessa had nodded as she pulled up her jean shorts. Two heart patches—pink and red—were sewn over holes at the crotch. "Yeah," she said. Why was she choking back tears?

"Can you believe we did it?"

Vanessa looked into his wide white face, his lips full and red, the dark brown roots of his hair showing through the blond. She had this profound feeling that he was not *her*. It felt in that moment that no one was, and also that she was not herself.

That night she saw H.R. hit Dexter McDonald, a kid from her math class who was thin as a stick of kindling but as bendable as putty, with the mike. The kid showed off his bloody wound all night. Sean nodded seriously when Dexter bent to show the blood on his forehead. Then everyone began to dance like crazy, harder than she'd seen. She watched the boys, who did not play soccer or lacrosse or rugby, finally finding a reason to throw their bodies into one another. They came at one another so hard, the club had to stop the music, warning that the second floor of the old building could collapse.

This shit was not on the radio. The radio was her father. The radio was Tatti, her classical records held tight to her chest. Then the show was over and after they'd dropped off several kids and their boards, including Dexter, who kept checking the rearview from the backseat to make sure the dried blood was still there, Jason and Vanessa went to her house and into the backyard, where they had sex again, at her urging, because she thought it would feel different this time, but it was just the same. Exactly.

Vanessa continued toward her mother's party in Dupont Circle, past the two roaring lions and onto the Taft Bridge. She flicked her second cigarette out the window and imagined it sailing down the Potomac, like one of those kayaks roaring along the Great Falls, crashing into boulders and heading over waterfalls. A protest was always gathered on the other side of the bridge, but tonight, in the dark, she couldn't tell which of the causes it was: gay pride or peace.

Over the bridge, down Connecticut, Kalorama on the right. Tonight would be horrid. She pictured Jason on his twin bed, listening to the Slickee Boys or White Boy and breaking the sealed plastic on some obscure music magazine to read an interview with Ian MacKaye. She imagined Jason helping his mother put the dishes in the dishwasher after dinner, Jason who threw off his shirt and ran around in mad circles with Sean as the Teen Idles played Reno. How was that the same person? She wanted everyone to be a single entity: all those nesting wooden dolls digested by the biggest one. Whole.

Vanessa circled the block, looking for parking; the Police sang, *I'll send an s.o.s. to the world. I hope that someone gets my . . .* She passed the house twice, a soft light in the dining room. The Police were so overrated, she thought, watching the Christmas lights still blinking on a massive tree, then the brighter, violent light of the kitchen in the next window, her mother passing by, arms cradling a basket of vegetables. The sound of Sting's voice seemed like a question, but not one whose answer was terribly pressing. And it was *so* radio-friendly. *I hope that someone gets my . . .* Vanessa continued to troll the block, waiting for a space to open, so she could get inside and get this night over with.

# CHAPTER 5

# Transfiguring

**September 1979**

When it came to deciding on college, Benjamin responded so clearly to his grandfather's voice of dissent. That, and Columbia had rejected him. Because I refused to give them money, Dennis claimed when the thin envelope arrived. Universities are just the same as corporations; they run on capitalism like everything else.

Once, who Ben was had seemed so clear to him: he was running down a long green field. He'd always sought a goal, and he was a swath of blue shorts, a swish of tanned flesh against the bright green AstroTurf, a body continually moving toward it. When he'd come home after soccer practice, stinking of sweat and dirt, but pleasantly spent through, he imagined his future in sports and a life of teammates, and practices and coaches, games won, and also lost, orange cones and deflated balls, nets ripped and sewn, whistles blown, yellow cards thrown, uniforms pulled on and off and on again, girls waiting on the sidelines or high in the bleachers, everything a part of this beautiful and knowable structure that being on a team had allowed him.

But last winter that image had begun to collapse. The resulting transfiguration was due largely to Sigmund. Ben thought of his grandfather on the white living-room couch rubbing his hands together, readying to speak: Without conflict, true true conflict, there is no movement forward, he'd begin. And the protests, the real protests, started with the workers! Any protest against the Vietnam War, any picket line, we can't really understand it without going back to the Bolsheviks; we really can't. Everything comes from before. We were really under the spell of that revolution—I was only a boy, but it was this amazing thing. The workers revolted! It was unheard of. And I could say, because this is my point of view, that everything from there is in decline. And people here started to believe it could happen as well. Of course capitalism is a very powerful thing, he'd say, and to prove his point he'd go get a box of cereal from the kitchen. Holding the box up high and shaking it, he'd rail about how that box was intended to make boys like Benjamin think merely to eat that cereal would transform them into strong athletes. Which Ben had of course believed it would.

That winter Ben began to listen, and in so doing his sense of sight seemed also to heighten, and he saw himself transformed. Now before stepping into the shower after practice, that image he once held so close—*of winning*—dissipated. What replaced this idea of running down a field was one of him alone at a desk piled high with books and papers. Benjamin was bent over his own work, but from where he looked in, he could never get close enough to see what was printed on those pages that held him there until long after dark. Was it a timeline, an equation, a symbol, a fairy tale? The image had such clarity, and at the same time, it was blank.

It was this voice and not the voice of his coach yelling at him, *Pass now!* and not the voice of his teammates screaming, *Here! Over here!* as they got closer to the goal, but Sigmund's voice Ben heard when he decided on Brandeis. And he heard his grandfather's voice when he turned around in the tiny dorm room that looked out over a stone-rimmed pond, to hug his father and gently tell his weeping mother, good-bye.

Unfortunately for Benjamin, his grandfather's perorations came too late. Because by the time he arrived at Brandeis University he'd missed everything. It was September 1979, and he'd missed History, those years of resistance and protest, which was the very reason he was here, and not at some Southern school with its emphasis on sport. What was he made of before? Snakes and snails and puppy-dog tails . . . that's what Grandma Tatti had always told him. Vanessa was sugar and spice; what a load of crap. Vanessa was filled with a lot of bullshit—no beer, no steak, no weed. She was empty! And anyway, since when did opting out *mean* anything?

Because he had left home, nerves exposed, and he was ready to opt in. He wanted in on all of it. But where the hell *was* everything? Where were the burning bras and draft cards? Where were the heirs to the Ten Most Wanted on the FBI list, who all had gone to Brandeis? Who would be the successors to Angela Davis and Abbie Hoffman? The first few days of school had revealed that the heirs to activism were a bunch of pre-law and pre-med students from New Jersey; it was good riddance to everything those sixties radicals had stood for. The only organizing Ben could find was a freshman orientation in the student center called Fun Fair!, no joke, and here Ben was partnered with several horsey, dark-curly-haired girls from New Jersey—he would soon learn this was the Brandeis *type*—and a dorm "meet and greet" where he and his dormmates were asked to reveal their best scar stories. Benji had bent his head and parted his hair to show the lightning scar, evidence of a fall off the bench freshman year that nearly cracked open his skull. (Yes, it's true, the ever-so-coordinated Benji fell *off the bench* . . . )

Arnie Lefkowitz's scar story was his nose job. Arnie Lefkowitz. How the two of them had ended up as roommates was beyond Benjamin, who had written his interests fairly earnestly on the form—playing soccer and ice hockey, watching baseball and basketball, sometimes football. The only thing he and Arnie had in common was that neither smoked. Arnie had a large, doughy body with disproportionately small feet and was from New Jersey. Ben was the only person in his dorm not from New Jersey. So far he had only met two people on campus who were not from New Jersey: Rajani Guptas, from India, and the delectable Rayna Zahavi, from Tel Aviv. And though this was not in any way a problem, Ben assured everyone, Arnie was gay.

Arnie and his identical twin brother, Michael, also gay, with or without self-knowledge, Ben was not sure, adored tap dancing and show tunes, as well as their twin jobs at the campus bookstore. *Hi, Arnie, hi, Michael,* the girls all sang when they went in for their Snickers bars and Yoplaits before lunch. But were they taunting them, or flirting? Both boys always giggled.

Not three days of school had passed when Ben walked in on Arnie blasting the sound track from *Follies* and tapping to "Who's That Woman?" Ben had opened the door to Arnie screaming, his hands moving in large circles, his little feet tapping away: *Lord, Lord, Lord, that woman is . . . Me! Me! Me!* he sang breathlessly.

"Sorry," Ben had said, quickly closing the door. He put his back against the door and breathed deeply.

After a brief moment, the music was turned off and Arnie cracked open the door, a towel slung over his thick neck. "It's okay, Ben. Sondheim just gets me carried away, you know?"

"Not really." Ben looked down and could see Arnie was wearing leg warmers.

"Come on, Ben! Sondheim!"

Ben found it impossible not to like him.

What else? The usual sign-ups for classes and clubs, the purchasing of outrageously expensive textbooks, and the barbecues and keg parties— slim pickings compared to the wild stories of drinking and debauchery and serious sportsmanship that Nick at Notre Dame would tell—that signaled an East Coast liberal arts education had officially begun.

Ben had already screwed an Israeli and gotten drunk at several "illegal" ZBT frat parties when it happened: finally, a sign. A ripple of dissent, a window onto the past. In response to the announcement that the university intended to serve pork and shellfish in the non-kosher dining areas, a protest had risen up, and proud signs were posted all over dorms and dining halls: *BLTs coming to you soon!* It was scandalous—serving pork at an institution founded in Jewish law? The uproar was tremendous, and protests were spearheaded outside all the dining halls, including Sherman, the cafeteria on the south rim of the Massell Quad and directly across from Ben's dorm.

Students stomped around the rim of Yakus Pond with handmade posters: *First it's shrimp, next the camps!* And *Pork is dirty* and *Kosher food is clean food!* The kosher and many non-kosher diners were livid, as were members of the larger Jewish community, who came in from Boston to give speeches on the singular importance of maintaining Brandeis's *history*. Quotas were mentioned several times, as were the hypothetical desires of the righteous Justice Louis Brandeis. Even Albert Einstein's opinion was considered on the *What would Al say?* placards, which was how Ben learned that originally the school was to be named for Einstein, but they'd fought over issues of fund-raising and spending.

Those who supported the university, in favor of pork and shellfish, were also represented, and these few protesters who were protesting the protest carried their own signs and banners: *Diversity is the spice of life* and *Internationalize our eating!*

Ben had to pass the dissenters at breakfast, and while he usually ate lunch up the hill in the student center near his classes, he passed them each evening at dinner as well, including an olive-skinned, black-haired, short, big-breasted, and as revealed when she held up her sign—*Get your rules out of our kitchens!*—very hirsute Rachel Feinglass. Yet despite her hairy armpits—the hairiest he had seen on any woman, or perhaps any person—he found himself brushing by her on his way to meet his new friends in Sherman.

"Come stand with me," she said when his arm touched hers.

"Me?"

"What's your name?" Her teeth were incredibly white against her tanned face.

"Ben."

"Benji," she said. "Sweet. I'm Rachel. Want to hold the sign?"

He shrugged and looked around at the scrappy group of protesters. It had been four days and the intensity had obviously waned. Just this morning it was reported in the Brandeis *Justice* that talks had resumed, and soon a verdict would be handed down.

"Sure," he said. "But can I just say? What's the big deal?"

"Benji." Rachel put her hot palm on his cold shoulder. "It's not about the pork and shellfish, you know that, right?"

"I know. But it kind of *is* about that, you know?" The sign seemed to wilt in his hands, and realizing this, he hoisted the wooden splint upright with both hands. "I mean, that's the issue at hand."

"Uh-uh." Rachel shook her head. "This is about choice. This is about making our own decisions, about being free. This is about truth, about what this university is supposed to stand for. This is a *participatory* democracy. I'm a vegetarian, what do I care if I can get a club sandwich here? But soon they'll be telling us we can't get birth control on campus."

Just Rachel's mention of those two words, *birth control,* uttered from the same mouth that housed those two straight rows of blinding white teeth, sent a shot of electricity straight down to Ben's crotch. He felt a line starting from his throat and bisecting him straight through.

"You're so fucking right!" He stood up straight and leaned the sign against his shoulder. He put his free hand in his pocket.

"You have to make your own revolution," she said. "We can sit here and just beat off, or we can do something!" Rachel looked over at the ten people on her side of the debate. "Every view must be questioned. And for every view there is an equal and opposing position."

Ben had heard this before, minus the beating-off part, but did girls really do that? Could they? He imagined what that might look like. Anyway, he shook the titillating image away; it all sounded new to him. It felt specific to *them*. This girl is phenomenal, Ben thought, though from this moment on, he would be Benji. And right then, as if to tether him to his own past that lacked any sort of political mobilization whatsoever, he envisioned Nikol Stathakis in her blue-and-yellow cheerleading uniform, her tanned legs and arms emerging from the polyester at her center. Nikol had been one of the few girls he'd balled in high school for more than a couple of weeks. Probably he thought of her now because of the dark skin. Or maybe because Nikol set Rachel, this voluptuous fount of radical thought, in relief. Opposite, but not necessarily equal, he thought, remembering the first time he and Nikol had sex in his bed when his parents were away, and though they'd had the whole evening, he had been quick, then they'd just lain there, not a thing to say to each other. He remembered the song on the radio: *Thinking of you's working up my appetite, looking forward to a little afternoon delight . . .* More due to his discomfort than his desire, though her body had truly been astounding, Ben had kissed her neck and rolled on top of her, entering her again. Nikol was rumored to have a porno video in her school locker and *Playgirl* pages torn from the magazine and pinned up over her bed. Once, after a country-club bonfire several blocks from the Goldstein house, they'd walked to his house and, though his whole family was home asleep, snuck into the basement—a cold room that smelled of his father's sweaty balls, with chalky walls that left markings on whatever body part had the displeasure of making accidental contact with them— and done it in an old sleeping bag he'd found rolled up behind the couch.

Unlike Nikol, Rachel Feinglass was incredibly short, a little bit stout, and had ideas; she had what he had come to college—to this college, the same college that was about to take away his right to choose what he ate—to find.

"There's a party in Rosenthal tonight." Benji pointed to the dorm of suites where Peter Cox and Roland Berger, juniors from his American Protest! class lived. "Want to come with? Around nine?"

Rachel reached for her sign. "Go eat." She pushed him toward the cafeteria doors. "I'll meet you right here." She kicked the ground. "At nine thirty."

Benji nodded. He looked up to see the pond, reflecting the tree branches in the still, clear water. The sun was setting and he could see his dorm darkening across the quad. He wondered if Rachel would be coming home with him tonight and if his roommate would be there— though whom was he kidding? Arnie never spent the night out.

Benji's back was to the hill, flanked by the practically brand-new library, and the social studies center. All of Brandeis had seemed modern, not like Columbia, where the buildings were held up by columns as old as the D.C. memorials.

When Dennis had been dragged to look at the school, he'd said to Ben, "Where's the fucking ivy?" But Ben had liked the new feel of it, the way it seemed as if nothing too important had happened here yet.

Up from the library and along the curved hill was the student center, where kids played Hacky Sack and Frisbee on the lawn, right in front of the glass window of the radio station, then up the steps to Rabb and Olin-Sang, where American Protest!, a popular yearlong survey course, and his World History class, ironically only one semester long, were held. Beyond all that was Waltham with its old redbrick watch factory, where women died from the effects of licking radium-filled paintbrushes to sharp points in order to brush teensy numerals onto watch faces. The beaten town did not seem terribly welcoming to the college or its students. The most birth defects per capita in the United States, the students all said. Boston's smelly armpit, they called it. Beyond the town, along the Pike, just ten miles, was Boston and Cambridge. But Benji had yet to leave campus.

He smiled at Rachel. "Sounds good!" he said. "I'll meet you here. X marks the spot." He jumped in place and then planted his feet firmly on the ground and handed Rachel back her sign. Rachel Feinglass's sign.

I fucking love college, thought Benji.

The zealots, or the batshit crazy Jews, as Benji would call them, won in the end. The day after Benji and Rachel met in front of Sherman Cafeteria, it was decreed that no pork or shellfish be served. Period. Alas, there would be no seafood salad, ribs, or strips of crispy bacon served anywhere on campus.

Rachel was crushed by the decision—not for herself, of course, as she explained several times—but after several days of letter writing and an expansive phone campaign, she decided it was time to move on to something more important and global, like freeing South Africa, for instance. Or anti-nuclear activism. She was the most passionate little thing Benjamin had ever met.

And she had gone back to his room with him after that party in Rosenthal. By some wonderful miracle, Arnie did not return to the room until long after Benji had examined her magnificent breasts, also a rich brown that seemed to go down many, many cutaneous layers. Her nipples were dark, the large areolas defined, brilliant suns setting against the sky of her skin.

After that night, Rachel and Benji spent lots of time in his dorm room when Arnie was at work or at madrigal practice, and after getting each other off without intercourse, they watched the building of an enormous sukkah below his window, constructed of branches and fig leaves and husks of corn. As Rachel gave Benji a spectacular blow job, he could hear the dry husks being nailed to wood, juxtaposed over the sound of Rachel Feinglass's Grateful Dead bootlegs she carried everywhere in her Guatemalan bag. The drum space was a perfect wall of sound he liked to listen to while nuzzling Rachel's breasts.

Benji was proud that they had not yet had sex, though even this brought much debate.

"This *is* sex, Benji," Rachel told him after he had let her know how delighted he was that they had refrained from sex, which, he told her, really changes everything. He had just come between her tits, which she wiped with the corner of his pillowcase. "Are you saying lesbians don't have sex? You have such a heterosexual view of the world." Rachel pulled on her sweater, and without her bra, Benji could see her nipples pressed up against the worn navy cotton weave.

As always, Benji knew Rachel had an inarguable point, and he accepted this and everything else she had to teach him. Still, Benji thought secretly, sex *can* ruin things. He thought of lying next to Nikol Stathakis and the uncomfortable silence between them, even with the radio playing: *Sky rockets in flight. Afternoon delight. Afternoon delight.* He thought of Erin Mackaby, with her bobbed hair and that single strand of baby pearls encircling her short neck, her penny loafers and her nearly diabolical dedication to being captions editor of the yearbook. She'd spend whole weekends in the *Wildcat* office, committed not only to correctly identifying every kid in each photo, but finding a clever way to caption that photo as well. Erin had lobbied for more candids, and she'd won. She'd put in a photo of Ben's sister sitting in class her freshman year, her feet up on her desk, her head leaning back over her chair—Vanessa's hair spilled out, long and wavy and highlighted blond from the beach, her giant smile revealing a large space between her teeth. *School's in?!* the caption had said. Vanessa looked like a little kid, like such a little sister, Benji thought now, which made him realize that when he thought of his sister at all, he pictured her as a seven-year-old, fighting for space in the backseat of the car, while he, at his current age, towered above her. Benji had always liked her following him around and copying everything he did, from wearing his baseball hats backward to using the same nicknames for teachers, to listening to the same 45s. It made him feel as if his decisions had always been correct. When she lost interest in him, he had sort of returned the favor, he supposed, or maintained the same veneer he'd always had around his sister. But he remembered being stunned by that yearbook photo Erin had found and captioned, most likely as a favor to Ben. Vanessa looked nothing like that anymore, but Sharon had adored the photo and had gone so far as to buy her own yearbook, just to cut out this picture of Vanessa not looking or acting anything like Vanessa and hang it on the refrigerator.

Ben and Erin had been friends since junior high algebra, where they'd had a teacher who wore a kelly green polyester jacket, used green chalk, and would say things like *You can factor this polynomial until Gabriel blows his trumpet* . . . And one afternoon in the fall of Ben's senior year, when he was walking home from soccer practice, he'd run into Erin, whose parents were at their house on the Cape. Erin's place was at the bend in the road, just before Ben turned off to his, and she invited him in and made a pitcher of sea breezes, then another, and then he'd taken her virginity, which she had given over quite willingly. They'd done it in her parents' four-poster bed; even now he remembered the eyelet duvet cover and all the pillows she'd thrown off the bed in haste. He'd felt terrible afterward, that he'd robbed his friend of the experience of having sex for the first time with someone who loved her. Her body had no curve or bend to it at all; it was somehow very unfemale, and its squareness made Ben unable to see her after that. He hitched rides from practice or took alternative routes along the train tracks so he wouldn't pass Erin's house, and he knew that no matter what Rachel said about heterosexual privilege, had he simply gotten a sweet little blow job from Erin, everything would have been just fine.

While he explored the creases and crevasses of Rachel's Rubenesque body and the parallel folds of her incredibly nimble mind, Benji also investigated the limits to his own consciousness, dropping his first hit of LSD, a little tab imprinted with a unicorn. Learning about the different layers of perception, he and Rachel, who had stuck out her tongue and said *ahhh* at Benji's mere suggestion, wended through the Brandeis campus on acid. They dragged their feet through the leaves on the many paths, sat on the lap of the Judge Brandeis statue, covered in birdshit, and walked three times around the reservoir. They ended their trip by climbing up to the water tower at dawn and making love below it, in the cold earth, looking out over Waltham, the red bricks of the watch factory growing deeper with the rise of the sun. It was mid-October and a light frost covered the grounds, melting as the sun came up, and Benji felt amazed at the new power sex could hold.

"See," he'd said after they'd rolled around on the hill for over twenty-five minutes, he on top and then she on him, then finally he from behind as she lay, her face smothered in his spread-open jacket, arms stretched behind her, his hands pressing earth, sinking into it, four knees brown with soil, as she turned toward him, "I told you."

Rachel Feinglass smiled at Benji. "Okay." She lolled from one side to the other, the dirt, now warmed by the sun, sticking to her ass and thighs. "You're right."

Benji dragged her up and they pulled on their jeans and picked leaves from each other's hair, then walked shakily down the hill toward Sherman for bagels. Rachel heaped scallion cream cheese onto her onion bagel, and Benji, still jittery from coming down, was unable to eat and watched her as the tip of her nose dipped straight into the cream cheese when she took a huge first bite. And another and another, her image becoming clearer and crisper to him, sharp lines delineating her body from the world she sat on and in.

Sex had a novel potency for Benji now, but learning, too, took on a new enormity. He had not yet been introduced to the intensity of his own scholarship, had never previously mustered the sort of passion he now found in Professor Schwartz's American Protest! class. The coveted course was difficult to get into for a reason. Here were ideas: movements leading to movements, and those to changing the way this country did business, radicalism in its purest form, its cycle turning and turning, making America; it had happened here on the very campus where Benji now stood. Then one late-November night at his dorm-room desk, his room filled with a muted yellow light, the scratch of winter at his windows, the image he'd had of himself back in Chevy Chase, Maryland, alone at a desk, was finally fulfilled. Here it was, the text he could never see as he looked so many times over his own shoulder: *The Decline of Socialism.* Here was Grandpa Sigmund, young then, perhaps twenty, here in blurred black and white, standing on a street corner in a wool overcoat, his face shaven, arm stretched out, a finger pointing skyward, addressing the gathering of men. *Trotskyite Sigmund Goldstein stumps for Socialist candidate Norman Thomas,*

*1932,* it said beneath the grainy photo. Erin Mackaby couldn't have captioned it any better. There was Grandpa Sigmund, a movement's vanguard, changing the dynamics of history, and now here he was, Benji Goldstein, his grandson, finally discovering what it really meant to be alive.

# CHAPTER 6

# The Chopping Block

**January 5, 1980**

Dennis thumped the steering wheel as he turned off Connecticut Avenue, and a shock of hair came down over his eyes. It was the Day After, and he knew the office would be in chaos—everyone called in on a Saturday—as it had become more and more clear that Dennis was not the only one Carter's people had not consulted before announcing the embargo. No one seemed to have bothered to talk to the economists either; the Treasury secretary was on bloody vacation last week. The private exporters had rushed in this morning with some fairly bad news: Monday they'd be dumping all that embargoed grain—to the tune of 17 million tons—on Chicago. The message from the grain companies seemed to be, just cancel the contracts and watch Chicago burn. It made no sense: futures on corn and soybeans were about to nose-dive, and in the end the Soviets would make out like bandits just as soon as they came back into the American market.

Dennis went over his first briefing in his head, but the rules were changing every moment. And the hostage situation—day sixty-one, Robert Conley had screamed yesterday on *All Things Considered*—was just going to further complicate their decisions. Suddenly—or not suddenly at all, depending on who was talking—the Soviets' military aggression in Afghanistan and terrorism in the Middle East had become intertwined.

Maybe this was his chance to move on. But to what? Worker bee, he thought, Bartleby. Dennis imagined standing in the audience, rapt, during one of his father's great labor speeches. The worker, the worker, the fucking maimed, dead worker, a slave to Corporate America, wheeling-dealing tools exacting every ounce of blood of the worker, no safety measures at all! Capitalist America is the source of all evil in the world!

Sit down! Strike! Boycott! The West was built on the measly shoulders of the Chinese; we all know how the South rose up, rose up, rose *up*!

It was a good job though. Far more administrative than he might have liked, but also thrilling: Novodevichy Park, an empty bench in the snow, meetings in the ministry, Stalin's skyscrapers winking to one another through the cold, long, black Volgas whisking him over the Fourteenth Street Bridge in D.C., confidential meetings with the CIA, he and Len waving to each other in the hallways as if they were merely passing each other on the way to the john in their dormitory. It was a kid's fantasy, the stuff of movies, this part, and he'd known the package when he'd signed on with the Foreign Ag service. He'd been relieved when, in the sixties, he'd decided—finally—on a career, but now it felt as if possibilities had closed up around him, the red tulips he'd planted last spring smashing shut, beautiful traps that held nothing. But what had those flowers captured? Everything Dennis might have pursued but had not: a career overseas, politics, the intended Ph.D. He felt haunted by the man he might have been, and this made him remember Gloria's appearance in that bedroom that reeked of sex, her presence in a slammed door, billowing curtains, the tilting of the mirror on the vanity. He had made a choice—to live a certain kind of life, to serve the greater good, a socialist conceit—but he knew there was nothing radical about what his life had become.

Dennis parked his car in its designated underground space and heard his own footsteps on the smooth concrete, watched his fingers press the lobby button in the elevator. He remembered Vanessa reaching up to press the button on one of the Saturdays she came in with him. Then he saw himself, his mother lifting him up so he could press the button to ride up the Empire State Building, where the CHORD offices were. Her brother, she'd said, was a musical prodigy. Misha. If only he could come and record here, she'd told them. Dennis did not meet his uncle until his first trip to Moscow; he had finally convinced his always reticent mother to give him Misha's address. Dennis had been sending him little pictures and drawings for nearly thirty years by then. I'll look him up myself if you won't give it to me, Dennis had said. His mother unfailingly gave in to this kind of pressure, which, Dennis reasoned, was a throwback to her Soviet childhood.

He thought of Misha now, barreling through Red Square in his big fur hat, to take Dennis to the GUM department store. Dennis had rung him up from his dreary hotel—he would never get used to those wearisome hotel rooms—and said, Would you like to meet me? Perhaps you can take me to find some presents for my son, he had said, as there seemed to be nowhere to purchase so much as a trinket. He knew this was an American conceit, as there was a shortage of any kind of consumer goods, yet still, if there was a way to bring Ben a gift and meet Misha at the same time, why not? Since that day Dennis had been to Red Square many times, but then he'd never before seen St. Basil's Cathedral, its colorful domed chapels and cupolas dusted with snow, or Lenin's stark, red tomb, or the Kremlin and all its towers topped with emerald green spires and red stars that spun in the wind.

"How many Bolsheviks are buried within those walls?" Dennis had asked Misha as he trailed him winding quickly through the square.

"Many." Misha looked down at his feet as he said this and he seemed to be laughing.

Misha brought Dennis to a raised area, which he now knew to be Lobnoe Mesto, the place of executions. It was perpendicular to the massive department store, and it was fenced off and guarded by sentries who waved them through. Dennis followed Misha up several broken stairs through a short wrought-iron gate that led into a circular area. In the center was a large cylindrical block that stood nearly three feet high.

"What is it?" Dennis asked, running his hand along the top of the stone.

Misha slid the side of his hand along his neck, indicating the block's function. The chopping block, Dennis realized, as his uncle explained in Russian that the raised stone was for the removal of heads that contained evil thoughts about Russian rulers during the reign of Ivan the Terrible.

Then they ambled back into the square, filled with people and police, their olive green uniforms stitched with red and gold piping, their tall hats rimmed in red and gold, the emblem of the Soviet Union golden at the center. The square smelled of sweat and garlic and tobacco, like the rest of Moscow. They went into the massive, ornate department store, which on the inside had the feel of the Paris train station with its glassed, arched roof with cast iron, light spilling in. Looking up the three stories, Dennis had remembered arriving at the Gare du Nord from Dordogne on their honeymoon, carrying his and Sharon's luggage, and a bag filled with tins of foie gras, through the enormous station. In contrast to the ornamented exterior, GUM's inside was gracefully utilitarian, like the general feel of the city's buildings, the floors and facades made of marble and red granite and limestone, the different levels crossed above by walkways, like bridges, throughout the enormous building.

The department store—resembling a cross between some kind of an oriental bazaar and Macy's—seemed to be the only place in Moscow where there was not a shortage of things. There appeared to be thousands of stores, and people were lined up outside each one, sometimes spilling out into the square, waiting to purchase goods.

"When Stalin's wife committed suicide," Misha said, guiding him in and out of the queues, "here is where her body was displayed for the people to see." He pointed to the floor, but Dennis couldn't tell if he meant this spot or this mammoth building.

They finally reached the wooden facade of a store, flanked by otherworldly sea-green limestone columns, on the second floor. No one argued when they cut the line and went straight to the front of the store. Dennis looked quickly among the colorful boxes and babushkas that lined the walls behind the counter and pointed to a box with a rooster painted on it. Without waiting a moment, Misha pointed to a different box, a troika scene, and without even asking if Dennis liked the choice, which he in fact did, bargained the shopkeeper down to just twenty-five rubles, a little over a dollar. He paid with a check, signing it with a big flourish and throwing it onto the counter.

Dennis was impressed. The whole country operated in cash—no one used scrip to pay. And for twenty-five rubles? It was a bit ridiculous. "You know this seller?" Dennis asked.

"We are old friends." Misha's nose was small and red and compact, and when he smiled, it crinkled white. "From school. He likes my playing." Misha's dark eyes twinkled, just like those of the Santa, ringing his bell beneath the Empire State, whom Dennis, making drawings for him at the kitchen table, his mother pulling burnt meringue cookies out of the stove, always imagined his uncle Misha, so far away in the Soviet Union, resembled.

"Thank you," Dennis said, grateful to have a gift for his son on the eve of his sibling's birth. Sharon would understand once he explained, There is really nothing to buy here. It is worse than you think. But Benjamin would want something, even if it was to appreciate when he was older.

"For my nephew." Misha slapped Dennis's already cold cheeks. "Anything," he said, before heading off, his gray wool coat flapping in the wind.

Now Dennis thought of the CHORD offices in the Empire State Building were on the fifty-fourth floor, at the end of the long, cold corridor, and Dennis could see the city laid out before him like a board game. We want to see the tippy top! his sister had pouted. We never got to the top. Instead they'd gone to drop papers off at the tiny office, and Dennis remembered sheet music everywhere, as if a wind had come in from where they stood so high in the clouds and blown things into chaos, old metal file cabinets haphazardly placed around the room, against windows, drawers hanging open like gaping mouths. Boris, his mother's boss, sat at the desk facing the door, and he stood up to greet them, jiggling change in the pockets of his enormous trousers. They'd gone ice-skating at Rockefeller Center with Boris. Come on now! Boris, such a sure and beautiful skater despite his heft, said to Dennis in Russian before he'd come up from behind in his big, thick coat and swooped him up. Accha! he'd said as they whipped by, beneath golden Prometheus, offering his mythical heat as they made their way through the cold.

Dennis headed out of the garage elevator and into the Agriculture building, through security, where he nodded at Clive, who touched his blue hat with the twisted yellow rope along the brim in hello, Clive who had been here even longer than Dennis, who was the first to tell him, The ID goes here. He'd touched his chest. Not here. He'd pointed to his breast pocket. Dennis headed over to the third wing, *click click,* tiny flecks of light bouncing off the linoleum floors, hallways like in high school, all the boys clinging to their books, backs against lockers, waiting for the girls they'd seen all summer at the pool to pass—Pitt Street Pool, goddamn, he still remembered those neighborhood girls in their capris and button-down shirts, scarves tied at their chins, disrobing, their new one-pieces beneath, and the way they slathered themselves in baby oil and spread out to cook, turning again to roast their backsides, deep lines from the plastic lawn chairs imprinting in their reddening flesh—then finally up to the fifth floor. He went into his office and threw his jacket over the desk chair; he loosened his tie and sat down.

Worker bee, worker bee, he hated the thought, then another image of Vanessa rose up. Here she was seven, still his, on the Halloween she dressed as a bumblebee. Her legs sprouted from a big, round center, a pumpkin costume Sharon had covered in black-and-yellow fabric, and a headband strapped to her skull, with two black pipe cleaners attached. Sharon could have Rosh Hashanah and Passover. She could have Sukkot; she could build a fort and hang squash from it like teats for all he cared, because Halloween was his holiday, pagan or not, and he took the kids trick-or-treating every year. That year Ben had been a disappointing Pelé, the most distinguishing feature of the costume a large 10 taped on his MSI soccer jersey. The number covered his usual, everyday number 12, on his back and also on the front of the shirt, right over his heart. Ben had tried to paint his face with brown paint, and Dennis had forbidden it.

"But why?" Ben asked. "Pelé is brown. Now I look nothing like him!"

Dennis had known this was an opportunity for discussion, but he felt exhausted by the idea of it. Later, he thought. I will tell him about Paul Robeson another time. I will tell him the way we all once sang together one day, but not now. "People are very sensitive about skin color," he'd said. "And when we paint our skin a color that we are not, well, that can be insulting even if we don't mean it to be."

Ben had looked at him cockeyed, and Dennis had looked side to side to see if Sharon had witnessed the pathetic exchange. So much about his life surprised him—why he didn't give his son some kind of window onto the imperativeness of civil rights and his sure view on this was one of these moments.

"That's so stupid!" Ben had said, stomping down the stairs. "Now no one will know who I am."

It was true, Dennis thought. Ben now looked nothing like Pelé.

*There are so many things that mark us,* Dennis had thought to tell him, but he'd stopped himself. He thought of his mother, her foreign accent as much a moniker as is skin, though she could choose to keep her mouth shut. He used to will her silent; sometimes he couldn't stand the sound of her voice. "Of course they will!" he'd lied. "The number ten is the dead giveaway. That's the important part."

Ben sulked the whole evening, dragging his bag for candy—a *Sesame Street* pillowcase that didn't help his cause—along the sidewalk and stomping up every ivy-lined walk in the neighborhood. This mood was worsened by Dennis's rule that the kids could not eat a thing until they had sorted through each piece of candy, ensuring that no wrapper had been ripped open, that the homemade cookies and caramel popcorn balls, the loose M&M's in sandwich bags tied up with orange and black, curling ribbon, had all been tossed. Every year his kids screamed to fight his policy, and they tested him blatantly, but crazies were out there, lunatics, even in suburban Maryland. Once a little girl at Ben's school bit into a candy apple and nearly sliced off her tongue on a razor blade that was hidden inside. That was what Ella Larson had said, though it had never been substantiated. Who could speak more to the threat of food than Dennis? He thought of DDT, still used to save crops from being eaten up by insects—might as well gas us all—long after the ban was in effect. He'd been there, working with farmers to find viable substitutes, but no insecticide worked better than DDT. It's why people used it on their lawns. Len's father had sprayed it on his, and Len had mowed the lawn every week, DDT-soaked grass swirling all around him in the summer heat. Maybe *that's* what made him a Republican, Dennis thought. It's easy to talk the liberal talk when you don't see people *starving*. DDT lets people eat! As a father, at least, he'd thought he could protect his own children, his lily-white, soccer-playing son, his little bumblebee of a daughter.

A worker bee. Dennis imagined himself now, a garment worker, or a furrier, one of the Russians Sigmund was always trying to unionize in that brief period after the Jewish gangsters had laid off the garment industry but before the communists swooped in. Perhaps Dennis needed mobilization after all; or was he in a position of power here in this government building? It all depended on how you looked at it. He still *believed;* he was the same man who cried when those soldiers stomped all over People's Park in Berkeley. The same man who cried as the hippies and the radicals actually banded together to turn that parking lot into a park, but he'd also cried because he had not been part of it, that he'd been here, *here,* worrying about his membership at the local pool club. The pools were not public in Washington, or not the good ones anyway. And here he was on his way to the administration building to discuss policy with the·person who would discuss policy with the person who would then discuss it with the president. The president of the United States.

Dennis closed the door of his office. At his desk he gripped the arms of the chair and wheeled it back and forth over the thick sheet of plastic until the front left wheel rolled off onto the gray carpet, stopping the chair suddenly. Dennis pitched slightly forward, like a crash-test dummy, his neck jerking forward. He stood up, flattened his tie, and went to open the locked cabinet to take one more look at the Landsat images before this morning's status briefing.

He rolled up his sleeves and lined the three most recent satellite images in a row. Dennis always thought the pictures—bright greens that marked urban spaces, reds delineating crops, and blues, the sea; colors as artificial as neon, set against black—were striking, far more worthy of a place over the living room couch than the ridiculous neutral painting on which Sharon insisted. He imagined mounting an image, hanging it in the living room, and having one of his Soviet colleagues over for cocktails. Though this was not protocol, the thought of Viktor Uspensky, with whom he'd developed a fairly informal if not personal relationship, thinking he was looking at a major artwork but seeing instead a satellite image that included his own home, amused Dennis. He pictured Viktor in his Stalin-era housing development, or in his little dacha, out in the front lawn, kneeling in the dirt and trying to coax his beets and carrots into growing big enough to eat. Would Viktor recognize his own home in these images? Of course he would; the Soviets knew everything. It was the Americans who were dancing so hard to catch up. Certainly we should know that by *now*.

By his untrained eye, he gauged whether there was more red—sustenance, winter wheat and squash—than there had been last month. People were paid to translate this stuff a hell of a lot more accurately, but they were holdovers from Ford, and Dennis couldn't stand them. He had a list of their names and extensions clipped on the folder containing the images, which were practically useless anyway, as they did not reflect the stockpiles. That's what Herndon Skye, the guy at the top of his list, had told him. They could have tons of grain hidden anywhere, he'd said, but you know that, right? It's entirely possible that the Soviets—those bastards—have been stockpiling for years. Now Dennis deduced that they would not feel this embargo in the least, and that the American farmers, DDT sprayers pried out of their white-knuckled fingers, would be the ones to truly suffer.

The CIA's job was to determine if there were stockpiles. People from Intelligence were now illicitly skulking through the country trying to estimate the grain on reserve. Could that be Len? Who knew, he was always so purposefully vague about his job. He could be doing absolutely *anything*. I'm just traveling, he'd say. You guys can have the house for the month. He was always so generous, but sometimes it was nice to be in Skatesville together. Len's wife, Annie, was a Southerner, and they had twin boys, and for years they'd take a weekend a summer together, despite Sharon's clear dislike for Annie. She thinks she's so damned sexy, Sharon would say, and it was true, Annie was always at the beach in a teensy knit bikini, swishing out of the sea, dripping with water, while Len smirked at her, burying his cigarette in the sand. She pawed at men when she talked to them—well, she did Dennis anyway—and she wore her hair long and parted in the middle, like a teenager. So what? Dennis would tell Sharon. So she thinks she's sexy, there are worse things.

Almost ten years ago, Dennis remembered now, they were all at the house together and the kids had finally gone to sleep. The four of them were sitting out on the porch in mismatched chairs drinking Len's mint juleps and talking about how much they hated Washington. The city, of course. Because Len would never discuss his job. Their distaste for the town and the bland people who inhabited it was a running joke. Or more, their disdain was not important because of the unacknowledged feeling that all this was temporary; back then Washington still had the potential to become *their* town. It was like the beginning of their marriages. Their offhand comments about the trappings of married life—arguments recalled, acted out, and laughed at in exaggerated public charades—meant little because it had not yet taken on a darker, permanent cast. Their marriages had not yet become what they now were, unchangeable perhaps, without the potential to become something else, something better, still magical.

Dennis looked over at Sharon as she unfolded her legs and got up.

"I'm going in," she said, looking straight at Dennis.

No one moved. The chairs squeaked along the creaking floorboards of the porch.

Len looked up at her and smiled. "So soon?"

Sharon crossed her arms and nodded.

"Well, sweet dreams, sugar," Annie said.

Dennis knew that Sharon, who had probably expected the party to disband with her leave-taking, had no choice but to go inside now. He waited to see what she would do.

When she turned toward the door, Dennis said, "I'll be in, in a bit."

Sharon quickly shut the screen door, and then Len got up, and Dennis and Annie followed him, the three of them stumbling out into the front yard and toward the woods. Annie's shapely hips and browned legs, emphasized by her frayed cutoffs and illuminated by the moon, sashayed in front of him as they walked along the loamy earth, thrashing through the night forest. When they got to the small clearing that marked the end of the property, they sat down on the thick, damp moss-covered rocks.

Len took a joint out of his crumpled pack of Luckys. "Can you believe this is our life?" he said after lighting it and passing it on to Annie. He stared up at the sky.

Dennis didn't know if this was a bad or a good thing. "This seems to be exactly your life," he said, inhaling. He could taste Annie's sugary lip gloss on the joint. "This was your plan, wasn't it? You don't seem that different than I expected, I mean. Other than the voting for Nixon. I don't know why I didn't anticipate that." Dennis laughed.

"I voted for Humphrey," Annie said. She was propped on her elbows, her head leaning back, dark brown hair spilling down behind her.

"You did?" Dennis turned toward her. "That's so sweet. I had no idea."

"Yup," Len said. "I never mentioned that?"

Annie giggled and took another drag on the joint. She crossed her legs, Indian-style, and Dennis, who was lying down, caught a flash of her pubic hair in the moonlight.

"Nope," Dennis said. He wanted to reach up and grab her hand.

"So. Your life is different then?"

"My life is different," Dennis said, sitting up. He ran his hand over the back of his head and felt his hair feathering along his palm. "It sure is."

They finished that joint and smoked another, and Annie and Len smoked several cigarettes apiece, then the three of them sloppily made their way back. Dennis stood before the house, the little picture windows glowing from the orange light of the living room and the wooden kitchen through the gray dark. It was all so pleasant, but it didn't seem real. Once they were inside, Dennis watched Len and Annie leaning into each other, giggling up the stairs—they always made such a goddamn show of it, Sharon was right—and he turned to go into the guest room.

"Hi," he said, after he'd peeled off his shorts and T-shirt and gotten into bed. The cotton quilt smelled of wet leaves and insects, and he slid under it, pressing against Sharon. He brushed her hair out of her face and skimmed his hand along the side of her neck, then her breasts.

Sharon looked up at him, her dark eyes shining. "How could you have let me go?"

"What?" Dennis instinctually lifted his hand and brought it to his hip. "Let you go where?"

"Let me go inside," she said. "All alone. You just left me here all alone and went off with them."

Dennis turned away from her, his heart racing. From what? The marijuana? His erection? His disappointment? "I thought that's what you wanted. To be alone."

"You did not," she said.

Dennis thumped his pillow. "Good night, Sharon." He lay back down loudly, trying to still his thumping heart and will himself to sleep.

When Len offered him the house for the month, Dennis had asked where he was going, and Len turned silent. *Hello?* Dennis had wanted to scream. *It's me!* But he was being ridiculous. Annie probably didn't even know where Len went off to or with whom he met, though Dennis didn't get the feeling that she really cared either. He tried not to be bothered, but it really bugged him. This was Len! And Dennis didn't even know what the guy did for a fucking living, though a few weeks later, when they'd gone to Skatesville alone, the only way to get Sharon there again that summer, Vanessa had found some Chinese jade medallions in a drawer in the living room, and Dennis had thought perhaps Len was doing work in China, for his beloved Nixon. This, based on a frigging piece of jade.

Gary Jensen, also with an elusive job description, was Dennis's contact at the CIA, and Dennis needed to be in touch with him about the Landsats. He had met Gary at Skatesville years ago and would have called Gary a friend, primarily at first because of his connection to Len. How else would he have found himself alone with him on the Chesapeake, sails unfurled, taut in the wind, the boat flying beneath the Bay Bridge toward the sea? Dennis, who as a boy had only watched the boats coming in from the Sound every Sunday, now opened sailing season on Gary's boat each year. For fifteen years they'd done this. By now they *were* friends. Dennis knew of Gary's two affairs, and that he'd almost left for the twenty-two-year-old secretary he'd schtupped for over three years every Tuesday in a room at the Mayflower. He knew when Gary's daughter went to Hazelton. Gary had rubbed the sides of his head when he'd told Dennis that she was getting electric shock, and Dennis had found this such an empathetic gesture, it had almost made him cry. He could not imagine living through that with his own daughter. Though he'd slowly become friends with Gary, still he couldn't help his resistance to the CIA; he would never shake his childhood association of that institution with the FBI as a hated branch of government. He heard his father's voice: *A tool of the ruling class!*

How different were these times, really? Dennis could still see those Rosenberg boys running from the loose grip of their unkempt grandmother. Though Sigmund had many doubts about the Rosenbergs' guilt, he had thought it shameful how long it took the communists to come to their defense. Sigmund had rescinded his allegiance to communism by then. Dennis was two when Stalin signed the pact with Hitler, and that was the moment when it was over for Sigmund. He'd ripped up his party card right then and there, he'd often said. From then on, as long as American communism had ties to the Soviets, it was not for him. Communism was synonymous with Stalinism, he'd say, and fascism too, and did no one notice the utter horror of the Moscow Trials? Where *is* everyone? he'd say, his fist shaking the kitchen table. It's like the whole damn planet has its head in the sand.

The American communists, they left those poor people to the dogs. Not until the Rosenbergs became a useful PR tool did they raise their pens in protest. Not until the communists started acting like the capitalists and realized they were as marketable as cereal. Then they embraced them.

Goddamned communists.

Tatti usually remained silent when Sigmund and his friends ranted about her homeland. But when the Rosenbergs burned, her horror seemed to give her voice.

"The chair!" Tatti had clutched her chest when the verdict came down. "A woman. Done in. By. Her. Own. Brother."

Dennis had thought of what his uncle must have been like then, imagining him as Santa Claus. He wrote Misha notes in huge print that his mother would translate into Russian. *We wish you were here with us,* he wrote. *This is a picture of my house,* he'd write beneath a crayon drawing of a brown house with picture windows and a green lawn, red flowers the size of trees bordering it, fluffy clouds hovering above. Dennis could not read Russian, and the Cyrillic letters in his mother's handwriting looked like a strange and unbreakable code.

"It's despicable," Sigmund had said. He read aloud from the paper. "'This description of the atom bomb, destined for delivery to the

Soviet Union, was typed up by the defendant Ethel Rosenberg that afternoon at her apartment at Ten Monroe Street. Just so had she, on countless other occasions, sat at that typewriter and struck the keys, blow by blow, against her own country in the interests of the Soviets.'" He shook his head and the paper rustled. "So they say Ethel Rosenberg does the typing, but maybe it was the brother's wife who did the typing, no? She was a trained typist, you know," he said. "A man protects his wife over his sister? Well, it's not right."

His mother had looked terrified. "You don't have a sister," she said, and Sigmund had laughed.

"And you don't type," he said.

"But how could this happen, Sigmund? How could this happen *here*?"

"How long have you been living here, Tatiana?" Sigmund snorted. "Where else? This country rubs your face in its own manure. It makes you eat your heart out."

Dennis had pictured his father pulling his chair up to the table, a fork in one hand, a knife in the other, leaning in to eat his own beating, bloody heart.

The CIA, the FBI, what was the goddamned difference? Only that now Dennis worked with folks at the CIA, he had cocktails on the Hill with several contacts there. Not three years ago when his parents had been visiting around Thanksgiving, he'd stopped on the way home from the office at Common Ground, a leftist bookstore he liked to browse in, just below Dupont, and an agent had followed him out. An agent! He'd known instantly—he would always be able to recognize them. You've got to be fucking kidding me, he'd thought when he heard the footsteps. He wished he'd bought something incredibly communistic that he could have flashed, not some shit copy of *Rolling Stone* with Linda Ronstadt on the cover. He had wanted to turn around and scream, *I am one of you, you morons. I too am a government tool. See?* He could have flashed his laminated ID.

But was he? Was Len? He managed to think of his old roommate as someone outside the Agency. Len was family, for God's sake. He was Skatesville and road trips and college and Annie and good fucking weed and Sissy Ford. He knew all about Gary's life, but what did Gary Jensen have on him? Because there very well might have been a file on Dennis. Any number of people had files now, open or not, and with his father's connections to the Communist Party, however broken, they had to have something open on him. Gary had asked gentle questions about his past—Where are you from? Where did you meet your wife? Len says your mother is Russian—normal, everyday questions that men might ask one another while eating steamers on the bay or at a Hill happy hour, but those questions cast in the buzzing fluorescence of government light could most certainly take on a different glow. Everything Dennis knew about Gary—his infidelities, his weakness for beer, his daughter's battle for her sanity—he knew only as it was happening, as if Gary lived merely in the present.

It was strange that his initial response was to rebel. Because in the next moment, he felt an electric surge of fear. Though Dennis knew this agent could very well have come from Gary, he also knew that a file of any kind would have come from his own set of mistakes, such as that first state dinner in January of 1964. He had been an idiot that night, at the Hotel Moskva in Moscow, and while one wouldn't call it a mistake per se, he certainly could have handled himself better, as he'd learned since.

The myth was that the hotel was built not on cement and steel, but on fear; it was said that Stalin approved two architectural plans and no one dared correct him. That cold night Dennis had tried to feel the fear travel through him, but he had felt nothing. Despite the rather grim facade, something was charming about the mismatched towers, the tilted windows, and the view of the Kremlin from the fifteenth-floor café. It being one of the few Russian buildings outside of the Kremlin that did not utterly depress Dennis; he was taken in by the rich history of artists and writers and politicians who had stayed there. He was still so easily taken in by bohemia! Sometimes, as if to harken back to the man he almost once was, he grew a mustache and let his hair go below his ears. Just to prove it.

Leonid Orlov, the mission's deputy chief, was hosting a dinner during a round of negotiations. The deals were done in cash, and so much was at stake for both parties that Dennis sometimes found it mind-boggling. Though Viktor was buying for the state and Dennis was selling, a fairly simple transaction, it often felt as if they were no longer acting as men, but as countries. But during these talks the effect of such gravity was often levity. It was all a game of Risk, the present juxtaposed over the past: the ghosts of Stalin and Truman, their hands hovering above a single button, dividing nations up like black cake.

The buttons were still there; would Brezhnev and Carter use them? What is loyalty? Dennis often thought. Which is more yours—your mother's country or your children's?

This question, had he ever asked it aloud, would explain why someone might revoke his security clearance, or why he was being followed leaving that lefty bookstore. He was shaking as he'd unlocked the car door. But even then he'd known he had most certainly never uttered aloud anything against something as sacrosanct as nationhood, and so he wondered, Would that agent have come after anyone in that store? Or had he followed him from the office? Dennis had tried to relax. Perhaps Len had sent him as a joke, though this was unlikely; Dennis didn't think a lot of practical gags were happening down at CIA headquarters. Or had Gary sent this agent as a warning? Yes, my mother is from St. Petersburg, Dennis had answered him. The Chesapeake sky was that clear blue of early June, before it faded into summer-white. Would this be enough to call out the dogs? But my uncle is still there, in Moscow. He's a musician, Dennis had said, tightening the lanyard. The sun was so perfect on his face. I don't remember what he plays, Dennis had answered. The drawbridge was up and a huge yacht was passing through. How unusual, Gary had said. How interesting that you never played music then, what with it being in your family, I mean. Dennis had shaken his head. My mother did make me play the clarinet, he had said, laughing. But it's true, I was absolutely no good. I did not get the musician gene, this is the truth.

In his car on the way home from the bookstore, Dennis had looked in the rearview and seen that the agent was now following him in a car. He drove along Connecticut, under the speed limit, and in trying to quell his nerves he thought of his mother and her fear when the FBI came to their neighborhood, when the Rosenberg boys were there. She locked the doors and closed the curtains. FBI, she said, her front teeth biting her lower lip. It was so village, Dennis thought as he drove toward home, this peasant fear of authority he always despised about his mother. As they walked down the street, it was always, say hello to the post office clerk, Dennis! Now shake the banker's hand, Dennis. She did this when he was sixteen! Her deference to bureaucracy drove him mad.

Was someone trying to terrify his mother, the foreigner? I will not be my mother, Dennis thought. Had someone known his parents were visiting then? He thought of his father—talking in that angry circle with his friends. Someone always banged a fist on the kitchen table,

covered in oilcloth, and Dennis remembered the teapot jumping on
the stove. They argued and railed long after he'd gone to sleep, and the
sounds of those deep, enraged voices was somehow more comfortable
than his parents' silence after dark, the apartment closed, quiet but for
the tick of his mother's knitting needles or the swish of his father's
newspapers as he aggressively turned the large pages. The sound of
argument might have been curious comfort, but as he was being
followed, Dennis wondered, What had those men been talking about
anyway? Had those heated debates been political quarrels or some sort
of schemes? Who was this agent here to frighten?

Tatiana had stepped out of the front door to meet Dennis as he pulled
into the drive. The black government car had idled on the street, but
no one got out, and Dennis saw her note the car, and he knew it was
coming: the Russianness! His mother and her Russian fears.

But this time the fear—that foreboding housed even in those
Russian buildings—did not seem to come. Tatiana had raised her
head unafraid, and her eyes had met Dennis's. After just an instant
she turned, guiding the storm door gently closed behind her. Dennis
carried his briefcase, his Common Ground book bag, logo turned
outward for anyone to observe, up the stairs and into the house. He
looked out the squares of warped glass and breathed out as he watched
the car drive away.

At that first dinner in Moscow, the men had insisted on Dennis's joining
them in some heavy drinking. This too was not unusual; he had been
warned, but he'd already known the importance of drinking if only
from the nights his mother's boss, Boris, had come back from a trip to
St. Petersburg, where they were always trying to get their music played
by Soviet orchestras. Boris had come with a hard, gray suitcase filled
with vodka and little jars of caviar, and those nights the whole family
ate blini topped with sour cream and caviar, and Boris would scream,
*Do dna*, bottoms up, before each of the many shots he knocked back
at the wobbly kitchen table, Leopold Stokowski's *Fantasia* recordings
playing on the record player. Boris always drank until he was red
with rage or until he melted into a puddle of his own tears. Dennis's
father never joined in; his idea of drinking was only celebration—two
short glasses of peppermint schnapps—and so it wasn't until college
that Dennis had learned to drink at all, with considerable help from
Len, whose childhood in Savannah and summers at Kitty Hawk and

Hilton Head with Sissy did nothing if not teach the essentiality of five o'clock cocktails. Dennis learned to drink claret until dawn, and he also acquired a taste for—as well as the hows and whens and whys of—scotch to begin the night, and whiskey to end it. Gin and tonics flowed freely each spring, but somehow he had escaped a necessary lesson in the flavorless, all-too-easy-to-consume vodka.

Dennis knew he would have to drink with these men to gain their trust, and he knew that, as he did so, the Soviets would try to extract information. So he had tried to prepare before the dinner by eating several large hunks of the black bread he'd picked up from a bakery in the Garden Ring and taking a salt pill he'd brought from home. Despite these efforts, however, he had one or two, perhaps three or four, even six, too many that night. Who could count? The bottle kept tipping and tipping; everyone drank. To respect the culture, as a sensitive representative of the U.S. government, Dennis stupidly, very stupidly, drank far too much. And his stupidity sang.

While the night unfolded, it all seemed as innocent as those first few months of freshman year, evenings that began with Lenny mixing cocktails in their room at Hartley, looking out onto Amsterdam Avenue, that continued at the West End until closing, then ended in a blur of the crooked walk back across campus at dawn. Dennis remembered the ease between him and his roommate those nights that could only have come from life before it was divided by politics. In Moscow, backs were slapped; glasses were tilted back, then slammed on the wooden table. Who actually brought up business, and who in particular wanted to discuss the Landsats, Dennis would never remember, but someone referred to them in passing.

"They're entirely legal," Dennis pointed out. He dismissed it with a wave of his hand. "What's to say?"

"But who," Viktor Uspensky said, "likes to be watched?" In addition to his work for the state-owned Exportkhleb, he also oversaw the state-owned flour mills, so he had a special interest in grain.

The whole country is watching itself, Dennis thought, thinking of those police stationed everywhere in Red Square.

The other men, also with Exportkhleb, and several ministers from the Ag department, including Leonid Orlov (it was rumored he was a KGB man, but what could they do? There was no getting out of doing business with Leonid), nodded in tandem as they tore off bits of bread and sopped them in the warm beef borscht.

"Of course," Dennis said in Russian, "it happens to all of us." Speaking Russian always made him feel as if he were a child talking to his mother as they made their way around the fountain at Seward Park.

"Besides," Viktor responded in English, "what do these images really tell you? They reveal nothing, of course. You know this, yes, Dennis?"

Dennis nodded sternly, an effort to override Viktor's implication that the Americans were fools who not only couldn't tell how large the Soviet stockpiles were, but who didn't even know the stock existed. What annoyed him most, however, was Viktor's shift to English. Dennis had excellent Russian, though his vocabulary was sometimes as limited as that of a twelve-year-old holding his mother's hand while shopping on Hester Street. Viktor's insult was yet another way of pointing to the stupidity of Americans.

"Yes, I know this," Dennis answered in Russian.

"Unless," Viktor continued, "unless you know a way to measure the reserves?"

English again! It enraged Dennis. Despite the drunkenness that had come over him slowly and rather sweetly, increasing in waves until he felt soaked in a clean, pure sea, Dennis could see the challenge laid before him, as if Viktor had unsheathed some kind of sword. And just as soon as the pure state of his drunkenness had come, it began to recede. In its place lay his unwashed anger, dry as sand, and he turned it to address the table of men, revealing a weapon of his own.

"What do you think the CIA is for?" he said in Russian, raising his eyebrows. He leaned back and wished that he were an enormous man who could place his large hands across his massive belly and sit back in a big chair with gravitas.

There was silence. Aleksandr Vishnevsky paused, his tiny glass at his enormous mouth, and Leonid Orlov stopped chewing his potatoes. Dennis wondered what exactly Leonid Orlov did in the KGB. Dennis turned to the door, for a brief moment expecting it to be stormed, by the Russians or the Americans, he couldn't determine. How had Orlov gotten the information he'd needed? How often? And how had he made it back home?

Dennis continued, the sack of butterflies inside his belly wild to be set free. "They're everywhere, crawling over your whole fucking country, over farmland, under bridges." They wanted English? He'd give them English. "Perhaps they are here right now." He placed both hands on the table, imagining that if he could not truly overturn it, he could at least turn the tables, as it were, so that the conversation was in his control. "Under this very building."

"Of course." Viktor brushed off this conceit with one flick of his pudgy hand. He made a most imperceptible move with his neck that Dennis thought might have been a tic, until out of the corner of his eye he saw Egor Demidov slowly get up to leave, his large body silhouetted over the Historical Museum, lit up behind him.

"Wait!" Those butterflies raged now, wings batting against Dennis's stomach. He could see the snow was falling, illuminated by the ruby lights winking to one another in Red Square. He thought of Ivan the Terrible's chopping block. *They looked at their Snow Maiden and were amazed at what they saw. The eyes of the Snow Maiden twinkled,* he heard his mother in the next room, whispering the winter fairy tale to his sister, the radiator blasting intermittently with steam. "I kid with you," Dennis said. "Come back, Egor. Have a drink with us." He swept his arm around the table, an imitation of Viktor's grandeur. "The CIA. What do I know from the CIA?" he said in English.

The men all looked to Viktor, who paused for a moment. He stared at Dennis. Then he lifted his massive hand and clapped Dennis hard on the shoulder. "A joker!" he said in Russian.

Egor Demidov sat back down. Aleksandr Vishnevsky tipped his head back and downed his shot, crashing the glass on the table. Leonid Orlov, whose party this was after all, resumed his chewing. "Greetings from Fanny!" he said to Dennis, smiling, a mouth of black teeth, and Dennis looked away, then suddenly the music played again, though Dennis wasn't sure it had ever stopped, or if all sound had merely been cut off by the ringing in his ears.

Everyone laughed heartily, including Dennis.

"What fun it will be doing business together. With such a comedian," Viktor said.

Dennis nodded and looked to his plate, still filled with borscht, the oil slick on the surface of the soup and on the suspended chunks of meat. This was the most famous dish of the restaurant. They had all said he must have it. "The people come here and beg for this dish," Viktor had told him. "They beg," he'd said, his hands heavy on the table.

That night in his apartment far outside the center, Dennis's high began to dissipate. All that was left of the alcohol now was the sugar. Before the hangover he knew was coming arrived in earnest, Dennis felt only panic. It was common knowledge about the CIA looking for stockpiles, was it not? People talked of it freely in the office, after all. It could hardly be considered confidential intelligence. But of course talk of the CIA at the Department of Agriculture was not the same as a conversation at a famous Soviet hotel—where Stalin was said to have celebrated his fiftieth birthday—right smack in the middle of Red Square. Red for color, Dennis reminded himself, red for beauty.

He closed his eyes and saw the Hungarian tailor from around the corner of his old block on Rivington Street being taken in by two FBI agents. The tailor's head was bowed and they walked closely behind. Kids got up from pitching pennies and shooting marbles to watch him go by. What had the man done? None of it was clear, but the Rosenberg children had just been taken from their grandmother; surely there was some kind of connection, the women leaning on their brooms said, and so did the men with the scratched-up briefcases at their sides. The old man's shop was boarded up as soon as he was gone. Dennis could see the agent who walked close to the buildings, so clearly, his mustache twisting up at the sides, his large ears protruding from the sides of his head like handles on a water jug. Dennis's mother had run out onto the street, his sister holding a meringue cookie and bouncing on Tatiana's hip. What is it, what is it? she had asked, then seeing the agent, she'd run back inside. The fear! The Russian fear. Even the *buildings* hold it.

Lying in bed, the mattress hard in his boniest spots, a simple bedside lamp he switched on and off, the flash of a plain, nearly empty room, Dennis had thought of his son, not even two years old; he saw his wife, her belly round and high. A girl, Tatti assured them. No question. It was true, Benjamin had sat low on Sharon, with a dark line down the center of Sharon's belly, which hadn't appeared this time. He had been reckless, and now he wondered if he should say anything of what had transpired to his boss. Perhaps he should call Viktor into a private meeting and lay it out again that he'd merely been joking, simply having a laugh with them, which is the American way. Or maybe he should do nothing, he thought. Say nothing. To no one. Never speak of it again. And as he gratefully watched the gray light come in through the single, tilted window, this is what he decided to do.

The next day, before leaving the country, Dennis waited for someone—Soviet or American—to confront him with tapes of the conversation. He thought to call Misha, to ask him his advice, but what, he rationalized, did an out-of-work musical prodigy know of Soviet intelligence? Yet he had been so assured when picking out this enamel box for Ben. Misha certainly knew more than him, Dennis realized. Back then, anyone would have known more than Dennis. What had stopped him from calling Misha was the knowledge the news would reach his mother and terrify her. He imagined her opening a letter, if Misha was stupid enough to write to her, and reading about Dennis's fear, and Misha's concern; the subsequent hysteria was something Dennis could not have borne.

Perhaps there would be a letter in the lobby, Dennis feared, or the driver would turn around, his large arm hooked over the seat, to tell him he would not be getting to the airport that day. Or at the airport, maybe someone would come out from a crowd and take him by his elbow. But there was nothing. Nothing. And upon returning home, he searched through his personal mail with dread, the only thing of interest a flyer for Goldwater that Sharon had left to amuse him. At work the next morning, he expected a discreet brown package to be waiting for him on his chair, set there by unknowing Glinda. When nothing appeared, he waited for Gregory Handel, his boss, to ask to meet him outside the office, on a bench in Lafayette Park perhaps, where Jerome Mooney had just been taken in after a stroll through the park two months previously. Dennis would be handcuffed and just taken away right there amid the protesters holding signs for civil rights. It was rumored that an espionage project, Venona, had been decoding Soviet spy messages and that Jerome, who worked in the Africa Bureau at State, had been caught sending messages to some Russian ringleader, that JFK knew about the Soviet placement of missiles in Cuba. How someone in the Africa Bureau got this info was no mystery: the government bled information. It seeped from one department to another; information was currency. Each day since March the protesters had stood in this park in front of the White House, and it would be among these committed people, these upstanding humans effecting change, that Leo would slip Dennis a manila envelope with photos and a cassette tape, proof of his utter lack of these benevolent qualities. Or mightn't it be proof of the opposite? The Russians, after all, were people too. They did not deserve to starve for politics.

Would Gregory ask him directly, Are you? Or would he just state it: You *are*. He would cut him off from the Soviets, perhaps; Dennis was already far too comfortable. Maybe they would send his mother back in return. He thought of Jerome—whose code name was rumored to have been Trusty—under house arrest, awaiting trial. The Commission's investigations had just been made public; had coincidence? Why had they only taken him then? Who w₂ what? It was always all about the way one looked at it.

Now we question everything; this, Dennis had thought, was what the death of President Kennedy had done. It made us look at *ourselves* differently. As a nation. But an individual could make himself crazy looking at a thing from so many angles. A prism, after all, fractures the light to throw a rainbow on the wall.

Dennis waited like a character in a Russian novel; none of these scenarios took place. The next time he saw Viktor, a month later in Washington, there was no mention of the incident. Dennis hoped, and soon he began to believe, that Viktor and all the others had been drunk as well, and that they too had forgotten the exchange. He trusted that it had been erased from Viktor's recall, just as the night slowly receded into the deep folds of Dennis's own memory. Now it sat in the same place as his childhood nightmares: a clarinet overflowing with spit, the Italians screaming at him on the corner of Essex Street, their faces as red as the Soviet flag, a shadow chasing him down the Bowery and into a flophouse lined with unshaven men on filthy mattresses. And also snippets of old recollections, his parents' arguments, the neighbor beating his wife and daughters, the light shining bright from the Empire State. Adult memories were also stored in these folds: innumerable fights with Sharon, and several (often subsequent) vulnerable declarations of love, small moments of his children's untellable grace, all moments from which he was protected. So much so, he could rarely find this place in his own mind. His heart safeguarded him for fear, and from fear, and it also shielded him from happiness—both, he found, could undo him—and he tried most often to sit by and just let his heart do its good, purposeful work.

What emerged from that evening in Moscow became less a fear of what would transpire, and more a cautionary tale. Drinking with the Soviets. He laughed about it at embassy parties, wagging his finger. Know your vodka! he'd tell anyone headed East. And he could pass it on to his son. When, a decade and a half later, they'd dropped him at the impossibly small and criminally expensive Brandeis dorm room and unloaded his duffel bags, after Sharon had made Ben's bed and wept over him, clutching his face in both hands to say good-bye, Dennis had pulled him aside. Have fun, Bennie, he told his son. Be yourself; always follow your heart. Be sure to have a good time, okay? Because this—all of it—will be gone in an instant. Like smoke through a keyhole. But whatever you do, stay away from the vodka! It is worse than a woman. Vodka is not your friend.

Dennis had not realized that the evening in Moscow twelve years previously had left him so alarmed until he had looked into the rearview mirror and watched that CIA agent following him, so closely, all the way home.

He'd save calling CIA Gary for later, but now Dennis wondered exactly whom the Soviets were buying their grain from. Briefly he had an image of the Russians gobbling up the planet's food supply. He imagined a map of the world: here was Africa, drought-ridden in yellow and brown, dropping off the map as the rich, bold, red USSR and its satellites got fat, their red land bleeding into the blue of the sea. Anyone could have leaked news of the embargo days before it was announced, even if Dennis hadn't heard a word. And anyone could be turning a profit right now.

As Dennis moved satellite images across his desk, he imagined the little houses in this large patch of many greens, the spaces where people lived. Perhaps right here was the Eastern Bloc housing to which he had grown inured. It was not so different a tenet from what he had been forced to live by. No more than anyone else. Enough for everyone, but there was always more than enough for some. Perhaps this was why his father turned on communism; he was not one of those idiots who hung on to Stalin for too long. But Sigmund sure continued to use enough of the lingo. He refused to leave the East Side and their third-floor walk-up on Orchard Street. His father felt that suburbia was death. Dennis found it amusing now that, in one of her torrents of anger, Vanessa would unleash some similar sentiment: suburbia (*which was not where they lived, goddamn it!*) was the death of culture, the death of freedom. Nothing is happening here! his daughter roared as she stormed out the front door and into an idling car. Jesus Christ. When had his daughter begun to roar?

Dennis would never shake his parents' first visit to his new home in Chevy Chase. How long would he look to his father to measure where he stood? Even in his adulthood, he had been unable to stop gauging his father's responses. Like any son, Dennis wanted his father's approval, to know that his decisions matched the pure and perfect quality of his father's beliefs. Only later would it occur to Dennis that Benjamin might look for *his* approval. Dennis had never felt the pull to sanction much of what his son did or said, and his son never seemed to need anything from him, so confident was he in the way his body navigated the world.

In one of Sigmund's articles he had urged his readers to "live your lives taking chances. Commit yourself in your hopes and your dreams." Dennis remembered looking at the page, the difficult type smashed together—so much rage and hope and knowledge to get onto that single blank page!—and he'd gazed up to see his mother staring out the small window over the sink, the only source of natural light in the kitchen. Was she looking up at the sky, or down onto the street? Her face was turned, her cheek illuminated by the gray light that lit the dim blue kitchen, and he had wondered what his mother was thinking. He wondered it now too. He was just a boy then, perhaps eleven, and he'd turned back to that page. Commit. Hopes. Dreams. Each word was such a lofty and incomprehensible concept back then; these terms were still perplexing, though he had made every effort to live by them.

Dennis had thought of that quotation often, as he greased the cork and put together his clarinet, as he moistened the reed and placed it in the mouthpiece, just as he began to play. He'd stumble through "Für Elise" over and over, in B flat, in the kitchen, and he could hear his sister giggling in the back room. He thought of these words at most of his life's crossroads and they made him ashamed of the career decisions he had once held pride in. His refusal to work for some corporation, for instance. Because the private sector serves only the self. And yet his children would have benefited were he able to leave them something more substantial. But what? A nice house with a fenced-in yard and the Jacuzzi Sharon wanted so damn badly did not fulfill a dream. It did not make a legacy. But what, Dennis thought, does?

Dennis had tired of listening to his father fight his friends: What is utopia? Is it dead? Are you still a radical? If you are not, who are you then, how will you change society? Screw the Zionists! they said. Screw the anarchists! Well, screw him! Everyone is doing the best they can.

It was not, however, lost on Dennis that many of his father's friends had headed to the safety of universities. His father complained bitterly all through the sixties that his friends were now protected in academia. Why was it safer to be on a campus than up in that shit apartment?

Dennis had wanted to tell his father when he complained of an old friend who had become a professor at Berkeley. What Dennis had said, though, was, No one is safe in the universities. Don't you get it? No one is safe anywhere! And that had been before those four students were gunned down at Kent State.

His father felt betrayed by his old cronies from City College. Caleb Blonsky, who had grown up on the same block as Sigmund, who had gone to school only three years behind him, took out an ad in the *Times,* Democrats for Nixon. His mother told Dennis that Sigmund had wept when he opened the paper and had seen so many of his like-minded peers from school listed on the advertisement. It seemed to Dennis that Sigmund thought the whole goddamn world was that cafeteria they argued in, that life was one big radical buffet. He got a dose of reality later, when Nixon was elected, and Blonsky—*Blonsky!*—who had argued so righteously for the workers, for revolution, was photographed shaking hands with the new president, Nixon, at a fund-raiser dinner.

"What?" Dennis had asked the first time he brought his father to his new home.

"Well"—Sigmund looked out to the living room—"why shouldn't we be comfortable? Why not? We all deserve it. But then, of course, you can't have the other part now, the authentic part. It's all diluted here." He flicked his wrists dismissively. "Because now, you see, Dennis, it won't be natural, everything will be a choice."

This was the kind of talk that drove Dennis bananas. What is *not* a choice? And who the fuck was his father talking to, an audience of thousands? Dennis was tired of the rhetoric. His father was losing ground. He'd lost half his friends to conservatism, yet still he couldn't embrace the next generation's agenda.

"Now come on," Dennis said. But the seed of doubt his father had planted had already begun to take root. Didn't he think of his father watching him as he sat at his desk, waiting for his administrative instructions? Brief this one, brief that one. Toe the party line. So often he saw this through his father's eyes. Where did he stand? It was confusing to him: working from within the government was both the most benevolently liberal thing he felt he could do, the most socialist really; had the last gasp of the sixties not been evidence of this? So why now did government work feel sometimes to Dennis like the nservative anti-individual, anti-independent-thinking move he ave made? Where did he *stand*?

"Okay," Sigmund had said, still gazing out at the living room. He smiled at Benjamin, who had come downstairs and was now leaning over the banister. "As long as you all are happy here, what's to discuss? Perhaps this is your utopia."

Utopia! Dennis wanted to pull out his hair. Happy. That fucking word again. Even if he heard mention of it in passing, Dennis couldn't help but question his state of mind. No, he was not happy. No, this was not *utopia*. At certain times perhaps: walking into a meeting, about to broker a deal. Happy? Sure: watching his daughter when he caught her unawares in the den, her legs curled beneath her, a hand on her bare foot as she chewed a pencil while looking into a book. Happy? Yes, but these moments were always bittersweet: they came with the deal not going through due to pork futures, or looking closely enough to see his daughter inexorably changed, her hair an awful inky black, her face so white, almost chalky against her scalp, the turned cheek of an old woman. Inevitably she would see him watching her and turn hard.

Dennis chastised himself that only at this moment did it occur to him that Sigmund had only been happy in his struggles, those seemingly unconquerable causes. He was only happy in the YPSL, the SWP, running the ISL, so many letters strung together it felt like Washington. It was a wonder Dennis hadn't become a goddamn Republican.

"Perhaps it is," Dennis had told his father as he listened to the sounds of his wife preparing dinner in the kitchen. "There are, after all, worse things."

The office phone rang and Dennis watched the light blink.

No Glinda on a Saturday. He picked up.

"Hello, Dennis," Sharon said.

"Hi. I'm just heading to my morning briefing."

"I was just thinking," Sharon said, a little too leisurely given Dennis's schedule if you asked him. "I want to visit Ben for parents' day this spring. I think it's important that we all go."

Dennis shut his eyes. One. Two. Three. Four. "Sure. We should go. When is it?"

"It's two months away, not until the weekend of March twenty-first."

"Surely we can discuss this later, Sharon. I mean, c'mon."

"We can, yes, but I just needed to make sure you were willing. We're going to have to bring Vanessa, you know. Unless I see some drastic changes by then. We can't leave her alone. I don't know what she'll do to herself."

Five. Six. Seven. "I have to go, Sharon. We can discuss it tonight."

"But I have the Epstein event tonight."

"So tomorrow, then. Tomorrow night. The next morning. We have plenty of time," he said. "We have our whole lives."

"Ha ha. I just felt like I needed to know now that you *wanted* to go. And you do, D, which is great, it's really terrific, and I'm sure Vanessa won't mind. I'm going to call Ben and tell him today. So put it on your calendar. In pen."

"Did he ask us to come?"

"No," Sharon said. "I read about it in the Brandeis newsletter."

"Maybe he doesn't want us there." Dennis started to get up from his desk, craning his neck to hold on to the phone.

"Why on earth wouldn't he want us there?"

Dennis was silent. He thought of how relieved he'd been that his mother, with her box of Russian tea cakes tied up with twine, her ghastly Russian sweaters, her vast hand gestures and thick accent, had left the dorm room before Sissy Ford got there.

"Well, we're going. It's decided. Good luck in the meeting, okay?"

"Thanks," he said.

Dennis hung up the phone and pictured the three of them driving up to Waltham for a visit with Benjamin. Perhaps it would be one of those important weekends that went so perfectly one could never imagine having experienced any trepidation. Briefly, this made him happy. *Happy,* he thought. But he doubted the weekend would turn out this way. He raised his head rather warily, as if he were the old man he saw his own father becoming. Thin, paper skin, legs as slight as a heron's. His mother, by contrast, seemed ageless, and he was sure there were a hundred reasons, Freudian and otherwise, for this, but truly, her skin was still lovely and luminous, set against her deep red hair. Perhaps she dyed it, but Dennis thought not; this type of vanity wasn't like his mother.

He took his khaki jacket from where it hung at the back of the chair, swung it around, and put it on. North Korea or Washington, Japan or the daily reports, the search for trade alternatives. Dennis threw his head back, brushed his hair from his face, and headed out of the office to see what would await him over the bridge.

# CHAPTER 7

# The Cherries

## January 5, 1980

In retrospect, Vanessa's gobbling up all the canapés for the Epstein event was a terrible omen for the evening. But at the time it just seemed to Sharon to be a small disaster that Marlene was able to fend off with the salted almonds and frozen fish balls and mini-quiche-lorraines she'd vacuum-packed and stacked in the Food Matters deep freeze a few weeks previously for such an emergency.

As for the rest of the meal, the women had it down to a science. Slow and measured in the kitchen, Marlene was a careful slicer, and she always left enough time to fluff the flour and then smooth the top of the cup with a straight edge for the exact amount. This made her a far superior baker to Sharon, whose temperament was precisely the opposite. Fast and frenetic, she was always racing to finish, so her juliennes were invariably slightly different widths, her chopped onions a complex range of sizes. Yet she could accomplish many tasks at once, and if need be, she could orchestrate the entire dinner on her own. In the time it took Marlene to unwrap the butcher paper, trim the fat, and salt the rack of lamb—they would be serving it Provençal tonight—Sharon had finished the filling for the stuffed mushrooms and had her new potatoes prepped for the oven.

Sharon far preferred more healthy and creative vegetarian cooking—she'd been doing a lot of experimenting since Vanessa announced she would no longer eat anything that once had a face—to meals like this, but she could certainly do formal and traditional. She appreciated Simone Beck just as much as Marlene did. Traditional—or conventional, as Sharon called it—was what Marlene favored, and that was the kind of party Marsha Epstein, wife of Felix Epstein, Mondale's advance man, had wanted tonight. Many luminaries would be at the event; it was already circulating in the kitchen that Mondale was in town and that he just might show.

Sharon put several baking dishes of her new potatoes in the preheated oven. The trick with potatoes was to add just a little water, steaming them before they browned. That Sharon knew from her own experience; you wouldn't read that in *Simca's Cuisine.*

Sharon had stopped in the office on the way in to pick up her knives and retrieve her messages from the new machine, as she'd obsessively done of late. *I'm sorry, Mrs. Goldstein,* the only message said, *but I can't make it today.* No reason, no solution, and, thought Sharon, no concern as to whether they would even get the message in time. Sharon couldn't imagine just not showing for any job, but she hoped she had raised her own children better. No-shows had happened far more when their business was just starting out, when she and Marlene, in an attempt at both selfish and altruistic hiring, had relied on their kids' friends. Even though they were being paid, the kids acted as if they were doing Food Matters a favor by simply waltzing through the door. Sharon watched in astonishment as one lithe, long-limbed girl with more split ends on a single head of hair than Sharon thought possible scooped a cherry tomato into the spinach dip, set perfectly in the head of a beautiful unfolding red cabbage, leaving a crater in its wake. And Ben's pal Jared, a lovely boy headed for Harvard, ate a chunk of chicken right off the tip of her skewer, then set it back down on the tray. These kids showed up unkempt, and she could tell sometimes they were stoned. They befriended the bartenders and snuck tequila shots behind the makeshift bars. Then every once in a while someone arrived showered and shaved, clean and sparkly as a razor blade, and did exactly what Sharon and Marlene asked of her.

But the gamble became far too stressful, and given their growing clientele, they needed professionals, or at least kids with experience, and now they had enough money and sufficient wherewithal to hire them. Tonight was an unusual glitch as they had a terrific and fairly stable waitstaff, which meant Sharon and Marlene could concentrate instead on making excellent, healthful food, setting a beautiful, welcoming table, and continuing to ingratiate themselves to the elite of Washington. Her father's town—Hollywood, USA!—might have run on money, but her husband's ran on pure power, and Sharon could see it tick and breathe each night.

No one on staff was available to fill in for the missing server that evening, and even more unbelievably, no one seemed to know a soul who could turn up, do a few spins around the room with a doilied silver platter, serve the rack of lamb without dripping blood on the Oriental carpet, and pick up the rim-kissed glasses at the end of the night. The old Sharon would have panicked. Or maybe she would have thrown her dish towel down and wept, made Marlene figure it out on her own. But that was the old Sharon, the *unfinished* Sharon. The new Sharon could attack problems with passion and find viable solutions. The new Sharon, though she still had her doubts, was *completed*.

And she made decisions quickly. Thinking about it no further, Sharon picked up Marsha Epstein's kitchen phone and called home.

"Hello?" Vanessa grunted into the phone.

"Darling?" Sharon was going to ignore the afternoon's fight and start fresh.

There was silence on the other end of the line. Sharon could hear her daughter breathing. "Yeah?" Vanessa said after a moment, sniffling.

"Do you have a cold?" Sharon asked.

"Nope," Vanessa said flatly.

"Thank goodness! Listen, I know you are probably busy this evening—or maybe you're going to Jason's?—but I need to ask you a big favor. Would there be any way you could help me tonight? One of the servers just didn't show up. Just did not show. Can you believe it?"

More silence. "Mom," Vanessa groaned. "You've got to be kidding me."

Sharon noticed Vanessa had not exactly refused, and seeing this window of opportunity, she forged on. "It would mean the world to me. I really need your help tonight, sweetie." She had not blamed her for eating the canapés, and she'd been firm and open, vulnerable and calm, just as she'd always wished she could be with her daughter.

"I can't."

Sharon felt it in her gut. It was more than the potential of the ruined party; it was the out-and-out rejection. "You know I wouldn't ask you if I didn't really need you."

"Uh-uh," Vanessa said. "No way."

Sharon clenched her teeth. Then she saw Vanessa, an infant in her crib, who hadn't needed her mother at all; she'd just lie there cooing happily to herself. Benjamin had cried and cried—he seemed to suffer terribly until she came for him, cradling his head and lifting him to her heart. Who was this terribly independent child? Sharon had been so depressed after her daughter's birth, she could barely rouse herself to feed her. Now she reasoned that Vanessa had been born this way, utterly unknowable to her.

But her daughter's body was so familiar. In retrospect, Vanessa, as she grew, even bored her with her sameness. Of course a girl had come from her; but a boy? This was strange and miraculous. Sharon had spent so much time watching her son lope across a soccer field and fling himself on the couch, his long arms draped to the floor, so many hours watching his limbs grow, that her daughter's body had escaped her.

"Listen here, Vanessa." Sharon had reached the point she nearly always went to—anger, white anger, that touched down like a match igniting in uncontrollable flashes—and there was no turning back. "You ate all my fucking crab cakes." Sharon remembered unsuspectingly opening the freezer only to be met by the black hole where her canapés once were. "All of them. There was not one left. And don't think I don't know about the cheese sticks. You owe me."

Vanessa breathed heavily into the phone.

"I've had about enough. If Daddy's not home yet, you call a taxi and you be here in the next twenty minutes, do you hear me?" Sharon said. "You be here, Vanessa."

"Dad's home," Vanessa said.

"Well, terrific. Now put on some black pants and a goddamn white button-down shirt and get in the car and get down here!" Sharon shut her eyes tightly, as if this would somehow allow her not to hear her own voice. She had so wanted to be good and strong and in *control*. "Now."

Marlene turned from the trash with a look that asked if everything was all right.

"Okay, Mom," Vanessa said. "God."

"Great." Sharon nodded to Marlene. "It's on Kalorama at Columbia. Right on the south corner. Thanks, sweetie, see you in a bit!" Sharon squeaked.

The florist had come in, and so had three of the servers, all waiting to be told where to place the nuts, what would be passed, what would be stationary. Sharon tried her breathing: I choose to, I *choose* to, Sharon said to herself on the exhale. She imagined she was seated on a folding chair in a hall at the Marriott off Rockville Pike, one among so many human travelers on like journeys.

"Marlene?" Sharon called to her partner, who was now ever-so-patiently patting the mushroom caps with a damp paper towel. "Can you manage the servers for now? Vanessa is going to help as well. She's on her way."

"Vanessa?"

"Yes," Sharon said defensively, as if Vanessa had been the best choice on earth. "Yes, she's offered to take Mary's place."

"How nice of her," Marlene said sincerely. She folded her towel in quarters, placed it carefully by the sink, and wobbled across the room, motioning the small group over to the flower-strewn table.

"It *was* nice," Sharon said after her, trying to fend off the gloom that, no matter where the occasion or how powerful or kind her client, always pervaded in these hours before an event. There was something depressing about being in someone else's kitchen, preparing for someone else's party. Here, among the silver and English china and crystal, the calla lilies and gardenias spread out on the kitchen farm table waiting for the florist to arrange, she couldn't help but think of her mother's disdain at her chosen career path. But don't you want to *go* to these parties? Helen would ask. Not be the *hired help,* for God's sake. Don't you want to help your husband's career?

Now Sharon had the tools to say, My image of my own success goes beyond such meaningless symbols. But yes, of course she wanted to help, and she believed she could, and had; she believed that people responded just as much to a sublime meal as they did to scintillating conversation. At the least she was providing a canvas, a platform for discussion. And wasn't food a central issue now? Dennis said it was only a matter of time before the whole world just starved to death, but that, even Sharon realized, was just how they talked at USDA.

When her mother asked such questions—more indictments—Sharon did wonder whether she should take the business further, open a restaurant, say, or write a cookbook. She had a whole goddamn shelf in the den filled with the *Moosewood Cookbook,* Mollie Katzen's recipes from her vegetarian restaurant in Ithaca. Sharon's friends, and her mother's friends, as well as many of her clients, had all sent her a copy when it came out last year. Each one was inscribed with a note to the effect of *You're next!* Or, *Who's this woman who stole all your ideas!*—which rendered each book nonreturnable.

Sharon had felt misunderstood; *Moosewood* wasn't her style at all. Something about the cooking was frumpy; it was neither refined nor beautiful. Reading that cookbook had made her run to her copy of *Ma*

*Gastronomie,* with its recipe for blood sausage made just from pigs who had eaten only pears. As ridiculous as this was—how would she know about the pears? Was she to feed the pig herself? She wasn't a bloody farmer—Sharon believed in cooking with great care, not throwing a bunch of garlic into a dish and calling it layered with flavor.

Sharon's aspirations had been so markedly different from her mother's. Whereas her mother had wanted to slip in among the powered and moneyed of Hollywood, during the Eisenhower administration Sharon couldn't wait to escape it and headed to D.C. Washington, she had foolishly believed, was where change happened. Yes, she'd been naive and misguided—what young person with ideals moves to Washington during the reign of Ike?—but only four years later she was there marching on the Mall on that stifling August day with massive crowds of people listening to Martin Luther King, Jr. Ben was strapped to Dennis's chest, and as the three of them, and Louise, stood with all the marchers, Sharon had felt nothing short of thrilled with her decisions.

That day she had felt like an adult, but now Sharon saw herself then as the young, immature girl she had actually been. She could not turn her head toward the memory of her husband, his impossibly young face, his hand, the slender gold ring glinting as his palm lighted on Ben's tiny head. Dennis mouthed the words to "We Shall Not Be Moved" so as not to wake their son. *Like a tree that's standing by the water . . .* Then later, the march for the mobilization to end the war, the four of them now, Louise far too radical to stand with a suburban family, Vanessa and Benjamin both reaching up, begging to be held on their father's shoulders so they could rise up above the crowd. The turned leaves—mustard, red, unthinkable oranges—were just beginning to fall off the trees lining the Mall, and it had been the kind of bright, crisp day that can only happen after a day of rain. She had looked up to Vanessa kicking at Dennis's chest, assuring Ben he would be next, and again felt a surge that everything she had done had been correct.

Sharon began to doubt her memory. Had she not thought then of all that had happened? There had been secret bombings in Cambodia. The Weathermen had just blown up that statue in Chicago. Hadn't she been *afraid*? Dennis had held Ben's feet and said, to Sharon or to himself, she didn't know then *or* now, "This isn't going to do *anything*. Pete Seeger can sing until he's blue in the face, but it's just a goddamn *song*."

In any case, Sharon thought now, turning away from both memories, two images split apart by history. At least, she rationalized, she had not spent her life chasing down invitations to this fund-raiser, or that producer's party, as her mother had. When they lived in that little bungalow with the tiny pond out front on Franklin Avenue in Hollywood, her mother had all the invitations she'd wanted. By the time they'd moved to Beverly Hills, though, the invitations—*to the right parties*—stopped coming.

Sharon would always associate the move to Beverly Hills, where Herb and Helen still lived, with her father's downward spiral. We're on the up-and-up! Helen had cheered as she rolled up her shirtsleeves and went to pack up the highballs from the sticky kitchen cabinet. Each time she set some glasses in a cardboard box, she'd pass by the window over the sink that looked out into their little garden, crammed with bougainvillea and jasmine and bottle washers. Sharon remembered that window now, plants nearly bursting through the glass, and how her mother wore a scarf on her head like a Bolshevik.

The Weissmans moved up to the Hills, just as the rest of Hollywood stopped working. That's when Herbert and that cigar-chomping, commie-hating Dick Yates not only worked through the hearings and the blacklist, but started producing more profitable westerns than ever before. Sharon had eaten dinner with Roy Rogers! Her father had made a huge show of ordering her a Roy Rogers that night, which had made her pout; she loved Shirley Temples. And it had changed the course of Sharon's promising youth. Once, on a dare, she and a boy drove out into the desert. They went out to the middle of Death Valley. Rattlesnakes shook their way across the desert floor, and the sun was so damn hot it was as if they were on the very face of it; only reach a hand out of the car and you would touch its bleeding border and would likely burn to bits; why, the sun too felt nuclear. Sharon gripped that boy's arm and told him to drive like hell and get them out of there, as if it were the A-bomb itself they could flee. This boy, his hair combed to one side with pomade Sharon thought would surely melt, burning his scalp the way all those Japanese faces she saw in magazines had been burned, his car idling in the desert, called her a traitor. Traitor! he'd said, as if he had been dared to bring her out into this blinding brutal world just to tell her this. She had thought he would leave her there, and her skeleton would be found, snakes wriggling out of her eye sockets.

But that boy had not left her there, and maybe everyone stopped partying once the hearings had begun. Or maybe television was taking over just as her father always said. Now the *Mary Tyler Moore Show* was filmed on that same lot where her father had filmed *Sheriff of Sundown*. God, how she wanted to throw a hat up into the sky that way; it was what she'd thought of when she'd started LEAP! I want to feel like Mary Tyler Moore, she'd thought when she'd found that blue card in her night-table drawer and called in that day. And when the phone was answered so brightly on the other end, Sharon's eyes leaked with tears: *You're gonna make it after all.*

Sharon might never have bolted from Los Angeles had her father been on the right side—which is to say on the left—of politics. With a father like Lester Cole, one of the original ten who'd refused to talk. He'd done *time*, and even by mere proxy his son was a hero at school. With a father like that, with the correct principles, there might have been a reason to stay. Then she could have been one of those earth women in Laurel Canyon baking bread for the neighborhood, spinning her own yarn and doing yoga beneath a picture of her very own guru.

Sharon knew now that Herbert Weissman hadn't been asked to name names, but she also knew that he would have wanted to be asked. She held an image of him waiting in the den, mumbling about the socialists from his old neighborhood. That's where they all come from, he'd said, my own goddamned street. He'd drum his fingers on the laminated phone table. What other call could he have awaited? From where she sat now, she saw her father clinging to his irrevocable immigrant fear of being sent back, sent *home*.

She pushed the cutting board aside, placed her head in her folded arms on the granite counter, and tried to conjure up her Essential Training. Sharon had almost completed Level 1 of her training, but still she remained unsure. Or more, she was not yet a *believer*. When had Sharon ever been able to give herself over to something? The consciousness-raising sessions she took part in a decade before were just women rapping—it was *good*, but there was no surrender in only talking. She'd wondered if she could really let go as the LEAP! session leader had stood at the lectern and described her own journey to self-actualization. The setup had felt very much like synagogue, which had made Sharon think of Marlene's initial advice: maybe Sharon was taking the wrong path and she should have gone back to Temple Sinai, as when the kids had been young. Perhaps the answer wasn't forging new ground, but treading backward, *returning*. Her father had revisited his faith only in his middle age, and she wondered if he was cheating death or if something more than thoughts of his own mortality, something true, had brought him back. Perhaps her father had been a stranger to himself and maybe now he looked in the mirror and could see through his aging—the brown spots and bits of hair, the sagging chin, and the puffiness below his eyes—to himself, to the boy he once was. How else does one age but like a tree, an entire past—fire, drought, flood, lightning attacks—all held within its maturing trunk, everything that ever happened to the tree evidenced by its growth rings. Every age we've ever been stored in our bodies. This is what Sharon had told Ben when he was learning about tree rings in the fifth grade, but she had said it quickly, to explain science to her son, and she had not really seen its import.

Perhaps she was wrong to turn away from God and look to something else for comfort. God was inside her. Or perhaps He was the spark outside her, the charge that came from a connection with another person, with nature. She had not felt that surge of connection—to anyone or anything—in ages. It had always been Benjamin. Even the women with whom she had gathered, who sat together in a tight circle and challenged conventional gender roles. She had wanted to feel securely fastened to them, but they were all unhooking themselves from the past, and despite a certain shared history, they were making their ways alone. Sitting in the Marriott looking for salvation might not be useful, it could also be just plain wrong.

Sharon thought of Vanessa emerging from the bathroom yesterday, her face red, her features unreachable and also hard, despite her swollen eyes and cheeks. That is not my daughter's face. My daughter's face is sweet and open; it smiles. I recognize it. My daughter is that girl drawing at her desk, flicking eraser crumbs off her work. My daughter is that yearbook photo from last year taped to the fridge; that is the real color of her hair, that is her true smile, her freckles. I have made the best choices available to me and I choose now to love her. I will not look at this as how it should have turned out between us. How Vanessa should have turned out. I have tried to live my life authentically.

Sharon lifted her head and, palm to her cheek, brushed off the bread crumbs. She remembered Vanessa standing on the lip of the lake at Monticello throwing crusts of bread to the ducks. But her profile was frozen—did she remember the event or was it only the photograph she saw? Why won't my memory *move*? Sharon thought. Vanessa wearing Sharon's enormous sunglasses by the woodpile in the backyard. She cleared her throat and straightened herself up, and steeling herself for the long night ahead, she went to put the cutting board, littered with potato eyes and flecks of parsley and garlic skin, in the sink for the housekeeper to wash with all the other dishes. I have made a choice, she thought of her daughter, a black cloud in a vintage dress. And now I have chosen to love you.

Elias Sanders, she knew, had also been her choice. Whether it was LEAP! that led her to him or he who led her to LEAP! she couldn't say. Sharon sat next to him at her third session, at the end of November, just after Thanksgiving. Dennis's parents had come, and for the first time Benjamin—who now insisted on being called Benji, which sounded to Sharon like the name of a sheepdog—was back home. That part had been lovely, but it hadn't lessened the stress, never mind the work she did for the dinner. An old friend from Los Angeles had sent her an article about Mexican Americans brining their turkeys, and this year Sharon had tried the technique. She had brined that turkey for days, bathing it with the kind of care saved for infants. Even as she held the bird, carefully lifting it from the brining pail, and turning it, rubbing its taut back and breast, she knew it was ludicrous. Then, in part because she had become so interested in Richard Olney's ideas about seasonal cooking, she made her usual trip to the Harley farm way out in Maryland for her root vegetables, then another trip out to the dairy for the whole milk and Gruyère she would use for the gratin, instead of the traditional mashed potatoes.

Had anyone offered to join her for the drive? Did anyone care? Briefly, the meal made everyone but Vanessa, who ate next to nothing, happy. Even Tatti, whose only non-Russian fare consisted of hot dogs, bran muffins, and her awful meringues, gobbled up the turkey and creamed spinach, scraping her plate with the side of her fork. But in the end, when the actual eating was over and done, Dennis still got incredibly wound up around his father, and Ben's new interest—more obsession—with Sigmund's past made Dennis even more clenched. Every time Ben asked his grandfather a question about union building, or what it was like to be a part of socialism when it was *real,* or why he'd turned against the communists in the end, the muscles on Dennis's neck bulged. As soon as Sigmund started to answer—union building was the most important thing he'd done; socialism is still very real, just look at France; I was more against totalitarianism than communism, but this is complicated—Dennis would make a noisy production of getting up to clear the table or change the music.

"What you need to understand, Benjamin, is that Stalinism was totally new to us," Sigmund droned on and on. "While it was happening, it was confusing. But communism and socialism are not the same thing. In fact, they were often in direct conflict with each other."

Dennis had gone to change the music and had put in one of Vanessa's tapes, "by accident." Instead of going back to turn it off, he came into the living room laughing. Of course, the effect of the screaming guitars was to completely drown out his father, if only for a moment. Still Sharon could not shake Sigmund's sad face tilting up to Dennis with such hurt and befuddlement.

Sharon found herself seated next to Elias on the Monday after Thanksgiving. He wore jeans and a wrinkled dress shirt, untucked, and he smelled of saddle soap. His eyes were electric blue, the whites of his eyes extreme against his tanned skin.

During a morning coffee break, as people stood outside smoking, shifting their feet to stay warm, Sharon and Elias stood among many in the lobby munching on bananas and soft pretzels.

He introduced himself to Sharon and she held out her hand.

Instead, Elias hugged her. "I've been wanting to do that all morning," he said.

Sharon's hands remained inert at her sides. It was all she could do to lift her shoulders in response.

"I've just come back from Africa, from Gabon. I was volunteering for UNICEF." His hands slid down her arms, toward her hands.

Sharon nodded. "How interesting," she said, shaking him off. She thought of the embassy party that had made her cooking locally famous.

"Can you believe I was a banker? Not too long ago, but I gave it all up." He scratched his chin through his beard.

"That's wonderful. So what brings you here?"

"I sold everything but my guitar." Elias's teeth were so white against his beard and his skin. "Don't even have a watch. I wanted to live an authentic life. I've looked into many things. Buddhism. Hinduism. EST. This will be only one of many things I will use to make my way, I think."

"To make your way?"

"Yes," he said. "Make my way through my life. Through the world."

"So you're not buying this?" Sharon imagined running her finger around the rim of a wineglass, wishing she had something to do with her hands.

"Well, I am paying, if that's what you mean, Sharon." He tipped his head back and laughed.

Sharon laughed. He was lean and she could imagine him in some dry field digging ditches, and just from the way he looked at her there was no debate in her mind: if this man who had given up his worldly possessions, who wore a leather band strung with one yellow African bead around his neck, and whose ass looked pretty damn good in faded Levi's, made a pass at her, she would accept it. A new decade, after all, was about to begin.

When they were all called back into the conference via bullhorn, Elias reached out and finally caught hold of Sharon's hand.

They took a room in the Marriott Hotel, along East-West Highway in Silver Spring, just a few miles from where she had lived for the past thirteen years. The room was twelve floors above the conference where they had each pledged to have no relations with other LEAP!ers for thirty days in order to let the high of the tenets dissipate a bit. One needs a more solid head, the leader had said. To decide such things.

Elias opened her blouse slowly, twisting each button with his thumb and third finger, then running his finger along her breastbone. When her shirt finally fell open, he studied her, then caressed her breasts. Was he putting her on? He licked her nipples, then moved his lips slowly down her stomach, and Sharon couldn't have cared less if he was. Elias removed her underwear, and kissing her just above her pubic bone, he slipped two fingers inside her. Sharon moved into his hands until he stopped suddenly, removing his fingers as if he'd thought better of the whole thing. While Sharon propped herself up on her elbows to see what had happened, Elias got up and opened his wallet. Was he moving to *pay* her? *Before?* Or worse—and now she thought of *Midnight Cowboy,* she'd been so scandalized by that film—was he expecting *her* to pay *him*? She wondered how much a man like Elias would cost.

Instead, he removed a joint from the wallet, took a lighter from his front pocket, lit it up, leaned over the bed, and passed it to Sharon, who took a deep drag. She passed it back to Elias, who, still standing, took another hit. Sharon unzipped his jeans. He wasn't wearing underwear, and Sharon could see instantly that he had a longer, thinner penis and was far hairier than Dennis, who always felt and looked unbelievably clean. Elias smelled dusky and deep, and as she leaned in, she was surprised to discover that he was uncircumcised.

After Elias had entered her and after she wrapped herself around him as he'd made love to her, allowed herself in that single moment to be carried, Sharon stood, zipped up her slacks, slipped on her blouse, and said to Elias that since he didn't have a house to go to, he could have the room, she was going home. But then he reached his hand out and grabbed her by a belt loop.

"Stay with me." His mouth was at her ear. He kissed her nape. "Don't leave," he'd said, unzipping her pants for the second time.

Again, he stopped suddenly. "Wait here," he said, just as he had removed her left pant leg. "I need to get something from my car." He let his fingers graze her crotch over her underwear before getting up from the bed.

Sharon sucked in her breath and fell back into the pillow. "Sure," she said. "Why not." Already she imagined being *one of those women*, waiting and waiting, flipping through the channels using the remote, a luxury they didn't have at home. There would be the hostage crisis, today was day number twenty-eight; how much longer could this go on? She imagined staring at the ceiling, which, as Elias had lifted her head and leaned over her, inching himself in, she had noticed had a wet stain on the yellowing stucco.

"I'm coming right back," he said, hopping on one leg as he pulled on his jeans.

"Okay." She wondered if he would leave her with the bill.

Sharon couldn't help it; she rolled on her side, leaned on her elbow, and watched him dress. She liked his lithe body, covered in dark, curly hair. It didn't really matter to her; it was absolutely for the best if he did not come back.

Elias left his wallet, she noticed, as he closed the door quietly behind him. Sharon rolled onto her stomach and kicked her legs in the air; she knocked her feet against each other and felt her crotch against the mattress, alive, its own animal, she imagined now, thinking of the first time she had been with Dennis. Because Elias was only the second man she'd had sex with unless one counted the surgeon, which would be absurd, if technically accurate. Because of course she had missed the moment when women became sexually liberated. By a hair, she had missed it. That first night with Dennis in Georgetown, after they'd gone paddle boating in the Tidal Basin, they'd gone back to her place on Q Street. The date had been only so-so; Dennis had gone on and on about architecture, the way D.C. was built. Just like Paris, he had said, sweeping his arm out as if the city had been his to show. She had not yet been to Paris, so she couldn't yet say yes or no, and she hadn't realized at the time that Dennis had never been either.

But her roommate had been away, and she knew they would be alone when she brought Dennis home with her late that afternoon. As he'd pointed to the cherry trees—they'd been blooming, she remembered as she waited for Elias; how prophetic, those trees bloomed for a matter of seconds—Sharon knew she would go to bed with him, just as she had known today with Elias. Dennis was teaching her about D.C., but his tone was neither bossy nor terribly preachy. And she liked the way his finger pointed at everything but her. She had desired him deeply— the blond duckling hair on his arms, his hazel eyes, his talk of making change from within the system. That's what Washington is *about,* he'd said. Her mother had warned her—Don't you ever do it before you're married! Men need the chase, darling, what do they want with what they've got?—but Sharon hadn't cared. She had, after all, been fitted for a diaphragm years before, in college, even though she had no need for it then. She had merely wanted to be the kind of girl who went to the clinic and got one.

The afternoon light had made its way through the blinds as she and Dennis began their lovemaking on the living room couch. While he banged up against her, meeting what he would later—a week later, in bed at Len Ford's place in Skatesville, when they were able to laugh about it just a little—say felt to him like a brick wall, hardly, he'd said, the way he would have imagined popping her cherry, Sharon was in excruciating pain. As he tried at her from different angles, Sharon wondered, had her mother gotten in there and inserted a barrier, somehow just walled her off? What of the horseback riding, or the time she fell, spread-legged, on the balance beam during gymnastics? Not to mention several late-night dry-humping sessions in Topanga Canyon and at the Santa Monica Pier, then in D.C., at more than one party where too many martinis had made her let many a Democratic finger dip in. How had her mother gotten *in*? Sharon thought as Dennis pushed harder and harder, standing on the rug now for leverage, his early gentleness usurped by this unaccomplishable mission. When she'd let out a cry of intense pain, they'd finally disconnected and headed to George Washington Hospital to see what all this suffering was about. Who could have known that Sharon had an unbreakable hymen? There, a surgeon went in with a scalpel.

Sharon could hear Elias returning in the hallway; already she recognized him by his whistle. *I'm goin' where the sun keeps shinin' through the pourin' rain. Goin' where the weather suits my clothes.* She knew all the words. And now she remembered the surgeon's face, looking up at her from below, his front teeth biting his lip, as if he were working hard to please her. Through the haze of the local anesthesia and the humiliation of the moment, a rush of blood and vaginal fluid poured out of her when finally—finally!—the surgeon broke through. She heard a small knock at the door, and when she sprang up to answer, there was Elias, smiling in the hallway, holding a guitar by its neck in his left hand.

Sharon was placing the mushrooms on platters, the browned caps heaped high with bread crumbs and parsley and garlic, and melted butter and Parmesan, when her daughter came into the kitchen, Sigmund's old trench coat wrapped tightly around her, bringing with her a rush of cold air.

Please let there be a white blouse and black pants beneath that awful moth-eaten coat, thought Sharon. When had her father-in-law ever worn such a thing anyway? She imagined him at some impassioned rally beneath the *Forward* building, his arm pointed straight to Marx and Engels, set in relief above the second floor. Maybe this black coat had been brand-new then; perhaps it gave him a sense of authority when he wore it to speak for the Workers Party.

"Hi, honey!" Sharon said, turning her head from the silver plate and smiling as if posing for a photograph in her own cookbook.

Vanessa unwound a chunky and endlessly long multicolored scarf her boyfriend had knit for her. Sharon still thought this odd; what seventeen-year-old boy knits? Apparently Jason McFinley did. He was a nice enough kid, but his dyed-blond hair, black at the roots, those weird pointy shoes, gave him less of an air of menace than they seemed to intend. To Sharon, he seemed like a friendly and well-adjusted kid who was always offering to help her in the kitchen, even if he'd show up at the house and Vanessa was nowhere to be found.

She tried not to watch too carefully as Vanessa removed the overcoat, which thankfully revealed a white oxford-cloth dress shirt, if rumpled and far too big, tucked into a pair of black corduroys. This would be fine under the white apron the servers folded down and wore tied around their waists. Vanessa threw the heavy coat over one of the kitchen chairs, and just as Sharon was going to instruct her as to exactly where she should put it, Marlene swept in.

"Thank you so much for helping us!" Marlene gave Vanessa a big hug as she took her coat from the chair. She looked like a bear next to Vanessa, so fleshy in contrast to Vanessa's bird bones.

"No problem." Vanessa looked at the floor, then up at Marlene. "So what should I do?"

"Well." Marlene scanned the room. She put the coat on the couch at the other end of the kitchen. "What do you think, Sharon?"

"Let's see." Sharon placed both hands on her hips and surveyed the chaotic room. "Do you want to pass, honey, or do you want to just clean up as people go?"

Vanessa ignored her mother and instead answered Marlene. "I'd like to serve stuff, I think. I mean, that's what I'm here for, right?"

"Absolutely," Marlene said. "Why don't you pass the fish balls, then?"

"Okay."

"You know, you hold the tray, let them dip in the sauce, and then pass a napkin. Like this." Marlene mimed the gesture.

"Got it," Vanessa said, and Sharon knew, were it she instructing, Vanessa would be enraged.

"It's not a huge party, and there are three other servers," Marlene continued. "Tom, Leslie, and Helen." She gestured to the table where they were piling mini-quiches on platters, and Vanessa looked over and nodded. "Tom and Helen will be serving champagne as the guests arrive and then the white wine, no red because of the carpets and the white chairs. You and Leslie are serving the hors d'oeuvres, and then they'll be helping with the empties. When the meal is ready, we'll be plating here." Marlene spread her hands rather tentatively over the kitchen island. "And you'll be serving at the table. So it's important to be very, um, well, proper. Then Sharon does the jubilee at the end." Marlene looked over at Sharon. "Remember the white chairs, Sharon," she said softly. "And voilà!" Marlene brushed her hands together. "Be sure to serve from the left. And you pick up from the right. But beverages, should you be serving, are always from the right. Basically, you never serve so the back of your arm faces the guests. Like this."

Vanessa clenched her teeth. "Okay." She rubbed her arms.

"Great," Sharon said, coming up from behind. The doorbell had just rung for the third time, and she turned to Tom with a strained face. "Now, Tom! The guests are arriving, you need to greet them with the champagne!"

"Showtime!" Marlene said, expertly popping open the second bottle of champagne, then quickly filling the flutes on Helen's tray.

Sharon heard only brief snippets of conversations as the servers moved in and out. Each time a server leaned into the kitchen door and walked into the hallway, it was like the brief roar of the ocean in a seashell. Then, when the door closed, it was as if the shell had been placed back down in the sand. She did get news that Felix Epstein was late due to some crisis at the office, which made his wife furious. Marsha kept coming into the kitchen and talking to Sharon, who was madly trying to carve the lamb into individual chops and plate it with the potatoes, while Marlene did whatever slow and ridiculously perfect thing she did. The vegetables, of course, the medley of spring vegetables.

"Would your husband ever do such a thing? On a weekend? What if Mondale comes, and Felix isn't here yet?" Marsha Epstein complained. "Not that there aren't plenty of people here already he should be here for. Senator Mathias is here. Ross Wilson is here, the brand-new consul general to—"

"I know them both," Sharon said, placing a chop on a plate. "Charles Mathias lives around the corner from us. He's got the most adorable golden retriever." She smiled to think of the senator trying to stay dignified as he walked the insanely playful dog. "And Dennis works with Wilson." Sharon and Marsha had actually been to many events together, both as guests, which was how Marsha had found out about Food Matters in the first place. See? Sharon had thought to tell her mother. Good to navigate both worlds.

"He's so young!" Marsha said. "Twenty-five years old, I hear. From Minneapolis, like our friend Mr. Mondale. *Very* interesting. Felix really should be here. It's appalling."

"It's the nature of the job," Sharon said, as she wiped blood from the plate with a dish towel. "Fritz will understand!" she joked. "Everyone understands. Besides, Mondale sees Felix all the time. Listen, Dennis didn't even show to his own daughter's birth."

"Really?" Marsha looked over at Vanessa, who was holding a tray with both hands as Marlene loaded it with individually portioned salads.

"He was in Moscow. Actually my mother was angrier than I was, at least until I had to actually give birth with my mother in the delivery room." Now Sharon added potatoes, about five a person, she thought, quickly doing the math as she garnished with chopped parsley. "She was convinced he was a spy."

Vanessa turned toward Sharon as she spoke, but she said nothing.

"Really." Marsha's eyes were trained on the closed kitchen door, as if she could see through it to the other side and down the hallway, to the front door, or beyond that to Capitol Hill, where her husband sat in some office, a phone to his ear. Or worse, Sharon thought as she watched Marsha Epstein grow more anxious, there he was in a room at the Willard Hotel, the long, impossibly slim legs of some Spanish diplomat wrapped around his neck. Who, after all, had nothing to hide?

"She still thinks so." Sharon imagined Marsha paying some man in a trench to sit in a car on Pennsylvania with a long-lensed camera, waiting for Felix to emerge with the brunette beauty, arm in arm.

"Well, screw him," Marsha said, as if she'd read Sharon's mind. She turned back to Sharon. "But you know there is a lot going on about the spies lately, my God. Felix has a friend at State who says there's this project called Venona, which has been decoding Soviet secrets for thirty-five years. And they're shutting it down! There's still a war on, you know." Marsha leaned in as if to whisper a secret, but maintained her normal decibel level. "Supposedly they're holding on to some cases from the forties and fifties, just to go out with a bang. Maybe one of them is Dennis!"

Sharon put down her towel, stained with lamb juice, and watched her daughter back into the door, heading out to the party with a tray of salads, just as Tom came in holding a platter filled with smudged, empty champagne flutes. Sharon looked back at Marsha. Even in January she wore coral lipstick, and her diamond and emerald earrings set off her olive skin. Her bangle bracelets jangled as she moved her hands, still talking.

"Not even in jest, Marsha," Sharon said. "Truly. And anyway, how old do you think Dennis is?"

Marsha laughed. "Right. Right. But can you imagine? People who may have slipped secrets to the Soviets à la Julius and Ethel could be right outside that door." She covered her mouth, and her bracelets clanked together like money.

"Oh, come on, Marsha, that was all such BS."

"BS? Oh, you come on! I bet the Venona transcripts will say differently; I hear there was plenty of traffic back and forth."

"Hear from whom?" Sharon asked, trying to get back to her plating. "I've never heard of Venona."

"I may look stupid, and Felix might think I'm stupid as well, but I've got my sources. I hope Felix is aware."

Sharon nodded at the plate she was wiping. Perhaps Dennis was gathering intelligence on her right now. "No one thinks you're stupid, Marsha."

Marsha popped a leftover fish ball, on a platter by the sink. "Delicious." *Clank clank* went the bracelets. "You want to know something? The Soviets, they'd find one another at designated hotels, and you know how they figured out if the person was correctly identified? Greetings from Fanny, the guy would say, the guy from the KGB—though then I think it was called something else—"

"The NKGB."

Marsha looked at Sharon and nodded. "Right. The NKGB guy would say, Yup, just like that, greetings from Fanny, and if they had the right guy—or girl—they'd respond, 'Thank you. And how is she?'"

"How very civilized of them," Sharon said.

"I'm sorry, but who knows. *He,* Julius, was definitely involved, Sharon, no question. No question. At. All."

Sharon shrugged and again resumed running the towel along the plates. There was her father again, banging the television, cheering for the Americans. Thank you, and how is she? How many times had he said that into the phone? How he'd cheered when the Rosenbergs went down; it never left her, his glee in these two people's deaths. Send them back to Russia! COD, he'd said, brushing his hands together, as if he were washing them of the whole affair. They had looked so regular to her.

"Who knew you were such a lefty!" Marsha said.

Sharon looked up from the plate. "Of course I'm a lefty—we all are, no?—but what does that have to do with it?"

"Now come on, Sharon, we're Democrats, not communists!" Marsha laughed. "I heard there were some cover names still unidentified. Ethel's brother went by Bumble-Bee. Can you imagine?"

"I can't, no."

"Oh, forget it, please, my God, let's save the politics for outside this kitchen, no? I'm headed back out there. By the way, your canapés were delicious, ladies." Marsha trilled her fingers next to her head as she went to the door. "Those fish balls are light as air!" she said, then the roar of the ocean was again upon them.

The dinner portion of the meal had been tremendously successful. Not transcendent by any means, but Marsha seemed happy with it, and the lamb had been perfectly cooked. The servers, including Vanessa, had been in and out quickly, and nothing had sat too long in the kitchen. Nothing dropped or broken; no one had been spilled on. This in and of itself was an achievement.

Sharon thought about Elias as she heated the cherries; even when cherries were in season, canned always worked best. She added a little arrowroot—far better than cornstarch—to thicken the sauce. What was he doing right now? She saw Elias lying back on the hood of his car, waiting. She thought he might have left a message for her at work, which was where he always called her; he, with no house and no job, was unreachable.

Sharon had halfheartedly tried to end the affair, but the pressure from LEAP! to see the training through was now all tangled up with her relationship, or more her dalliance, with Elias. It became so difficult to tell which was helping and which was not. Which part, if any, Sharon wondered, was the self-*actualizing* part? Barring the fact she had no way to reach him, seeing Elias had been absurdly easy. Dennis was always away, or were he not, she simply claimed she was out at an event outside the Beltway and so would be staying the night. Her husband never questioned her, nor did her children. Did no one think her able? The ease of it made Sharon think often about what had been there before Elias had surfaced. Meeting Elias had happened, and her life moved in and around the event to accommodate it, like a sponge. Sharon imagined him carrying his guitar case, a blade of grass singing between his teeth, as he turned to head out West. He had often spoken about an Indian reservation in Taos, outside Santa Fe, where he'd once been to a sun dance. Perhaps he would head there and sing and eat fry bread and camp on the reservation until some Indian woman took him in with her stories and her long black braid and her big big love.

Because Elias would not be staying long with a woman like Sharon, she knew, not someone so tethered to materialism, so unattached to a colonized narrative, and whose sole involvement in politics was cooking for Democratic fund-raisers. Every time—including the one just two nights ago—felt like the last, just the way it had been that first night. She was both haunted and liberated by the feeling that he might leave and not return, and that perhaps she would be grateful to have him do so. Perhaps my life is Dennis after all, she'd thought those two nights ago, remembering her honeymoon in France. They had stayed in a château in Sarlat and eaten breakfast on a terrace, a blue peacock dragging its feathers in the garden below. She had buttered her brioche then and thought, This will be my life, and she had turned to see Elias roll onto his side in the unmade bed; she had heard the door click so loudly behind her as she left him there.

What she needed was a sign from Dennis, and this was why she'd entreated him with her call this morning. Call it a test: she thought of her mother-in-law and her talk of curses and hexes and omens. If Dennis said yes, yes, I will visit Ben at school with you, then things would not forever be undone. She had trembled dialing his office, and when he'd answered, she realized her voice was shaking as well. Then Dennis had said yes, he had tried to put her off, as he always did, but the answer had been yes, and he had unknowingly said yes to the prospect of their becoming whole again, a family, and so here she was once more, that girl on the terrace, and the peacock was about to spread its feathers in the garden below; there was nothing but possibilities.

Now Marlene helped her prepare the rolling cart with a green tablecloth, the copper flambé dishes atop the two small burners they used for these occasions. Sharon—it was always Sharon, Marlene was far too self-conscious for such work—would add the brandy tableside, then light it. Tom and Helen would follow with trays of vanilla ice cream in crystal goblets, Leslie with trays of linzers and shortbread for the table, and as soon as the flame went out, Sharon would spoon the warm cherries and liquor over the ice cream at the table, which they would pass one by one to the guests.

If Mondale did come to the party, he didn't stay until the cherries. Everyone clapped when Sharon emerged from the kitchen wheeling the cart, and in addition to cheering the prospect of the grand display they were about to witness, they were also clearly applauding the meal. She bowed to the guests, two tables of thirty apiece, to Marsha at the head of one table, and to Felix, who had finally arrived at his own dinner party—before or after the Spaniard, who could say?—and was now seated and waving at the end of the other. She saw Senator

Mathias, and the man—more boy—Ross Wilson. She wheeled her cart to their end of the room to nudge herself in between the two tables and turned to face a bay window with a view onto the large garden. She nodded hello to the guests she knew, then smiled down the long tables as she poured the warmed kirschwasser into the cherries. She stirred the mixture, then took a matchbox from the cart drawer, a lovely box that featured a pink swan, one that Dennis had brought back from Moscow. Sharon lit the long match, then touched it down to the copper dish. Instantly, the spectacle made this the most rewarding part of the meal for Sharon; the cherries were aflame in a ring of fire and a blue halo of the alcohol. The guests oohed and aahed. *Oh, Sharon!* someone, Marsha probably, exclaimed, and Sharon turned to her and smiled, thinking already about her next party, how she would prepare a more complicated crêpes suzette.

In this moment out of the corner of her right eye, she caught sight of Vanessa. Her daughter stood out in the garden in the freezing cold. She wasn't wearing that old coat. What was she doing? Please tell me she's not smoking out there in the middle of the garden for everyone to see, Sharon thought. The tables continued to cheer and Sharon turned to view Vanessa in full and was met by the image of her stuffing herself with lamb Provençal and potatoes. The pockets of Vanessa's serving apron were bursting with food, and Sharon watched her move behind the leafless trees, crouching down now as she tore the meat from the chops like a wild dog.

But Vanessa is a vegetarian! Sharon thought.

Sharon closed her eyes. Then she thought of her anchors: I have chosen to love you. She remembered Elias just then, cross-legged on the hotel bed, his nakedness covered by his guitar: *Asking only workman's wages, I come looking for a job, but I get no offers . . .* Sharon had lain on her back running the tips of her fingers over her belly as she listened to him play. I am returning, I will return, I have returned to you. *Li la li, li la li la li la li.*

Vanessa looked so cold out there, alone and primitive, and Sharon could feel her own heat, a huge warmth crawling into her, such a contrast to her daughter's state. She remembered the medieval castles rising along the banks of the Dordogne; it was a setting for a fairy tale. But it wasn't hers. She and Dennis screamed at each other as they'd tried to canoe upstream beneath the beating sun. They paddled and paddled—each claimed the other was steering—but the boat only moved sideways. Sharon had already begun to think of their marriage as something from the past. Now Sharon heard more screaming, and she thought of the hostages, all in a room together being tortured, and she wondered what would become of Jimmy Carter in the upcoming elections. She would serve peanut brittle for dessert at her next fund-raiser, or perhaps her next fund-raiser should be for something entirely different. Women's health issues, she thought as a great white heat began to overtake her. What is Venona? she imagined demanding, turning on the light quickly and questioning Dennis in the middle of the night. Why was she so warm, safe and inside, when her daughter was freezing? There was a rancid smell, like tires burning. And then Felix Epstein, Mondale's advance man, was upon her, there was a terrible crash, and then the night went black.

# CHAPTER 8

# A Witch's Mask

**March 22, 1980**

On the night before they left to visit Vanessa's brother for parents' weekend, the Goldstein house was toilet-papered. Vanessa watched it happen. She was smoking at her window, and blacking out the Government Issue lyrics she'd written weeks ago on the rubber strips along the insteps of her Chuck Taylors, furious that her mother had insisted on dragging her along, citing the Epstein "episode" as the reason Vanessa could not stay in the house alone. Joni Mitchell's *Blue* played softly on her tape deck—*I wish I had a river I could skate away on.* This was not frilly Joni, but a gateway into an interior life—Vanessa's perhaps—that ached with want and celebrated it.

I wish I wish I wish . . . *I'm selfish and I'm sad* . . . This song was a journey, a feeling Vanessa was after, and she didn't need to scream and raise up her fists and stomp her feet to match some unknowable part of her precisely. Jason could play her 107 tracks of a Ramones bootleg, listening for new information, a breath, say, a pause, anything that would reveal something different about a song and so about the men playing it. He and Sean Flaherty traded tapes and obscure Buzzcocks and the Damned LPs the way Ben had once swapped baseball cards. Vanessa understood the desire to search for more than what you are merely given in a studio album; she could listen to any number of versions of "River," just to hear the way Joni Mitchell's voice seemed reshaped, saddened in new places, the way her voice lifted, paused, rejoiced. Tom Waits, too. Vanessa had found a recording of a radio program in San Francisco in '74, and the way he had sung "I Hope That I Don't Fall in Love with You," more jagged by its live nature, played faster, and sung with irony—it had changed it from a sorrowful song about missed opportunity to one about perhaps. Love had a chance in the live version, which made it less devastating than the one on *Closing Time.* Vanessa listened to that album over and over, wondering as it spun, would that be it? Life, a series of fumbled chances, and of wanting only what cannot be had.

Music had a purity, and Vanessa agreed with Jason on the reverence they should have for it. But for the most part the music they saw at shows depended on being there in the room with it; it was contingent on reaction and that feeling of being present, alive with intensity. This got lost and not deepened on all the recordings. Other than a stunning bootleg of the Clash in Leicester, England, where Joe Strummer actually belted out, *Let's kiss to another Clash love song!* the live punk stuff didn't hold much interest for her.

Vanessa turned off Joni Mitchell when she heard the skateboards against the road making their way down the block, then the squeak of the stopping wheels, the scrape of wood against asphalt as the boards were lifted. Flicking off the light and looking out, she was met with the sight of four kids lifting their boards at the side of the house. Then there was the near silence of their treading on the lawn.

It was just whom she'd expected: at least Sean Flaherty was. He was accompanied by George from the now defunct Tellers, and two Georgetown Day School boys, Georgetown punks whose parents were all high up in the administration, or at State, not exactly from the broken homes she had once imagined. They wore backpacks and pulled them off and swung them to the ground, at their ankles, then bent into them to remove rolls and rolls of toilet paper. Now Vanessa wanted to play something loud enough—White Boy maybe—so she could hold it out the window as these assholes made their way across the yard.

She could hear them laughing as they crossed the lawn like soldiers, their large white arms swinging toilet-paper rolls, little grenades, into the sky. Sean's shaved head was a negative silhouette, and a darker black seemed to outline him, setting his skull against the blue-black of the night. Sean Flaherty was wound tight; he'd already grown into himself, and his muscles were carved, made more of stone than flesh. The smooth head was an extension of his taut body, waiting to be sprung. Vanessa watched as they pitched roll upon roll over her father's prized dogwood, the massive oak, even the hydrangea, bending beneath the assaults. As the arc of one roll traveled by her window, followed by a stream of paper, a shooting star, which then caught and broke on a single branch, she wondered at their meaning, Sean's meaning, as she reveled in spying on them. Come in! Boys. They glowed over the dark as Vanessa wondered at the way they moved so stealthily along the periphery of the house.

Watching the toilet paper loop over the trees, Vanessa thought of climbing up the cherry trees at the Tidal Basin with Jason. After a Tiny Desk Unit show at d.c. space in November (Tiny Desk Unit: kind of a new-wave jam band that Vanessa liked because the lead singer, Susan Mumford, was sort of a cool, striking girl), they'd parked on Independence Avenue and gone over to the Tidal Basin, and Vanessa was shocked to see Jason scramble up into the interwoven branches instead of staying below, with her, pushing urgently against a trunk and pressing against her, the way he had so many times that summer. She'd never been to the Tidal Basin at night, and she followed Jason, climbing carefully so as not to step on the delicate limbs as she made her way up. It was cold, and Vanessa remembered the stripped branches, slippery with frost. She'd looked up to Jason on a stronger, higher branch, wrapped up in his parka, and had wondered then, What does this person want from me? A web of blossomless boughs was in front of her, a cross-hatching against the backdrop of sky, and Jason had looked terribly white and frail, as if he were caught inside it. Why, Vanessa wondered, does he still take me along with him?

Then, bizarrely, she had thought of the Mills scandal her father had delighted in several years previously. Wilbur Mills, chairman of the Ways and Means Committee, had been discovered drunk, in an altercation with an Argentinean stripper, and when the police arrived, he'd jumped into the Tidal Basin. Or perhaps it had been the stripper who jumped. Right here, Vanessa had thought then, imagining the splash, the putrid Potomac surrounding the body in slime. She wondered just how much had been thrown into that basin. Sometimes people in this town can be fun, her father had said. But they always get punished later. Trapped in the network of cherry branches with Jason, Vanessa looked out to the Jefferson Memorial, a round dome shining with light, and she thought about what lay at the bottom.

Vanessa knew why Sean was here. Not three weeks ago Jason and Vanessa had gone over to his house intending to get him to go downtown with them. They'd pulled up to his house, then tiptoed through the side door, into the kitchen. A large wooden table stood on the other side of the Formica counter strewn with papers and folders, all stamped with the round green-and-blue seal of the U.S. Department of Energy.

Vanessa noted how much more kicky this seal was than her father's, which looked like a children's-book rendition of dried corn, some kind of wheelbarrow stuck in the foreground. She had such fond memories of parking at her father's office before they went out to a museum or ice-skating on the Mall, and her father always made them run upstairs for a few minutes so he could pick something up or return a file. She and Ben used to swipe correcting tape and Wite-Out from the supply closet. Once, Tatiana had been with them, and Vanessa and her grandmother had stolen a few sheets of her father's letterhead, giggling, while he was out at the copier. Tatiana loved to be in her father's office; she was so proud to have a son who worked so high up in this city, this country. She had come from this faraway land, a place Vanessa would never be able to truly imagine as real, no matter how many dolls and music boxes she stacked on her bureau, or how many photographs her father showed her of lit squares, a building shaped like an ice cream.

At Sean Flaherty's no one was at the table or in the living room they passed through, the blue velvet drapes tied back with golden stays, with a gleaming black grand piano, silk flowers and family photos framed in silver placed neatly on the sparkling surface.

Vanessa and Jason had quietly walked up the stairs, shushing each other, a painting of an elephant in an Uncle Sam hat, seriously, hanging from the brown walls above them. They crept into the hallway, toward the door leading into Sean's attic room.

She had been up here before, after Sean had driven her to Annapolis last September, to get fake IDs so they could get into eighteen-and-over shows. Jason already had his, and it was the first time Vanessa had ever been alone with Sean. They went out to the place everyone went to—run by two Arab guys who didn't give a damn how old you were just as long as you didn't say you were Jewish—after school one afternoon, and they'd been stuck in so much traffic, they'd turned right around and driven back in silence, their new laminated IDs still hot in their hands. Vanessa tried to think of things to say that were not necessarily what she would ask Sean when in the presence of others.

"Are you really a Republican?" she asked.

"Fuck yeah." Sean hadn't been playing any music at all, which seemed in that moment connected to his Republicanism.

Sean Flaherty Junior, she thought.

Vanessa didn't know many kids who were named after their father, and she didn't know many Republicans; the arguments she heard in her house, as she wove in and out of the tiki lights during her parents' patio parties, or even as she listened to her grandfather and her father, were the arguments between liberals.

"I don't even know what that means really," Vanessa said.

"It means Carter is the best thing to ever happen to us," Sean said. "What a joke!"

She did not ask what he did believe in. The draft, the death penalty, no money for the arts or education, tax breaks for the rich? Nixon?

"So what does it mean to be a Democrat, then?" he asked as they drove toward Bethesda.

If she said the right thing, she knew she would be going to Sean's. "It means you're against the closing of Varsity Grill, where non-desirables hang out." She laughed ironically. "It means you do something when Madam's Organ is shutting down."

He scoffed. "That place smells like shit. And if a bunch of punks can't come up with three hundred and fifty bucks to pay the rent, then they don't deserve to use the place anyway."

Vanessa was silent. She had thought there was a universal point of view, at least among the kids, on the terrible injustice of the impending closing of Madam's Organ. The place was disgusting; really, it was dirty, and it stank of beer and sweat and something unnameable that Jason and she thought was the smell of insects having sex, but still she had thought keeping it open was a sure position.

Sean turned onto Wisconsin Avenue toward his house anyway, and soon they were in his driveway and heading upstairs to his room. His room! He had pushed Vanessa against the wall in the stairway to the attic, where a large Anarchy poster, a white symbol on stark black, a Stiff Little Fingers show poster, and a photo of a punk singer Vanessa didn't recognize, shoving the chord of a mike into his mouth, hung by clear pushpins and silver thumbtacks from the flowered wallpaper peeling away from the stairway walls. He took Vanessa's hand and led her up the steps to the bedroom, the ceiling sloped so much at one side they both had to tuck their chins before stumbling onto Sean's unmade bed. As soon as she'd hit the mattress, Vanessa had reached up and pulled off his shirt, revealing the tattoo below his collarbone at his left shoulder of a kid gripping a skateboard, knees bent to his chest, jumping out of flames, an image she'd previously seen only from afar.

Sean took off her skirt and her underwear and they did it quickly. She had held on to him, her ear to his chest as if she were listening to his heart, and she had not felt sad. When it was done, she'd dressed and he'd pulled on his boots to take her home, and as they had shifted back to who they had been, Vanessa tried to be the girl who could just *do it herself,* play the bass, goddamn it, *start a band!* or at the very least fuck the bass player. But Sean wasn't in a band—and he was a Republican. And he was also Jason's best friend.

Creeping up those same attic stairs, sneaking up on Sean with Jason, she looked up from the stairwell to the slanted ceilings, and the exposed wooden beams she'd seen as she'd leaned back sideways on the bed.

"Boo!" Jason said as he hit the top stair.

Then he turned around so fast he bumped into Vanessa, pushing her down several stairs.

She caught herself on the banister. "What the hell?"

"Sorry, man," Jason called up to Sean over the banister.

"What?" Vanessa peered over to see Sean seated, naked in his bed, sheets pulled over his very erect dick. She stared at him. As she turned away, Jason in front of her heading down the stairs, she caught sight of his rumpled bed, strewn with magazines.

Vanessa let herself be pulled all the way downstairs by Jason, fast and loud, offering evidence that they were getting farther and farther away.

"Should we wait?" Vanessa said, breathless, in the dining room. She was both disgusted by the idea of Sean masturbating and delighted that she'd been spying and caught Sean exposed, merely the mortal boy he was. Whom had he been thinking about? she wondered, remembering the feel of his muscled back, and how she wished she didn't bite her nails just as Nana Helen had always told her, so she could scratch them along it.

"No way," Jason said. "We're leaving."

"I feel bad, though." Vanessa looked at the table of papers. "This seal is kind of cool, don't you think?"

"No, I don't really think. It's a fucking government seal."

"It looks like a 1950s textbook." She took a few sheets. She folded them and put them in her pocket. "It could be some retro album cover."

"Vanessa. Come on."

"Don't you think we should wait until he comes downstairs?"

"Believe me, we should *not* be here when he comes downstairs. It looks like we're spying on him!" He took Vanessa by her elbow and led her down the driveway, and she didn't resist.

She got in the car and turned to Jason, in the driver's seat. She could eat lunch with him at school each day, she could spend afternoons in the back room of his house listening to the comforting sounds of his mother preparing dinner, she could drive with him all over town, speeding along the Potomac, past Watergate and beneath the awning of the Kennedy Center, over to the Lincoln Memorial and around the Washington Monument, momentarily breathless for the beauty of this town, and never once would she think about having sex with his friend. "So do you?" She pointed upstairs.

"My God! No!"

"But don't all guys do it? I mean, all the time?" If he wasn't having sex, what was he *doing*? Because for several months now, sex, as in *doing* it, had rarely come up between them. Or Vanessa now didn't bring it up and Jason never instigated it. Never. She began to wonder if he hadn't forgotten to tell her he'd sworn off sex as he had drugs, as so many of the kids she saw around were vigilant about being sober, and disconnecting from the earlier punks who got so heavily into drugs. Detaching themselves from the dirty hippies who fucked each other so recklessly. You took drugs; that's what you were. A smelly goddamn hippie. And also a total cliché. All these things, they alter us, Jason told her. We need our wits about us, he said. It's all a way for the government to keep us down, Jason had said, and Vanessa had cocked her head and looked at him to see if he was serious.

He was serious, and Vanessa could subscribe to the idea of being a pure self. She wanted to be righteous and uncontaminated. With all this recent talk about cleaning up the Potomac, that's what she imagined she would be: purified. Now Jason and she spent nights lying on the couch in his parents' den, a blanket draped over them, disguising all that was not passing between them. They listened to music. When Vanessa played the live Tom Waits on KPFK in Los Angeles, Jason had listened so thoughtfully, nodding his head. "I get it," he, said. "I totally get it. He's so the real thing, you know? Like Ray Charles or something. And this is us."

But there was no missed beat, nothing lost, only Vanessa convincing herself she could stop wanting anything else, all those things that had once both defined and polluted her: beer, pot, burgers, the sticky, sweet spareribs from Hunan Village on Georgetown Road. The more she gave up for political reasons, the easier it was to do so, and her body reflected this, waxing and waning depending on her dissent. She was relieved also to let sex go.

"Maybe," Jason said now. He started the car. "But not me."

"What's the big deal?" Vanessa asked. "Ben says guys do it all the time. Like they have to or they'll die."

"That's ridiculous. That's what your brother tells girls so they'll fuck him."

"Is it a Catholic thing?" Vanessa asked, ignoring the comment. Perhaps she and Jason were *both* boycotting sex. Vanessa remembered the wet leaves against her legs and back, the feel of earthworms crawling around at her ankles, the leaves whispering into the summer sky on those first few nights at Valley Hill with Jason. She remembered the vestal beginnings of sexual desire, then the stifling heat and sticky floor of some kid's basement, the great roar of an out-of-tune bass, and the anticipation of waiting for the singer to stand up and scream them all down. Was there something awful about wanting? When had she become so terribly herself, conscious of her awkward positioning, the soft cushion of earth beneath her, the tires humming along the highway, her body grown ungainly and graceless flung against the cold, damp earth? Her own longing—for most anything, it seemed—had been burned away, like fog. It was replaced by the comfort of Jason's unthreatening presence.

"Please, Vanessa." Jason put the car in reverse. "It's not a Catholic thing. It's just no big deal."

"Why are you making it seem like such a big deal then?"

Jason shrugged. "Please. Can we just go?"

"I think it must be a Catholic thing." She crossed her arms and sat back in the seat.

"Fine!" He put his long arm over her seat and looked out the rear window, reversing out of the driveway.

"What*ever*." Vanessa shrugged, realizing that Jason may have been just as drawn to Sean as she was. She remembered Jason watching Sean fling himself off the rocks at Great Falls. Looking at a guy like that was *not* Straight Edge. Sean's arms and legs circled in the air, his chest puffed up toward the sky. Vanessa had been so sure, as he dropped down, that before hitting the water he would rise up, his feet pointed, arms together over his head, heading toward the sun.

She watched Jason shift gears from reverse to first, then second, with ease as he drove fast, toward Wisconsin Avenue. She remembered him patiently trying to teach her to drive stick and how she rode the gearshift of Mrs. McFinley's Corolla evening after evening in the high school parking lot. He was so assured at some things, such as driving, and directions, and who was playing where and all their bootlegged recordings, and exactly how to get downtown to see them. Vanessa thought of Bee's talk of rim jobs and blow jobs and the many boys she'd fooled around with. What made Bee need sex, or male attention, while Vanessa needed food or the inceptive warm feeling food proffered? She looked over at Jason, rewinding his *30 Seconds Over DC* tape to hear the Slickee Boys again. His fingers tapped along the gearshift when "Attitude" came on.

She reached over and mussed his hair. "It's no big deal at all." She would accept it, she thought. Because it let her off the hook too? Because this way she would not have to be Bee; she would not have to be one of those brave girls who made their own way, or one of those who just picked up their guitars and drumsticks and screamed. This way she could be no one.

Jason smiled, looking straight ahead. He nodded his head faintly to the music.

She had this strange desire to be experiencing anything before now, for her body to be made small again, before it had curved and ballooned, grew dangerous and disappointing. It occurred to her that people made a choice: they lived for the past or they lived for the future, and only now did she question why she would choose the former. What had been so fucking great about the past? It was easy, she supposed. The future had not yet given way to the present, which felt so leaden and irremediable.

Vanessa thought of the near past, her mother, on fire, and knew she would never shake the mental picture, however old she became. Vanessa had risen that night from her crouch in the Epsteins' garden, and she had watched her mother through the window, calmly, as if she were looking at something incredibly beautiful and unusual, a solar eclipse or a low-hung harvest moon. It took several moments for her to translate the image into fear.

The paramedics would not cut away her mother's clothes, and her shirt was charred against her singed skin. Felix and Marlene had gone in the ambulance, and Vanessa had taken a taxi with Marsha Epstein, whom she barely knew and who was hysterical. On the ride there, Vanessa thought about her mother's shirt, burnt black, and also how she would rid herself of all that food. All that meat that had been wrong to eat. She could feel the stone weight of the potatoes, the fat and gristle

from the lamb in between her teeth and at the back of her throat. Her
father had been called and was on his way, and so it was the Epsteins
and Marlene and she, all in the sitting area at the ER at Sibley, hoping
for the doctors to come out soon with news. Vanessa couldn't help
herself; she'd gone to the bathroom off the waiting room. She had tried
to be quiet, but in the end she hadn't really cared if anyone heard her.

Perhaps she would always see that bright light at her mother's chest
and arms, an embrace of flames, when she looked at her mother.

She remembered her mother's scarves and the way she used to roll
each into a flat band to hold her hair back, a knot at her nape, the silk
flowing down her back. Vanessa would take the huge sunglasses off
her mother's face and place them on her own, seeing the world for just
a moment veiled in pink: childhood. At the time she imagined that
was what her mother always saw too. She remembered Benjamin's
birthday parties, all his friends running through the backyard and she
watching with a mix of admiration and envy. Desire? She remembered
these purple pineapples on the floors when they'd first moved into the
house on Thornapple Street. They had made the rather formidable
new house seem friendly and accessible, a place where a child could
live. Then one day some man with a huge metal machine came to the
home and erased them. Where did they *go*?

Where does childhood go? Did it disappear beneath Jason last June
or beneath Sean that afternoon last September, or was it years ago,
the day the Great Dane came in and bit that blond girl, Trudy what's-
her-name. Or was it one of those nights when her parents argued so
hard her father slammed the front door, got into his car, and sped
away? Vanessa had this strange and rather sickening thought—more
sensation—that people, her parents, had children of their own so that
their childhoods would not be lost, but would be carried on, and on.

Instead of Jason's Slickee Boys, Vanessa wanted to hear the
Carpenters: *I'm on the top of the world lookin' down on creation, And the only
explanation I can find* . . . To be taken back to being a camper in musty
cabins, in fields of blackberries; Herbal Essence swirling down the
cement drain, girl feet, girl hands, girl tears; she and Lisa Stern on top
of each other, kissing each other's hand-covered mouth, practicing;
sneaking past the night watch and meeting David Sherman down at
the lake, the orb from his flashlight bouncing in the dark woods.

Bee and Heather and Jessica and Vanessa listened to the Carpenters
as well. What were they doing right now? Vanessa remembered her

foursome in their running shorts and tie-dyes, getting ready for the Bicentennial. They were too old for the neighborhood block parties, but too young, her father said, to go down to the Mall by themselves. (Today? On the Fourth? With all those crazies in town? You must be out of your mind.) Heather's and Rachel's parents were going to let them take the brand-new Metro, but Bee's mother had also said no, so they'd decided to just stay in the neighborhood. Every station was playing Elton John and Kiki Dee singing "Don't Go Breaking My Heart (I Couldn't If I Tried!)." Even though they knew they were too old for it, and a little bit because they were way too old, they'd tied red, white, and blue streamers on the handlebars of their bikes at Bee's suggestion—Jessica and Bee had ten-speeds and she and Heather their old Schwinns—and they rode screaming through the neighborhood. Heather had a little pink-and-green-flowered bell and she'd ring it every time they passed a house they knew, on Underwood and Glendale and Woodbine, including Ed Brady's house on Primrose, before he was gone. At Rock Creek they'd wended around Beach Drive into the District, to Pierce Mill and then back up Rolling Road and Summit, until dark. Then they'd settled on the lawn at the Presbyterian church on Shepherd Street to watch the fireworks burst over the 4-H Club. Someone had handed them a joint, and Bee had lain crossways, her head on Vanessa's legs, and passed it back to her languidly.

Vanessa had wanted to escape those girls, change, try on punk like everyone else, *be* punk, not just watch it bloom around her as she observed, shifting her feet along the viscid floors of fetid clubs. But did stomping around in boots or shaving your head make you into something? Who were those Brits beneath their pink Mohawks, *really*? Vanessa saw postcards of them everywhere in Georgetown. But despite a foray into temporary black hair dye and a brand-new studded black belt, she remained the same. Going to shows with Jason and Sean, she spent less time with Bee and Heather and Jessica, becoming keenly aware that most of the kids in this particular scene were not the disenfranchised youth in search of belonging, but were instead the rich sons and daughters of judges and senators and diplomats dictating what belonging meant. In comparison, Vanessa—and even Bee and Jessica, Heather not so much—were far less privileged. Combat boots and ripped black anarchy shirts were stepping out of Mercedes and Bimmers before heading into someone's basement for band practice. The Tellers played two gigs at Fort Reno, then broke up when the drummer and the bassist went to college in September, to Vassar and to BU. The scene outside of D.C., which she could learn about at Yesterday and Today in Rockville, seemed different, more real—the Cramps, say, and their frenzied blues from New York or the general insane panic of the Buzzcocks, from Britain—but Vanessa wondered even then if that was a matter of proximity. Up close, everything seemed so phoney, and Vanessa wondered, Can you try it on? She would see interviews in Jason's British magazines, which covered the D.C. scene before any of the U.S. magazines did, and these Georgetown kids were quoted as saying they understood what it felt like to be black in this country due to the abuse they took for their shaved heads and tattoos.

Were the girls putting on their eye shadow and Orange Crush Lip Smacker and going out to some upperclassman's party? They were so shiny! Something about the thought of them was sweet, a relief compared to some of the violent shows she'd been to. Kids no one knew were coming in, and the raging circle of boys' bodies had gotten so big. Where were the female singers anyway? All this just-go-for-it bullshit, anyone can, and still it was the guys she saw kneeling and screaming; she missed the brave, freakish, egomaniacal girls who fronted bands. Vanessa missed drinking warm beer with her friends, talking to soccer and lacrosse players, and getting chased into the woods by the cops for being underage and drinking in public.

As Jason dodged the traffic lights, perfectly timing the drive down Wisconsin, for a brief moment Vanessa really missed her old version of high school.

What was so goddamn powerful about the pull of Sean Flaherty? Vanessa didn't bother to get up and switch windows to get a view of the boys casing the backyard in toilet paper; she knew what it would look like. As they moved out of sight, she thought about what Benjamin would do were he still home. Jason, with his large hands and feet attached to skinny arms and legs, was far less strapping than Sean, and her brother's strength was also different. Jason held no menace in the way he moved, as if he had not yet grown into his man's bones, his muscles still struggling to wrap around an adult skeleton.

The boys tramped beneath Vanessa's window, making their way from the back of the house, and she dodged out of view. She visualized them at her father's hammock—how many nights had she looked out from the porch into the backyard, calling her father in for dinner, and seen him only in quick, tight flashes as he swung batlike beneath his cave of trees—and she imagined it now, a wrapped, empty cocoon.

They'd soon completed their mission, and now Sean and his friends retrieved the skateboards from the edge of the lawn. She heard their voices, then the smack of wood and metal onto asphalt, then the wheels turning along the road, and they were off. She looked out again to see them disappearing down the block until they were completely erased by the mottled suburban street.

Very early Saturday morning, even before her father had gone out for the *Post,* he turned to Sharon in the kitchen. "There couldn't be a worse time to leave for the weekend, you know," he said.

Vanessa had just come downstairs, and she threw her overnight bag on the landing, waiting for someone to either register her bag's ill placement or notice what had transpired the night before. Instead, she watched her mother turn from wincing at Vanessa's luggage to look at her father. Her eyes turned to slits.

"But you promised!" her mother said, and Vanessa heard her own young self, importunate about that Barbie head that she was never allowed to have at home. Now she was chastened to have ever wanted such a ridiculous object. Nana Helen had gotten the Barbie head for her and hid the outrageously large thing in her closet for when Vanessa came to visit. They'd spent hours lavishing that head with preposterous amounts of makeup and brushing the stiff blond hair into extravagant styles topped by colored silk ribbons and pearly barrettes.

"Dennis, you did promise," her mother said again. "We talked about this *months* ago. In January." She sniffed. "Months."

"I never said I wasn't going." Dennis sounded resigned. "I'm just saying I've got a lot going on here, Sharon."

"Really?" She sounded more guarded now, like an adult. "Like what?"

"Like a lot is what. Like phosphate exports were suspended last month, did you know that? So this hinders fertilizing on the Soviet end, and yet Canada and Argentina are still supplying them with grain," he said. "There's a lot going on because it's impossible to enforce an embargo. So that's what."

Her mother looked into her coffee cup and nodded. "Well, there's a lot going on with me too, you know. It's an election year, my God, do you know how many parties I refused so we could go this weekend?

And we all know I've lost a hell of a lot of work." She held up her arm. "I've got to finish packing," she said, climbing off her stool.

"He didn't say he's not going, Mom." Vanessa knew her mother would never leave packing, even for a trip to the market, to the last minute. She watched her cradling her left arm, which had suffered the worst burns. *And I have things too,* Vanessa had wanted to say. *I'm here too.*

"Of course I'm going to Boston," Dennis said, sighing. "Like we'd planned, Sharon, don't worry." Any day would have been the same: her father kept expecting the embargo to be lifted and, the very moment it happened, to be called back to Moscow for a meeting with shipping agents before he could tell his family *dasvidaniya.*

Sharon continued up the stairs. After all the bandages and dressings had come off, her skin had been the most tender along her hand and forearm. She took morphine for the pain, which made her more oblivious than ever as she wandered around the house, her hip hitting tables, her toe stubbing corners. But the scars had turned out to be hypertrophic, which, though hideous-looking, the skin stripped of pores and hair and striated with dark, ropelike scars, was not anywhere near as wretched as contracture scars would have been. These, they were told, created a permanent tightening of skin, which more often than not affected tendons and muscle, limiting mobility. The implications of this on her mother's life were not discussed, not in Vanessa's presence anyway, though whether Sharon would need surgery had been much deliberated. When her parents debated this, Vanessa imagined her mother rendered unable to cook, now incapable of whipping cream into mountain peaks or kneading her breads and pizza doughs, her fingers no longer smelling of garlic or yeast when she went to brush Vanessa's hair out of her face.

Despite a good deal of concern about her arm, the doctors had been relieved that her head had somehow managed to stay away from the flames. You're lucky as hell your hair was back, a nurse whispered as she'd adjusted Sharon's IV. And your face? Whew, you really are a lucky lady. When the nurse said it—*lucky lady*—it looked as if she were clucking. While Vanessa had pictured her mother's face burnt as coal-black as her shirt, and beneath that the oozing, red wound, what Sharon seemed to take from this most was that she could have lost her hair. Her hair! And, as the nurse told her, that doesn't always grow back.

Her mother's hair: it was long and fine and even in winter it retained golden highlights. When she cooked, she wore it up in a bun held with a red-lacquered chopstick, or in two tortoiseshell combs.

Thinking of her mother without her hair was worse than imagining her unable to prepare food. Vanessa pictured her wearing some kind of a wig, but the only wig she'd ever seen her father had found in a trunk in the attic. It had this appalling scratchy mesh that showed through the dark strands. He'd forced her to wear it as part of a costume one Halloween. Her father, who was spastic about Halloween, had insisted she go as a witch that year so he could make a mask of her face out of papier-mâché. She'd lain on the basement floor beneath his towering purple and green sculpture made of the same material—it's my medium, he'd said as he placed her head on pillows taken from the musty couch. Vanessa hated the basement, covered in a film of dust, and always with some rank, primitive smell that she mostly recognized to be her father's sweat from his naked sun salutations, which Vanessa had had the unhappy pleasure of witnessing on the several occasions she had been sent to the extra freezer for a can of frozen orange juice or a container of pasta sauce while he was practicing "yoga."

She remembered her father breathing heavily as he lay long bands of newspaper dipped in water and flour along her face. Each long piece had been shockingly cold and horribly slimy, and despite the straws he'd inserted in her nostrils, Vanessa couldn't breathe when he placed the strips over her mouth. After she'd gotten up, dizzy, her mouth filled with the drying paste, her lips crusted with it, he'd fashioned a witchy nose out of crumpled newspaper and attached this to the mask that for a brief moment had resembled her face. Vanessa reached up to touch her cheek, as if to ensure that her face had not been taken. Over the next twenty-four hours her father checked the mask often, tapping it with a pencil to feel for the right resistance, and when it had finally hardened, he cut holes out for eyes and a mouth with an X-Acto knife. She'd put it on only to discover that the holes had been cut inexactly and she could neither see out of the right eye nor breathe from the nose holes. Yet her father insisted on her wearing the mask he'd worked so hard on for her. This mask, he'd claimed as he'd painted the mole on the terrible witch nose, was *art*.

Dennis maintained that the wig was made of genuine horsehair, as if this made it a good thing, and that it must be worn to complete the look. With the mask on, she looked like someone else entirely, though she could only truly see this stranger in full when she took the whole contraption off and looked at the Polaroid taken by her father before they stepped out into the night. As Vanessa had stumbled up the block gasping for breath the whole evening, Ben, who wore a cardboard box fashioned into a tombstone, a huge space cut for his face, changed merely by gray Pan-Cake makeup, loped ahead of her with out-and-out disregard. And when she'd blindly held out her bag for candy—candy she would not be able to eat until her father had inspected it for the razors and poisons he never found, not once—she'd been unable to shake the thought that somewhere some poor pony was without his mane and tail.

When they'd arrived home from the hospital, both her mother's hands bandaged, she called out from her bedroom. "Vanessa!" she'd screamed.

This is it, Vanessa thought. She had waited for the moment when her mother would confront her about that horrible night at the party. Vanessa felt she would do anything to the person who came between her and food. She had become in these past few months quite unstoppable. At the Epsteins', when she'd sneaked into the garden and ripped the meat off the bone, she hadn't even liked the taste of it. Vanessa didn't eat meat, which had something to do with loving animals, something to do with politics, but mostly to do with restricting her diet, and she was filled with self-hatred for the way she'd consumed something she so detested. She heard the taunting of the punks: meat is murder! And even worse, she thought of the images of children starving in Africa, their bellies distended, flies swarming around their foaming mouths. She thought of the Russian children living under the iron fist of communism and eating only potatoes and stale rolls, made when they'd had U.S. grain. She thought of the starving, tortured hostages getting typhoid from fetid water, and she thought of powerful punk girls who would look down on her and rub their big black boots in her face, could they see her in this state, the exact opposite of powerful, extremely contrary to *Do it yourself!*

Whenever she was finished, she always thought of how mind-boggling what she did was when she knew the world was on the brink of starvation. Night after night her father discussed this impending, global food shortage. She knew! Your children could go hungry, he'd tell her and Ben. Norman Borlaug can work until the cows come home, but one day, the food will just be gone. Her father swished his hands together. But Vanessa knew this was also a trick to make sure she had been listening closely enough to know that Norman Borlaug was the genius who'd doubled wheat production in Pakistan and India and Mexico and had won the Nobel Peace Prize for his efforts. She knew! Her mother talked continually about the quality of food, where it came from, how it was overly processed and refined, how we just ate wheat and not soy, or why we ate corn and not wheat without question. Vanessa had grown tired of so much talk of food.

As she coaxed what she'd eaten back up, she was forced to endure the same humiliation in reverse, as well as experiencing again the horror of what a little brat she was, a lucky American, a total JAP, and by the time she was done, empty and again laid bare, she was stripped down and small again, with only her little-girl memories. Tatti's Russian folktales: *Once upon a time there lived an old woodcutter and his wife who had no children. On a cold and bitter day in the dead of winter, he went into the forest to chop wood and his wife came along to help him. We have no child, said the woodcutter to his wife. Shall we make a little snow girl to amuse us?* Nana Helen's pointed nails running along her scalp, through her hair. Thoughts of growing up, her fears, the way her body would always betray her, were gone, and for this single instant there was peace, purity, no knowledge of what was to come, of what it will in just one moment feel like to hate yourself so utterly for all the things you've had the privilege to do to yourself.

"Vanessa!" she had heard her mother call again.

She walked into the room, hoping to finally let out this secret that was no longer exactly clandestine, to tell her mother how she did it and how much and where, and also the reasons why, which were furtive even to her, as if she were the girl in her witch's mask, unable to breathe or even to see her own face. Perhaps, Vanessa thought, her mother would stop her.

She saw her mother's back, her face reflected in the mirror, her eyes bright with tears. "Will I be able to use my hands?" Her arms were swaddled in gauze, making them look like paws. "Do you think my skin will grow back again?"

"Yes," Vanessa told the mirror, but how did she know? The doctor said Sharon might not have the use of her hands. I'm here too, she thought. *I wish I had a river I could skate away on* . . . She wanted to go to her mother and put a hand high on her arm, lean in, hook her chin onto her mother's shoulder, but instead she did not move.

Her mother turned toward her. Her paws framed her head. "Thank you."

Vanessa nodded and turned away.

★   ★   ★

"What on earth?" Dennis said when he finally opened the front door to see if the morning paper could have arrived at this ungodly hour. They were to leave by 6:30 a.m. and Vanessa was at the kitchen counter. She leaned to the side to watch him head into the gauzy, white down.

Dennis came back in from the yard empty-handed, shaking his feet as if to brush off snow. "What is this?" he said to himself. "Vanessa!"

"I know." Vanessa was eating her usual breakfast of two hard-boiled eggs, yolks popped out and set aside to be thrown away. More waste, but what could she do? She pushed away the image of barefoot children on dusty roads and looked out into the hallway from the kitchen.

Vanessa felt her anger rising. Why hadn't her father asked her, *Who did this?* Why hadn't her father turned to her as he once had, filled with love, if a little too much intensity, and said, *Who did this to you?* Why hadn't her mother just pulled her from the bathroom and *stopped* her? Why had nobody stopped her? She began to say something—about the skateboarders, about the perfect location of the house, the ideal trees—but stopped herself.

"It's not my fault!" Vanessa said to her father, placing the last of the egg white in her mouth without touching her lips. "I didn't do anything." It had been thrilling to watch them, her hand pressed to the screen as she blew out smoke; it had been like standing by as her house was being burgled.

"I have to call Zachary before we go," Dennis said, referring to the gardener. "There's no way we're leaving with the house looking like this. Sharon?" he sang upstairs, half delighted. "We have a bit of a delay."

"It's six in the morning," Vanessa said. She went into the hallway as her mother looked down from the top of the stairs.

"What is it now then, Dennis? Let me guess. Stalin has come back from the grave and he's called a meeting. Wait." Sharon held out the burned hand and curved the other over her chin. "No, no, it's Lenin," she said, as if she were guessing at charades. "We might still get to leave if it was Stalin."

"Ha ha," Dennis said. "Only it's neither—why don't you look out the bedroom window, smarty-pants?"

Sharon retreated and Vanessa could hear her whoop from the bedroom. "What happened?" Sharon returned to stand again before the black-and-white Joe Strummer poster hanging from Vanessa's bedroom door.

"We got toilet-papered," Vanessa mumbled.

"And now *we* need to call the landscaper," Dennis said.

"We. Got toilet-papered." Sharon cracked a smile. "What does that even mean?" She shook her head. "I wonder what will be next, Vanessa. Tell me. What will be next?"

Vanessa shrugged, out of her mother's view.

"You're going to call him now?" Sharon said.

"Yes, I am."

"Let's just hurry up, Dennis, okay?" Sharon's voice sounded farther away. "Wow," she said from inside the bedroom. "It looks like it snowed out there."

Vanessa went back into the kitchen. She hoped they wouldn't be going up to Boston now. She resented being dragged on this ill-fated family trip, and if its cancellation was the outcome of last night, so be it. As it stood now, she was going to have to miss going to the Bayou tonight, and even though the bouncers there were total assholes, the worst in town, she liked going to shows there. Vanessa's fake ID was really bad; it was one of her short life's greatest ironies that, after that whole bit with Sean Flaherty, her ID from that day was essentially unusable while his had turned out perfectly. Every time she held it out to the bouncer there was the stress of the ID's failing, which it often did, and the humiliation of being turned away. The shame of not being let into a show while everyone else sailed into the throng of buzzing energy would always lead her to think of that afternoon at Sean's, the way he rolled off her and lay flat on his back, his legs exposed and dangling over the bed. She remembered his feet, so narrow and very white, five protruding bones leading to long, yellowing nails.

Vanessa brought her plate to the sink and headed outside into the lightening morning to see the damage herself. The mid-March day was neither lion nor lamb, and she wove her way through the mess, down to the sidewalk, then turned to face the house to get the full view. Paper looped expansively over the tall branches, as well as along the bushes at the side of the house, continuing, she could tell, into the backyard. Toilet paper was wrapped along the railings at the top of the stairs, and it came down like streamers from the gutters. The swaths of paper hung like loose bandages. Her mother's bandages; the oozing wounds seeped through for weeks. Then the itching began. She needed help with everything: brushing her teeth, bathing, chopping fruit and opening yogurts and jars of vitamins for the smoothies she was supposed to drink for nourishment, so she would not lose too much weight and her skin would grow back dewy with good health. Vanessa remembered Sean's nakedness that day, and also the other earlier days, when the three of them had gone to the Virginia side of Rock Creek, and Sean and Jason had jumped off the small cliffs into the river, deep and wild in those parts. It was as if they were all kids again. Jason's chest collapsed into itself, but Sean was beautiful, his tattoo aglow in the sun, his body nimble as he ran off the ridge screaming, arms circling madly in the wind, white against the blue horizon. Why hadn't she jumped? Vanessa had sat on a rock, warmed by the sun, her knees drawn to her chest. Once she'd been the kind of girl who had always jumped.

Vanessa went upstairs to her room to call Jason.

"Hi," she said. "What are you doing?"

"Umm, sleeping." She could hear him stretching. "What time is it?"

"So why'd you answer the phone then?"

"Because I knew it would be you. And I wanted to get the phone before it woke my mom."

"Did you go out after I left last night?"

"Didn't you leave pretty late? Like after midnight?" Jason laughed, as if to conjure up last night's activities of lying on the couch under a blanket, waiting for *Midnight Special* to come on, as they did on so many Friday nights.

"Did Sean come by?" Vanessa didn't laugh back. She'd left when the Village People came on the show, another rerun.

"No, Van, what's up?"

"Well, he came by here. With Tim and Seth, those assholes from GDS, and George."

"Tim and Seth are great," he said.

"Really."

"I mean usually they are, yeah."

"And I know how you are about Sean," she said.

Jason was silent on the other end of the line, but Vanessa could hear his breathing.

"Well, anyway, they came by and completely toilet-papered the house."

"No!"

"Yes. My father is totally pissed. We're supposed to be leaving this morning."

"Did you see them do it?"

"Yup. I watched the whole thing," Vanessa said.

"So why didn't you do anything?"

Dennis picked up the phone from downstairs, and Vanessa heard the sound of the rotary dial turning. "Hello?" He tapped the receiver several times, trying to get a dial tone. "Hello!"

"Dad, I'm on the phone." Vanessa tried not to sound as exasperated as she felt.

"Well, how about getting off it then?" he said. "It's a little early, isn't it, guys?"

"All right, all right, one second."

"Is this Jason?" Dennis asked.

"Hi, Mr. Goldstein," Jason said. "It's me."

"I'm sure Vanessa updated you on last night's activities. I've got to call the landscaper. Okay, guys?"

"I'm getting off!" Vanessa said. "Can you hang up.the phone for a second, please?"

"Okeydokey. Bye, Jason."

"Bye, Mr. Goldstein."

"I've got to go. Really I was just wondering if you knew about it, like if you'd seen them before or after," Vanessa continued.

"Of course I didn't. How can you think that?"

"Hmmm."

More silence from Jason. "Well, we'll miss you tonight," he said.

"You and Sean, you mean?" She pictured them together again, tapping their feet and bobbing their heads in time with the bass. Everyone was screaming. What was anybody *saying*? "Me and everyone," Jason said. "It's going to be a good show is what I meant."

"I probably wouldn't get in anyway. Nope, it'll just be me and bitter Dad and burnt Mom heading up to my hippie brother's dorm to be a family. Sounds amazing, doesn't it?"

"Stop it. You'll have fun. You miss your brother, you know you do."

"I'll call you when I get back. Have fun tonight. Give Sean a kiss for me."

"Stop it! I'm totally going to find out what happened," Jason said.

"You do that. You investigate thoroughly and find out why they didn't do *your* house," Vanessa said, and hung up the phone.

"Dad, I'm off," Vanessa screamed down to her father. "It's all yours."

# CHAPTER 9

# Paths in Utopia

**March 21, 1980**

Neither Benji nor his roommate could figure out where the stench that had overtaken their room for the past few weeks was coming from. So they just left it there, spending the nights out, Benji across campus at Rachel's in Ridgewood and Arnie at his brother's next door in Renfield. Though they both held tight to the belief that the smell would one day just disappear, it had only deepened, becoming all-encompassing, spreading into the cement walls, the bed linens, and the faux Oriental rug Arnie had brought from home, and the roommates took to dashing into the room while holding their breath, to grab clean clothes or stray books, which had also begun to stink, then racing off to class.

It was Arnie who discovered the problem in a brief fit of cleaning brought on by his preparation for parents' weekend. Not two days previously, Benji came in from Rachel's dorm, only to walk in on Arnie wearing a frilled apron, pink plastic gloves, and a nose clip. He thrust out a swollen can of Campbell's chicken-and-stars soup in Benji's face.

"This was under your fucking sweatshirts," he said in an even more nasal voice than usual, his nose still pinched by the plastic clip. The soup can had the tiniest slit along the top, as if someone had started to open it and had then gotten too tired to pull the can opener along the rest of the lid. "Positively disgusting, Benji."

"No way," Benji said, walking right by the can. "Shit." Benji had a vague memory of being drawn to the wondrous miracle of stars in his soup late one night and having started to open the can, only to realize he'd much rather eat a less beatific but more satisfying pizza. He'd put the soup back on the shelf of freeze-dried noodles and cans

147

of pineapple—he got these incredible cravings for pineapple, which always reminded him of home—and called Sabatino's.

Arnie made a big production of putting the bloated can into a garbage bag. "Next time do your bong hits after you open the soup, okay? I can't live like this! Really, I just can't."

"Sorry, Arnie," Benji said sheepishly.

Arnie peeled off his rubber gloves and threw them in with the soup tin, opened the door, and chucked the bag into the hall, his nose scrunched up and his mouth pursed.

"Thanks for cleaning," Benji said. "Really. I'll do the rest."

Arnie let out a cackle. "Gee thanks, Benji," he said, his arm outstretched to the cramped room. "There's so much left to do here."

Benji promised Arnie he would tidy up his desk and make his bed so the Lefkowitzes didn't have to look at a disgusting mess when they came up from Teaneck. These tasks alone, in addition to doing over a month's worth of laundry, would have been overwhelming—Benji rarely paid heed to housekeeping—but now, to top it off, the Goldsteins were also on their way here.

Benji was already trying to finish up schoolwork so he could go with Rachel and some friends to see the Grateful Dead, playing three straight shows next weekend at the Capitol, in Jersey. Benji's first ever Dead show had been last November, on Long Island, and it had changed him completely, utterly, and powerfully. He would never be the same. Never. Benji was instantly drawn to the sense of community and understanding, this insular world that shirked all preconceived notions of what happened outside it. From the moment he stepped into the Coliseum parking lot before the music started: happiness unadulterated. Pure utopia. Seeing the Dead live was revelatory, a moment of intense connection rarely experienced at all, and yet here it was, among so many. Benji was not prepared for how much this would eclipse his early exposure to the band, those midseventies bootlegs playing loud and hissing with noise from Rachel's tape deck as they dove under her huge down comforter to fondle each other.

He thought of hitting the parking lot at the Nassau Coliseum for that first show with Rachel and their friends Schaeffer and Eliza, whose parents lived nearby in Bethpage. He walked the lot with Rachel, a silver anklet jingling against the flash of skin between her jeans and her sandals. Her jeans were frayed at the ankles and had holes at the knees and one on the ass, which was partially obscured by a roughly sewn-on Steal Your Face patch. Her billowy white peasant blouse emphasized her large breasts, which pressed against her fringed suede jacket, the color of Bambi. The soft, light suede set off her dark skin, still tanned, even into November, and Benji felt entirely connected to her, cell to cell, molecule to molecule. Because of this he felt totally tethered to the world. Kids were throwing Frisbees, playing recorders, listening to bootlegs of past shows, eating homemade veggie burritos and sausages, laying out beaded necklaces and tie-dyes and bells and beads and batik clothes for sale or barter out on the ground or on card tables. Everything was separate from the real world, yet this new world was a place in which he could make a true home.

Benji bought treats, four tabs with two crossed peppermint sticks stamped on each square, from a shirtless guy in a long skirt, and Rachel, Schaeffer, and Eliza opened wide, closing their eyes and sticking out their tongues. Slowly, before the doors had even opened into the show, something magical began to overtake Benji. He held tightly to Rachel's hand and knew that she, in turn, held to Eliza, who held in hers the hand of a benevolent world. Here, everyone was equal. The strangers they walked among turned quickly into friends, and Benji's single longing for something beyond the parking-lot borders was for his friends from home to be here with him now. Where were they right this minute? Where was Ratner? He imagined him on a field, a city skyline rising above the rim of the stadium, lights clicking on on the field and simultaneously in the skyscrapers above. Benji did not miss soccer, yet he found himself indebted to the time he'd spent playing and training. He felt utterly fulfilled by his new life, and grateful that the old one had taught him how to move in tandem with others in earnest. He felt he could always return to it, that soccer was there for him, as reliable as the sun. What soccer inspired, however, and what Benji wanted to discard from his life, was this useless concept of winning and losing. Benji could no longer embrace the idea that only one team is victorious in a game. His life now was about winners. No one was a loser, and now Benji only hoped they had not taken the tabs too early and that they wouldn't peak too soon, before the music had really begun.

The love Benji felt that night was shameless and fierce, and he felt it for his new friends, his old friends, for the many splendid people he danced among, and for his first big all-over love, Rachel Feinglass Rachel Feinglass Rachel Feinglass. And for the Grateful Dead. He was overwhelmed as well with love for the band, for the Grateful Fucking

Dead, who spoke to him through their music and brought this new world together. Amazingly, Benji found that he was able to break down the division between band and audience by affecting what the band played. Last week he and some friends had taken magic mushrooms and listened to "Fire on the Mountain" over and over. Benji wished they would play the tune tonight. And sure enough—and only, he knew, because he'd wished it—there it was: *Long distance runner, what you standin' there for?* Jerry had read his mind.

Benji had gone completely bananas and had felt in control—the sort of control that he could give up and share, but control nonetheless—over the circumstances in the world. Had he been old enough to join those Vietnam protests he would soon start reading about in class, he was quite certain he could have been an instrument of change. He informed such circumstances with his own thoughts as they—as history—had informed him, as it informed his parents, and his grandparents. Now his grandfather came to life on that street corner, speaking to an audience. And the people spoke back to him. What was the difference between the two? For that matter, what was the difference between Benji and his friends, the concertgoers, between himself and the band? Nothing; despite all this physical space, there was no separation. Bowls of weed and opium, mixed, and hash joints rolled with tobacco were passed among the people surrounding them, and they danced for hours and hours, shoes kicked off, their T-shirts and long hair damp with sweat as the Dead played "Looks Like Rain" and "Don't Ease Me In" and "Candyman." They just played and played and played.

After the final note of "Good Lovin'" rang out and the show was over in earnest, a mere pause until tomorrow, the foursome walked down the path, back to the parking lot, where the party was still raging. Those who hadn't had tickets and had stayed listening to bootlegs on tape decks in the lot sat around on deck chairs by the trunks of their cars, some naked and drooling, others passed out, draped over the hoods of their cars or sprawled flat on little patches where the grass had not been completely tramped down. People streamed out of the stadium, heading to their vans and VW buses to continue the evening, lighting up barbecues and spreading out silver rings and anklets and beaded necklaces on sheets of black velvet. The two couples searched for Eliza's car for a few minutes, or perhaps they spent several hours meandering through the cars and the Deadheads until they were in

the car, speeding toward Eliza's mom's place in Bethpage, where they
would stay until they got to come back again tomorrow afternoon.

But that first night, after they had walked over the magical line that
separated this world from the one they lived in, and after Schaeffer and
Eliza had gone to her childhood bedroom upstairs, Benji and Rachel
headed to the pullout in Eliza Blaunstein's basement. They were
finally alone, and only now did this seem as if this had been the goal
of the entire evening. Benji, releasing gently from his trip, went down
on Rachel for what felt to him like several magnificent hours, and he
would then realize, in between moments of stupendous joy, that what
had happened was about both self-determination and community, a
transcendent moment when love and music and fate and beauty all
met up. He would appreciate that this was something unstoppable
and good, and that, were this energy harnessed, it could do amazing
things in the world. Sigmund was wrong; revolution was possible in
this country. The Dead! The Dead; it made Benji think of ghosts, the
friendly one, that Gloria, whose presence he'd once felt as he sat on the
edge of his bed at Len's house in Skatesville, and then the ones he had
heard of but had never seen. Where did Trotsky go? Once someone had
told him Mexico. But where was the ghost of Ethel Rosenberg?

Who came before his grandfather?

Benji lapped Rachel up, with vigor and abandon, Rachel, who had
allowed him entry, Rachel, who had showed him everything. He knew
he would do whatever he had to do to feel this way, and to help others
feel this way, over and over.

There was no way he was going to miss those Jersey shows. Still, he
would rather have more of his work done than he'd had last semester
when, after the second show in Nassau, he and Rachel had gotten on
a friend of a friend's bus filled with MIT grads taking a break from
string theory and quantum physics to tour year-round. They made gas
money selling veggie pizzas and whole-wheat spaghetti in the parking
lots before and after shows, and Benji and Rachel traveled with them
to Providence, Philly, Maryland, and Buffalo, making red sauce with
locally grown zucchini. Eight days after they'd started, Rachel had
had to drag Benji away from the hot plate, off the bus, and back to
Waltham, or he would most likely have continued on to Ann Arbor,
then out West, never returning to school.

★　★　★

"Why don't you come another weekend?" Benji had asked his mother a few days earlier. "When it won't be so crazy here."

She sucked in her breath. "But this is *family* weekend! I told you we were coming up ages ago, Ben. Ages ago."

Benji leaned back and closed his eyes. Please don't let this be one of those conversations, he thought. "Okay, first of all, it's not family weekend. It's parents' day, but it's also just a really busy time is all."

"Why would they plan family day at such a busy time?"

"It's *parents'* day, Mom, Jesus!" Benji said. "It's okay you're bringing Vanessa, and Rachel is fine to have her stay with her in the dorm, but can we just call it parents' weekend, not family day? It's not camp. And who is *they* anyway?" Benji had a fleeting thought of sleepaway camp, all the parents lining up to meet their children, and his mother stepping up first to take his hand and hold it to her heart. Then he thought of working at that day camp out in Potomac, his hands on the shoulders of his favorite campers as their parents greeted him hello and thanked him for improving their corner kicks.

"The planners!" Sharon said. "And sure, honey, we can call it whatever you want, but we've all carved out time this weekend to come up, and this is what we're doing. As a family. Besides, how will you feel if everyone else's family is there and you're all alone?"

He remembered his mother then, stepping away from his father and greeting him by the flagpole; she looked tan and young and pretty, not the way he saw her when, after hearing of her accident, he'd come back from Rachel's parents' house to see her arms and chest bandaged, her head propped up and lolling from side to side from the morphine. I am risking vulnerability today, she'd said when she saw him. Today I hold out my hand of trust, she'd said, extending the arm that was not bandaged. Benji took her hand without hesitation and sat down.

"None of my friends' parents are coming, Mom." Benji quickly discounted Arnie from this category. "Because it's No Big Deal. But you know what? Forget it, just come up. Okay?"

"Great, sweetie. We'll be there, don't worry. And we're all thrilled to meet Rachel. We'll see you in a few days!"

When Benji had hung up, he was surprised to find himself relieved. Why relief was the dominating sensation, he couldn't really say, but when he thought about it, he could pinpoint its arrival around the moment his mother referred to the event as "family" day. Meaning she did not have the impression it was mother/son day. Because Benji could not have endured one single minute of mother/son day, which he imagined as one extra-long afternoon of his mother splayed out on his beanbag chair listening to *The Stranger*. He remembered her fingering the record cover featuring Billy Joel gazing at that faggy white mask, and she'd said to Benji, We all wear masks, you know. Benjamin— she'd looked up at him with watery eyes—can you see mine?

No, he couldn't, he thought now. And he did not want to. He remembered his mother wandering into his room nonchalantly after he got home from practice and lying on her back on the floor, her hair fanned out behind her head while he played Elton John and Jim Croce. In this way someone else played his mother his own emotional sound track. In the seventh grade he'd made out at a dance with Holly Martin, an art-club girl with long hair and freckles and blue paint beneath her fingernails, to Joe Cocker's "You Are So Beautiful," and though he hadn't told this to his mother, he had played the song for Holly.

His mother had cried. *You're everything I hoped for; you're everything I need . . .* Joe Cocker's psychotic singing fused with his mother's tears. "Do you think anyone will ever say this about me?" she'd asked him, her hands splayed over her face. "Benjamin, honey, life can be so disappointing." Instantly his associations shifted from Holly's soft, wet mouth, her darting animal tongue, and her lithe body that shook just a little in his arms from first-time fear, to his mother.

Since her accident, Benji had received several late-night calls that he had not told anyone about, not even Rachel. His mother sounded as if she were speaking from a phone booth beneath a torrent of rain. He would picture her pulling her coat around her and pushing the glass door shut, trying to stay dry. She always seemed thousands of miles away, like his father had the time he'd spoken to him when he was in Moscow. Benji had been told that his father had called from Russia the day Vanessa was born, but he held only the most vague memory of that day, a foggy image of his grandfather Herbert sitting with him at the kitchen table watching as Benji wound the yellow telephone cord tight around his index finger as he talked into the huge receiver. In these late-night conversations his mother would tell him how she could no longer talk to his father, or that sometimes she wanted to stay in her dreams. She worried that her own father was dying. *His skin,* she would say, *is so thin, so thin, Ben*. We're all getting very old.

Benji could not fathom why his mother insisted on handing over so much, as if he were a vault where she could store all her emotions.

He hung up with her and then crept across campus, around the pond, no moon visible tonight, the still water a sheet of black, past the art museum, to Ridgewood. As always, late-night partiers were hanging out drinking from a massive jug of red wine and playing guitar in the courtyard, and he nodded at them as he went up to Rachel's suite, into her room, and, finally, completing the journey's objective, into her warm bed.

She yawned into him, her body hot with sleep. "Hey, you," she said, poking his side. "What's up?"

She smelled of pot and sandalwood and mint-chip ice cream, and Benji lifted her T-shirt—the yellow *Maryland Is for Crabs* shirt he'd gotten in Ocean City years ago, faded from beach sun and walking on the boardwalk, watching for girls at the funnel stands and the Tilt-A-Whirl—to run his palm over her fleshy belly. All the weed-smoking girls he now knew had an extra layer that spilled out over their diaphanous, long skirts, their tie-dyed tank tops, and along the peripheries of their round happy faces. Benji grew to love this, in Rachel in particular, and he could see her abundance even on her toes, the silver toe ring, tight around the second toe. Tonight he'd wanted to curl up in her flesh without explanation. This was why, he thought now, he enjoyed tripping. When he was in transit from one world to the other, all that was so inarticulate was not negative at all, but wholly transforming.

The little, everyday stuff was also transfigured when tripping. Just the previous week he and Rachel and Schaeffer had eaten mushrooms and taken the train into Boston. They'd ended up on the Common, where a million dogs dotted the park. There were huge Newfoundlands and Great Danes—like the one that had lived across the street from Benji and had almost bit off that girl's face—and there were bichons and vizslas and springer spaniels and cairn terriers and poodles and also mutts of all sizes, colors, and combinations.

Benji approached the owner of a Saint Bernard. "Excuse me. What a lovely species! Is there some kind of a dog show here this evening?"

The man had looked at him strangely, and Benji wondered if he could tell he was tripping. "Umm, no. It's six o'clock and folks are home from work and we're all just out walking our dogs."

"Really! You are all very lucky individuals, these are spectacular creatures!" Benji had said as Rachel and Schaeffer giggled a few yards away.

Not all trips, however, were good trips, and tonight there was no trip at all. Benji wanted to disappear in this bed and not be asked why, as Rachel was wont to ask. *Why* are you feeling freaked-out tonight? *Why* does this word—*family*—upset you so much? Are you feeling bad about your mother's accident? All were fair game and it would be exhausting. But she had merely turned toward him sleepily. I can't explain it, he'd wanted to tell Rachel without telling her, and so his finger trailed down her soft stomach and into her wild bush of hair, and then, as if this would name his feeling, made its way urgently inside.

Benji put his family's imminent visit out of his mind and turned to his American Protest! work. It was really the first class of its kind, Professor Schwartz, one of the youngest professors at the university, told the students often. After all, *curriculums change more slowly than the living events of the world,* he'd said, quoting from the "Port Huron Statement," Benji realized only later as he went over the document line by line with a pink highlighter. The rumor was that Professor Schwartz's girlfriend had left him to become a Manson follower and had somehow—maybe tangentially?—been involved in Helter Skelter, though no one had the balls to ask him about it. How could one be tangentially involved with Manson anyway? It seemed as if you were in or out when it came to Manson. Reports, perhaps faulty as well, had also circulated that the professor had fucked Sharon Tate before dating said girlfriend. It was a series of strange and unusual coincidences. Or *was* it? the students all asked one another. Perhaps, they said, it was all connected in some grand and divine plan. Whatever the case, it gave the professor a certain amount of cred to teach such a subversive class; he could be student and university, establishment and anti-establishment, everything at once.

The yearlong course—because two semesters, Schwartz had written in the course description, was as long as he needed to teach it—had already ambled through the history of social movements of the thirties to the resistance of the forties, and on to the era of conformity that was the fifties, a time Benji still could not completely wrap his head around, but for the past few weeks the class had become about the sixties and the sixties alone. The sixties; The Sixties! What hadn't happened in the sixties, the mother of all eras, when it came to radicalism. Berkeley! Civil rights! Student revolts! Psychedelia! This was what the students had all been waiting for; it was why they'd taken the class in the first place, and each and every day Benji sat in a lecture, he wished he'd been born a decade and a half previously. He'd had no idea how much social protest there had been, and how much of it had happened here at Brandeis University. Black, feminist, anti-war, gay, environmental, social-class, student, all these forms of activism were incredibly edifying. "The Port Huron Statement" was old, but still it rang so very true: *The decline of utopia and hope is in fact one of the defining features of social life today. The reasons are various: the dreams of the older left were perverted by Stalinism and never re-created.*

Were the older left and his grandfather truly this dismissible? The class had learned about his grandfather's generation last semester— the many ways they had built on the Debsian tradition of socialism, how they had brought it into a universal, national debate, and how they were once a great force in American democracy. But they got *lost,* Schwartz said. They didn't take *action,* man! They were apologists for Stalin. Benji thought of his grandfather stepping out of a train with Tatti, several disco compilations tucked under his arm. Perhaps this was the look of a man who had lost his way.

Thanksgiving was the first time Benji had talked to his grandfather about all he'd learned. He'd stepped into the house on Thornapple Street and it had seemed tiny to him, a dollhouse with minuscule rooms and miniature pieces of furniture; even the plates and silverware seemed to have shrunk since he'd gone.

The dining room table was formally set—light green linen tablecloth, Sharon's mother's silver, her wedding china, ringed in gold—for six, and just as everyone was poised to pull out his or her chair, Benji stopped suddenly. "Wait!" he said, clearing his throat. "Before eating of this most beautiful bounty, we need to take a moment to remember the Native Americans. Thanksgiving was, after all, a day of mourning for the original Americans, and so today we should all remember the injustices our people inflicted on them."

"Not my people," Vanessa said, pulling out her chair. "My people were being killed somewhere else."

"You get what I mean," Benji said. "Jesus."

A few moments into the meal, after Dennis had served the carved bird, and Sharon had spooned gratin, too hot to pass, on the plates beside the meat, Benji turned to his grandfather.

"I have a question," he said, before stuffing himself with turkey and cranberry sauce. "Did socialism fail because all you guys at City College hung on to your beliefs in Stalin for too long?" Benji had thought about becoming a vegetarian, like Rachel, who had such good reasons for abstaining from meat, and who told him about them nearly every time he ordered a burger. But he just couldn't do it. He loved his meat, he thought now, chewing his mother's most excellent turkey. A man needs his meat, he laughed to himself, knowing he would never say this to his feminist girlfriend unless he was in the mood to be pummeled.

Sigmund's nostrils flared. "That is entirely incorrect. Who told you such a thing?" he asked, sitting up in his chair and quietly putting down his fork.

Dennis cleared his throat and shot Sharon a look across the table. Benji thought of the previous Thanksgiving when he had still lived at home and his mom's parents had flown in from Los Angeles. Helen said she'd had enough of the uncivilized trip to the East Coast, just to gnaw on a turkey leg and listen to Sigmund drone on as he did. This year, they had gone to some club in Palm Springs, and during the cheese and crackers before the meal, there had been much conversation about why they hadn't come and, more important, why they would ever join a club that only began to let in Jews two years ago. Benji imagined them now, eating turkey and stuffing alone at the club with a view of the golf course. He'd have felt bad if he hadn't known they were having a far better time there than they would here, Helen screaming over to Tatiana, as if she were not foreign, but deaf, and Herb talking about bonds for Israel and baseball and his Olympic-coin collection, reaching right over Dennis for salt and gravy. Benji knew few people with less to talk about than his grandfathers.

Now Benji shrugged sheepishly at Sigmund's question. "I can't remember who told me. My protest-class professor, maybe?" He felt protective of Schwartz for some reason. "But I'm not sure; we haven't gotten to that time period yet. I'm reading a little ahead." He put out his plate for his mother to serve him more of the gratin, then took a massive forkful of cheese and potato and shoved it into his mouth.

"You like it!" she said, smiling too brightly.

"How often are we here as a family? Ben's home." Dennis clapped his hands together in a false manner of exclamation. "Ben, why don't you tell us a little about your life at school?"

"Everyone can call me Benji now." He looked around the table. "And this *is* my life at school, Dad. This is totally my life now."

Dennis took a deep breath and Vanessa giggled.

"You'll see, man." Benji turned to his sister. "Laugh now, but you'll see the way it is when you go to college."

"Oh, okay, Ben," Vanessa said. "The flower child hath spoken."

Benji shook his head. "So sorry, little pseudo-punk girl, to offend your sensibilities."

Vanessa pinched her nose. "Do you smell that?" She turned to both sides of the table. "It stinks like a hippie, worse than it stank of jock when you lived here."

"Let me guess," Benji said. "You've lost your appetite?"

"Enough!" Sharon said. "Please—"

Sigmund interrupted, "Why don't you tell this professor to do some research. Is he over twenty, Ben? Because we were not infatuated with Stalin, not ever. This was a nuanced time. We believed in the Soviet Union, yes. As a model, absolutely. But please ask this professor of yours if he's ever heard of Trotsky."

Tatti coughed. "Excuse me," she said, her hand fluttering to her neck.

"Why don't we start questioning the university now?" Dennis said.

"Come on, Dennis." Sharon looked up from her plate. "Sigmund is a teacher, after all. This is the kind of discussion we should embrace. We should always be questioning, right? Isn't that what we believe in?" She threw up a meek fist.

"*Okay,* Mom." Vanessa shook her head. "God."

"What do the rest of you think of the potatoes? They're from a farm in Maryland, and so are the onions!" Sharon said.

"They're just fine, Mom," Benji said earnestly. "But this is important!" He turned to his grandfather. "I will ask him about that, about Trotsky. Thank you, Grandpa."

"So it's settled then." Dennis resumed eating. "And the potatoes *are* delicious, Share."

"See the problem with all this is context, Ben," Sigmund said, ignoring Dennis. "It was a confusing time. No one had ever seen anything like Stalinism before. It's your teacher's job to put things in historical *context.* You've *got* to remember, remember the revolution: there is no way to ever start new. And while he has a point, separating my generation from the next, he is not right to disown it. I mean, he's got twenty-twenty vision on his side now, but we were inside it. We would have done anything to keep the Soviet Union in business. Absolutely anything; it was going to save this country. The Soviet

Union meant that there would be no poverty, no inequality. That's what it meant to us then. In light of all these tenets of the sixties, this insistence on rather violent questioning, it's also important to question where your professor is coming from as well."

"The revolution?" Dennis said. "That was a thousand years ago. The sixties was revelatory too."

"I need to write all this down." Benji put down his napkin.

"Not now," Sharon said, putting her hand over Ben's. The gesture was also meant for Dennis. "We're having dinner."

"Yes," Tatti said. "We are eating this beautiful dinner Sharon has worked so hard to prepare." *Pre-pare,* she said, her *r*'s a long trill of the tongue between her teeth. "You may write it down later."

Sigmund nodded at Sharon. "Oh, the way you talked then, Dennis. But it was like you'd never listened to a word I said. It was like you'd never heard any of it before once you had Vietnam." He turned to Benji. "Just *listen.* Please. What's *his* point of view? Look at your grandmother—why is she here, after all?"

Tatiana brought her water glass to her lips.

"Why *is* she here?" Benji asked as if he'd never considered it.

Vanessa looked at their grandmother.

"I departed, first to London, just before what you here call the Great Purge." Tatiana placed her glass back on the table. "My father was a bureaucrat and he got me a job at a Jewish theater troupe when they came to Leningrad. Stalin allowed this then—he'd appointed the director to an anti-fascism campaign. There were quotas here then; not many people got in. And there was, of course, this irrational fear of communism."

"They thought there was going to be a communist revolution here, in New York City and Philadelphia!" Sigmund interjected. "Imagine."

Tatiana smiled. "There was still a hangover from that scare when I came. But I snuck in with a lead actor. We were not farmers! We were well educated; we were the bureaucrats and artists. George Balanchine, also from St. Petersburg, though it was Leningrad then, we came the same year. We were not peasants."

"She always does this," Sigmund said. "Who cares you weren't peasants?"

"Your country," Tatiana said.

"She was very lucky!" Dennis said. "Right, Mom? I mean, you were really, really fortunate. And later, well, it was awful."

"What if you had stayed? What would have happened?" Vanessa asked.

"One never knows," Tatiana said. "It was not good for us there. Not for Jews. Zionism at the time was actually a crime against the state."

"Well," Sigmund said, "Zionism *is* just a form of nationalism, now isn't it?"

Sharon put down her fork. "You can't be serious, can you? So persecution of the Jews in the Soviet Union is justified?"

"I said nothing of the kind."

"He didn't say that, Sharon," Dennis said. "But we know, Dad, your socialist beliefs preclude your belief in Israel."

"Wait," Benji said. "I'm getting totally confused."

"And, let me say," Sigmund said, "that my views on this are changing. I can see the argument for Israel now, let's say. I can see it clearly."

Dennis nodded. "How interesting. I don't think I've ever heard you say any such thing before."

Sigmund smiled. "Well, I'm getting older."

"Wow, how scary," Vanessa said. "Leaving your country."

Tatti nodded in agreement.

"Why didn't your brother come?" Benji asked.

For a second, his question hadn't seemed to register. She tilted her head. "Oh, Misha. He didn't have to come. Music was such a part of our lives. George Balanchine was already successful. He was lucky! He was wanted. But what would Misha do here? Many people were coming here only to drive taxis!"

"But wouldn't Stalin want your brother out too?" Benji asked.

"Well, yes, of course. But he was okay. He played music with the company and took care of my father."

"Just listen, Benjamin," Sigmund said, ignoring Tatiana's rather faraway expression. "You come to our house one weekend, from school, we'll talk. About all of this."

"Well," Dennis said, "it's an apartment."

"I've been to their place, Dad." But it had been years. Benji remembered the taxi pulling up on a crowded street and his father dragging him up the stairs, covered in worn rubber treads. Vanessa and Sharon had come up behind them, and he remembered looking back at them and the smell of cabbage and the sharp scent of unfamiliar spices.

"Rent control in New York City is a beautiful thing. There's a lot for us to discuss," Sigmund said to Benji. "It's just so wonderful to know that you are interested."

Tatti turned to Dennis and said something in Russian.

Dennis nodded.

After a pause, Sharon put down her fork for the second time. "What? What did you just say? We're all sitting here talking together, it would be nice if we all knew what was being said, don't you think?" She looked at Dennis, then at Tatti, and back at Dennis. "Hmmm?"

"I'm sorry." Tatiana wiped her mouth with the linen napkin. "I was saying that the potatoes are good, yes, but so is the turkey. The turkey is very wonderful, Sharon."

"She was, Share," Dennis said.

Sharon smiled sheepishly. "Oh!" she said, breathing. "Thank you. You know I brined it. For five days."

"Brined?" Tatti said, looking closely at a forkful of the bird. Then she looked up at Sharon. "Well, it tastes like he really appreciated it."

Benji took his grandfather up on his offer and visited his grandparents on the way home to Washington over the winter break. Despite Benji's protests that he could easily take the subway downtown on his own, Sigmund arranged to meet him at Penn Station. But it was all turned around: instead of running to meet his grandparents at Union Station, now his grandfather, his cap pulled down over one eye, leaned against a pole waiting for *him*. Is this reversal, Benji thought, what it means to get old?

Benji was grateful his grandfather had come—it was a more complex journey to the Lower East Side than he'd anticipated. They got on the A train, and after an excessive amount of stairs and train changes, and Sigmund's insistence on running to get in the car that would dump them closest to the proper exit, they finally ended up at the Delancey Street station, just at the turnstiles.

Trying to move through the crowded streets with his grandfather, Benji realized how little time he had spent in an actual city, even though he considered himself to be a city kind of person. He didn't feel he had grown up in the suburbs, like most of the people he now knew at Brandeis. He'd spent a good deal of his youth in Georgetown and Washington bars—Vanessa used to beg him to take her with him to the Charing Cross, peopled with its frat boys, and girls just back from Rehoboth Beach, as black as beans. Though now, in Waltham, he rarely went into Boston unless it was to go to a movie, or when he and Rachel decided to go to a club or see music with one of her friends in Cambridge.

That wasn't *city*, though, Benji thought; it was not navigating streets and avoiding traffic, fighting through the throngs of people, taking public transportation. His grandfather guided them south, showing him Hester Street, which once, Sigmund explained, holding out his arm, had a street market where people spilled out of their flats and bought anything from herring to work pants to chickens killed in the kosher way, bleeding from the neck. He grabbed his own neck and stuck out his tongue by way of example, then took Benji over to Seward Park, and to the *Forward* building, and the Henry Street Settlement, which, he told Benji, was once the center for Jewish life but now, thankfully, was the center for every kind of life, as it should be.

Accosted by images and smells and chaotic sounds, Benji understood he could never live this way: so crowded in; terribly fearful. He'd never held such fear in him, fear of anyone walking toward them, fear of getting lost in the maze of streets and beneath the overhanging bridges, which he also feared would fall and crush them. He was embarrassed by the way he clung to his grandfather, so at ease as he strolled along past all the kids hanging out on the chilled street with huge combs sticking out from their Afros, the kids with bandannas tied over their faces, their breath hanging in front of them in the cold as they bunched together conspiratorially.

"Is this neighborhood even safe, Grandpa?"

Sigmund waved it off. "It's fine. When you live somewhere, it's not dangerous. But it certainly has changed. Absolutely. You should have seen it in the thirties and forties, all Jews, communists, and socialists screaming in the streets over who was what and then banding together anyway to turn on the anarchists, who then went for the Zionists. Now it's the Puerto Ricans and the Dominicans. Before them, the Chinese, the Mandarins. This is where all the immigrants come, even now." Sigmund pointed to the Manhattan Bridge, just slung over the city like that, a crisscrossing of roadways suspended over carts and tin-can fires, little figures in fingerless gloves hovered around the heat, hundreds of screaming people beneath it.

And then—finally!—they were at his grandparents' place on Orchard Street, though Benji couldn't say how the hell they'd gotten there. He would certainly not have been able to find it again. Once they walked up the three flights, the smell was exactly the same as when he'd come as a boy. And inside the place, he remembered the tall ceilings and molding along the doors and windows, and the open dining area and kitchen.

"You're too young to know, but rent control," Sigmund said. A radiator sang with heat. "We pay next to nothing, and see?—we have a lot of space. Plenty of space for two."

Benji wondered what it must have been like for four as he kissed his grandmother hello and sat down in the chair Sigmund waved to, at the Formica kitchen table piled high with books: Buber's *Paths in Utopia;* Stephen Cohen's *Bukharin and the Bolshevik Revolution;* an anthology, *Why Is There No Socialism in the United States?;* issue upon issue of *Dissent,* many with his grandfather's name listed in the table of contents, Benji noted as he flipped through them all respectfully.

Then, just as he had finally sat down as if to rest from his labors, Sigmund stood up suddenly. "Wait. Have you read *this*?" He came back with a tiny book, almost a pamphlet, with a plain red cardboard cover, worn thin. "Please, if you haven't read this, you must read it now. I'll wait." He crossed his arms.

Benji felt the soft, faded cover and nodded. "It was the first book we read in class." He handed *The Communist Manifesto* back to his grandfather.

He heard Tatiana let out her breath.

"Well, thank God for that," Sigmund said. "At least some things don't change."

As Benji listened to his grandparents for the afternoon, he finally decided what he would do for his American Protest! class. They had choices: Organize and run a campus workshop! Prepare a pamphlet! Document the oral history of a movement! Develop a network of former and current activists! Start your own protest! Base your project on the past, Professor Schwartz had said, but look toward the future. That's revolution.

Benji decided he would do an oral history not of a movement but of a *family.* Just before the Great Purge, Tatti had said, we ran four city blocks, holding hands. Once I went to Moscow and I skated in Gorky Park. She'd described the meat pies and the scratchy records an old woman played as the skaters in their fur caps and dull skates went round and round. Later the Jews were being persecuted but Misha was okay. My father had protection. Communism was not all bad, she'd said, winking. The ballet, it was beautiful. I came over the same year as George Balanchine. For the Ballets Russes! Like nothing you have ever seen. Benji had thought of the only ballet he had been to: *The Nutcracker* at the Kennedy Center, his mother in the red velvet seat next to him hitting his leg every time the sugarplum fairies scampered onto the stage in their stiff white tutus.

Sigmund had dismissed her. "That's ridiculous, Tatiana. Art has nothing to do with communism."

Tatiana had smiled.

"But see, Ben," Sigmund said, "communism there, it was very different than here. That is the major thing people don't understand. About the failure. It was never going to work here. These are two different cultures. There is more than a world between us, and it is wrong to say that only economics would link us. Even this country, this single nation is so varied. In the end, what was of vital interest to the farmers in the dust bowl was not going to be important to the factory workers here." Sigmund waved his arm at the kitchen window above the sink, where Tatiana had stood, her cheek illuminated by gray light. Sigmund smiled. "But I'll tell you, down here, on the Lower East Side, was the most interesting part of the Soviet Union!"

"Now that's ridiculous," Tatti said. "This is not the Soviet Union."

"The most interesting part, I said. Here, at least we could have a discussion about the struggle between Trotsky and Stalin. There was no discussion in the Soviet Union. You are forgetting everything!"

"I'm forgetting nothing." She turned to Benji from the sink, where she was slicing cucumbers. "You know I met your grandfather at a Communist Party meeting. Or maybe it was a benefit of some kind. For the striking seamen, I think." She turned back to her slicing. "I wasn't interested in the politics; everything was art for me then. But I missed home! I wanted to see some Russians. Of course there wasn't a Russian in the place." She turned to face her husband.

"Why you didn't think you'd get deported still unnerves me," Sigmund said.

Tatti ignored him. "Who was singing, Sigmund?" she asked instead. "I want to say it was Ethel Rosenberg, but I know it couldn't have been she." She turned to Benji. "She did sing at meetings sometimes. She had a very high soprano voice. It was lovely in its own way. You know about Ethel Rosenberg?"

"Yeah." Benji imagined her again, as a ghost. "I do."

"It was just awful what they did to that poor woman." Tatti looked over to her husband. "Maybe it was Helen. Sigmund, could it have been Helen singing?"

Benji's grandfather shook his head. "Your grandmother Helen." Sigmund threw his head to the right, as if Helen Weissman were just outside the door. "She sang all over the neighborhood. I remember some picket-line stuff, that time in front of Orbach's, a lot of Spanish-loyalist activity, but not at CP events, darling, what are you talking about?"

"You knew Grandma Helen?"

"No," Tatti said. "We didn't know her, and it was only when Dennis was getting married to your mother that we realized we had heard her sing. She was the opposite of Ethel Rosenberg; low and very sad. A very nice voice. I had thought it was at a meeting, no?"

"Most definitely not. She was decidedly unpolitical," Sigmund said. "How else could she have married that man? No values! Just works for whoever pays. Capitalist pig."

"That's enough," Tatti said, looking nervously at Benji.

Benji thought of Herbert handing him one of his collectible Olympic coins. It was fulgent, smooth, brand-new. To start your collection, he'd said, pressing it into Benji's palm. That was capitalism.

"You know this is true, Tatiana." Sigmund crossed his arms. "You know this."

Tatti nodded, her mouth pulling down at both corners as if tugged by two strings. "Well, anyway then, the day we met, on this particular day, Sigmund and I both stood in the back. In the beginning this is where your grandfather stood, before he left and went to the young socialists and learned how to get on a soapbox and scream his head off."

"Unlike your grandmother, who went to people's doors," Sigmund said. "Or whatever she did at people's doors."

Tatti reddened. "I was campaigning for Roosevelt. I believed in his New Deal. I don't see how you couldn't have."

Sigmund grunted. "Yeah, I sure didn't. But see, Ben? Dialogue!"

Tatti shrugged him off. "And also, you remember my work at the record company, when the children were in school. Remember 'Chattanooga Choo Choo'?"

Sigmund laughed. "'Chattanooga Choo Choo.' I remember when Boris tried to change the title." Sigmund rubbed his forehead and looked up at his wife. *"Won't you choo-choo me home?"* he sang. "How about some music?" he said, rising. Benji thought Sigmund might ask his grandmother to dance.

Instead he went to the phonograph in the living room, and Benji leaned against the table as he watched him set the needle down. It was Donna Summer! His grandfather sat back down at the table ensconced in an old and sudden afternoon light, his face turned toward the golden stream of it, motes of dust dancing above his head, and somehow he ignored the growing crescendo of her singing. "We laugh, but that was a special time, Ben," he said. "It sounds ludicrous now, but we felt things so fiercely. We were getting smaller, and history was getting bigger and bigger and bigger!" The space between his hands increased with each word. "And we thought it would bend to our submission. I went about my life, but I remember the way the movement claimed me. It was all very exciting."

Ben thought then of watching the Dead playing as the sun went down on some other coast he couldn't see. It was the most exciting moment of his life—he felt as if he were waiting, asleep in the snow, for someone to kiss him awake—but in the end, it was about nothing but happiness. Was that enough to claim a man? He couldn't help but think of Sigmund: The workers are hurt, they can't support their families, how can we help? Don't eat biscuits from the National Biscuit Company! American democracy is hardly democratic enough.

"I was under the spell of the Russian revolution for a long, long time." Sigmund nodded his head a little to the music. "But when FDR took office, forget it, the communists were by then all hapless instruments of the Russians. For me, communism became merely an extensive arm of the NKGB. You look skeptical, yet it's true, Benjamin."

Tatti went to the living room, where she removed the needle from the record. "Why?" she asked. But Benji wasn't sure if she meant Donna Summer or the thread of the conversation. "Something else, please," she said, placing the arm of the player back in its holder and coming back into the kitchen, where she stood over the table. She nodded, at the silence perhaps, crossing her arms.

"But your grandmother and I had already fallen in love." Sigmund looked up at her. "For me it was always the heart above the country."

Tatiana smiled down at him.

"But I would never go to the Soviet Union," Sigmund said. "Never."

Tatiana came up from behind and put her long, thin arms around

Sigmund's neck. "Now how would we go there? How, Sigmund?" Then she let him go and turned to take a platter from the kitchen counter. She placed it on the table in front of them: black bread and herring and cucumber salad. "Enough with communism." She raised her chin. "Now eat."

Professor Schwartz began his section on the sixties with the Free Speech movement, and Benji could see that his grandfather had a point. Professor Schwartz saw the left in two camps, he told the class. Ideas and action. Period. Yes, the earlier leftist movements were focused on labor factions, but that left, the twenties and the thirties left, just refused to get their hands dirty. With that, bam, the lights had gone, and black-and-white footage of students going limp in the arms of policemen, kids being dragged down the stairs of various city halls across the country, lit up against the wall.

After the film was finished, a little, nail-bitten hand emerged out of the dark in the large auditorium. "And what, then, became of the New Left? What did getting one's hands dirty lead to?" asked a long-haired girl in a peasant shirt.

Professor Schwartz shook his head at the girl. "What did it *lead* to? Perhaps you mean what *didn't* it lead to? The very fact that you can sit there and ask this question is because of what happened in the sixties. Social activism was born, my dear, there was a hell of a lot more out there to mobilize than the workers. The effects are still to be determined, of course. We will be seeing the effects well into the next century.

"Not sure if that answers your question." Schwartz looked in the vague direction of the young woman.

"So you're speaking about white males then. That's what this class is, about the men in history, those who are responsible for the destruction of human life and environment on the planet today. Yet who is controlling the supposed revolution to change all *that*?" The young woman sat down with a snort and a flip of her hair. The girl seated next to her patted her on the shoulder.

Professor Schwartz smirked. "And with that," he said to the class, in the same manner Benji's father would talk to him and Vanessa when trying to show the lunacy of their mother, "with that, I'll let you go." Schwartz looked at his watch. "But *do* think about it: think about what happened in the fifties, how students, who were really a very privileged group of kids, they were the children—men *and* women—of children who had worked very hard to get what their parents never had. This was the first generation to really question the status quo. Because they *could*. This is what I'm talking about. I am not talking the bona fides from the old-timers here. I'm talking about questioning authority. Actively, not sitting in a room and writing about it. *Activism,* as we know it now, the reason you can pick up a sign and march around on campus for whatever piddling little thing you believe in, we owe that to what happened in the sixties. Plain and simple. Okay." He flicked his hands in front of him in a motion of dismissal. "Be free," he said, as at the end of every class. "Be free, think about those class projects, and think about your freedom."

Which revolution is my model? Benji thought, walking down the steps toward Usdan, where he ran into Schaeffer, on his way back from his Victorian-novel class.

"That class is loaded with chicks," he'd said when Benji had first made fun of him for taking such a course. "There are literally two guys in the class." He'd recently broken up with Eliza, which had put a cramp in the foursome, though both parties still claimed to be the *best of friends*. Often Benji and Rachel saw them sharing a cigarette in Usdan, or happily throwing a Frisbee on the lawn, Eliza's head scarf trailing behind her.

"I could never just hang out with you as friends," Benji had said, squeezing Rachel's hand.

"That's because you are so invested in ownership. We don't own each other, you know. And we don't merely share sexual experiences together. It makes perfect sense to me."

Benji had started to make an argument for loyalty; he'd taken a deep breath and was about to tell her what bullshit she was spewing, but he'd stopped himself.

"It's loaded with chicks for a reason," Benji had said to Schaeffer. "It's such a girlie class."

"Naaah," Schaeffer had said. "It's pretty damn interesting. What, reading is for girls? Come on, Benji."

He'd nodded, conceding. It was so easy to change his mind, Benji thought, does that mean I have no point of view?

"I think it might be my favorite class," Schaeffer said. "And the professor keeps talking about these clitoral moments. I swear to God, she'll say"—Schaeffer raised his voice to a pitiful squeak and spoke with an English accent—"'this novel is composed of a series of clitoral moments, not the traditional trajectory of upward action with only a single climax in mind. These are clitoral moments, many small climaxes that, as we all know, are far more pleasurable for the duration.'"

"Is she British?"

"Naah, she's from Texas, but you get what I mean. It's hysterical, most of the girls nod their heads, and you know, or I know, they're all thinking about how many times they can come in one night. I mean except for one or two, they've got no idea what she's even talking about, I can tell."

Now, seeing Schaeffer, several spiral notebooks and a copy of *Adam Bede* slid under his arm, Benji wished he had signed up for the class, which struck him then as far less confusing and somehow less personal than what Benji was beginning to realize he'd taken on. Those Victorian texts had a narrative. Clitoral moments or not, there was a beginning, a middle, an end.

"Hey, Schaeff," Benji said now, coming up from behind.

"Oh, hey!" Schaeffer said. "Where you headed?" Benji thought about his plan to quickly grab a falafel sandwich from the Nature's Way stand in the dining hall and go back to the dorm, to clean and get some work done before ending up at Rachel's for the night, in preparation for his parents' arrival. At the least he'd thought he'd clean up his desk as he'd promised Arnie, and definitely outline what his American Protest! project would be.

"I don't know, I've got so much shit to do. So of course I'm thinking about blowing off the rest of the day." Benji laughed.

"Me too."

"Are your parents coming?" Benji asked.

"My parents?"

"Yeah, for parents' day."

"I didn't even know it was parents' day," Schaeffer said.

Benji stopped walking and closed his eyes. "Really?"

"Your parents are coming?"

"And my sister."

"You *told* them?"

Benji let out a long sigh. "My mother read about it in some newsletter."

Schaeffer started laughing and hitting his hip with his notebooks.

"Shut up," Benji said. "Please. I can't fucking deal with them coming."

"Oh, it will be fun!" Schaeffer cleared his throat. "I bet Arnie's parents are coming too!"

"Let's go smoke," Benji said.

"At my place," Schaeffer said, as they wended their way through the student center quad. "I've got better weed. And we wouldn't want to smell up the room with Mummy and Daddy arriving so soon."

When they got to Schaeffer's suite, he put on *American Beauty*—No bootleg today, he said, I kind of want to hear it clean and shiny and produced today—and handed Benji the bong, a red Plexiglas cylinder covered in multi-colored dancing teddy bears. He lit the bowl and Benji took in a deep hit. Exhaling, he felt himself loosening. It was as if his body had been curled up in a drawn net, and now the fastening had been cut. His shoulders fell, as if they'd previously been tied to his ears, and his stomach and chest opened. He handed the bong back to Schaeffer, who filled the bowl up again. Schaeffer leaned back and lit up, the red tube now a massive line that looked to Benji as if it were cutting his friend in half.

"You going to make it to the Jersey shows?" Schaeffer asked, blowing out smoke.

Through a keyhole, thought Benji. "Absolutely. You're coming too, right?"

Schaeffer nodded. "Feel better?" he asked after they'd each taken another hit.

"A little." Benji did not admit to the vague feeling of paranoia fluttering in his stomach. What would it be like having his family up here? He didn't want to stop his life, but he didn't want it on display for them either. He knocked his head softly against the wall, where Schaeffer's Janis Joplin poster hung. "I think I gotta get going."

"No way! I get you stoned and you just take off?"

"Okay, okay." Benji sat back.

Schaeffer filled the bowl again and they each took another hit. *If you should stand, then who's to guide you?* Benji loved this song. He just loved it. They were silent for a while, listening to the rest of it. *If I knew the way, I would take you home.* It almost brought him to tears every time. Just as the tune was ending, and with a burst of energy, Benji said to his friend, "Let's get something to eat, and then I think I really have to deal."

After Benji and Schaeffer ate huge sandwiches with pickles and mayonnaise and mountains of turkey and Swiss cheese on dark rye at Sherman, Benji walked around the pond toward Deroy, the trees still without leaves, old ladies' fingers clawing into the gray sky, which looked as hard as porcelain. He imagined reaching up and punching it open, into spring. The pond was a sheet of black glass, no telling what lay beneath. He squatted down and dipped his hand into the half-frozen water. The water was numbing, but it also felt soft and comforting. It was true about ripples in still water. Now they traveled out and out, and Benji watched as his small presence expanded along the surface.

He wiped his fingers on his jeans and heard a cosmic amount of noise coming up from the field, where he and Schaeffer had passed a makeshift rugby game earlier. Chapels Field, surrounded by various religious houses: a synagogue, a mosque, a church, each place of worship was built to stand alone, none in the shadow of the other, Ben was told on his campus visit last spring. It had been raining like hell as Ben and Dennis and Sharon, along with several other prospective students and their parents, sank into the mud of the field.

"It's a remarkable feat of architecture and a beautiful metaphor wrapped up in one." The tour guide had smiled smugly and held her umbrella unsteadily against the downpour.

"If this isn't an omen," Dennis had whispered to Sharon, loud enough for Ben, the tour guide, and the several other drenched kids and their parents to hear.

Sharon swatted Dennis's shoulder, as Benji wondered whether his father meant the rain or the architectural achievement.

The tour guide continued, "Like so much here at Brandeis University, Chapels Field is about freedom. And equality. That's what Justice Brandeis stood for as well." She'd held out her hand to the field and was immediately smacked by rain.

Benji thought now of high school: being on the field at practice, the leaves turning, the smell of autumn, that ethereal golden light of afternoon on the field. He thought of the feel of the ball on his knees and thighs, on the tips of his toes, on his forehead, the way it became a part of him on the best days, another limb. He remembered the irreplaceable feeling of running down the field, how it had felt that nothing could possibly come between his body and what was in front of it. Everything was ahead. He saw the bleachers filling, his mother shifting from side to side on the hard seats; he saw Erin and Nikol and every other girl he had ever known or kissed or fucked, cheering for him. Now he was on a different path.

The screaming Benji thought he'd heard coming from the field drew closer. He thought of the rugby games in Maryland, the rugby queen, that poor girl who never seemed to mind getting the keg turned over on her head followed by the mighty yelps and screams of the players and the bystanders. Surely they didn't have such sexist practices here, Benji thought as he turned toward the field. All this noise wasn't simply over some lacrosse scrimmage. He walked from the pond up the stairs, toward the growing din, some kind of a protest. It was streaming down from the student center up the hill. Athletes were gathering on Chapels Field—some of them were suited up as if they were just about to play— soccer, baseball, basketball, tennis. Brandeis had no football players, just as his high school friends had warned, and he found himself aching for that promise of a football game, the fall air, alumni filing in with their ugly carnations stuck in navy lapels, the sight of players on the field all stuffed up in their padding and helmets. Today, bats and balls and mitts and rackets were strewn all over the field haphazardly; it looked like a sports extravaganza, some kind of twisted jock fantasy.

Two soccer players, still dressed in cleats and guards, came running toward the steps just as Benji had taken the last stair.

"What's going on?" Benji tried to stop them. "Wait!" he said, struck by fear. Something was happening without him. The sixties, Port Huron, the Grateful Dead: how could he have *missed* so much? And Brandeis! History had already come and gone here. He'd been mistaken about the architecture; the newness was no more a blank slate he could write his own future upon than a blackboard, gauzy with layers of erased chalk. Effaced or not, everything had already come to pass; these buildings had previously been overtaken by angry students. Bombs had exploded; all the one-legged soldiers had come home. The sixties were finished and he'd missed it here, as he'd missed it everywhere. Watching footage of Woodstock, even if it wasn't exactly the Dead's best performance, was unbearable. He should have been there! He was meant to have been there. At Brandeis he had this unshakable feeling he'd been born too late, and now he was relegated to learning about his missed opportunities in a college classroom.

"You haven't heard?" one of the kids with the number 12 on his chest said, jogging in place. "Carter just announced an Olympic boycott."

Ben looked at them blankly. "The Olympics?"

"Yeah, man, the Olympics, in Moscow. The Americans aren't going this summer!"

Moscow. His father with a tin can on the other end of a long string. Hello, Bennie? It was as if he were asking his name. Greetings from Moscow! His grandfather sat across from him, repeating, Do you know how expensive this is? What's this I hear about you having a new baby sister! his father had said. But Benji couldn't have remembered this. And yet he had the enamel box—a winter troika scene—that his father had brought back for him from that trip. He remembered that, hadn't he? His father handing him the golden lacquer box, red horses braying across the painted top, before his father went to the hospital to bring Vanessa home. To store anything you want, his father had said. Or nothing at all. So many times he had looked at the box as a kid, the old man about to beat his horses, a woman sitting back, waiting for her journey to begin.

"Wow," Ben said to the athletes.

"Can you believe it? My brother is a long jumper." The guy, number 8, shook his head. "He's been training for this his entire life. I can't fucking believe it."

"No way," Benji said. "God, I'm so sorry." What would it have been like, he wondered, to be cut from the play-offs because of politics? It was unthinkable, and that had only been high school soccer. For a moment his heart fluttered at the thought: winning. So many people in the stands, cheering for him. Victory. But this way of thinking—that some win and some lose—it's useless. More than useless; it's negative.

"It's fucking fascistic, is what it is," Number 12 said, and he and Number 8 were off and running down the stairs, slower than Benji could tell they'd intended, handicapped by their cleats and shin guards.

At the bottom of the stairs, Number 8 turned around. "We're going back to our rooms to make signs—grab what you have, come out to the protest!"

"They can't take away our right to participate!" Number 12 chimed in without turning. "The Olympics is about the world!"

And then they were off. "The whole world!" they screamed, fists raised high in the air.

# CHAPTER 10

# The Protest

**March 22, 1980**

Benji thought of the soccer players' plight as he watched them disappear into their dorms. So much really was at stake; the Olympics *was* about the world. And it was also personal; watching the games with his mother created an unrecognizable but radiating joy that circulated in his stomach. Now he remembered the girls spinning on the ice, weightless and bewitching, his mother close, cheering wildly when Dorothy Hamill performed her Hamill Camel perfectly. It had made Ben want to create a signature move on the soccer field, a reverse scissors perhaps, the ball rolling sideways across his body, that he thought he'd call a Rolled Gold, which he'd never got around to making unique enough to call his own. Then it hit him the way seeing his grandfather in that textbook at the beginning of the semester, the way seeing Rachel holding her little sign in front of Sherman, had. *There are many ways to win: there is nothing more mine than this fight.*

And Benji decided to take political action.

He walked over to Chapels Field. There, with most of the soccer players, the baseball and softball teams, basketball players, even the club teams, the rugby players and the touch footballers, girls who were once gymnasts, anyone who had ever loved a sport and who knew it could be elevated to art, anyone who knew what it was like to step onto a field, or a court or a balance beam, anyone who understood what it meant to use his or her body to be victorious, Benji made signs well into the evening. Everyone was banded together, working in the gloaming beneath that scattering of sunlight in the upper atmosphere illuminating the field just before dusk, and it felt then just as it had in high school on those nights they'd been able to continue practice before the lights clicked on and the lightning bugs and mosquitoes came out.

As Benji sat out at the makeshift tables filling in his hammer-and-sickles on red poster board with black ink, he thought of all the work he wasn't doing, which in light of the Jersey shows made him want to put down his marker and go to the library to get some actual reading done.

Then it came to him. "Let's have a rally, like a real rally, not just a bunch of us hanging around with signs!" he'd yelled into the crowd of athletes. And if it worked? An extra bonus that this could also satisfy his American Protest! class project.

Bent over their own signs, the kids next to him had flinched, startled by his outburst.

"We can have speakers and we can get athletes from all over Boston to come," he'd said, a little softer. He'd looked out onto the field and was met with a dozen athletes sticking their fists in the air. "Yeah!" they screamed. "Ra-lee!"

Several kids started throwing around a football, and as a game of touch developed on the field, Benji and Number 8 and Number 12, Larry Fuchs and Andy Shapiro, as well as Peter Cox and Roland Berger, juniors from Benji's American Protest! class, went back to his dorm to plan the event.

They decided to call their fledgling organization STAB—Students to Abort the Boycott—well, it almost worked and Larry thought that STAB could also mean "stabbed in the back," which was what this country was doing to its athletes by not letting them compete. Benji put Moscow out of his head, the Moscow he heard on the other end of the long string that led to his father, who he now imagined had sat on the edge of a tautly made bed in some Stalin-era hotel, drinking Stolichnaya. Vodka, he'd told Benji as he rose from the just made bed to leave Benji's brand-new dorm room, it's worse than a woman; vodka is not your friend. It was such an unlikely thing for his father to say. It sounded as if he were channeling some Russki spy who'd grown old and now lived on a hill in Calais overlooking the sea and was telling his life story to a foreigner. Surely there are far worse double crossers than vodka. Like the government, for instance! Like the U.S. government!

Forget the Soviets. Benji willed himself not to think of Tatti's story, his grandmother, young, cheeks flushed red with cold, ice-skating to scratched records in Gorky Park, hot potatoes in her mittens, an image now as frozen in his mind as Moscow must become in winter. Why expunge the memory? Benji thought, as he realized only in this moment that what he was actually protesting here was the American government and the way it exploited people, the way it used the erroneous—grain, for instance—for political gain. People were not weapons, he thought, but as he thought it, he wondered, were weapons involved, would he not be protesting them as well? There was little now, Benji thought, that was not protest-worthy; how does it end? How did the sixties end? Did people run out of protests; did they forget the violent way so many people had been killed?

Well, he hadn't gotten that far in his class, but he had already read *Rules for Radicals* and *A Time to Speak, a Time to Act,* so he knew that things changed. Groups factionalized. Agendas split. People went berserk; they seized revolution. Now Benji remembered being one of many in that huge stadium, his body rocking back and forth, eyes closed, his face tilted back as "Box of Rain" enveloped him, each note, each lyric, so many stars tumbling over him. Nothing was wrong in this, Benji had thought at the show, he and Rachel sewn together, her curves sutured to his bones, unless pure joy had also become something to rise up against and beat down.

Through simple, divine word of mouth, the college teams all over the Boston area began to hear news of STAB and the rally. Athletes, Benji told himself, were as networked, if not as sweet-smelling, as the Washington politicians he grew up around. He remembered the smell of D.C. insiders—the scent of perfume and liquor and tropical flowers—that lingered on his mother's clothes when she came in from some catering affair. Ratner at Columbia, whom Benji called with news of the protest, knew a dozen players at Harvard and Tufts, and it went from there. Benji, who had once been in this athletic network, felt a pang of jealousy at the speed at which his news was traveling.

Andy, who was from Worcester, had interned one summer with an assistant coach of the Celtics, and he tried to get Larry Bird to come speak. Instead he'd ended up with Robert Parish, who, Andy had on inside information, would most likely be sent to Boston from Oakland next season. This was far less impressive, and Roland was concerned about Parish's growing reputation for silence.

"I mean, are you sure the guy will actually talk?" he had asked. They were using the blackboard in the lounge to brainstorm over who might speak and had come up with a list of the Celtics past and present, peppered with one or two New England Patriots. Roland went to the board and began to erase them all. "Because he doesn't say a whole hell of a lot."

"Actually," Andy said, folding his arms and pushing his chair back on two legs. "That's a lie. I've heard he's a terrific public speaker." His chair slammed back onto the floor.

Roland threw the eraser down hard, and a cloud of dust puffed out around it. "So what's with the mute-Indian rep then?"

"Shhh." Benji placed his hands palms down on the table and looked around the room, making sure no one outside their group had heard the slur. "Come on, man, none of that shit here, okay? And anyway, he's called the Chief."

"Why is that?" Larry had asked.

"*One Flew over the Cuckoo's Nest,* baby!" Peter said. "The Indian who did Jack Nicholson in."

"Oh, yeah," Larry said. "Yeah."

"Talk about the sixties, man," Peter said.

But such a prominent player lending support was exactly what they needed to give some credence to their cause and to assist Benji with reaching out to the media. He called contacts from the *Boston Globe* to the *People's World,* to local NPR, to the nightly news, all from a phone list provided by the Campus Action Committee. Benji left long, heartfelt messages on STAB's plight for producers and editors well after eleven o'clock that evening. Several even picked up, including a producer at CBS's *Evening News,* who told him, "Pray for a slow news day, kid. If all we got tomorrow is who shot JR tonight, and more of this hostage crisis, we'll be there."

Well after midnight, Benji climbed eagerly into Rachel's bed, anxious to tell her about his day. His amazing, came-out-of-nowhere-important, life-changing, life-affirming fucking day.

"I'm not sure I believe in this, Benji," she told him, curling into herself as she put her underwear back on.

"Are you kidding me?" Benji flipped onto his back, his dick softening.

"No, I'm not kidding." Rachel sat up. "It's important only to protest what one really believes in. Otherwise one's voice is a muted voice; one will be taken less seriously. We can't just jump onto every cause. I mean, I'm supposed to go to every protest on campus?"

"I met you at a pork rally, Rachel." He brushed his growing hair out of his face and began vigorously twisting a curl. "You're a fucking vegetarian."

"Make fun if you want. The pork and shellfish debate was about the university's larger issues, which I believe I explained to you." Rachel thumped her head against the wall, crossing her arms over her naked belly, conscious, Benji noted, of the skin that folded into her stomach like a stack of thick, fluffy pancakes when she sat up.

"Lighten up, Rache," he said, simultaneously wondering if Larry, who was responsible for contacting teams all over the Boston area, had cast a net as wide as they needed to get a decent crowd. And if Peter had organized the buses correctly, one for every school, with the corresponding pickup time. "And anyway, *I* believe in it," Benji said, propped on his side. "And I'm one of the organizers. Isn't that enough?"

"I believe in a cause because my boyfriend does? Well, that's impressive."

Benji had made signs supporting abortion rights—*Take your laws off my body!* He'd painted that for Rachel. He had marched to protest nuclear testing after Three Mile Island, and he had run a half marathon to free South Africa, a marathon at which, he noted now, Rachel had merely greeted him at the finish line. That day he had also signed a contract to never use Shell Oil, a company that Rachel had told him paid hundreds of millions to circumvent oil sanctions in South Africa while they had half a billion dollars invested there. And he had done it all willingly, happily even. Learning from Rachel was part of what drew him to her; her ideas and the way she articulated them separated her from any other girl he had known. To watch her get all fired up in public, then be the one that she chose to be alone with later, the two of them smoking hash off spoons and listening to Dead bootlegs as they made love, was one of his newfound and necessary pleasures. Benji accepted what Rachel believed not because he was without his own ideas, but because she believed them and he loved and trusted her.

"We always go to your things. What about mine?" Benji lifted Rachel's duvet and scanned the bottom of the bed for the underwear he'd kicked off not twenty minutes before when he'd entered Rachel from behind, cupping her breasts with his hands as his chest pressed into her thick, warm back. He had felt so excited and stressed and filled with anxiety over all he needed to do for tomorrow, being inside her had been a tremendous relief.

"Okay, well, why do you believe in it then?" Rachel's mouth was raised at one side in a smirk. Her fingertips rubbed her elbows.

"Because I do, is why. It doesn't matter; that I do should be enough. And I've done a lot to plan this."

"And you should go to it."

"I am going to it. And so should you." He found his underwear in the tangle of bedsheets and struggled each of his legs through the white cotton. "You don't think it's worthy? Even if it's important to me, you won't come?"

"As I said, Benji, I'm not sure we should be there—in Moscow, I mean. It's very complicated, all these issues. You're acting with your heart, not your head. I mean, isn't this more about being on a soccer team or screwing a cheerleader?"

"What?" He pulled up the briefs, the waistband snapping.

"Sorry," she said. "I mean, it is about the soccer, though. You missing soccer."

"That is so condescending! We all, I should hope, act with our hearts. I understand the issues, you know. I'm fucking Russian for one. When they come and clear all the Russians out, when there's a Russian holocaust, I'll be gone."

"What the hell are you talking about? Come on, Benji, you're as Russian as anyone else here. And there's no holocaust."

"I am too Russian," he said, though he had never considered himself so until this very moment. Isn't that when identity is determined? He'd read it somewhere: the second there is opposition, you become what is being opposed. Just look at the Holocaust, he thought.

"Fine." Rachel rolled her eyes.

"Well?" he said sheepishly. He now chose to ignore what he'd brought up, this inevitable dialogue overheard in every crevasse and corner of this institution. Will there be another one? Could there be? Will it be here? Who will be taken? "And, just for the record, I grew up in Washington. I was going to protest marches on the Mall while you were shopping in the strip malls of New Jersey, you know." His rally, he was beginning to see, was effectively a mobilization to support the Soviets. Was Rachel correct to tell him he had not thought the issues through, that he had in fact been swayed by the heart; by aching memories of cheering crowds and locker rooms and, yes, cheerleaders? Because this rally protested the Americans, and in plucking this one aspect from the complex web of history that went back and back, as Sigmund had told him, to the original Revolution—1917!—the one that had worked, the *only* one, Benji had landed quite staunchly on the side of the Russians. So did this make him a communist? Sigmund would say no. His father would say, please, please, no. Wouldn't he?

"And I also feel for the athletes; there's nothing wrong with knowing both sides. I have absolutely no idea what this has to do with balling cheerleaders."

"Well, didn't you?"

Benji couldn't stop himself; he thought of Nikol Stathakis in her short polyester gold skirt with navy pleating tucked in crisp, secretive folds obscenely slicing the skirt and revealing the blue fabric within when she moved. She wore the little team Skivvies beneath, and when she walked, the big *W* stamped on the ass revealed itself in parts. The image alone seemed to prove Rachel right. She was always game, Nikol. Once he'd finger-fucked her beneath the bleachers, smack in the middle of a football game. She'd sauntered over at a third down, retrieved him from the top seats, and led him there herself.

"I have, yes," Benji said, remembering the view of asses and legs and shoes they stood beneath as he felt his way to her.

"I really hate that about you." Rachel's left hand—every digit but her wedding finger, including her thumb, wrapped by a silver ring— tapped the opposite arm.

Benji looked at her, squinting. "Really. And why's that?"

"That you were once that kind of a guy. Who went out with cheerleaders."

He stared at Rachel. She had always seemed so secure, above the usual forms of female pettiness. "Yeah, well, I did. That was me. I was him."

"I know that." She brought her chin toward her chest and took a deep breath through her nose.

"What does it matter?" Part of him wanted to offer comfort, alleviating those insecurities he'd never known her to have. He recognized in Rachel what he had begun to see in his sister, that all her hates were merely fears turned around. The other part of him, however, wanted to say something horrid, demeaning, unmentionable. But for better or worse, his anger stayed closed, a bee trapped inside a soda-pop can dropped on some sunny field, unable to find the opening out. "This is about people, athletes, who are having their dreams stolen right out from under them. Even cheerleaders deserve to have dreams."

Rachel was silent, working both arms with her fingers and rocking herself.

"And who were you anyway?" Benji asked. "What made you so special?"

He didn't wait for an answer, but turned away from her, slamming onto his side. Smoke curled around the window in fading, delicate wisps, and he could hear people out in the quad. Someone strummed an out-of-tune guitar as several girls sang "Puff, the Magic Dragon," and the soapy smell of opium permeated the air the way honeysuckle does. He thought now, though he hadn't remembered it until he'd mentioned it, of driving downtown and parking in his father's office garage and walking out onto the Mall, mobbed with people. His mother had been tense. He could tell she was afraid, but his father made his way surely through the crowd, the three of them linking hands, Dennis holding Vanessa, and weaving toward the Reflecting Pool. All around young people screamed with rage. He still remembered one girl's face, a deep shade of angry red, her nose had snot streaming out of it, her eyes were tearing, and her mouth was open in a scream, and yet she was covered in yellow flowers, long strands wrapped around her neck and ankles and wrists, at the crown of her head. Both her arms reached into the sky, and Benji followed them up, to see her fingers flashing the familiar $V$ of a peace sign. All around her, kids were screaming, *Hey, hey, LBJ, how many kids did you kill today?* and his mother's hands gripped tight on his shoulders. Peter, Paul and Mary had been singing, he remembered. *Painted wings and giant rings make way for other toys,* the girls continued below the window, and Benji's heart rose in his throat.

He feigned sleep, a trick he used to will himself calm.

"Who said I was special?" he thought he heard Rachel say just before he fell asleep.

Benji woke up early, a little after eight, and he slipped out of the room without waking Rachel. As he walked back to his dorm, the morning gray and cold, Skatesville was on his mind, and he thought of one of those few weekends in winter when he and Vanessa were kids and Len and Annie were there with the twins, and the family had slept in the one guest room together, to stay warm. Ben and his sister slept on cots until they crawled into the big bed in the cold mornings, under an old, smelly quilt. Benji remembered that feeling of pure invincibility in the warm, dry love of their four bodies, a single unit. Now the campus felt depressing, cold, and terribly small. It seemed discharged of people, as if students had been poured out of the jar of it, and the buildings looked as if they were made of cardboard, so new did they seem to him. Benji wondered about his friends from high school at their old Ivy League campuses, vines covered in thick, waxy leaves climbing up redbrick and white-columned buildings opening onto porches, and inside dark-paneled rooms, old oil paintings of men and spaniels hanging along the walls.

When he got to his room, Benji found a note from Arnold pinned to his pillow: *Your parents are running late!* He had signed it with a smiley face and pinned it to his pillow! Benji gritted his teeth at the thought of Arnie bending down and grasping at the fabric to attach the note with its impossibly small gold safety pin. How had he opened and closed it with his plump, nail-bitten fingers? Many times he had asked Arnie to leave notes for him on his desk, but he was always met by his roommate's defensive claims that Benji never found said messages on his disgustingly messy desk, and that he always blamed Arnie when he didn't receive them. Either way, Benji was relieved to know his parents would be late.

It was only 8:30 a.m. but he had so much to do before the rally, he didn't know where to begin. He pulled off his sweatshirt, grabbed a T-shirt from the mess on his bed—Rachel's *Grateful Dead Winterland* T-shirt, so soft, a faded blue, almost the color of fog, with a skull wrapped in a crown of roses over the left breast—and over that, he pulled on a sweater. He didn't bother changing his underwear. Benji went to fill a bowl from the bag stashed in his desk drawer, then decided against it, realizing that the day might demand quite a bit of him. There was too much unknown, and how much better to have the first smoke of the day be later, he thought, when it was over, before another oppressive family dinner.

The Action Station, a makeshift booth intended to be the head-quarters of the event, was already being set up. Benji nodded at several girls from the Action Coalition who were stacking up papers and pulling tops off Magic Markers, checking their potency. "Hey," he said, pointing to a sign-up sheet. "What's that?"

"A sign-up-to-vote sheet," one girl said.

He looked at her quizzically. "This isn't about voting!" He began to panic that they all had the wrong event. *This is STAB,* he'd wanted to scream. *STAB!* But he had remained calm.

"We do this at every rally, Benji," the girl said instructively.

He smiled at his name. Then he looked to the one bending over to open her knit bag. Alice was her name; she had helped him secure a permit for the rally at the eleventh hour last night, while Larry was arranging for buses from the neighboring colleges. Benji had heard a rumor that someone had stumbled upon her in the wee hours of the morning several months ago, behind Rosenthal, doing it doggie style with an activist from Northampton who was here for a rally to fight homelessness. Benji watched her stand up with her pile of folded pamphlets pressed to her chest, and he thought of the way the morning light must have reflected off her blue-white body, the flash of her ass, her hands and feet planted into the earth taking root, like young trees.

"Because voting is, like, the whole point. To everything. It's the basis for what we do, no matter what we're fighting for." This one was a freckled brunette with long, curly hair and green eyes. He noted that she too seemed to have an extra layer of fat, even around her eyes, which almost disappeared when she smiled. "Can't vote; can't get anything voted on."

"Got it." He shrugged. "Sounds like a good plan."

"Andy's over there." She pointed to the pay phone. "I'm Gwen."

"I know," Benji lied. "Gwen."

He walked over to Andy, talking animatedly into the scratched-up pay phone.

"Everything okay?" Benji gestured.

Andy nodded, twirling the phone cord the way Vanessa used to do back when his sister was a regular girl who did regular-girl things, such as talk all night with her girlfriends and refuse to let him even speak to his friends to so much as confirm a spot to hang out. Fleetingly, he missed Heather and Jessica and Bee, all matching in their scuffed-up brown cowboy boots and satiny blouses, their hair so feathered and wispy, lips oozing root-beer-smelling lip gloss. One night he had come home late and was sitting out on the screened-in back porch when Bee came downstairs in her nightie. She had stood in the doorway, the kitchen light shining from behind her, illuminating her curved body and her nipples, dark against the diaphanous fabric of her light pink nightgown. They had made out in the hammock for hours, tiptoeing back into the house just before dawn.

Andy got off the phone and announced to Benji that in addition to Robert Parish, he'd just now secured Kathy McMillan, the long jumper who had won the silver medal in Montreal in '76. "Yeah, she was visiting her sister in Roxbury this weekend, just randomly. Her sister is friends with my brother, and word got out, so I just called and she's up for it. It'll be cool because she can talk about being in the Olympics and what it feels like to not go this year."

"No shit," Benji said. "It's just so unfair! Hey, anything happen with the flame?"

Roland had thought it would be bangin' to get the real Olympic flame electronically transmitted, the way it had been in Montreal, but orchestrating it proved far beyond what these five guys were capable of managing technically.

"Yeah, here, check it out." Roland walked Benji outside and over to the fake wooden podium, which two guys from the radio station were helping to wire. A huge Olympic flame, the fire constructed out of tissue and stiff tulle or chiffon, hung from the window of the radio station.

"Wow," Benji said.

"Lana did it. Art major." Roland held out his palms as if to ask, *What can I say?*

Benji laughed. "It looks good!" he said, even though it was hideous.

He looked around to see if perhaps Rachel had awoken to massive amounts of guilt at abandoning her devoted boyfriend and had decided to come. Though she was not among them, many kids had begun streaming in to the rally, carrying steaming cups of coffee and pink and white boxes of doughnuts. With any bit of luck, today would run smoothly; all that Benji could do was hope the speakers showed, that there was a good crowd, and everywhere from the *Brandeis Justice* to *World News Tonight* would report on it. Perhaps, he thought to himself, this event could actually effect change. How amazing would that *be?*

Around eleven thirty, buses started chugging up the hill. He watched them pull into the circular drive out front, which brought to mind the children's book about the train his mother had read to him; she'd curled around him with her smell of spicy perfume and ChapStick, and he remembered the train's smiling face carrying all the toys to all the needy children: *I think I can I think I can.* To his surprise and delight, the buses were as filled with students as that grinning blue train had been with toys. Kids spilled out of them, some in full sports regalia, and others in their school colors or sweatshirts with school names blazoned across their chests. Benji looked up at the thick gray sky and imagined a whole other universe behind it, begging him to stomp through, a thought he'd once had while tripping on a cold day beneath an overcast sky. The thought of an entire people, their faces and fists pressed against the sky waiting to be let in, had never left him.

He had a brief flash of his parents making their way up 95 in the

Volvo, Vanessa sulking in the backseat, his parents up front bickering over when to get on the Jersey Turnpike. *I think I can I think I can.* The train reached the top of the hill. Bring it on! Benji thought. Anything.

Still Benji watched for Rachel as Tuesday Twilight, the more popular of the campus cover bands as it featured Matty Schlangel, a cherubic political science major who resembled Jerry Garcia, played. They covered a few Dead tunes as Benji greeted the buses. He also helped adjust the mikes, and assisted in stapling two-by-fours to the backs of thick poster board: *End the Cold War Now!* and *You Can't Keep Us Out of Red Square!*—even the random ones from the Communist Club that caused some minor disagreements about varied purposes and agendas: *What Would Karl Say?* and *Capitalism Is Evil!* As he worked, Benji constantly checked each entrance to the quad in hopes that the next gust of chilly March air would bring Rachel loping up the path and out of the gray day with her just-fell-out-of-bed tangle of black hair, that fringed jacket, her tan suede boots that wrapped around the shapely gams he'd been twisted up in just last night. Matty Schlangel dedicated their next song to the youth of today and began: *Comes a time when you're driftin'*. Rachel held in her a radiating heat that went from her stomach outward, and he craved the inside and outside of her. *Comes a time when you settle down . . .* His mouth watered for the taste of her, he couldn't help himself, and he blushed as he put down his sign to turn to see if maybe she had arrived. Because he did not know what he would do if she didn't show.

Benji watched all the athletes and hippies and socialists, the communists, the lesbians, the gays, the environmentalists, the feminists, the militants, and, he noticed now, several Russian Jews, famous on campus for the asylum Brandeis granted them, fill the outside of Usdan, all singing and clapping their hands. And another one for us and our buddies who should be in Moscow! Matty Schlangel declared. *He's got the whole world*—Come on now! *in his hands!* Matty let his guitar hang at his hip, and turning to the two other members of Tuesday Twilight, he clapped his hands together above his head.

Several star activists were in attendance, the strongest voices—despite their claim that every voice, each human's story told, was evidence of another's silenced—at every campus rally, their mouths practically eating the mike as they galvanized every crowd into action. Today, however, there was also a new contingent: the athletes. Not just Brandeis athletes, which would most certainly have limited the number, but players from neighboring schools, each wearing a team uniform or their school colors, a team jacket and sweatshirt. Scanning the crowd now, Benji saw three football players from Harvard, several from the MIT soccer team, a few Boston University hockey players, some of the Wellesley lacrosse players in their little plaid skirts, and rowers from all over the area, including Tufts. *He's got the whole world in his hands.* Matty Schlangel lifted up his brawny fist, and the crowd sent up a scream of applause.

Here Benji's past life and the present converged, and he remembered how he'd once felt his body move in parts; he had controlled which muscles grew, which ones diminished, the coordination of his limbs and muscles directly corresponding with what he visualized. Now he inadvertently flexed his calves and bunched up his fists. It was so crowded people were standing on the brick walls surrounding the center, holding signs and lacrosse sticks and footballs. He smiled to himself; it was just like before a game, just like the moment before he was about to rush onto the field and play.

Organizers and friends swatted Benji on the shoulder, nodding to the music as they shuffled into the outside circle of the student center, streaming in from all entrances, and he nodded back at them, smiling, also noting several newscasters walking around the student center. They held microphones beneath students' noses and happily asked the reasons for the rally and if anyone, anyone at all, felt the protest might become violent.

This, he thought, in this magnificent crowd of committed people, was a worthy cause. Tuesday Twilight sang their final song in harmony: *The river is deep and the river is wide, hallelujah.* He remembered his family, all of them singing along with the crowd, led by Peter, Paul and Mary. *Milk and honey on the other side, hallelujah.* Benji felt the past stitched inside him like a secret pocket. The future would be sutured where? he wondered.

You cannot take away a dream, Robert Parish had said after Matty led the crowd in the final round of "Michael, Row the Boat Ashore" and bowed off with the rest of the band. That was pretty much *all* Parish said—that mute-Indian rumor had evidently gotten started for a reason—but he did have a point, and his sheer tallness, as well as his blackness on such a glaringly white campus, gave him the presence they needed to begin the day. It centered the rally. Andy had also spoken and introduced Professor Schwartz, who then gave a speech about tradition.

"The sixties is always with us," he'd said. "Look around you. Herbert Marcuse was here, may he finally rest in peace. Abby Hoffman was graduated at Brandeis, wherever he may now be. So was Angela Davis, a Phi Beta. Were these students, now legends, embraced by the system? Were they embraced by this university? They were not! But never will their legacies die."

Before Kathy McMillan got up to speak, anyone could say whatever he or she pleased at a free mike. This was always the wildest part of any rally—individuals with their own agendas, ranting and raving. Some hippie went up, half naked and drooling, and begged to drink bong water, God's juice, he said. The crowd watched him in silence. Then a slight, brown-haired woman with a head full of split ends, upright golden threads reflected in the noonday sun, spoke about Free Schools.

"It is a dying movement, but so necessary when we have schools, not unlike this very one"—she pointed a finger to the sky—"that turn out merely manageable workers, obedient consumers, and malleable voters. That churn out willing murderers!" she said, raising her tiny arm above her head. "Stop the domination now!"

Benji heard one of Rachel's sayings, *Everyone's voice deserves to be heard,* and nodded at the memory and in the spirit of his egalitarianism.

Several athletes also spoke—Larry talked about his brother, who would have been here today to represent the ripped-off, but he was too distraught to travel. He had trained for the Olympics since they were children.

"Who knows what the next four years will bring? What," Larry asked the crowd, "does this teach our brothers?"

"*Lies!*" the crowd answered in unison.

Standing as part of the crowd, Benji could see so plainly his history and his future, and how everyone, all of them, he thought, had a past they were running from or running toward; why couldn't Rachel see and appreciate this? Kathy McMillan went up to talk about her Olympic experience. Going to Montreal—such a foreign country!— was, she said, the most amazing experience of her life, hands down. Being in the Olympic Village was like being in the League of Nations. She'd never known, she said as she bowed her head, that the world was so large.

The crowd was steady, people filing in and out, bringing in burritos and sandwiches at lunch, drinking from bottles of beer and cans of Coke and orange soda, their signs leaning on their shoulders as they took huge bites of their burgers and slices. After one o'clock, someone—it turned out to be Schaeffer—began handing out tabs of acid imprinted with the Pink Panther, though when it reached him, Benji declined, laughing to himself about the prospect of tripping when his mother arrived.

It was already past three o'clock and the permit stated the area needed to be completely cleared out by four. Rachel had not shown; now Benji remembered seeing her that first time, standing in front of Sherman with only those several protesters, holding her wilting little sign: *Get your rules out of our kitchens!* She wore all white and she was so brown; he had wanted her from the moment he saw her.

He looked up to the podium where the crowd waited for the next speaker. Benji watched Professor Schwartz milling about, hands in his pockets, indicating he was merely an observer here, and not a terribly impressed one at that. His gait seemed to be saying, In my day things would have been done differently. Benji thought of his father holding him up into the intense sunshine, Peter, Paul and Mary singing on the steps of the Lincoln Memorial. *It's the song of love between my brothers and my sisters . . .* Benji shook his head for a moment to counter his daze, and only when he was able to again focus on the here and now did he realize that someone was calling his name, that he was next, that now, he thought, as Schaeffer pushed him toward the microphone, now it was his turn.

## CHAPTER 11

# I Spy

They were on the road up to Waltham by seven; Vanessa tried to be patient. She even brought some of her music to play for her parents. Dennis had slipped in the Bad Brains cassette just as soon as they'd turned onto Connecticut Avenue. By the time they'd hit the ramp for 95, he'd ejected it.

"I just can't," he said. "I'm sorry, honey, but it's too early and life's too short."

"Why do we have a cassette player in the car if we don't put it to good use?" Vanessa said. "I had thought I could explain it to you." It was a rare moment where, briefly unhindered by embarrassment, she felt she could say, This is Bad Brains, they created punk in this city, and they believe in a powerful mental attitude. At least H.R. does. He's the singer, she'd have told them if they'd asked. When he plays you kind of believe him; you feel like you can do whatever you want to do—is that weird? And yet. And yet, she would not tell them, the whole punk ethic seemed sometimes to Vanessa like the cheer of a frat boy: just do it yourself, who cares if you can't sing—*sing!*—play the drums if that's what you're into, start a fucking *band*. Because, Vanessa thought, growing more and more skeptical, how does one really make that leap of faith?

She'd felt guilty about the toilet-papering; she wanted to give something back, a bit of herself, even though saying *punk,* just the word, made Vanessa feel like a poseur. Here she was with her parents in their Volvo driving up to Brandeis. How punk rock was that? She half expected to hear a driver scream, *Poseur!* from the car in the next lane, just like when someone showed up at Madam's Organ in a new coat or sneakers because they'd read about the place in *City Paper. Lame-ass fat fucking suburban poseur!* She looked out of her window at the wood-paneled station wagons and Bugs passing by, but no one seemed to notice her.

Dennis looked at her in the rearview mirror, and Sharon turned around in her seat.

"That would be great, honey," Sharon said, twisting with so much enthusiasm that Vanessa thought of those cartoons where Wile E. Coyote's body twirls into a spiral, then spins back to himself. Her mother was like that, all fast, tense movements, coiled to spring. "Explain your music to us."

"You need to be listening for me to talk about it," Vanessa said. PMA is a little like Mom's stuff, she was going to say, with *empathy*. She would not be against her mother, she promised herself, as she had been on so many occasions.

"Put it back in, Dennis," Sharon said, her arms still gripping the headrest, her body turned to the backseat. "We want to hear about Vanessa's new music!"

"Oh, God. Forget it. It's not my new music." Vanessa should have just had them play the Tom Waits and be done with it. How could she really convey how exciting and frightening that first Bad Brains show had been. The building had nearly collapsed! From people responding to music, retaliating against it. It had felt completely life-altering. And yet it had seemed to have nothing to do with her.

"I'm sorry; I can't," Dennis said. "I'm the driver here and it's a hell of a long way to Boston."

"Well, tell us anyway!" Sharon said.

"It's not such a big deal, will you please stop making such a big deal about everything? Jesus." Vanessa felt her goodwill toward her parents dissipating in quick, receding waves.

"I'm not," Sharon said, finally facing forward. "I just wanted to know a little more about you."

"Believe me, there's nothing to know."

But of course that had been a lie, and she knew her mother recognized it as such. Would she like to know that Sean had toilet-papered their house because she'd had sex with him six months ago? Or perhaps her parents might want to hear how she could feel her body growing beneath her, right now even, that she could not escape her fat and muscle and hard bone, not ever, even her skin felt wrong and foreign to her. Can someone be in the wrong skin? She was wrong, a sausage that didn't fit in its own casing. How, she wanted to ask her mother, though she never would, not in a million years, how does one escape her body? It was ruining everything, and everything Vanessa tried to make it go away—sex, music, television—only made her more aware of it.

Inside that skin wasn't a whole lot better. Inside was a pit of black; she was hateful and mean and worthless and stupid. It was far easier to worry over the outside.

Had her mother felt freed? In that fire, that awful fire, her mother had ascended from the table like a paper doll burning, rising into the air.

What, Vanessa wondered, did freedom feel like? Perhaps it was like those few passing moments when she did not think of food. Because her thoughts of food were not like those of her brother, who ate for nourishment, when he was hungry, stopping when he was full. Or of her mother, who went over recipes and drove out to rural Maryland and Virginia, over rolling hills and into farms, cooking to bring happiness. Nor was she like her father, who worried over what the lack of food would do to entire countries. Vanessa thought only of herself, of getting food and stuffing herself with it. When she gave in to this constancy, the deepest thought she had was where the food would reveal itself—on her enormous hips and thighs, in her cheeks—and how she could rid herself of it, what types of food she could eat to make the ridding easier. It was such a weak and shallow conceit.

"I know there's lots to know about you, but if not today, that's okay," Sharon said. She gave Dennis a knowing look that was not quite a roll of the eyes, but nearly so. "I know! Let's play I Spy!"

"Mom," Vanessa said.

"Come on. I'll start." Sharon closed her eyes. "I spy with my little eye . . . something . . ."

"I don't want to play." Vanessa looked out the window at the cars driving parallel to the Goldsteins', an old, mustard-colored Volare filled with poodles dropping behind.

"Well, I do," Dennis said, which felt like more of a statement against Vanessa than support of the game they'd played on every road trip. I spy with my little eye! Anything. A multicolored Super Ball. Daddy's newspaper. Mom's sunglasses, two rose-colored lenses the size of their tires. Vanessa and Ben would go wild to see who would be the first to find the object, but most of the time it was Vanessa who could rut nearly anything out. Dennis would always turn in the driver's seat, his hands gripping and releasing the steering wheel. You're a great spy, Van. Turning toward the road again, and looking out at the flat horizon of 95, he'd say, We should all be very careful.

"Go right ahead," Vanessa said. "By all means, play all you want." She thought of riding with Helen in Los Angeles on some endless sunny highway. Out there they were always driving somewhere. Where had they been going? Somewhere silly like Grauman's Chinese or the Santa Monica Pier. Or to Canter's Deli, the one place that wasn't the Polo Lounge where Helen would eat breakfast. Canter's was so dark, a sharp contrast to the constant sunlight. The smell of smoke permeated the plastic-covered banquettes and the waitresses wore drooping false eyelashes; they pinched Vanessa's cheeks and called her toots.

Ben had also been in the car, in the backseat, Vanessa's turn to sit in front, yet another special treat not allowed at home. That day Vanessa had said, as she always did on long car rides at that time, I Spy! She'd turned to her brother to see if he was up for the game, and as she'd twisted back around, she saw a Mercedes in front of them, its blue plates with yellow writing: *California!* What a strange and lovely place. The lettering of the plate was hazy behind the exhaust, and she looked up from it to see Nana Helen turning from the road to stare at her, wide-eyed. Vanessa saw her grandmother look momentarily unhinged, wild, and then, before she could ask her what the matter was, Helen grabbed her arm. Her nails dug into the meat of her biceps.

"What?" Vanessa said, rubbing her arm when her grandmother let go. "What did I do?"

Helen said nothing, just gripped the faux-shearling-wrapped wheel and looked ahead, continuing to drive. Toward the hills, Vanessa remembered now, because she was going to I Spy the *Hollywood* sign, and she had known that Ben and Helen would be able to guess it while they drove because it would be staying with them for the drive the way the moon did.

Helen had shaken her yellow, spray-netted helmet of hair and sniffed loudly. "That's not a nice game. Not nice at all. Did your father teach you that? Anyway"—she'd turned gaily to Vanessa and then to Ben, via the rearview—"should we get ice cream?"

"Yes!" Ben had screamed. "Yes! Yes! Ice cream, Nana."

Helen had then started singing, *How much is that doggy in the window,* and not ten minutes later Vanessa was happily licking her strawberry cone.

"Something red!" Sharon said, her hand on the handle of her door.

That was usually for the newspaper—*black and white and read all over*—but Vanessa was willfully not getting involved.

"Is it in this car?" Dennis asked.

A little boy in a blue knit sweater played in the backseat of a yellow Datsun, his face intense with concentration, his tongue dangling from his mouth. Were Vanessa and Ben ever that young? Her memories were images: her father imitating Rodin in the Hirschhorn Sculpture Garden; sitting at her father's desk, her legs kicking the air as she typed on her father's letterhead on the electric typewriter with two fingers— *tap tap tap*—pretending she was typing Daddy's documents while their father talked on the phone and wagged his finger at her in warning; lying in bed with Nana Tatti, her long arms wrapped around her as she told the story of the Snow Maiden, her skinny fingers jabbing the air, as if that were where the story had been written. Now Vanessa had a crippling sense of her own aging along with the prescience that she was also impossibly young and incapable of handling the process.

"Yes!" Sharon said.

Dennis grinned at Sharon. "I know. It's your underwear!" He looked down at Sharon's waist.

Sharon clapped. "It is; it is! How did you know, I thought you'd never get it and you got it on the first go!"

As quick as a shot, Dennis snapped the elastic of Sharon's panties. "I got it!"

Vanessa threw herself back in the seat. "That's disgusting!" She crossed her arms. "And anyway, it's supposed to be something you can *see*. That's the point; it's spying. Do you have X-ray vision or something?" She knew she sounded childish.

Dennis shook his head. "Uh-huh." He nodded in the direction of Sharon's lap again. Reluctantly Vanessa looked over to see a hint of red lace peeking up from the waistband of her jeans in the back.

"That's ridiculous." Vanessa folded her arms.

Sharon giggled. "Good one, D." She slapped his leg. She kept her hand high on his thigh. "Okay, your turn."

"Let's see," he said. "I spy with my little eye . . ." Dennis was smiling, looking ahead, both eyes on the road. "Something beautiful."

Benjamin was not in his room when the Goldstein family arrived at the dorm.

"Hello?" Sharon called, banging on his door. "Ben!"

Dennis paced back and forth. "For God's sake!" he said, mostly to himself.

"Ben, come on!" Sharon said, still banging, and then she set her cheek to the door, listening for life inside. "Let us in," she said quietly.

"He's not there." Vanessa kicked at the floor and her boot squeaked on the linoleum. "You're making a scene. Can we not make a scene, please?"

"Hello!" Sharon smiled cheerfully as two boys who looked exactly alike—plump, tall, broad noses—came ambling down the hallway.

"I'm Arnie. Ben's roommate? And this is my brother, Michael."

"Do you know where Ben is?" Dennis asked. "We don't exactly live down the street here."

"I think he's at the rally. There's been a protest all morning at the student center," Arnie said.

"A rally!" Sharon clapped and had a vision of her son holding a placard that read *We Demand Freedom Now!* A rally. She would not be like her mother, she had thought as they'd marched on Washington sixteen years ago—more walked, really, stood even; it was fucking crammed with protesters. Dennis's gold ring had glinted even in the gray morning light. Her son was at a rally. Perhaps he would choose the road that she had wanted to choose then. Sharon had thought she would better the world; she would not always take and take, never to be satisfied. Her father, working through the hearings. It was a constant crossed picket line as far as she was concerned. Benjamin had been asleep on Dennis's chest, his tiny head exposed, and Sharon had resisted the urge to protect his ears from the noise so she could watch her husband run his hand over his downy hair and know that her choices had been good ones. The Lincoln Memorial was packed with people but for that perfect rectangle of the Reflecting Pool, shimmering silver, miraculously still, untouched in the middle of such chaos.

"A rally," Sharon repeated. "How wonderful."

What if Ben, her athletic son whose biggest passions mere months ago had been the play-offs and cheerleaders and Maggie's Pizza, carried it all on? What if something about that day when he was just an infant had gotten in and formed him into a committed person?

Vanessa groaned. "Jesus!"

"Your brother has obviously become very involved in politics, Van, which is a wonderful, wonderful thing." Sharon remembered at the March to End the War, when Ben was seven, and how he had turned to sit on Dennis's shoulders. He had clapped his hands and cheered wildly as people around him chanted, lifting their fists. She had wanted to reach up and still his applauding hands. Who celebrates a bloodbath? Ben had seen the first images on television as she and Dennis had seen them. A reporter in a Vietnamese field commenting as marines flicked the tops of their Zippos and torched the thatched roofs of the village to his back. The reporter did not try to stop it. Ben had gone up to the television and pressed his face up close, and Sharon had run to her son and swept him up, as if his close proximity to the screen placed him in that field and that village and that war.

That 1969 march had been relatively peaceful, with a glorious blue sky. The morning had had a nearly implausible clearness, the trees so striking against it, but she did remember that day as one without hope.

"He was one of the organizers." Arnie looked at his watch. "It should be winding down soon."

"See?" Sharon turned to Dennis. "One of the organizers!"

"I'm not going," Vanessa said. "It's going to be a bunch of hippies smoking pot."

"And so what if it is," Sharon said. "So what."

She hadn't been able to cauterize the memory, so there it was, there *he* was, so suddenly, Elias, naked, lying back on the bed in the hotel room, his tanned arms behind his head, the dark hair of his armpits and crotch exposed, passing her a joint, the end wet with his saliva. She pictured his penis, finished, flung at his thigh, shrinking before her. She had straddled him, reaching for the joint. Her hand was beautiful then. She was told she had been quite lucky that she still had use of her hand. A very lucky lady you are, the nurse had said, and Sharon had momentarily felt young and new and fortunate.

What had happened was not so tragic when you considered all the people who were suffering on that burn unit; when you considered those villagers, or the soldiers burned by napalm, the people who survived that bomb, that bomb, that bomb, Sharon told herself. None of this was lost on her, but pain can make a person selfish. And vain. Now she wanted to duck from the image of leaning into Elias, feeling his stomach and chest first with the very tips of her nipples as she slid up him, reaching for the joint. She wanted to shirk the embarrassment of a moment when she had thought she was someone she was not. The fire had taught her this: she was not Carole King, or a girl who had bedded the boy who played acoustic guitar at the coffeehouse; she was not Judy fucking Chicago liberating vaginas by serving them for dinner. She had never been any of these people, and now she was a middle-aged woman, married she might add, who had bedded an out-of-work, middle-aged man she'd met at an empowerment conference in a hotel lobby. And not a terribly nice lobby either. It was a little, well, run-down. She still heard him playing guitar with his long, tapered fingers, and she could feel them at the same time on her body, the calloused tips brushing over her as he strummed: *After changes upon changes, we are more or less the same.* Sharon was not who she once was, or whom she had the potential to be, and she was acutely aware of this. She knew who she was not. How embarrassed she was! Now Sharon Goldstein was only—merely—whom she had become.

Dennis said nothing, even as Arnold looked at him, expecting him to add to the discourse about the rally and how wonderful Ben was to have organized it. But Dennis merely shot his chin outward, as if to ask the kid, *Where is the damn thing?* Because he was tired of rallies; how many times could he protest? Sometimes one doth protest too much! And looking back, he could see it had accomplished nothing. Not until people grew violent. The prospect of watching his son go through it all the way he had, the ignorant hope, then the futile knowledge! The light! The sad, unshakable belief, the sanctimony, the morality, then the realization it would all come to nothing, and so the anger, the grief, the subsequent inaction, well, it made him weary. It was what he felt about Sharon and her cult, her pyramid scheme, her foray into self-improvement; he felt sorry for her and was simply waiting for the moment when she would come to him and ask him, *What the fuck was I thinking?* Then he would welcome her back. Dennis wondered what was left of any kind of a movement now, if anything true lay beneath the unending fashion of radicalism, and if his son would find something real there. Because Dennis couldn't picture what the movement was anymore. Perhaps it was a function of his own age that he was no longer clear on what his kids' generation was fighting for exactly.

He remembered that first day of work at USDA, the squeak of the shiny linoleum against his new shoes, brand-new Florsheim loafers, bought for work in an office, and the feeling—no, the *knowing*—

that government service was a worthy continuation of a tradition his father had begun. His tenement neighbors were dealing in diamonds or shoes or, God forbid, braziers, even pickles, while the Goldstein family business had been activism. Had Dennis ever viewed his work as protest? Because really that's what the family business dealt in. His mother also. He had heard she'd campaigned for Roosevelt until he was born, and he imagined her cinching her coat and going out into the cold, knocking on people's doors to canvass. *Sign this, take a look at that, here are the many letters that make up the names of agencies, this is the new* utopia. *This,* he imagined her saying with her thick accent, *is the true New Deal.*

Twenty-five years later when Dennis had first set up shop in that windowless office at the end of that long corridor, he'd thought, And here I am too. He'd thought how his son—Vanessa was not yet born—would soon see by example the importance of working from within, the tradition of the New Left. His mother had practically begged him to take a job in Washington. He had been surprised; when had his mother wanted him out of her area code? This is what the revolution looks like, he'd thought, looking at the scratched-up bookcase, the beaten file cabinet, then placing on his desk a framed black-and-white photo of Sharon in profile, her face in Ben's cheek, her long hair cascading over her slim shoulders.

There had been other opportunities for change, openings brought to his attention in the private sector, but even in government he had many options. He was not surprised when he was approached, both in the USSR and here. The requests were simple: to make intelligence available for a few hours so it might be copied and returned to him hours later, this sort of thing. He was asked by the Soviets to merely turn away, and also by a few surprising Americans he preferred not to think about so as not to remember them should he ever be called to. By saying nothing was he saying something?

He remembered his panic as he lay in bed that night after his first dinner in Moscow. That had been before he knew what would happen in Vietnam, and still he had felt his country shifting. He could see it all the way from the Soviet Union. We were not so fabulous now, were we, with JFK shot dead. But what was to come was even worse! Everyone died in Vietnam. Questioning the world around them would be instinctual to his children. Even though Dennis had sat at the dinner table listening to his father criticize government for years, he'd had to teach himself to constantly challenge it systemically. He could see it in Vanessa now, this fundamental mistrust of information. This was the difference and this, he could now see, was his generation's gift to the next: welcome to a world you cannot have blind faith in.

Rumors now, from State, said Venona was being canceled. Would all those decrypted messages be made public? he wondered. Because these people were not bad people; in fact, their ideologies he might even call admirable. These people believed in something. Anything, he was told, could be useful information—the Landsat images were cited—although the Soviets were more excited for his close access to presidential advisers. He had not said anything. Why would he? But he had not been sure one day he would not.

Lending intelligence would be of little risk, he thought now, and it would have been Dennis's own protest, much more a link to the family tradition than what his job had become, especially since the travel hiatus. Activism had been the hushed surface of the family business, but something violent lay beneath that call to change. Were he to walk away from his desk, the locked cabinet left open, just once, say, he too could protest against the idea—blaspheme—that food could be as viable as weapons. Weapons were what should be weapons, but he was against those too. Dennis had thought then, as he thought now, was starving a nation into compliance morally correct? *Were* they actually starving?

Picturing his son in the crowd at a rally annoyed Dennis; it lacked originality. He wished not for a passionate life for his son, as he'd often hoped in the days he'd watched him run back and forth and back again on some green field tromped brown, but for a livable one. Not even Jimmy Carter could have believed for one second that the effects of his embargo would remove a single Soviet soldier from Afghanistan. Be a fucking lawyer, Ben, he said to himself. Be free.

"Where is the student center, Arnold?" Sharon asked.

"I'll take you over there. Do you want to stay with Michael?" Arnie asked Vanessa.

She pushed herself off the wall with her boot. "Naah, I'm coming," she said quickly.

"Let's go to the rally!" Sharon almost screamed.

Arnie muffled a giggle. "Follow the yellow brick road!" he said, marching down the flight of stairs and out the door onto the quad. Yakus Pond shimmered, whispering a secret. "I'm the cowardly lion."

Arnie turned to watch the Goldsteins in step behind him. He brought both of his hands out in front of him and bent his fingers into claws. "Grrrr," he said, and turned back toward the hill.

Dennis kept his head down as they followed Arnie. Sharon oohed and aahed over buildings and fields, smiling, half deranged, at the students who passed by. More and more he couldn't help thinking that the unbroken chain of events was a load of crap, and what was needed for success was impossible. Ally support was faltering: already Argentina and Canada were not abiding by the embargo. There was no way to gain complete control over the private sector either; that was capitalism for you. The less concrete, more psychic, need for the American farmers to think beyond their own farms, beyond their own needs, was hardly in effect, just as Dennis and his colleagues had warned. How were farmers supposed to view the greater good of the country when their lives were wrecked by it?

"And here is Chapels Field." Arnie swung his arm broadly to his left. "Did you know that each place of worship was built to stand alone, none in the shadow of the other?"

"We'd heard that, yes," Sharon said, following Arnie's substantial arm. She turned to Vanessa. "It's really remarkable the way they've done this so everyone can feel free to worship whatever and whenever they choose."

So much had happened since they'd visited here last spring, she thought. The fire had altered Sharon, even just the actual moment of it, the heat crawling toward her chest. It had been reassuring. It was a new feeling of something big and warm and wonderful approaching her heart. She'd thought it could be God—God's love!—or maybe, she'd thought, this is my changed, enriched self, turned over to happiness; this was what everyone in that huge Marriott conference room was gunning for. Perhaps it was only later when she had tried to make sense of what had happened that she had these comforting thoughts, because of course it had not been God at all, not even His verification: neither a burning bush nor her self leaving her body in order to return enriched, fulfilled, beautiful, reborn. It had not been a perfect her, but merely fire itself, fire from the liquor poured over her cherries, evidence only of her carelessness. She realized this was not an event for which she had always waited.

The fire was taking with it all the layers of her. She imagined herself the anatomy model in her high school science class, the diffused desert light illuminating the classroom and the insides of the plastic dummy, the skin on the right section pulled back, arteries and veins and layers of muscles revealed in red and blue plastic, the organs and sex parts removable and interchangeable. She had thought her skin was gone from the fire, and she'd wondered, before Felix jumped upon her to put out the flames, and before she'd passed out, what she would be, and how she would exist, without her coverings.

"It really *is* about freedom," Arnie said, Chapels Field behind them, as he herded the Goldsteins up the hill. "That's just so true."

Dennis looked up and faced Arnie. "Did you read that in a brochure? Not to be rude, but we had a tour guide tell us the exact same thing last year. Verbatim actually."

Arnie laughed. "You sound like Benji!"

Dennis smiled.

"I know, I know, you can always count on me to drink the Kool-Aid, as they say," Arnie said.

Dennis looked hard at Arnold Lefkowitz. Was this kid for real? Was he talking about Ken Kesey's LSD or Jim Jones's grape-flavored cyanide? Certainly these kids could not have slept through news of the genocide at Jonestown, barely a year ago. And surely they couldn't be so insensitive . . . It occurred to Dennis that Arnie might not be referring to either, that he might not even be aware of the reference, that the phrase had already come to mean something so different and benign it was now rendered meaningless. Why even *say* it then?

Dennis thought, with a strange longing, of Len Ford, seeing him now on that first day at Hartley, blowing in with Sissy and her teased blond hair, her whole being strangely arousing to Dennis as she touched his warm, dry hand; even the way she ruffled her son's hair seemed languidly sexual. He and Len would never have been friends now, not here, thought Dennis, not on this campus, where, in all its talk of freedom from religious prejudice and ethnic shackles, it felt more pious or holy or *Semitic* really than anything he had previously experienced. Lenny Ford, and anyone like him, would never have come to Brandeis, which made Dennis realize the diversity his son would miss out on.

"Not me," Dennis said to Arnold about the Kool-Aid.

"Oh, I don't know, D," Sharon said. "We all drink the Kool-Aid sometime or other, don't we?"

Dennis started to respond, but stopped when Sharon slipped her hand in his. "I hear the rally!" she said.

"We're approaching!" Arnie said. "It's so exciting, I would have totally been here earlier, but my parents, you know. They're not big protesters." He laughed. "Anyway, it's kind of about the athletes. I'm more theater."

Dennis could see a crowd, and he heard someone speaking over a bullhorn or a loudspeaker. "Athletes? How bizarre."

"This is to protest the boycott," Arnie said. "It was actually Benji's idea!"

They were at the student center now, and the crowd had spilled out onto the main walking road, where they stood.

"Look!" Vanessa pointed into the pack of people.

"Wait, this is a protest against the Olympic boycott?" Dennis felt his fingers digging into his palms. "In Moscow?"

"Wonderful!" Sharon said.

Dennis looked at her. "Not much of something to rally over, is it?"

"People love their Olympics," she said. She looked away from Dennis and Vanessa, still smarting from watching this year's winter Olympics all alone.

"It's true, we all love the Olympics," Arnie said. "Everyone does."

"There's Ben!" Vanessa couldn't mask her excitement, though her brother seemed so far away.

Sharon saw Benjamin standing at the podium, so tall he had to stoop down to speak into the mike. His long fingers gripped the sides of the lectern, and his dirty-blond curls bounced across his face. My son's bones, she thought, remembering him unscrolling the Torah by its wooden handles with the rabbi at the bimah, his voice high and then low, just breaking, his face so tiny but for the wide nose, a suit too broad for his narrow shoulders, room to grow. Even then she'd thought, He's so grown up! Soon I will lose him. No more room to grow, she thought now.

Just then she connected her son's voice with the words being broadcast over the crowd.

*We need to know that in this country, what we work for will be appreciated. That if we spend our lives training—which, let's not forget, is serving our country—and then we are told we can't compete, well, what does that tell young people?*

*Lies!* the crowd responded.

*That our voice doesn't matter?*

*All lies!* they said.

It was the call and response of synagogue, Vanessa thought. And so did Sharon.

*Well, today we have made our voices heard!*

There was applause, and some whistling, and cheering.

Vanessa and Arnie clapped wildly.

"Ben!" Sharon screamed out suddenly just as the crowd had started to quiet. "Ben! We're here!" She waved her arms dissolutely and started to charge into the mass of people.

Dennis got hold of her arm. "Sharon, don't. We'll embarrass him."

Vanessa just shook her head and covered her eyes with the fingers of her right hand.

Benjamin looked over to the sound of his mother calling his name, and he nodded in their direction.

*This has been a wonderful day!* her son said. *I want to thank everyone for their participation . . .* Ben began to tick off a list of all the people who had helped make the day possible.

Dennis thought of his father; any corner, anytime he saw a group of people, he just stood up and began. This is the way it is, Sigmund would say. Let me steal you away from what you think you believe. Why must you eat your heart out? There are other ways, Dennis thought. Talking isn't everything. In fact, it's nothing.

Sharon was grinning maniacally. "That's my son." She turned to a clutch of students passing a bowl between them. They were dressed for winter in wool hats with flaps over their ears or with long tips that folded back and swept across their shoulders like old-fashioned nightcaps, and crassly knitted mittens, parkas hugging them tight. They turned and smiled.

He was mobilizing for the Olympics, which Sharon knew was a rally for them both. In an instant, she forgave him for last month when night after night she watched alone as Eric Heiden took gold. Nothing had made her miss Ben more than when the United States won the hockey. Sharon didn't even like the sport; she had a crazed fear of what those kids would do to one another with each play, the multitude of injuries they had to have endured. And the fear of the Soviets winning never left her.

Benjamin didn't even call when the Americans won! Here it was, the *miracle on ice,* and when she'd given in and called him two days later, she'd been distraught to find that he hadn't even watched the game.

"Or maybe I did," he'd told her distractedly. "I mean, it might have been on in the background."

Sharon had resisted the urge to cry into the phone. She wanted to cry for everything: for the fire, for Dennis, who was always leaving, for Elias, and for Elias's absence. For Benjamin, who would never be the all-over presence she hadn't known life would be unbearable without, and for Vanessa, who was so clearly suffering. She had wanted to cry for her youth, and for the way she had never enjoyed it and now it had slipped away, first so slowly and then with about as much warning as her first fall on the ice. Was her son still young, or was he now old? Suddenly, there was no in-between, and she'd tried to tell Ben this when she'd called him after the game. He had not been responsive, and she had felt her insides draining, like when her water broke. She'd been at the stove when it happened, frying up steaks Diane, Dennis's favorite.

There he is, Sharon thought now. When did I ever cook steaks Diane? she wondered, reorganizing the unhealthy menu in her head. She found her body unburdening, relieved that after so many months, finally she could set her eyes upon him, and soon—soon!—her arms around him.

There he is. He leaned into the podium and brushed his hair from his face with those long, attenuated fingers. Those are his bones. People cheered. Sharon took everything in. He is here.

CHAPTER 12

# A Sealed Box

The party at Larry and Andy's suite in the Usen Castle had been in full swing for hours by the time Benji and Vanessa arrived. The delays had been many. For one, Benji was in charge of the cleanup after the rally, and though the area had been left surprisingly clear of trash, he and Peter had picked up the few paper plates, the hamburger wrappers and beer cans and Coke bottles left behind, piling them into huge black trash bags. As Benji had thrown one of the bags into the Dumpster behind the building, exactly the way the permit had instructed, he thought with more than a little spite, What is the point here? Is a protest a protest if it's sanctioned?

It made him think of Professor Schwartz, surveying the scene from the edges of the rally. There was something patronizing in the blasé way he held his hands in his pockets and rocked back on his heels. As he'd milled around during the rally, Benji had caught Schwartz's eye and had gotten no wink of encouragement, not even a nod of the head, just an empty stare back with the glassy and condescending expression of a generation that had dropped to the ground and was pulled out of courthouses by their hair, the same people who now had houses in the suburbs and listened to Woody Guthrie and Bob Dylan on their turntables and hoped their kids would become doctors and lawyers. It was such a lie! Benji thought. That American Protest! class was a crock of shit and so was the rest of it. Who could learn anything worth a shit in the sealed box of a classroom?

On his way back to the student center, Benji thought of Schwartz's newsreels: kids being dragged down the stone steps of city buildings in flowered dresses and thick black eyeglasses, their bodies limp, and he felt soiled, as if he'd said yes when he had meant no, and he began to

relate to the way his sister opposed everything. She was anti-corporate-
branding so much so that you couldn't refer to a tissue as a Kleenex or
gelatin as Jell-O. She was anti-animal-testing and anti-leather and had
begun to wear an array of Chuck Taylors, the plastic at the toe and
around the soles of the sneaker filled in with blue-penned doodles and
colored markers. She was anti-nuclear-testing, anti-drugs, anti–South
Africa, and anti-caffeine. That summer before he'd left for school,
each day she'd come home with some new thing to rail against, and
only now, stomping back inside, did he get it: you had to go all out.
There was a war on. He imagined wearing big black combat boots
(leather) and brass knuckles, his exterior finally a testament to his
inner grievances about the many ways the government disregarded its
committed youth.

The last of the buses was pulling out of Usdan, driving off in a cloud
of black diesel, kids hanging out the windows, some with pom-poms
shaking in the wind, when Benji came around in front of the building
with Peter to help Alice and Gwen take down their registration booth.
As they pushed in the table legs and pulled thumbtacks out of the
banners, Benji couldn't help but again picture Alice on all fours, her ass
pitched high in the air, her back arched. She had one of those curved
backs, he knew she did, and he imagined that divine space where her
waist met her bottom and fanned out. Rachel was shaped that way
as well, and as he watched Alice bend to take down the banner taped
across the front of the table, he realized it was Rachel's figure he was
in fact picturing, Alice's blue-white skin somehow slipped over his
girlfriend's body like the fabric of a newly upholstered couch.

How could she not have come today? Benji scanned the room at
the party, now jam-packed with people who had been at the rally,
and he spotted two of her suitemates. They waved to Benji and he
nodded back to them. Matty Schlangel sat perched over a bong, next to
a starstruck girl on the ratty burgundy couch, his guitar still strapped to
him as if at any moment he might just burst into song. Several people
danced in the middle of the room to Zeppelin's "All My Love," which
played achingly loud; they threw their bodies toward one another in
no particular rhythm, arms swinging in slow motion above their heads,
hips swiveling so slowly they seemed geriatric. But he didn't see Rachel.

Benji felt bad about ditching his parents tonight, and now he thought
about today, how when he was done speaking, his mother had come
at him, hugging him and sobbing a little on his shoulder. Ben, she'd

said. Ben. He had hugged his father, then had gone to ruffle Vanessa's thin, brittle hair, but stopped himself, wondering if it could take such playful abuse.

"Your hair is so long!" Sharon exclaimed, stroking it with appreciation. "It's too long, Ben, but it's so thick!"

Benji shook her hands out of his hair as if his scalp had been invaded by large insects. "Your arm looks so much better, Mom," he eked out. He pictured her in bed, her dry mouth reaching for the straw stuck in her milky drink.

"Really? You think so?"

"Hippie boy," Vanessa said. "Fucking hippie."

"Yeah yeah," Benji said. "Sure."

"Nice speech, son." Dennis grabbed Benji by the shoulders. "You were really good up there, for what it's worth."

"Thanks, Dad. That's worth a lot actually. I think Grandpa would be proud too, don't you?"

"I do." Dennis shook his head. "Absolutely."

"He'd be proud until he realized you're, like, campaigning for sports," Vanessa said. "You know there are hostages in Iran right now? You might have wanted to mention that."

"That's enough," Sharon said. "This is about much more than just the Olympic Games. The Olympics is about everything. Everything. Isn't it, Ben?"

Yes, he'd meant to tell her, but he'd turned away, distracted by the thumps on the back and the hugging by his fellow organizers.

Perhaps Rachel had already left the party, Benji thought now as Peter, jolly as hell, filled cups up at the keg, planted conveniently by the bathroom. Benji couldn't imagine she wouldn't wait to see him, unless she was irritated about dinner. He had dinner with his parents and Vanessa at Franca's—the only brick-oven pizza this sad town had to offer, which he knew his mother would appreciate. Rachel was to have joined them, and he had looked so forward to her cramming in between him and Vanessa in a little red booth, impressing his parents with her brilliant ideas. But that had been planned before she hadn't shown up at the rally, and he had just walked down the hill with his family, retrieved the Volvo, and left campus without so much as giving her a call.

When he told his parents he and Vanessa were going to a party, his mother looked as if she would be sick, her nose flaring at the nostrils and her mouth, also exposed, quivering a bit at the sides. Benji felt horribly guilty, though he had made the right gesture with his sister, whom he wasn't much dying to bring either. Would she sit in someone's room alone biting her nails to the quick, refusing every offered drink or pill or pipe, or might she—might she?—just this once join in and have some fun? Bee and Heather and Jessica had been licentious, decadent girls; though he had pretended to ignore them, he had enjoyed their reckless presence and the titillating possibility of fleshy, mostly drunken Bee in the bedroom next to his. Now Vanessa was the opposite of that; she was serious, earnest, incapable of fun.

"We're off then," Benji had said, getting up from the booth where he and Vanessa had faced their parents during the meal. The remains of a spinach-and-ricotta pizza was on the silver plate before him. *Hmmm!* his mother had exclaimed when it came to the table along with a mushroom-and-sausage pie; she had brought out a margarine container filled with wheat germ and offered it around the table before sprinkling it over her own oozing slices.

His father looked pissed but said nothing.

Vanessa had stood as well, brushing off invisible crumbs, as if she too had partaken in the gluttony that was Benji and Dennis and Sharon descending upon the bubbling pizzas when the waiter placed them on the table. What Vanessa had actually done was pick at the spinach and say that her stomach was bothering her.

Benji turned to Vanessa. "You coming then?"

Not long ago, when Vanessa was the old Vanessa, the one smiling in jeans and Sunshine House T-shirts and macramé platform sandals, who named her hermit crab Joni, who fought with him over the cubes of meat they'd stick in the hot oil of the fondue pot trying to knock each other's chunks off their skewers, this Vanessa and Benji would steal bottles of wine from the Magruders' bags in the basement and drink in the backyard, straight from the bottle, just the two of them. He could not recall what they had talked about then, though he remembered the comfort in looking up to the filmy suburban sky and the feel of the grass on his neck, the damp of the earth seeping in through his T-shirt, and the relief that he could lie next to his sister in silence without the pressure he felt with any other girl, to lean over and kiss her, and then move on from there, and from there, to a place where he had to take different routes home or skip classes or do it all over again.

But tonight Vanessa was a ghost of that girl, and Benji half expected her to rise and hover, shake some teacups, slam a window, then disappear into the smoke-filled air.

Now, Andy and Larry came out of their room—one of the funky circular ones with walls curved by the castle tower—joined by Schaeffer, who still appeared to be tripping. The three of them made their way over to Benji and his sister.

"We did an amazing thing today." Andy slapped Benji hard on the back. "Let's celebrate our victory!"

"Hello, sister," Larry said. "Sister Goldstein." He put his hands together at his chest and bowed his head.

"Vanessa," Benji said, halfheartedly swinging out his right hand. "Larry and Andy."

"Hey," Vanessa said.

"Vick-tow-ree!" Larry said, his hand in the air, fingers forming a *V*. Andy did the same.

"Goldsteins." Schaeffer draped himself over Vanessa's and Benji's shoulders, the hand hanging over Benji holding a full cup of beer by the tips of his fingers. "Gold. Steins." The beer slipped to the floor, landing miraculously upright. Beer sloshed onto their shoes, but Schaeffer made no move to acknowledge this or to pick it up.

Larry and Andy were right: there was much to celebrate. The rally had been well attended—more than eight hundred people according to one of the designated counters, which had been another one of Alice's solid ideas—and according to her, thirty-six people had also signed up to vote, all registered Dems. It was, she pointed out, going to be a serious defensive fight this year.

"I saw you on TV!" a girl whom Benji had never met said as she walked by.

"Yeah," Larry said. "You made it on the news."

Benji headed for the keg, Vanessa in tow, kicking himself for not having designated a proper spokesperson to talk to the media on behalf of STAB. All the news organizations had been directed to Benji because he had made the initial calls, but he had been the wrong guy for the job.

He'd had a great and supportive interview with the *Justice,* the campus paper, and the *Phoenix,* the alternative Boston weekly, then a reporter and a cameraman from the local NBC News affiliate had made their way to him.

"What do you expect the rally to achieve?" the reporter had asked. He was balding and jowly, a paunch evident even beneath his trench coat, which was far too light for the cold March day.

"I expect it will stop this boycott, that's what I expect," Benji said. He thought it strange that a man in this physical condition could have a job on television. "Our athletes should be going to Moscow this summer!"

"Really? What are you doing to get the message to Washington?"

Benji shifted his feet and stuck his hands in the front pockets of his jeans. "Well, we're hoping people like you will get the word out on what we've achieved here."

The reporter looked at Benji searchingly, as if he were just now seeing his interviewee. He brought the mike back up to his mouth and turned to the camera. "And what, young man, is next?" he asked, turning back to Benji. "What if there's silence from the White House on this? I'd say you all need to move fast." He held the mike up to him. "Summer is coming up quick." He turned to the camera, raising his eyebrows.

But they had moved so speedily! They'd done all this in a single day. One fucking day, man. Benji pictured his message, written in some secret code on a folded piece of paper, making its way to President Carter at that desk, the desk where anything of import was announced. It could be that easy. He could almost get Carter that slip of paper himself, thought Benji. After all, he had *been* there; he'd seen the White House close up on a number of occasions, and once he'd even been on a special-access tour for the kids of political officials. Nixon had been president at the time; his father had said it over and over as they'd walked through. That little shit, he'd said, and then he'd smiled as the guide had ushered them all right into the Oval Office. This is where it all happens, the guide had said, clicking his tongue and lifting the red velvet rope at the door to the room. Benji had circled the desk with several other kids. Right here, bills become whole laws, and here is where they break; just vanish into thin air, the guide had said, snapping his fingers. It takes a lot to get by our president, the leader of the free world. Benji remembered a feeling of access, his feet planted on the Oriental rug, his hand close enough to swipe a finger across the Pledge residue skimming the mahogany desk. How could he be this near? Benji's nose was pressed up so close to the window that looked out onto politics, he could see those gears turning and turning. But to what end? he'd wondered, even as an eight-year-old. That's what it felt like to grow up in Washington.

A blurred memory of the energy crisis came to mind, and how he and Vanessa imitated the way Carter said the phrase—*inergy crass-is*—for days. He imagined Carter taking the note and opening it slowly, smiling slyly, then looking into the cameras, yelling directly at the television, "The boycott's off!"

Perhaps the way to ensure the president heard their pleas would be to *do* something to stop the Washington machine. "Accidentally" torch one of the campus buses, say. Pull a Patty Hearst: *I'm Benji, up against the wall, motherfuckers!* He imagined pointing a gun, anywhere. Or, on a slightly saner note, perhaps every university and liberal arts college could have a rally of its own. A map of the states came to Benji's mind, different universities marked instead of by pushpins, by flames.

Benji had smiled at the reporter and said "What's next?" It was an angry smile that did nothing. "Revolution?" he'd said, shoulders high, palms up. "Yeah, because this government manipulation must stop." Maybe he should kidnap someone and demand it: stop the *manipulation*!

But what he had really, truly thought was, when would it be enough to simply *believe*? It was sad for Benji because he had briefly touched the faith he'd held as a child, those moments on the Mall, Pete Seeger with his banjo, everyone swaying back and forth. Everyone now! Peter Seeger had said. All together. Pete Seeger hadn't wanted to sing alone, and the whole fucking crowd had sung with him, *We shall overcome some day ayayay.* Everyone held hands—Benji felt as if the whole goddamn world were holding hands—and his mother was crying. When had she started shedding tears merely for herself? *Deep in my heart, I do believe,* and now Benji wanted so desperately for that feeling again, for that conviction that was not what Grandpa Herbert found in a synagogue once a week, reaching out to touch their heavy story, stored in scrolls, not the faith Benji had never so much as considered looking out from the bimah the first Saturday in the month he'd turned thirteen, but Sigmund's faith, faith in people, in every song, every speech, every man, every movement, for all of this to finally ring true, but he was old enough to know that the time for that had already eluded him.

The reporter had laughed and again turned to the cameraman, making the universal sign at his throat for *cut it*. "Choose your battles, kid." He looked back at Benji. He was laughing at him. "There's a hostage crisis on, you know that, right? I mean, sure, maybe you're bored of that story, but do you really think it's correct, a bunch of kids just wanting to swim some laps and jump as high as they can for communism?"

Benji stared at him and saw instead soldiers in the rain, trudging through a forest, covered in mud. He saw a president bleeding on his wife's chest. He saw men in the lotus position bursting into flames. He saw bras burning. The sixties. "Every generation needs something," Benji said halfheartedly.

"It certainly does," the reporter, that *ass,* said.

"But it's not for communism; this is for freedom."

"Communism, kid," the reporter said, shaking his head, lassoing his wires together in his meaty palms, "is no joke."

After he'd left the interview, Benji could have killed himself for not having stated the obvious: that the Olympics were not about politics at all. They're supposed to be above politics, about the world coming together, and leaving the political machinations behind them. Benji had not been quick-witted enough—perhaps his mind was not as fast as his body—and after that he refused to speak with the media. Peter, and also Andy and Larry, for better or for worse, talked to some local papers, and they made good, happy spokespeople, though the message was beginning to get muddled by their cries for victory and their personal stories of being jilted by the government. The damage had already been done; Benji could feel it as he handed Peter a cup to fill.

Schaeffer followed the siblings across the room. "I have presents," he said. "Gifts from above. Come, shepherds." He beckoned them closer with one finger. "Shepherdess." He nodded at Vanessa. "Partake in some pure, unadulterated allover love."

Vanessa crossed her arms; Benji held out his tongue.

"You're kidding," she said. She looked around, momentarily forgetting her disgust at such excess, alarmed now at being at a party where she knew no one, on a campus in a town where she knew no one, with her brother, whom she hardly recognized, about to head off into the sunrise of an acid trip. When had he become such a goddamn *hippie*? She almost preferred him as the asshole jock he'd been in high school. But now she saw in him the strength that had once made her friends want to follow him anywhere. Getting ready to go out on weekend nights at Vanessa's house, Bee would lean down and kiss her mirror; her bubble-gum-flavored Bonne Bell lips would leave an indelible imprint. That kiss is for Bennie! she'd say, annoying Vanessa by calling her brother by a nickname used only by Dennis. Once Bee had lifted up her halter top and, her nipples erect, shoved her tits against the glass. Vanessa had quickly wiped the two dots of fog away, though their impression, and those kisses, left a smudged swath that distorted Vanessa's features the next time she looked into it. The girls would all wait at the top of the stairs for Ben to yell up to them that he was leaving, that tonight would be the one he would take them out with him.

"What the hell am I going to do?" Vanessa asked now. She hugged her stomach; she pictured the grease from the mozzarella at dinner burning through her digestive tract. She felt the cheese attaching itself, blowing her up from the inside out.

"Ummmm." Benji looked at his wrist for a nonexistent watch. "Hmm. I don't know, *chill* maybe?" he screamed over Robert Plant. "It's been a stressful day is all, and I want to have some fun now."

"Might as well, might as well, might as well . . . ," Schaeffer began to sing.

Benji thought then of sitting on that bus heading north on 15 through Pennsylvania on the way to Buffalo after a night serving whole-wheat veggie pastas to all the 'Heads at the Coliseum show in Maryland. Rachel and Benji cuddled together on one of the ripped vinyl bus seats under a red and black Mexican blanket. One of the women, Sarah, an aeronautics major, her long hair in a thousand braids, wiped pots and placed them in the airtight storage boxes, and these two kids up front—planetary science Anthony, and chemical engineering Gerald—picked up their guitars and started to play. Several joints were passed around, and they began to sing "Dark Star." Benji and Rachel had tripped on mushrooms for that show, and it had felt good, easy and mild, but still joy overtaking. He'd almost taken the acid and the mushrooms together, the best of so many worlds, merged, but he had already eaten the mushrooms and he absolutely needed to drop the acid first, otherwise, he knew from experience, he could get really sick. Benji had felt perfect with the gentle combination of 'shrooms and beer and a little weed, and now the sky was this incredible midnight blue, stars were pushing their way through, tiny needles punching into the heavy night fabric, the titanic swarm, Anthony had told them before picking up his guitar and singing, we ourselves are starstuff and we are heading into the titanic swarm. They played and sang softly and Benji held Rachel against his chest. He felt his heart beating at her cheek, and he felt the kind of love that was not of the earth but that floated down, blanketing them from the sky above, released from the clouds perhaps, or the bubbles and gas tendrils of exploding stars, in the galactic spiral of dust and stars and gas, somewhere deep within the time and gravity lost and then gained around some dark hole in the universe.

"It'll be okay," Benji said to his sister, who looked as if she were about to let out a howl. He missed Rachel. "Don't worry about it so much. It'll all be fine."

Vanessa felt for a brief moment as if she would cry, then she gathered up her features and made them strong again, her heart now obdurate, closed, and she took a plastic cup from the stack by the keg.

"Thata girl," Schaeffer said, nodding in her direction. "Straight Edge is for pussies."

Vanessa squinted and drew up her mouth at him as Peter Cox filled her cup.

"The golden potion," Peter said, holding the tap at the side of the cup.

"Hey, man," Benji greeted Peter. "That's my sister's first drink in, what, Van, how long?"

Vanessa rolled her eyes and crossed one foot over the other. "It's been a while, Ben. A while. Okay?" She took a sip while looking at him harshly; it was all coming back to her: her inability to refuse a dare, her continual search for obliteration. Sometimes she thought the straight-edge stuff was not really her at all, but more a way to keep herself at bay. Protect herself, even, but it was selfish in this way; it did not consider the betterment of the world, as she claimed. And a lot of the people she saw at shows were having fun. They were drinking beer and they were unplugging the amps and they were dancing wildly and they weren't taking themselves so seriously. The music was theirs too; everyone needed to have hope, everyone needed a way to let loose. She thought of Sean, rushing so soon after he was done to pull on his pants, his tattoo disappearing beneath his T-shirt just as quickly as it had appeared. She thought of the skin magazines strewn around him as she and Jason crept up the stairs. Sean was as self-righteous as anyone she knew—he wouldn't even read magazines that had liquor and cigarettes advertised in their pages—and taking another sip, she wondered, did he do his drinking in private, the way he looked at porn, the way he did his fucking?

Vanessa hated to be the kind of girl who was not game. Bee might have been the leader in the sex department, but it was Vanessa making out with one of the locals under the boardwalk at Heather's beach house, Vanessa sneaking vodka and running naked into the sea, Vanessa out getting the dime bags in Dupont Circle while Bee and Heather and Jessica waited, looking at *Rolling Stone* and *Seventeen* in Common Ground.

I protest myself, she thought now, turning to Peter. "It's been a while." She took a sip. "Drinking can be seen as a way for the government to keep you down, you know. I realize this is a stretch, but it's what some people do believe, and it's not totally off."

Peter nodded solemnly. "That's so true." He looked at his cup of beer. "It really is."

Benji smiled at Vanessa, who was slowly turning back into the girl he knew, and he was relieved to hear Janis Joplin come on the stereo with a scream. That's when the smell of sandalwood and that Herbal Essence—the yummy-smelling shampoo that smelled of wildflowers and the woods, in the green bottle on the edge of Rachel's shower—overwhelmed him.

"So, no dinner invitation tonight?" Rachel said, coming up from behind them.

"You," he said, turning, both accusingly and with adoration.

"You must be Vanessa. The famous Vanessa! I've heard so much about you." Rachel held out her hand.

"Famous? I doubt it." Vanessa shook Rachel's hand and moved her head ever so slightly to the music. Janis was *good,* Vanessa thought, bringing the beer to her lips. She wasn't flower power at all, but soulful and bluesy and jagged and raw, and Vanessa wondered why she had always dismissed her and what it must have been like to see her perform live. Famous! She had to laugh at Rachel's comment because she knew Ben had rarely considered her. He was older; the only place he looked was ahead. Then she thought, Ben's girlfriend is fat! Vanessa was trying not to add up the calories she herself was consuming—each beer was about 240—and instead tried to concentrate on feeling once again sprung loose, the way she'd felt with Bee and Heather and Jessica, drinking at the bonfires at the country club, then running like hell through the bushes and out into the street when the cops came.

"I've heard a lot about you too," Vanessa said. Rachel seemed incredibly comfortable with herself, Vanessa thought now, looking at her fresh, clean face, her many silver pendants, strung on different lengths of brown and black leather, slung along the cotton of her tie-dyed shirt.

Before Benji said anything, Schaeffer gave Rachel a big, sloppy hug. "Where ya been, baby? Need a little instant Zen?"

"Sure do." She opened a suede bag that crossed her chest diagonally, bisecting her enormous breasts. She took out a plastic Snoopy wallet.

"No way!" Schaeffer pushed the wallet away. "I got this round, been handing these out all day." He laughed. "In honor of the *protest*." He slipped a blotter stamped with Pink Panthers—about a third were left on the sheet—from a delicate wax-paper sleeve, like one you would use to collect postage stamps.

"So where *have* you been?" Benji hadn't yet begun to feel the drug's effects, and he wanted to stop Rachel so he could actually talk to her in real time. Instead he watched her place the tab on her tongue.

"Dada da*dumm,*" she sang, her neck bobbing.

Vanessa stared at her. She imagined the girls Ben brought home those afternoons. Most of them had been coltlike, thin and incredibly lean and long-limbed, utterly enviable. Some were athletes, mostly runners and field-hockey players, though there were more than a few cheerleaders, and she vaguely remembered a tall volleyball player named Michelle, and an arty girl who wore a sweatshirt painted with a huge *A* for "anarchy."

"Crazy day," Rachel said, tilting her head back. "Lots of studying for soc, and I ran into Cambridge to meet up with a friend from high school. Anyway, how did it go today?"

"Really well," Benji said slowly, dumbfounded. "We could have used the support. But clearly you had a friend to see. From high school. I mean, we didn't need it—it went amazingly well—I just mean, like, I could have used it."

"It was fucking awesome!" Peter poured Rachel a beer from the keg. "Totally radical." He started to laugh.

"You sure you don't want a little bit of my pink sunshine?" Schaeffer asked Vanessa, twisting his neck so he was looking up at her from below.

"Who *talks* like that?" Vanessa asked.

"I do, I guess," Schaeffer said.

"Yes." She turned her head. "I'm positive."

"I just took mine now," Rachel said to her, reaching for the beer Peter offered. "We'll be peaking at the same time, not to worry."

Vanessa nodded and sipped her beer.

Schaeffer pulled off a tab. "It won't hurt a bit! Open wide!" His face was obscenely close to hers, and her eyes crossed looking down at him.

Benji pulled him back by the elbow. "Cut it out, Schaeffer, she doesn't want it. She's never tripped before."

At first Vanessa felt a surge of gratefulness; she was so thankful that Benji cared enough to not let her get lost in this muddle of strangers. But as quickly as it welled, her anger and embarrassment burgeoned. This was the first time he was going to stand up for her? Over a tab of acid? She was tired of being Benji's younger sister. She remembered waking up in a kid's car in the parking lot of the Carousel Hotel in Ocean City two summers ago. Jessica was with her in the backseat; Bee was gone, down to the beach with the guy who'd been driving, it turned out, and Heather, well, Vanessa had a hazy memory of her perched at a slot machine with a handful of nickels.

"It's okay. God, Benji, lighten up!" She laughed. "I'll try it." She intercepted the Pink Panther tab. "It's no big deal." Vanessa looked with meaning at her brother. But instead of opening wide for Schaeffer, she placed the tab of acid on her tongue herself.

"Nanoo nanoo," Schaeffer said.

Benji shook his head at them both. "You're in for it, little sister." Then, so as not to freak her out, he said, "I'll be here, okay? Just take it easy. Easy."

He turned from his sister to Rachel. "You didn't come." He could smell her shampoo, that shampoo!—it was irresistible. And she looked incredibly foxy with her tight T-shirt and that black hair cascading down her back. He had never wanted anyone else, he never would want anyone else, the way he wanted Rachel. "How could you not have supported me?"

"Benji." Rachel turned to face him. "I do support you. In everything. But I don't support your cause. Two totally different things."

Sometimes, though, he had to admit, she got on his nerves. "I've gone to everything with you. Everything. Just because you were there." Benji was starting to feel the LSD; it was not coming on in the waves of love stretching time that usually overtook him, but was approaching more in sealed boxes, love and time stuck inside them. As he looked at Rachel, he began to see her only in parts, as if she were an anatomy model, her tits and her pussy removable, her face peeled back, no longer her face.

"I'm sorry if I disappointed you, Benji, but I told you I wasn't going to be there."

Benji nodded. "Yeah. You've really disappointed me." He thought of the plan for Vanessa to sleep at Rachel's, and he no longer felt this would be possible. He wasn't sure now if Rachel's parts—her removable organs, that plastic heart that gave nothing, a heart he could just detach and examine, smash even—should sleep near his sister. Arnie would be out tonight anyway—the Lefkowitzes were staying together at a hotel, like a *family,* Arnie had said, hugging himself—so Vanessa could stay with him now. It was by far the best plan anyway. "You've really let me down," he said to Rachel.

Rachel put her hand, her warm hand that he felt for a moment, before it turned plastic, on Benji's forearm. She leaned in. "I will make it up to you." Her smell! That smell was what held her muscles and organs together, it was all that made her human. "You know I will."

"Yeah?"

"Yes."

He crossed his arms.

"Okay?" she asked. "Ben?"

"Benji," he said, nodding, still looking at the floor. He felt her whole body around him, only it was plastic. "My name is Benji." He looked up. Her body was sharp and hard; it hurt him. "What's your fucking problem? Can't you even remember my name?"

# CHAPTER 13

# Parents' Day

Dennis and Sharon watched incredulously as their children got up to leave the table.

"Good to see things haven't changed," Dennis said as Vanessa slid out of the booth at the pizza parlor after Ben. "We pay; you split. Welcome to parenthood."

"Sorry, Dad," Benji said. "I feel really bad, but we have to go to this party, you know? It would be totally shit city if I didn't show."

"Well, we certainly wouldn't want that," Dennis said.

"What are you talking about?" Sharon said to Benjamin. "Who are you? And where, by the way, is this girlfriend of yours?" He hadn't said anything about her all through dinner.

"She was busy tonight."

"Too busy to meet us? Sounds like a nice girl." Sharon brushed the tabletop with the palms of both hands. Wheat germ fell like sawdust around her. "Another one of your nice girls." She smiled at her son.

"She is nice. You'd totally like her." Benji remembered the glass jars lining the door on the refrigerator—Kretschmer wheat germ, with the red label. His mother had started using it like bread crumbs, on chicken and fish, rolling anything she could in it, just to coat her food with it and shove it into them. No wonder his sister was so messed up about food.

"So where is she, Ben?" Dennis was starting to lose his temper. He'd had it with his children and this little frigging road trip.

"We got in a fight, okay? We had a fight. All right? Happy?" Ben said, as if stealing his father's thought.

Sharon paused and sat back. "Of course we're not happy to hear that, honey. We're very sorry." She looked at Dennis and then at her son. "*Very* sorry."

"Hmm," Benji said.

"Do you think you two will be able to work it out?" Sharon asked. "You really like this girl, don't you?"

"Woman. I really like this woman."

"Mom's just trying to help," Dennis said.

"Anyway, can you guys take us back to campus now?" Benji asked.

"Okay." Dennis looked at his watch. "Let me just pay here. Share, what do you want to do? It's early."

What brings about negative feelings? Sharon tried to call up something from her training, anything that might indicate that those sessions had been purposeful and transformative. Most often, negative feelings come from the way we *think* things should be, she thought. Let perfectionism go. It's up to you—it's up to me—to decide; resentment, is my own interpretation. Sharon threw her balled-up paper napkin, veined with sauce, onto the aluminum pizza tray, making a mental note to suggest to Marlene that they make mini-spinach-and-ricotta pizzas for their next outdoor affair. Elegant, and also comforting, she thought as she slipped the wheat germ back in her purse.

"Get back to campus on your own," she said. She held an image of her rage: there she was in her own home, punching out the windows of the living room. You are being *reactive*, Sharon thought. And then she thought, Damn it, this isn't *working*! Even Elias had packed off for another way. Least that's what she'd heard—someone from their basic training had said he had started over at PRISM, which espoused a totally new philosophy based on the play of light as taken from Genesis. Perhaps it had potential, she thought, trying to pull her hands away from the shattering glass in her imagination. "We're not your chauffeurs."

"Mom!" Vanessa said.

"Seriously, go on, go to your party." Sharon motioned for Dennis to stay seated and she smiled at them both. "Have fun!"

"Yeah." Dennis also smiled up at them. "Have a groovy time," he said sarcastically.

"You're not serious," Benji said. "Right?"

"No, I am serious," Sharon said. "Serious as a heart attack. We came all this way, and what have we done? We've waited for you at the dorm, we've waited for you at the student center, and now we're supposed to go back to the hotel and wait for you some more?" Sharon couldn't believe she was staying at yet another Marriott. Because it was such a long drive from home, they hadn't been there yet. They'd driven straight to Ben's dorm, but Sharon could imagine it with the same stain on the stucco ceiling as in Silver Spring. She remembered pulling back the thick polyester curtains for a view out onto the parking lot. "Well, we're tired of waiting for you. Your dad had a lot of work to do—you know there has been just so much stress with the embargo still on. Do you know what this has meant for your father's career?"

Dennis looked at her. What *had* it meant? he wondered, motioning for her to stop. "It's okay, it hasn't been that bad," he said, though he was tired of being in flux; he was tired of waiting to see what would happen.

"No, I won't stop," Sharon said. "It has been awfully stressful and it's just wrong, Benjamin, really, really wrong."

"Well, I'm sorry," he said. "But I hardly think you can blame me for the grain embargo."

"You should have boycotted that," Vanessa said as an aside. "You can be the boycotting boycotts specialist."

"I don't think I was blaming you, Benjamin, I'm merely explaining the context of the trip." Sharon tuned Vanessa out. "This was supposed to be fun!" she said, placing both palms gently on the table.

"Well, to be honest, Mom, I didn't ask you to come this weekend. If that's how you feel about it, we'll walk."

Vanessa looked at him. "Maybe I should just stay with Mom and Dad."

"Whatever!" Benji threw up his hands. "Do whatever."

"You should go too, sweetie," Sharon said, appealing kindly to Vanessa to increase the effect of her anger at Ben. "If we can't all be together, you should at least be able to spend a little time with your brother, whom we never see anymore."

"Okay, we're going," Benji said, not moving. "We're going to *walk* back to campus now."

Sharon ignored him. I choose not to risk vulnerability, she thought as she looked straight at her husband. She pictured him that first night in her Georgetown flat, looking down to unbutton his pants, a shock of hair falling over his eyes. Through the large window she could see onto the street; a young couple watched a police car whiz by. She wondered now where the couple had been headed. She was moments away from excruciating pain; how had she thought losing her virginity would be pleasurable? When, she thought now, was losing anything pleasurable? I want to take a risk, this is my choice. She remembered drinking wine with her husband, and eating foie gras on toast in the plaza of Sarlat after the day of boating so many years ago, and how all the buildings surrounding the plaza seemed so old and perfect they looked fake, drawn in by Walt Disney himself. When will this seem real? she had thought then. Her marriage? she had wondered. Her life? Or just that town?

We all have the possibility to break through. Sharon ran a finger along the fake wood of the pizza-parlor table. The pizza had been good, she had to admit; Ben had been right about the pizza.

That night in France she and Dennis had stayed in a castle outside town; the travel agent had told them it was advertised as haunted, by a woman from the sixteenth century whose husband had found her in bed with her lover. She'd been imprisoned there for more than twenty years. They had thought it would be fun to see a French ghost; a change from small-town American Gloria. Why not see as many ghosts as possible? Sharon had thought, before she became one herself. She and Dennis had sex in the enormous bathtub and, lulled by the warm sparkling wine they had bought in Vouvray and had drunk in their bathrobes, they went to sleep only to be awoken by streaks of lightning flashing in the room, while outside it was a clear, starry night. Then in the early hours of the morning a bat swooped in and flapped its wings over their bed. After Dennis had swept the bat out the window, he told Sharon he had felt a presence on the bed, a comforting weight seated next to him.

She had thought that the weight might be an omen to the future—everything that was to come. Now she saw so vividly that this ghost was not friendly—she was angry and spurned and wanted escape, and her weight was the unshakable weight of the past.

"It's far, you know—campus," Benji said. "It's pretty far and it's kinda cold out too."

"Hmm." Sharon ignored Ben. "What do you say, Dennis, wanna hit the town?"

Vanessa cleared her throat.

"Why, darling," Dennis said to his wife, "that sounds like the most marvelous idea."

After watching their children storm out of the pizza place, after they'd paid and gone to the parking lot, where they sat in Sharon's Volvo, waiting for the heat to kick in, Dennis came up with the idea.

"Let's go to the bar at the Ritz." He gripped the cold steering wheel tightly. The Ritz, on the Commons, was where Len used to take his Radcliffe girlfriend—one of the many Seven Sister coeds he'd dated— back when women were only allowed at the bar when escorted by a man. He didn't mention this part to Sharon, though he was sure the seventies had to have feminized the place.

"The Ritz-*Carlton*?" Sharon turned to face him. She looked down at her jeans—Calvins, yes, but not exactly Saturday night at the Ritz. "I'm not really dressed."

"Who cares?" Dennis could feel the moment deflating. Soon there would be endless debate, then it would turn into a search for another, more appropriate place somewhere deep in a city he barely knew. Dennis recognized that he would soon be sent back in to look in Franca's yellow pages, or worse, Sharon would ask people on the street without discretion. Well, he'd rather go watch the evening news at the Marriott on Route 128 and call it a night. But in an effort to abort what would surely be a depressing evening, what he said was "Don't be silly, you look great!"

"You know, you're right." Sharon swung her left shoulder out and smiled coyly. "Who cares, who the hell are we going to run into in this old town anyway?" Sharon slapped her leg. "Let's go!"

They pulled onto the Mass. Pike toward Boston, and simply by following signs to the Commons, they surprisingly got to the Ritz without so much as having to stop and ask for directions. This made Dennis proud, and he pulled up in front of the hotel, where the doorman, his double row of golden buttons sparkling, the metallic threads entwined in the ribbon shot through with light at the brow of his wool cap, a look not unlike that of the Russian police, waited for the car to stop.

"Welcome to the Ritz!" he said, opening Sharon's door, the gold braid appliqué along his sleeve illuminated in the lamplight. "Are you staying with us?"

"Just here for the evening." Dennis leaned over and winked, nodding to the enormous building, surprisingly modern. "Only a drink tonight."

"Well, have a lovely time, sir," the doorman said, taking the car keys in his white gloves, a gleaming button that snapped the glove closed at the white underside of his wrist.

Sharon took a deep breath and rubbed her palms on her thighs, as if she were readying for a jump. "Thank you," Sharon said, offering her good hand and stepping out of the car.

Even though it was a Saturday night, it was early enough that the lounge was not terribly busy. Sharon pounced on a cozy table with a candle flickering in its center, positioned by the far wall looking out onto the spectacular bar, shining so vibrantly it looked like fractured pieces of moonlight were reflected off its surface.

"Shouldn't we sit at the bar?" He hoped she would say yes; there was something so wonderful about saddling up to the bar and being greeted by the bartender, whether at Malarkey's or the Mayflower. The bar was always comforting, and Dennis appreciated that one could be any age or class or color, and still you were seated together, while also being pleasantly separate. Besides, he liked the long, sleek slab of polished wood so sturdy beneath his glass, able to withstand whatever he chose to place heavily upon it.

"But this is such a nice little table, all to ourselves," Sharon said.

He shrugged and imagined eating dinner at home with Sharon on so many nights, Vanessa out at the library or with her boyfriend, this table meant to sit four at the least. What was so great, so coveted, about just ourselves? "Whatever you want to do," he said.

"You know what?" Sharon interrupted, standing up. "The bar looks so nice and civilized tonight." And it did—the black veneer was set off by the dazzling array of liquor bottles and glassware behind it. "You like it up there, so why not?" She smiled at him and walked over to the bar. The year before Ben was born, she had met Dennis for lunch at the Dubliner on the Hill. They hadn't realized it was St. Patrick's Day, and due to the crowd and the limits on Dennis's time, they'd sat at the bar and eaten corned-beef sandwiches and drunk several pints of green beer. It turned out to be one of the more pleasurable meals she and Dennis had shared together, and she remembered being giddy from the beer and the buzzing crowd of congressional staffers and local Irishmen. They'd gone back to Dennis's office; Sharon had followed him along the long, gray, squeaky hallway, his secretary seated at the very end of it. They'd greeted her and walked into Dennis's office, where he'd shut the door behind her and kissed her so slowly against the wall. As she climbed onto one of the tall bar chairs, she remembered the slow, soft feel of his tongue that day and the hard Sheetrock against her back, the Freer Gallery just outside his office window.

"Hello," she said to the bartender, who came forward immediately. He was a young man with dark hair and sweet brown eyes, set a bit too close together. If she'd been in Washington, she would have thought perhaps he was some kind of Carter aide making extra pin money; in New York he'd have been an actor; surely he'd be a ski instructor in Denver; but she had no idea what this made him here in a town like Boston. He was too old to be a college student; perhaps it made him a handsome bartender.

"Hi." Dennis leaned on his hands and lifted himself onto the seat next to his wife.

"Welcome," the bartender said. "How are you tonight?"

"Just fine," Dennis said. "This is our big night out." He squeezed Sharon's hand below the bar.

"Well, what can I get you two?"

"What's good?" Sharon asked.

The handsome bartender smiled, which made Sharon think of politicians. "Everything's good; our cocktails are famous. But our martinis are infamous."

Sharon laughed. "I bet you've used that once or twice before."

"Never," the bartender said, smiling again. He had a dimple in his left cheek.

Several sturdy, frosted cocktail glasses were lined up behind the bar, stacked into a pyramid. "A martini sounds good." Sharon rubbed her hands together, imagining the clean, cold feel of the drink, a complement to that long-ago kiss. "Doesn't it, D?"

"Make it two." Dennis threw up two fingers with his right hand. "Lots of olives in mine."

"Vodka or gin?"

"Gin," Dennis said quickly.

"Real martinis are always with gin," the bartender said. "But people like their vodka."

"That they do," Dennis said. There he was again in that dining room of Soviets, shot glasses hitting the wooden table over and over as they plowed their way through bottle after bottle of Stolichnaya. He even ached for the most precarious parts of his pre-embargo job.

"Can you believe this weekend?" Sharon asked. "We've barely seen Ben at all."

Dennis shook his head and put aside his thoughts that in all the years of this war, such measures had never been taken. Never. What would have happened if the Export Admin Act had not been put into effect the year before? This embargo wouldn't have been able to happen, is what, Dennis thought. "Well, what did we expect? He's in college. I think we should be happy he's so busy. He was just terrific at that rally, wasn't he?" Tonight, Dennis resolved, I will focus on what is here and not what has gone missing. He laughed to hear himself thinking in one of his wife's LEAP!isms.

Sharon nodded, watching the bartender shake their martinis in his cocktail shaker, polished to such intensity she could see the reflection of the Japanese businessman two seats over, his face distorted in the curved silver. "He was great. Just great."

"A rally against the Olympic boycott? Only in college." Dennis shook his head again. Yet he and Ben were on the same page. Cutting off grain, cutting off sport . . . was it terribly reductive to wonder how different the consequences were?

"The Olympics are a big deal!" Sharon started. Then she laughed it off. "Well, you know how I love the Olympics."

"I do." Dennis smiled.

After a brief silence, Sharon said, "So we never met the infamous Rachel."

"Not yet. His first love." Suddenly Dennis visualized the first girl he'd fallen in love with. Ellen Brown. In many ways his adoration for her had been inspired by meeting Sissy Ford; Ellen too was blond—everywhere—and strewn with pearls, her accent straight off the boat, as in *yacht,* at Newport. "We'll meet her if she sticks around long enough," he said, but he didn't have a lot of faith in that happening. The martinis showed up, wobbly and perfectly chilled, his with four olives, hers with two.

"I just hope Ben isn't too upset." Sharon nodded a thank-you to the bartender. "He seemed like he really liked this one." She fingered her cocktail napkin, the Ritz lion's profile stamped in the center.

"Let's talk about something else. You know what would go well with this?" Dennis brought the martini to his lips.

"What?" Sharon leaned her head down and took a sip from her full glass.

"Pineapple!"

"Ha ha ha."

"I miss those skewers. Why did you ever stop serving them?"

"God, I don't know. I think it was after that awful dog nearly chopped off the Macintyre kid's head. Do you remember that?"

"Do I ever, my dear, I had to call Barry Brady just in case we got sued. That was before his son lost his mind. That poor family. Barry's partner says the kid's still in Psychiatric Institute. I hadn't realized Vanessa was actually friends with Ed Brady."

Sharon nodded, sipping from her glass. "This is delicious." Then, to the bartender: "This martini is magnificent!" She held it out for him to see.

Tonight his wife's insistence on involving herself with the bartender didn't annoy Dennis as it often did when they were out to dinner and she'd persist in engaging with the waiter or waitress, discussing anything from the weather to the hormones and chemicals in even the most select cuts of beef. "You served those pineapples years after that. This *is* tasty, isn't it?" He fished out an olive and popped it into his mouth, savoring the punch of salt against the smooth, clean gin.

"They weren't really good friends, I don't think."

Dennis looked at her.

"Vanessa and Ed Brady. I don't think they were good friends." Sharon took a big sip. "I think it was just boredom."

He nodded. "Well, what friendship isn't?" He laughed, then for a moment stopped, caught by his wife, who was so at ease tonight, her eyes glittering, lit by the candles around the room, the flames throwing shadows over the faces turned toward each other by the walls, and the twinkle of the crystal glasses, the many-colored liquors illuminating the back wall. He was even getting used to—appreciating, he might say—her more casual look: dungarees and turtlenecks, her hair down. He missed the way she wore it up when they went out, in a twist, with long, dangling earrings. He could still smell the faintest whiff of her perfume—it was a sharp, bright scent, not sweet at all. And he remembered a dress she wore—a Leonard of Paris dress; black with bright pink and yellow flowers splashed across it—that looked fantastic on her. She was a knockout in that dress, and Dennis realized he hadn't seen her decked out like that in ages.

They'd once gone out often, and they'd also had lovely, relaxed parties with Sharon's friends from college, with his colleagues, couples they had met through tennis and even some parents from the kids' school. Sharon would make fondue or paella, and the party—often bipartisan—would go into the morning. People argued over everything. Vietnam, China, ERA, John Updike, Watergate, Woody Allen. Fighting was how he and his friends talked to one another in those days, and Dennis missed that ease he no longer felt in Washington. He remembered Sharon in a long batik dress, the brown and mustard fabric crossed sexily at the neck and tied at the back, entering the living room with a huge steaming pot—she might as well have been carrying it on her head like an African—and placing it unceremoniously on the coffee table. Everyone ate with plates on their laps and drank wine from juice glasses.

Maybe, he thought, Sharon stopped throwing these bohemian parties when she started catering bashes for everyone else in town. Her parties at home got smaller and more uptight. They moved from sitting Indian-style in the living room to the dining table, draped in linen tablecloths and set with her mother's wedding china, from listening to Jim Croce to Vivaldi's *Four Seasons*. Dennis had thought, This is what aging is: more and more formality until you're in a tux in the goddamn grave. But maybe they had also outgrown their friends: some moved when Nixon was re-elected; some became diplomats and went overseas; some never had children and spent their free time traveling or in French cooking class together; a few just grew too exhausting. For the most part their friends were now extensions of their business acquaintances, and who wants to dip bread and gherkins into a hot pot of cheese with people who don't feel the least bit like family?

When had this all changed? The embassy parties they'd once loved for their little blips of glamour in a fairly frumpy town of government buildings filled with stuffy bureaucrats had become rote. They still went out to make and solidify connections; Sharon looked for clients higher and higher up in the echelons of Washington society, and Dennis was climbing higher into the bureaucracy of the town. What could he say? The closer one got to the president, the more likely one became a political appointee or, even better, a cabinet member. The election did not look so hot for the Dems, and by most accounts it looked as if Reagan would be the Republican nominee. And Reagan's big thing? Lifting the embargo, of course! After freeing the hostages. What an impossible town it will be with Ronald Reagan in office, thought Dennis as he sipped aggressively at his drink. It wasn't the first time he'd thought he might secretly vote for Anderson.

"What are you thinking?" Sharon leaned toward her husband. Since the accident, she felt she lacked any powers of seduction she may have once tenuously possessed. She knew she hid beneath her sweaters and her long pants, her hair.

Tonight, though, she felt relaxed, and as close to Dennis as she'd felt in those days before they'd decided to marry, when even the city looked new and clean and blooming. She noticed the crow's-feet at the corners of his eyes; other than this, and the little bit of a tummy, he hadn't really aged much. Most likely, she thought, from all her healthful cooking and the tennis he still played beneath the bubble at Racquet and Health each Saturday. There was no gray to speak of, nothing receding. In some ways this terrified Sharon; she had aged. She knew that she had, and she knew that she would. She was changing all the time; what if Dennis stayed the same?

"I'm thinking you look great," he said. "I'm thinking about that Leonard dress your mother bought you in Paris. I love that dress, do you still have it?"

"Oh, God, I haven't thought about that gown in ages. It's old!" Sharon pushed up her sleeves. She also adored that dress, the way the sleeves were slit up the side, giving the blousy effect of a kimono, and yet the way it was fitted at the waist and hips, tying at just the right place. It always made her feel sensational; why had she stopped wearing it? Fashion, she supposed, and she could no longer carry such a dress, not with this burnt-up arm, she thought, running her fingers over her scar. She still couldn't really feel with her hand, and touching it with the other produced the strangest ghostly sensation. "I wonder where it is," she said, picturing her closet, now filled mostly with long batik African shirts and turtleneck sweaters and blue jeans.

Dennis felt riotously happy and ordered them another round of drinks. "To ditching our beloved children," he said when the second drinks arrived.

Sharon gulped down the rest of the first. "To a great weekend after all!" She held up her glass and resisted her nearly reflexive urge to bring the handsome bartender over so she could find out exactly who he was and how he made such marvelous drinks.

The bar was filling quickly, but Sharon and Dennis hardly noticed. They continued to talk about nothing in particular, about their daily lives, which were inevitably connected—if sometimes chained—to the past: a dining room table regrettably not purchased, a lobster roll at Reds in Wiscasset on the way to Rockport the summer before Ben was born. Their lives were constructed on so many diminutive moments, and not all of them, Sharon noted, had involved their children.

After the third drink, Dennis excused himself from the bar and returned several minutes later. He placed a key on the bar in front of her.

"What's this?" She laughed. "A key to your heart?"

"No." Dennis looked at her sheepishly, and she thought not for the first time tonight of that young man she'd turned to see shuffling his feet as she opened the door to her place on Q Street. She had thought, I will take him to bed, and she had felt terribly transgressive, her mother's warnings hardly registering. Then we will see, she'd thought. "A room with a view."

"Dennis!" She swatted his hand. "With a view!" She threw her head back just a bit, her hair swishing behind her. "But we already have a room."

"We are not going to that dismal Marriott over a wretched highway." Dennis leaned over his wife and, placing his hand at her nape, kissed the top of her head. Then he sat down in his own seat. "Our bags are still in the car, my dear, and tonight we're staying at the Ritz." He told the bartender, when he finally got his attention, "One more round." To Sharon he said, "I confess, though, I couldn't drive back to Waltham if you paid me right now, and a room with a view was all they had left."

Their bags had already been retrieved from the car and carried to the room when they entered, and the curtains were pulled back, leaving in their stead a midnight blue sky and a lit skyline with the white steeple of Park Street Church bisecting the center, pasted over the night. Washington, D.C., is so low to the ground, thought Sharon as she ran to the window, only to trip on the leg of one of the overstuffed chairs crammed into the beautiful but small room. She toppled onto her side and sat up on the plush rug.

"Your arm!" Dennis gasped.

She held it up, laughing hysterically. "Still here."

Dennis remained by the doorway, shaking his head. "You are such a klutz!" The moonlight cast an eerie light in the room, and for a moment Dennis considered a moon salutation.

Sharon sat on the floor, her legs splayed before her. "I know." She wiped her eyes and went to lean on the chair for leverage.

Dennis came over and reached down to help her up. "You have to be more careful, Share."

She groaned more than necessary as she rose to her feet. "I'm getting old!"

"You're getting clumsier, if that's possible." Dennis held on to both of her hands. His thumb traced one of the thick, corded sections of her scar. What if she had gone up in flames? It was not like him to think so catastrophically, but he imagined Sharon in her eighties and falling this way. Really, he thought, she needed to pay more heed to her surroundings.

"Thanks," she said. The sky opened up behind her, luminous and lovely, an invitation toward any horizon.

The mood had rather abruptly shifted from the gaiety of the bar, the clanking of glasses, music, their drinking and general good cheer, and it felt suddenly as if they'd been on a date, and now that awkward moment that would decide if there would be a kiss, if the evening would continue, or if it would all just end right here.

There was silence between them as there hadn't been in hours. Sharon walked to the window, her original destination, and she stood at the side of it, gazing out over the Commons, her body silhouetted against the sky. Dennis watched her face in profile, that long nose reaching down, the static in her hair setting several frayed ends vertical. He imagined taking out his clarinet—something he hadn't done since the kids were small—his own silhouette bending back, his instrument held high, set over the sky as he played.

He made his way over to her, and Sharon watched in the glass as he came toward her, his body moving between the lights and the modern buildings, fractured through the branches of the leafless trees. The high from the drinks was already turning into an ache at the front of her head, and she felt overwhelmingly sad for what she had done. She would take it back if she could, take back everything that had come after the day she walked into LEAP! If she could, she'd return to the time when she and Dennis were first married, when the Jews and the blacks sat together, before Selma, before Kennedy was shot, before Vietnam. Everything was happy then, who cared that it was pathologically delusional? What had happened—to them, to the world—in between those two frames?

"Dennis." She turned toward him. "Darling, I've missed you." She was sobbing when Dennis took her slowly and silently into his arms, and they stood for several moments embracing beneath the city lights.

Dennis bent down to kiss away his wife's tears, first the left eye, then the right, then the cheeks, wet and salty, down to the mouth his lips had not touched other than to peck hello and good-bye and good night for longer than he cared to remember. Her mouth was soft and wet with sadness, and it kissed him deeply, as if it were the first time she was discovering the taste of him.

As they made their way to the bed—pulling back the comforter that neither trusted to have been cleaned, not even at the Ritz—Sharon imagined that what they were doing now erased what had been done before. Removing Dennis's shirt and unbuttoning his pants, helping him step out of his briefs, then peeling her own jeans and shirt off and crawling into bed with him, she believed she could obliterate the memory of Elias, his body coarse and spent and enjoyed by many, in comparison to Dennis's fleshy and pristine skin, which appeared less used. She had certainly slept with Dennis since she'd started up with Elias, but tonight as she crawled into her husband's body, she felt as if she were going back into her casing, back home, returning to who she was when they'd first met, to that first weekend in Skatesville.

Her past, the far past, rose to the surface, and as she wrapped a hand around Dennis, already erect, she thought so sadly of those heady days of sexual languor. She saw an open window, sun pouring in the late morning, that focused eastern light, an altogether different feel from the expansive light that fell over Los Angeles. The exquisiteness had even kept jittery Gloria quiet. There had been dinners, the two of them, just pasta and butter and some grated cheese and jelly jars of crappy red wine, and afterward they'd brought their glasses onto the porch and sat on the splintered wooden porch swing, her head in his lap, his fingers tracing her forehead and moving strands of hair from her face, slowly rocking, the trees heavy with the flapping of birds' wings and the prospect of rain. Once a white-tailed deer had run up to the house and stopped suddenly, as if embarrassed. The deer had looked straight at them. Sharon had risen slowly, to face her, but she had quickly spooked, running off toward the mountains.

And now as Dennis made his way into her, the two of them facing each other, Sharon saw both their past and the future, whose promise she'd forgotten somewhere in between shopping for farm-fresh produce, ordering minerals by phone, leaving business cards tastefully by the door of every catered affair, and fucking a homeless person. She imagined Dennis as an old man, his eyelids sagging as his father's had, his fair skin, his mother's legacy, wrinkling suddenly, one summer of too much sun at Rehoboth, and she imagined fitting into him this way still. This gave her what she had not felt for months now, which was relief.

She had not realized when she'd marched into the first LEAP! training session that it was this, and not freedom, she was seeking. What was freedom anyway? She had marched for it and had picketed for it, and, yes, she had cooked for it, but what *was* it? She had not found relief in the arms of another man, nor had she found it on her own personal, if unfinished, journey. A crooked passage. Children, she thought now—still with a pang for Ben's departure, the day she watched him throw that huge green duffel into the trunk of the Volvo without even a look back to the house they'd raised him in—they bring you closer, yes, but they also separate you. They bring your bodies together, then they insist on their separation. Children divide you, she thought now, though it was not a pleasant thought. Our children have divided us.

Dennis was inside his wife, and her breasts were sealed to his chest, her legs pulled so tightly around him, her heels gripping his bottom, and he felt that he was going to come. Just like those times when he was still stunned by the warm, pillowy sensations of her body. He stopped for a moment and kissed her ear, then her neck, which made Sharon rock harder, the pressure in him welling. He sucked one nipple, then the other, and she groaned, moving harder against him, and Dennis loved his wife, he did not know how he had forsaken her, and he did not know how he had lived without that love. Perhaps leaving the country as often as possible was a way to alleviate its loss, but here it was before him, around him, and it was also in every memory they'd shared, their bodies young, and now aging, their children, they had *children* together, and their children would both be gone too, and it would be just them, back to when it had begun, and tonight, Sharon had chosen him. He had not felt his wife, the center of her, which he was touching now, for a long time, and she began to breathe heavily and he could feel her pulsing as she moaned into his shoulder, then finally, as if it were the first time, he had finally—finally!—broken through, he let himself go.

"We should call the kids," Sharon said. The curtains had remained flung open to the beckoning city, and the moon illuminated their luggage.

"Whatever for?" Dennis asked, running his fingers along her forearm. Her hair stood on end and her flesh goose-bumped.

"So they know where we are," she said, sitting up. "They're our kids."

"Don't remind me."

"We always make them tell us where they are. Nice to return the favor." Sharon reached for the phone and dialed Ben's dorm room.

"How egalitarian of you."

"Thank you." She smiled. "And we should make a plan for having a meal together before leaving, don't you think?"

Dennis nodded.

"I'm not going to ask. I'm just going to state it as fact." Sharon bobbed her head decidedly.

The phone rang—even Sharon had no illusions that her son would be there—and she got his machine. It was Arnie: *You've reached Arnie and Benji!* He seemed so thrilled to say their names together, which Sharon understood. *We're not here, so leave a message and maybe we'll call you back!*

Sharon spoke clearly and distinctly into the phone. "Hope you had fun tonight, kids. Let's have breakfast together before we head home, okay?" She hit her knee with her fist for not making the sentence imperative. Say what you mean and it will be, she thought. "We'll be by before ten." She also explained their change of plans and where they could be reached, just to provide an *example* of considerate behavior. "At the Ritz," she said, trying not to giggle. "We decided to stay at the Ritz tonight."

They lay naked, Sharon sprawled across Dennis's chest.

"D, I'm so sorry," she'd whispered after, and there it was. She had not planned on saying it, and as it had slipped out, she hadn't wondered at what her husband would do with it later. But she *was* sorry. She knew this was really the end with Elias. Somehow she had always kept it in the back of her mind that she could call him, that she might call him. That if she decided to go on to the next phase of her training, she would see him there again. Maybe he would leave PRISM and come back, a blade of grass singing between his teeth, his satchel on his back. But tonight she knew she was done with all of it.

Dennis was grateful that she hadn't said more, hadn't reduced a stereotype into agonizing cliché by telling him, *You've just been away so much* or *You didn't see me* or *It's not that I ever stopped loving you.*

He did not trouble himself with the details or with imagining what she had done with someone else, the way her back dipped when she clenched her thighs around this nameless, faceless person. As soon as he tried to picture the man, he could see only himself, and only himself as he appeared in photographs. There he was in a green army parka beneath her; or in shorts and a faded red T-shirt, *Capitalism Is Boring* printed in black, a hole cut out at his hip where in his imagination Vanessa was excised from the photo as he made his way into his wife from below her. Tomorrow it will be different, Dennis knew; there would be details that would thrust him out of this image, the way someone is pushed from the tight frame of a crowded photograph. He thought of getting off the plane in Moscow, and slipping into the backseat of the car and thinking that life stopped everywhere but here. No one moved when he left them; he only saw evidence of his family in photographic-like images when he was away: Benjamin just after scoring a goal, his arms stretched above his head; Sharon at the kitchen table, planning a menu; his parents eating soup, the kitchen at twilight. He had been ignorant to believe their lives had stopped and only resumed when he returned. He felt Sharon twitch over him, and he made to accommodate her at his neck. Then, as he reached for a new image, one from tonight, the night he found his wife again, Dennis slipped quickly to sleep.

# CHAPTER 14

# Trips

**March 23, 1980**

The harsh ring of the telephone jolted a still-tripping-but-somehow-managing-to-sleep Benji out of bed. At first he had no idea where he was, so he called out to the dark for assistance. Hello? he said to the room, whose walls were caving in, the keys of the typewriter on the desk swirling, a line of books above it dancing on the shelf. The response came from the receiver.

"Hello," a man's voice said. "Hello?"

The blind that shaded the single dorm window—each plastic slat heavy with dust—was furled open, and the light from the buzzing safety lamps lining the quad cast a blue haze over the room and helped Benji's eyes adjust to the dark. He soon registered that he was in a dorm room, and that it was, thankfully, his own dorm room. He tried to let himself go. Don't fight it, he thought, just let it come in. Easy. Slowly the images of the next bed, empty but for two large stuffed teddy bears—*Twins!* Arnie had proudly said—with which Benji had a vague recollection of trying to copulate came into focus. He'd had the idea they were really twins, hot little girl twins, last night.

Last night!

"Yes, hello," he said into the phone.

"I'm looking for Dennis C. Goldstein. Is this he?"

What did the *C* stand for? Benji wondered. He'd never heard it used before; he never knew his father even had a middle name. "This is his son. Who is this? It's . . ." The voice sounded so . . . conservative. Benji craned his head to look at Arnie's clock radio—his had stopped halfway between 1:38 and 1:39 over a month ago, and it was still caught there like an eyelid frozen while blinking. "Nearly four in the morning."

Benji's heart rose in his throat. They're confused! he thought.

They're coming for me because of my protest, because of that stupid television interview. Because of *communism*.

"I realize that."

Perhaps this was a joke. "Schaeffer?" Benji said tentatively.

"No."

Benji was still tripping—how had he ever fallen asleep? The teddy bears beckoned him with open arms, radiating blue in the lamplight, and he was momentarily aroused by them. He thought about sex easing the journey into and out of the two worlds and how rarely he had come down from a trip without it. Sex and pot. Perhaps, he thought now, this was due to endorphins.

"I am looking for Dennis C. Goldstein."

"Okay, you said that." Benji sat up straighter. "Are you a friend of my father's?" Benji knew his father counted several Republicans among his friends, including Len, who Benji always found incredibly Southern and dangerous. He smoked rolled cigarettes, ignored his two sons, and mumbled lewd comments about Sharon's mother.

"I'm afraid I'm not at liberty to discuss this. I'll just say there's some government business. If he's not there, could you please tell me where he can be reached?"

Benji paused.

"We can just as easily find him ourselves, son. Boston is a very small town."

"How do you know he's in Boston?"

"We know."

Was that a joke? "They're at the Waltham Marriott," Benji said, but as the words came out, he had a shadowed idea that this was no longer correct. He remembered coming to his room. He hadn't been alone but he had heard messages. "Wait. I think they may have left that hotel."

Had one of the messages been from this guy? Why would his father switch hotels so suddenly? Perhaps, Benji thought, his father was on the *lam*? Just as Nana Helen always said.

Benji stood up. "If you hold on a moment, I can tell you for sure."

"All right then," the man said.

Benji placed the phone on the bed and went over to the answering machine on his desk. He pressed play. *Dude! That was boss today . . .* Benji fast-forwarded to the next call. *Benji,* Rachel said. *Hope it went well today. I hope I get to meet your parents later, I . . .* The next: *You're on*

*TV right now!* . . . Then: *Hey, big guy, I just saw you on TV!* And finally, his mother's voice: *We're at the Ritz,* she said, giggling. The sound of her laughter—intimate and secretive—repulsed him almost as much as her exhaustive tears had.

"He's at the Ritz," Benji said, finally picking up the receiver from the folds of his bedspread. A roach sat on the table by his bed, and he scanned the table for a lighter. "My parents are at the Ritz.

"You're so fucking welcome, man," Benji said into the receiver when he heard the click on the other end of the line.

He found a lighter under his pillow and lit up and lay back. Just let it come, he thought, fending off the raw, dirty feeling, his insides scooped out. Easy. Perhaps he should call his parents? Wait, he thought, staring up at the ceiling, peering at the stars pasted in the shape of all the constellations. Rachel had put them up a few days after they'd come back from the all-too-short bus trip with the science grads. She had come in when Arnie was in New Haven with the Madrigals, and Benji had been in class, and not until they turned out the lights and crawled into bed did he see the entire solar system, the stars and planets, the rings of Saturn, and the constellations, her sign of Gemini designated by the largest, brightest stickers, his Scorpio as small and insignificant as the rest of the zodiac. He couldn't have been asleep long; they were still lit ever so dimly, as if they were dying, Benji thought now, old stars.

Wait, he thought now, what just happened? The night was vague to him—blearily he tried to focus on how he had gotten home. He remembered walking through a thick fog, aware of each individual dust particle, every single hanging drop suspended, and together as one body, creating the mist he walked through. He had felt as if it were a doorway leading to another world, though he was traveling there alone.

The phone call had to have been a joke. Schaeffer or Peter Cox was having a belly laugh over Benji's fear and the way he'd just did his father in right now. But the joke would surely have been that some government official—from the CIA or the FBI, say—was looking for him, not his dad?

Benji looked at the phone for several moments and decided to call his parents. He dialed information for the number of the hotel, then promptly forgot the number just as soon as he'd hung up. He picked up a paperback from the night table—*Pilgrim's Progress,* from Arnie's humanities class—and an uncapped pink highlighter and wrote the number down on the inside back flap of the book on the second call to information. When he got through to the Ritz, he was told by the receptionist that the line in his parents' room was in use.

Where was Arnie? he wondered, quickly distracted by the thought of how, whenever he might have appreciated his roommate's absence, he was always in the next bed ready to chat about his day selling textbooks and Mead notebooks and *Brandeis Judges!* T-shirts and pencils at the campus store. Even if Rachel was with Benji in bed, Arnie would blather on and on about his studies, his drama group, the set list for his next recital. Night, guys, he'd say, before leaning over to turn out the light, and Benji would be unable to keep his hands from at least skimming over Rachel's warm body.

Wait. Benji sat up. He looked over at the empty bed. Wait, Benji said out loud. Just wait! He cut the air with his arm.

Where the fuck was his sister?

Like Benji, Vanessa had no idea where she was when she was roused by the sound of incessant drumming, punctuated by several shrieks and yelps. A lava lamp—the shape-shifting globs of red and yellow—shed a wan aura of golden light in the room, faintly illuminating a desk scattered with a half semester's accumulation of books and papers, a luminous typewriter. Balled-up socks, dispelled from the mass of laundry by the closet, littered the room, along with several basketballs and baseballs and an assortment of tapes, some crushed, ribbons unspooling, others flung out of their cassette cases, all glowing, like a range of rare insects crawling throughout a tropical-forest floor. Two enormous bongs—one by the bed, a red cylinder circled by colored teddy-bear stickers and red, white, and blue skull stickers, the other by the closet, a clear shaft marked in gradations from light to dark by evidence of smoke. Smack in the middle of these two anchors, there— here—was Ben's friend Schaeffer, incandescent in the changing colored lamplight, pacing the room and slicing the air with karate chops, each cut interposed by a grunt or yell.

Vanessa closed her eyes and lay back down on the bed, slamming her head onto the stripped, stained pillow, where she was overwhelmed by the heady mix of smells: the scent of Ben's room after practices— sweaty balls and armpits, old socks, jockstraps—and also bong water and patchouli. The sharp and crushing fetor made Vanessa feel she would soon asphyxiate, and she lifted her head from the pillow to sit up. But it wasn't just the pillow; the air was also thick, acute with the stench of old beer, the sickening sweetness of pot or maybe opium, thick cotton layers of trapped cigarette smoke. Vanessa leaned over to open the window and dangled her head into the unenclosed air, breathing in the eerie predawn. The odor of dew and stored, impending weather, the tree branches with their scent of crooked, brittle bones, also became unbearable, and Vanessa ducked back inside, hitting the top of her head on the sill.

"Ouch!" Vanessa rubbed her fingertips in circles along her head, both to ease the blow and to check for blood. She brought her hand close to her face. The red light from the lava lamp cast a warm glow over her skin, and for a moment she thought it was blood.

Her head began to ache, an all-over feeling at the front of her forehead, more like what she had once called a hangover than the focused pain of an injury. She remembered throwing up the morning after a Crosby, Stills and Nash concert at Wolf Trap, where she and Bee and Heather and Jessica had drunk several beers out of massive plastic cups and sat on the lawn on Heather's mom's quilt. An older couple, ex-hippies seated cross-legged on a Mexican blanket, kept passing them joints, the woman telling the girls over and over, *You remind me of me! All of you!* as her husband rocked to the music, hands placed on his knees, his eyes closed.

Vanessa recognized a hangover, but she was also subdued by confusion; she watched Schaeffer for clues, searching for information about him, something that might indicate anything about herself. What time was it? She realized then she had no idea what time *was,* or how it operated, the way it moved and flowered, creating forward motion, age and wisdom, escape from the despondency of youth. Until time stopped, and with it, life. She was starving. Or, no, was she dreadfully full? She imagined filling herself up without remorse or redemption from her toes to the tippy top of her head, but as she envisioned herself at some baroque table filled with torn-open melons and figs, the cooked thighs of massive beasts, golden goblets overflowing with wine, feasting with kings, she realized that her mouth was not her mouth. These were not her teeth, she thought, knocking on a front tooth with the knuckle of her index finger, unable to feel the impact.

"Can I have a cigarette?" she asked Schaeffer.

"Hey!" he said, as if he had neither seen nor heard her wake, nor registered the thrashing up and down in bed, the opening of the window, the screech from the head wound. "How's it going!" he said cheerily. He came over to the bed and shut the window. "Brrr, kitty."

The music bore down on her with a steel weight; she felt her head would explode from the pressure of unending drumming. The torturous sound came through the walls and began entering into her body through her pores. "I need a cigarette," she said.

"Absolutely." Schaeffer handed Vanessa one of his Camels. "Here you go." He unfolded her hand carefully and placed the cigarette inside it, a gift, gently folding her fingers around it.

"Why are you up?" Vanessa placed the cigarette between her lips, where it dangled for a moment. I am James Dean, she thought. Then she gagged and spit the Camel out. "What *was* that?" she said, feeling the waxy sensation of a candle.

"It's a cigarette, sweetie." Schaeffer cupped Vanessa's face in his hands. "Just like you wanted." He smashed her head to his heart. "Just what you needed."

"Okay." Vanessa's face felt good in his hands, supported, and she waited a moment at his chest before looking down to fish for her lighter in the pocket of her jeans. How long had it been since she'd left the party with Schaeffer? She remembered being on top of the tower of an old castle. They'd wandered around and found an entrance to the stairwell, through the laundry room, and run up the spiral staircase, the old brick walls filled with decades of graffiti, the hauntings of previous parties; perhaps Abbie Hoffman had written on these walls, she'd thought. Angela Davis. *Criminals!* They'd reached the top and gone outside, where they'd stood stood at the lip of the tower, shivering. He had placed her head in his hands then, and Vanessa remembered a kiss, the swell of air, the grand sweep of a foreign town blanketed beneath a sky pierced with stars.

Vanessa's fingers—no longer her fingers, did that make them Schaeffer's?—skimmed her hips as she searched for her lighter, but they could not locate her pocket. These fingers could not locate the jeans either. "My clothes!"

Schaeffer, who had darted back across the room, sat at his disorderly desk, the chair turned out, his legs crossed. He grinned. "I just took another tab about an hour ago, you want one?"

Vanessa shook her head. She remembered clearly racing back down the staircase of the tower, then slowing as they hit the ground and began walking back to his dorm, her hand welded to his. Vanessa had a less clear memory of warmth and safety, the feeling of the heavy weight of animal skin spreading over her. She remembered the sweet feeling of mutual desire, of two people wanting to trade pelts.

Now she felt confusion and also tremendous, unmitigated fear. She had imagined she was a princess in that tower, a Barbie princess, just like the one Nana Helen had gotten for her. A princess like the one her mother had relented to let her be one Halloween. Go ahead and let her, Sharon, she's a *girl,* her father had pleaded on her behalf. You always insist that feminism is so damn flexible. Vanessa remembered closing her eyes as her mother brushed blue and purple eye shadow along her fluttering lids and tied long white ribbons in her hair with a sigh, then turned her around to resignedly zip her long pink dress up the back.

When had Vanessa stopped wanting to be a princess? It had probably been the day her father had cast her as a witch. Wearing that awkward mask—living for an entire Halloween night behind it—had been uncomfortable, yes, but it had freed her. And who's this? everyone said so loudly upon opening the door. Appearing unrecognizable and ugly made her sink into her inner state, and she had enjoyed watching people scan her for some clue that might give away the identity of the clumsy girl behind this perverse, bulging mask. How much easier it was to be a witch. No one would ever know you.

But now Vanessa's thoughts turned from fairy princesses and ivory towers to sleeping in a row of girls in a moldy camp cabin. She remembered Raymond, who taught photography, dark and enigmatic; all the girls scampered with their hands over their mouths when he came to their side of camp. She remembered a darkroom, the photos coming to life beneath the red light. Like this light, Vanessa thought, watching the lava lamp throw colored shadows onto the wall, remembering the smell of the chemicals and his close breath. Look here, he'd said, through this little pinhole. She had been picked by Raymond; she had felt chosen and wanted, and only when she had become a counselor herself had she thought of how she had been crushed by that challenge. She was careful with her own campers to make them feel equally adored, though it was hard not to always take the hand of Laura Erlinger, who sat outside the group at lunchtime, the one who made spectacular God's eyes, and whom Vanessa knew would one day bloom into someone magnificent.

From the castle to the cabin, to here in this dorm room and the devastating realism: I am in the world alone, she thought, angered at her brief, delusional period of wanting to be beautiful. She thought of Jason and felt the weight of her metal heart dropping. "I'm all alone!" she said.

"No!" Schaeffer hurled himself to the edge of the bed. "No, you're not ever alone. We're in this world together." He took both her hands in his and shook them, then kissed the top of her head. "Wow. I see so many colors in the fibers of your hair. A whole kaleidoscope of colors."

Vanessa threw the covers back from the bed and stood up. Did he really have *Sesame Street* sheets? Big Bird soothed her temporarily, for a moment tethering her to the happy memory with Ben on their parents' bed, arms flush, chins in their palms, waiting for everyone to see Mr. Snuffleupagus already! Ohmygod, where's Ben? she thought. She had waved to him from the tower above as he'd stood outside with his girlfriend. Had it been his girlfriend? Just as she tried to remember the figure of the girl silhouetted beside her brother, Vanessa was overtaken by the sound of outrageously loud drums; she'd never heard music this amplified. As she stood, the air felt cold around her body, and she went to wrap herself in the sheet, but stopped herself in brief appreciation of all her body's parts, pleased that she could see all of her at once.

"I'm going," she said.

"Okay. You sure?" Schaeffer had pulled his chair in close to the desk and was pressing random typewriter keys, his head tipped low. At the same time, one hand kept pushing the release lever, the platen moving back and forth and back again.

"Bye."

"Whatever is best for you," he said, his eyes now trained on the type bars.

Vanessa walked into the community part of the suite, empty but for the colossal mess, that disorder special to careless, privileged young men, and then into the stairwell leading out of Rosenthal. She felt the cold tile beneath her bare feet as she took the stairs two at a time, rushing out the back door of the dormitory. Outside, she breathed in and out, stomped her feet, and rubbed her naked arms for warmth. A mentholated breeze blew through her legs, and before her the field, the same one Ben's roommate had made such a fuss over, appeared out of the gloaming. Vanessa imagined the grass receiving her gladly, each blade of the lawn with its own soft welcoming, and she could tell it smelled only of grass, deeply of grass, grass like summer camp, grass like the front yard of her parents' house, plain green grass like Randall Park, where once she and Jason and Sean had all gone together. She remembered the way Sean had skated alone, jumping onto the rails, bending his knees and reaching down to grab his board, making sure they were both watching him. How they had both watched him. He was so lithe and easy in his skin; they both loved him. It was a perspicuous image, its outlines as clear as the image of the *Hollywood* sign she would never forget driving toward so many times with Nana Helen—There it is! Helen would say. Don't let it break your heart. And Vanessa thought of Jason, warm, safe Jason, who expected nothing from her and so received it.

The soft earth against her feet besieged her entire body. She wanted such intensity to stop, and for the whole night to end, to go backward prior to this weekend, before Sean had wrapped their house in toilet paper, before she'd climbed into the backseat of the car and driven with her parents to this dreadful place. Vanessa was freezing and she looked down to see her body, white against the earth and the lightening sky. She noted how thin and frail she looked, her skin goosefleshed, each pore bristling with the erection of its tiny hair, limbs trembling.

Vanessa stood in the middle of the field and held up her arms, exalted. In this moment, this one single moment in a lifetime of moments, she did not look at her body with disgust. She mimicked a salutation to the sun, picturing her father in the basement.

Ecch, Vanessa thought now, lowering her arms. She went to spit out the memory, but her tongue was stitched with thread, each strand hanging from her mouth. She tried to direct her tongue into forming words by moving these threads as one would impel a marionette, but there was only sensation: the smell of her father's sweat and Ben's sweat, and also the sweat of Schaeffer's room, and Schaeffer's sweat, slick on his skin, and then her own when she skimmed his stomach as he moved her on top of him, skinning her.

Vanessa lowered herself down to the earth and onto her side, curling up in the grass, just as soft and silent as she had hoped and known it would be.

In that eerie moment between night and daybreak, cloud cover reflected in the inky water of Yakus Pond, Benji got out of bed to look for Vanessa. He'd debated it for what seemed like a while, then realized what he'd first dreaded: his sister was still not there. Leaving the dorm,

Benji pulled on and zipped up the frayed gray hood of his high school soccer sweatshirt and set out toward the castle. As he tromped along the edge of the pond, he wished for daylight savings, for dawn to break early, for the long, sunlit days when girls ran around campus braless, their nipples, cold and hard as buttons, pressing into halter tops worn long before encouragement from the weather.

Memories of the previous night made their way to him in a series of undulations, gaining and receding in his consciousness. He remembered Andy and Larry's room in the tower, the rounded walls swelling as if with breath, and he remembered sitting Indian-style facing a girl on Andy's bed. Alice! It had been Alice, from the registration booth, showing him how to place his hands, palms together, at his heart center. He had closed his eyes and breathed, as instructed, a loud *ohhhm,* humming pleasantly through his body, calming him.

Had he left the party with Alice? He remembered walking out the door, past Rachel, wishing instead he'd had a cheerleader on his arm. Now he couldn't believe his cruelty; he'd been so pleased by Rachel's face, fallen, like one of his mother's soufflés ruined by the dribbling of a soccer ball through the kitchen. He remembered kissing Alice at his desk—her skin was freckled and white; her mouth was dry— and then she had sat on his answering machine, the messages playing Rachel's voice: *Hope it went well today . . .* Benji was brought out of his momentary miasma of wanting a newly upholstered Rachel, someone who came to his rally and worked there, and he had pulled back and asked Alice to leave. Just like that; Benji thought he might even have pointed a finger toward the door, because he had thought, I am just like Lincoln, and he had imagined the memorial, Abraham Lincoln's stern finger pointing out across the Mall and toward the Washington Monument, along with all the people who stood, brave and beautiful, chanting for the war to end, now, now, NOW.

Poor Alice, he thought, remembering her hesitation at the door, a watery look, beseeching him, before she opened it and walked out. How he could have done that—*regressed*—he had no idea, but now he looked south at the horizon, the clouded darkness suspended above him, and knew it was the same sky suspended over Rachel, curled up, warm, asleep in her room. He tucked his hands in the center pocket of his sweatshirt, the fingers of each hand touching the thickness of the zipper that divided them, as if he were being banned from his own body's warmth.

But now Benji's body sang with guilt. He thought of Rachel, then the look on his mother's face, astonished that his evening plans did not include her. And his sister! Her eyes had cast downward as he placed the hit of acid on his tongue and closed his eyes. The weight of their disappointment! Then the defiance in his sister's eyes—those huge eyes, lidded heavy like a movie star's, he'd always thought—as she placed the tab on her own tongue. Had his sister been there when he'd left with Alice? His memory stopped there, and ashamed at his selfishness, he wondered at the places on this campus—or worse, in town—she could have ended up.

Benji quickened his march up the steps along the path to Usdan, on his way to the Castle, a decent place as any to start his search. It was nearing six o'clock, anyone still at the party and not crashed-out would be a disaster. His shame transformed quickly into paranoia. What had happened to his sister? he thought as he headed toward Chapels Field. What had he allowed to happen to her?

Walking toward the field made him slip back to yesterday, the high of the rally, then the worry over what he'd told that reporter. He had actually said the word *revolution*. He thought of his grandfather: we were under the spell of it, Sigmund had said. It all went back to the workers, 1917. Yet couldn't anything new have meaning? Let's just say it didn't last; was there no value in something sudden and vibrant and, yes, important, even if it could not last?

Benji knew their protest had been fruitless, that it had stood for nothing. He saw Professor Schwartz's face, his raised eyebrows, which managed to tell Benji, *This is wrong and your grade will reflect this*. The sixties, Schwartz was always telling them, is gone. What will replace it? *This? You?*

Why *not* me? Benji thought, looking out onto the field, where only two days ago he was one of many at the beginning of an idea they believed would inspire change. They had sat at tables and had conviction in the promise of their cause, and inside the pleasant bubble of his fervor, Benji had felt purposeful, as he had when he'd stood anywhere with Rachel, for anything she'd wanted, as he'd felt swaying back and forth, the Dead playing in the waning autumn light, as he'd felt that day he came upon his grandfather in a history book, everything connected, the time line extended by the tip of a finger to meet his.

Now he felt severed from the cause, unbound to his personal history, his future, estranged from his own limbs. He noticed something stacked in the center of Chapels Field, at the very spot where all the shadows of these religious buildings met, cast-off tennis rackets and lacrosse sticks left behind yesterday perhaps. It looked like the land of misfit toys. Yet as he moved toward the equipment, stark white even in the moonless, predawn sky, the pile seemed to stir. Or perhaps I am just still tripping, he thought, tiptoeing closer and closer, his heart filling with dread as the wooden rackets and field-hockey sticks turned into a pair of legs rising and falling in the grass.

"Hello?" he called out.

Dawn was breaking; Benji could see a sliver of orange peeking out from beneath the cloud cover. He heard a groan.

"Hey there!" he said, running toward the sound, and now, standing before it, he saw the naked figure, a bag of gray bones spilled out onto the grass.

"Vanessa," Benji said, kneeling down. He unzipped and removed his sweatshirt. "Sweetheart." He turned her over from her side and tried to cover each part of her nakedness, the tiny breasts and sunken belly, hip bones protruding, the sparse brown-haired triangle of her crotch. A line of fuzz ran up from her pelvis, bisecting her stomach. "Vanessa." Benji tried not to cry as he propped her up from behind and wrapped her tightly in his sweatshirt and then in his arms, and then, even his head, tucking his chin over her shoulder. There she was crying on her bed, the wooden figures of her Russian doll in chaos before her on the wrinkled brown and pink bedspread. I think I lost the littlest one! she'd sobbed. "Come on," he said, lifting her now. She turned toward him in the driver's seat, tanned and freckled, a space between her teeth revealed only as she laughed, the Volvo jerking out of the driveway. And there—just there; smoke through a keyhole, it was true—they were together, side by side on the hammock, hands outstretched in the heavy netting as the soft lights in each room of that red-brick house clicked off one by one. One day we will live in a city, they'd said, looking up at the variegated suburban night. So many years and yet here on this field that seemed to be gathering its own light she weighed nothing. "I'm sorry," Benji said, shaking off many burdens. Still he heard the song. *If you should stand, then who's to guide you?* "I'm so so sorry." His focus here was clear. *If I knew the way . . .* He wondered, just as he said it, what it would mean exactly, but still he told his sister, his little sister, "Vanessa," he said. "Let me take you home."

# CHAPTER 15

# Eat Your Heart

**March 23, 1980**

The phone woke them both suddenly, and Dennis, weary from sleeping hard, a hangover slowly emerging at the tip of his skull and at the bottom of his throat, momentarily unsure as to where he was—what country, what state, what town, which hotel, what room—reached over to pick up the line.

It was four o'clock in the morning and he sat up and leaned against the headboard in the dark, the phone to his ear.

Sharon rose slowly, also misplaced, her eyes adjusting steadily to the dark. The moon had moved on, perhaps to bless another couple with its otherworldly light, and she began to see her husband, a ghostlike shadow beside her, nodding in the dark.

"Yes," he said, sitting straighter. "This is he."

"What?" Sharon whispered. No one but Ben knew they were here! How could anyone be calling? "Who is it?"

"Gary." He put his hand up to stop her from talking.

"I see." He paused for a while. "But I'm in Boston now."

There was another silence, and Sharon contemplated her husband's face.

"I'd like to drive, if that's all right. But I won't be there until afternoon." He looked out the window. "And my father?"

He listened for a bit, then took the pad of hotel stationery and the pencil on the night table, and without turning on the light he wrote something down. "Got it. Yes. I'm leaving now."

Dennis hung up the phone but did not move. Sharon watched him turn from shadow into man as he sat, not breathing, for several moments. Tonight, she waited.

He knocked his head several times against the headboard. He took a deep breath. He let it out. "Sharon," he said. "There's something I have to tell you."

Dennis watched his wife turn away from him, wrapping herself up in the sheets, hugging the bedding to her stomach. He turned on the light on the nightstand. He had not told her everything because he didn't know much more, but also because he could not have borne it. He told her that Gary had been kind to call. Terribly kind, and he had remembered Gary pulling the jib and tying it, then pulling at it again to make sure it was secure, then describing his daughter's shock therapy, his fingers pressing his temples in empathy, and Dennis had felt heartbroken by that image. He rubbed his own temples now and told Sharon that he was leaving for Washington immediately. We were very fortunate to have this chance, he said. Most people don't get a warning, he'd said.

"Boy, we're really lucky, Sharon," he'd said, and she had snorted.

His bones felt creaky and brittle as he got up, and he thought of his father, hands on his knees, taking a deep breath before getting up from the couch. Dennis wondered if he was seated at the table now, a knife and fork poised upright at each side of an empty waiting plate, readying to eat his red heart.

"So I have to go now," he said, going to his bag. "I've got to drive down now."

Sharon lay in the fetal position. The white sheets were knotted around her body, her white hip, striated by stretch marks, exposed. She didn't stir.

"Do you hear me, Sharon?" For a moment he stood, observing her. Because let's not forget his wife had also committed a crime here. "Are you coming?" he asked, when she still did not reply. He went to the bathroom for his toiletries. He remembered the Bay Bridge opening, as if just to let them in their little boat through. Had it been Gary? Dennis had been so careful with Gary. Yes, my mother is from Russia, but she never goes home. She has never been back, he'd answered, feeling terrible for her, so far away from home. My only relative is a musician from Moscow, Uncle Misha. He'd laughed, trying to remember, as he'd said it, what instrument his uncle had played.

"I'm not coming with you," Sharon said when he came out of the bathroom, flicking the light off behind him. She held the sheet at her waist, and her small breasts hung lightly, only slightly pendulous, the pinkish nipples pointing out from the center. Her hair was tangled and her eyes were shot with red lines and puffed beneath, dark with shadows. But she looked just like the girl with a hangover who used to drag herself out of bed to cook them popovers, before Vanessa and Ben were born.

"Okay." Dennis knelt down to place his Dopp kit in his bag. "Just have the concierge get you a taxi back to Waltham. You can get a bus with Vanessa from there then."

He zipped up his bag and swung it over his shoulder. Again he paused at the bed and leaned over, kissing Sharon on her head. "This could not be helped."

Sharon was silent.

Dennis opened the door to leave.

"Dennis?"

He turned toward her.

"Good luck, Dennis," she said, before lying back down and placing the pillow over her head.

Morning was just breaking over the Commons as Dennis pulled onto Newbury Street, where the shops were preparing for the long day. A young man with a large mass of curly black hair and a full apron tied twice at his waist came out from the back of a bakery with a tray of rolls he set down on the glass counter case. Dennis paused for a moment to watch him draw the back of his hand across his forehead, leaving a faint trail of flour.

Lights clicked on in a coffee shop as he drove down Newbury Street on the way to the highway. A girl was taking down wooden chairs stacked on top of small wooden tables, her long blond hair swinging from side to side. Dennis slowed the car and peered out from his window to look inside the café, its brick walls decorated with brightly painted canvases. The girl turned to lean on the counter and looked into the street, her chin on her elbows, her legs shifting weight, swaying a little from side to side with bored languor.

Oh, to be bored! thought Dennis, who sped up as soon as she looked out the window and met his eye.

Youth! Coffee shops! Hot rolls! Dennis actually put his hand over his heart. How at a time like this he could think merely of his own aging, he didn't know. Yet he was cut off from every image available to him: he could no more be that kid in the bakery than he could be the one sauntering into that café to talk up that girl.

Had the call this morning never come, would he still have this nearly existential feeling of regret? Because now Dennis felt overwhelmed by the what-ifs: What if he had stayed in San Francisco and waited for the summer of '67, waited for revolution, so what if he was already too old? What if he had never entered Sharon's Georgetown apartment that day when her roommate was out of town? Then, as he'd tried to make love to Sharon, the spider-plant leaves spilling out from a planter on the sill above the couch and practically crawling up his ass, he had thought even then, this should not be so ridiculously difficult.

He went over it again. It overlapped and looped around the past. His father walking ahead of him on the busy street; it always felt as if he were trying to lose Dennis. Then his father would wait at the doorway of Yonah Schimmel's, the heat streaming out from the small, brown shop, the woman screaming in Yiddish, *Zei nit kain vyzoso*—Don't be a fool! She'd gesture wildly for them to come in and close the door against the cold, and Dennis would give in to the comfort he was about to receive from biting into a hot knish. *Me ken lecken di finger,* his father would tell the woman as he peeled back the napkin. One can lick the finger.

It was like following Misha as he wound through the crowds and the police in Red Square. We'll take this one, Misha had said, pointing at a shelf lined with wooden babushkas. That one there, he'd said, pointing to a red doll with a purple kerchief. For the girl, he had said when Dennis questioned him. Of course it will be a girl, and Dennis had thought of Sharon's belly; she was carrying high with this pregnancy, and craving sweets. It's a girl for sure, Tatiana had said as she watched Sharon inhale chocolate after chocolate. Girls like the sweetest things, she'd said, rubbing his wife's back, and she had not been wrong, had she?

Dennis quelled the rising thought of his mother, her hands in her lap, her head down, being questioned, as he headed down the Mass. Pike. His father stood outside the door working the brim of his hat with his fingers. Dennis saw Ethel Rosenberg, her round, fat face, her unshakable pride, and he thought of her children, rabid as dogs along his block, their grandmother barely noting their escape into the street. It still amazed him that she had been brought in because of that bumbling fool husband of hers. Because he had been. He had been so obvious. In the end, he was an awful spy, but Ethel was murdered because she had said nothing. Yet how would she have lived with herself—and her children—if she had?

She would have been that woman who turned her husband in, and her children would have hated her. Because now those two boys, who grew up nice in the end, who seemed sort of normal, if intense, they fought every second for their parents' innocence.

Dennis thought of his mother in the kitchen, a mixing bowl filled with egg whites, and the way she brushed her hair from her face and pulled back the checkered curtains—they had blue-and-white-checkered curtains!—and looked out onto the street when those two boys were taken by the state.

I'm in for a long drive, Dennis thought, lifting the wooden box of tapes up from the floor onto the passenger seat. This was Sharon's car, and he bemoaned not having his own music, *his* music, not his daughter's screaming crap, this indecipherable headbanger shit, and *please,* not Sharon's *Stories of Transformation,* or that sulky Billy Joel album Sharon must have taken from Ben's room. One hand on the wheel, he picked up a tape and fed it to the tape deck, which swallowed it hungrily: *Well . . . it's closing time . . .*

Tom Waits, also his daughter's. But this was a song he had always loved. The song marked one of the few moments in recent memory that his daughter had sat still with him, playing him the song. *I search the place for your lost face . . .* Dennis hoped he had not lost every opportunity. Even loving his wife; he hoped it had not eluded him. He had not wanted any of it, a wedding in a temple, a reception at a hotel, Jesus Christ, but he had gone along, gritting his teeth; he had signed the ketubah and walked to meet her beneath the flowering chuppah, then—and then!—he had lifted Sharon's veil and there she was, her freckled face. Then he'd gone willingly.

Dennis longed for his own music. Harry Chapin! Dennis used to twirl Vanessa in the den as they played his record, the wall of books rising before them, and as he'd held his daughter at her chest, her legs flailing behind her, he had yearned for each one of those books to reach her; to grab her and take her into knowledge. He had wanted to hold her up to them and shake her a little, say, Learn! It is what we do in this family, *this* side of the family anyway, and he had thought this as Harry Chapin sang, *The girls were told to reach the shelves while the boys were reaching stars . . .* That was Sharon's generation maybe, and Tatiana and Helen's, yes, but thank goodness, he had thought, keeping Vanessa clasped to his heart, my daughter was born in a time when women could be exactly whom they wanted to be. So be everything, please! he had thought. Now is your chance to be everything.

*His* music was Harry Chapin, and then he thought of Stravinsky, his mother's records, *Rite of Spring* playing on the turntable just as soon as spring tipped its bright felt hat in the direction of Orchard Street. Not even a day of good weather before that street began to stink of piss. His father and his friends! But his mother, she only had Boris. Sometimes Dennis would come home from school, and the two of them would look up suddenly, as if, though he came home at the same time each day, his mother hadn't been expecting him. Even as a child, Dennis knew nothing romantic could pass between them: Boris was a cow. How could he—a Russian!—have been her only confidant? Were there no other Russian women to go trundling along Brighton Avenue with? She would take the train out there with his sister, then head straight back in. I feel sorry for them, Tatiana said on one winter day when the four of them walked the beach at Coney Island. An old man jogged by slowly, his chest bare and red, his mustache frozen at the tips. Several women in furs held their kerchiefs on their heads against the wind. Who comes to this country to be with the Russians? It makes no sense, she'd said, reaching for Sigmund's hand.

It makes absolutely no sense, Dennis thought now, remembering his mother bringing out her meringues with those cherries, American cherries, she reported, hard as stones, for his birthday. The kids sat around the table with crooked little paper hats and nearly broke their teeth on those cookies.

Today the beginnings of spring were already evident; a few of the trees planted along the highway boasted diminutive green buds, and as morning came on in full, he could feel it warming up, even in the car. Despite the rush of the highway he considered opening the windows. It had been such a long and terrible winter; one could almost call it spiteful.

Dennis pulled into the Roy Rogers parking lot off the highway for some coffee and breakfast. The biscuits reminded him of his father-in-law, and as he got out of the car and slammed the blue door shut, he imagined a young Sharon at dinner with Roy Rogers in a ten-gallon hat.

Dennis made good time; he pulled up to the house just before one o'clock and parked the Volvo on the street so he could take his own car. His little red Beetle. God, he loved that car. He walked up the steps, leaning down and picking up stray bits of soggy toilet paper, and glancing up to the roof to make sure the gutters were clear, he went in through the front door. He dropped his coat across the banister at the landing and went to change into a suit and tie. After pulling back the curtains and peering out onto the street, which for the moment appeared empty but for the neighborhood Dodge Darts and Pintos, the wood-paneled station wagons, he took a look around his bedroom. How silly he was being; it was not going to end this way for him after all—it simply couldn't.

He considered phoning Len, even though he was sure it was Lenny who had insisted Gary call him and give him this unorthodox opportunity. There would be security, of course, which is the only way the CIA operates. The CIA! How had Len become this man? He thought of Annie, her head thrown back, her bare shoulders exposed, her chipped painted toenails. She was so loose. This was not whom a CIA man married. And how have I become this man, Dennis thought, knowing he had no one to rail at now; he was grateful this was the path his old friend had chosen. Gary had been kind to call him. He had been kind to tell him they'd been sitting on this awhile now, gathering information. There had been a long lull, then, when the activity had started up again, well, they'd had no choice but to stop it for good. Venona was ending.

Len knew more, Dennis understood this, but he couldn't make that call, not even if he pulled off the highway and called from a pay phone as he'd thought to do in Milford and Fairfield and Port Chester. He was grateful—he was—but as bureaucratic as this town was, there were always favors; everyone fucked up sometime. Dennis couldn't count on both hands the number of times he'd "accidentally" thrown a memo away or let something slip in a briefing. Looking at that black phone on Sharon's night table, the rotary dial with its numbers like hands of a grade-school clock, it occurred to him that this phone was undoubtedly tapped. When had they come in? he wondered, picturing slim men in ski caps prying open the front door and slipping into his bedroom to slap a tap beneath the phone. He remembered the bug found inside the Great Seal that hung on the wall in the U.S. embassy in Moscow. The Thing, they'd all called it. It was inside the replica of the U.S. seal that had been presented by Russian schoolchildren, and it had hung on that wall gathering information through radio frequencies for nearly fifteen years until the baffled Americans finally figured it out and shattered it.

What he needed was a bug detector. One of those briefcase-size receivers that could isolate radio waves, and he had to laugh to think

of opening such a contraption and locating the source in his own
bedroom.

He thought of his mother meeting his gaze that day the agent
followed him home from the bookstore. When he had come inside,
she'd returned to her timid self and asked him, Where did they see
you, Dennis? She'd grabbed his wrist. What is your job, *really,* Dennis?
And he had turned to her and said, How do you know who was in
that car, Mother? She had raised her head and released her arm. I am
Russian, she said. And you work for the government.

The extent of Dennis's wiretapping knowledge came from
government myths and James Bond movies, which made him go
downstairs and run his hand over the lock to the front door, checking
for forced entry. He tried the lock several times, the dead bolt shooting
out and in, out and in, but aside from making him think of one of
those hollow dead drop bolts that he knew were used for stashing
information, he noticed no difference. Ella Larson from across the
street, who looked a lot better since she'd gone away and, according to
neighborhood gossip, kicked the pill addiction that had started when
her kids were in school, waved to him from the sidewalk. Dennis
waved back before slowly closing the door. Then he turned and took
the stairs by twos, running back up to the bedroom.

He sat down on his wife's side of the bed and put his hands in his lap.
He hooked the handset on his neck, then, pressing the receiver buttons
down with his palm, he turned the phone over. There was nothing he
could see; perhaps the tap was inside the phone, he thought, peering
over it. Or maybe it was on the den phone, or the kitchen, though he
wondered how they would manage to get into a phone fastened to a
wall. Dennis set the phone right side up and placed the handset on the
cradle. He might not be able to find it, but it had to be there.

He thought of his parents making their way down to Washington
separately. Was his father here yet? Where were they keeping him? He
had no way of knowing. Dennis saw his father so clearly now; he stood
alone, and he saw his father's face gone slack, weakened and unsettled.
Sigmund looked as if he were trying to speak but had realized that
no one was listening any longer. What must that feel like, Dennis
wondered now, to become aware of your irrelevance? And Tatiana. He
wondered was his mother broken yet.

Dennis slid open the drawer of Sharon's night table. He did not
know why he did this; he had never before looked inside this drawer.

Her diaphragm sat in the front left corner, and as soon as he saw it, he heard that *click* of the case opening, the barrier emerging, the *click click* of it closing. She had not brought it to Boston, and last night they had done without it. The evening had come back to him in waves on the ride home—the lightness of drinking at the bar with his wife; it had felt as if he were shot through with light, that finally his insides had become hollow, so easy now to carry. And in the room later, the moonlight had shone off her face, and he thought of the gentle way the past had come to sit with them. A plastic container of pens was in the drawer, and a lint brush, several fine, light hairs clinging to the red velvety fabric. I'm sorry, Sharon had told him. He picked up a stack of green Food Matters business cards and placed them back in a straighter pile next to the hand lotion and gobs of wax he soon realized were the earplugs she wore in the early mornings on trash days. Sharon could not take back what she had done. Dennis thumbed through a stack of photos that he recognized as photo-album rejects: there was Sharon grinning, a huge turkey on a platter in her outstretched arms, her eyes two red points of light; Ben running down the field, his body blurred in motion. Dennis had seen more perfect versions of these same photos—Sharon's real eyes staring down at the perfectly browned turkey with affection, Ben dribbling on a green field, his leg muscles as defined as those of Michelangelo's David. A wrinkled envelope, folded in half, the unsealed flap tucked inside, sat atop two thick, well-worn paperbacks, and Dennis picked it up. He unfolded it and turned it around in his fingers. Two green guitar picks slid onto his lap.

# CHAPTER 16

# Perilous City

The shades were still pulled back in the hotel room, and Sharon could see the city spread before her, alighting as the dark blue of the sky clouded over into morning.

She crossed her arms over her bare chest as she listened to Dennis speaking, his voice a ringing she couldn't answer. It was difficult to focus on what he was telling her, and she saw his mouth forming words, but couldn't quite make out their meaning.

He paused, and Sharon said, "Yes," even though he was not asking a question. "Okay," she said at other silences. When he reached out his hand to her across the bed, she did not take it.

She'd registered enough to know that it was shameful. Caught. One day those Venona transcripts would be leaked, and she would be able to see for herself how it had happened. How long had it been happening? How long had it been kept from her? She did not know those things yet, but she knew it was appalling, reprehensible, and, yes, shocking. It was disgraceful that her husband had sat naked in the dark and disclosed it: a spy in the family.

The details were not of interest to Sharon now because she realized that their whole lives had been condensed into this single secret. And Sharon seized on this. This, this *spying* could have been the cause for everything that had gone wrong for them, that had taken them from the bright moment when they'd stood staunchly on the Mall, their fists raised with such *conviction*—and at this word, Sharon stifled a sob, because she had always thought that above all it was what they had shared. They had always believed that what they would pass down to their children was not the good fortune their parents had fought for and handed them readily, but the intangible splendor of hope and dreaming.

How, she wondered, would she ever explain this to her father?

These secrets were *ours,* he'd said as he strung up the American flag. Those two got exactly what they asked for.

And as Dennis had gotten out of bed slowly, like an old man, she remembered her father watching the flag snap in the wind, then standing on the front lawn with his hand over his heart like some asshole, she'd thought then. Theirs was a town torn to bits over what that flag meant and who would carry it. How many times had she heard her father say it? They're more commies here than on Hester Street, he'd said, to any producer or script doctor who came over for cocktails. What, he'd implore, pointing his finger toward the door, is *happening* out there?

And maybe he had been correct, Sharon thought now. Because this was a great country. *America* is a great country; where else on earth would she rather be a citizen? Nowhere, Sharon thought, tearing up again. There was nowhere else. Maybe the Rosenbergs had not been heroes after all. She saw them frying at Sing Sing—is that what would happen now, all these years later? She tried to imagine it, though she couldn't stop herself from thinking that perhaps the Rosenbergs had gotten precisely what they'd deserved.

Her husband turned on the light on the nightstand and she blinked several times.

"Okay," she said to Dennis because there was silence.

Sharon watched from the bed as he dressed in the half-light.

"So I have to go now," Dennis said.

She had expected this when, last night, she had given her blurred, feeble apology about Elias. Just a murmur before they fell asleep; he might not even remember it. She had thought Dennis might leave and that she might have to fight for him to stay, but this morning it had become irrelevant and so Sharon offered nothing.

"I've got to drive down now. Are you hearing me?" He turned to look at her. "Are you coming?" he asked, when she neither moved nor made a reply. He passed the bed and went to the bathroom for the toiletries he'd set by the sink last night.

But all Sharon could see for this moment was arrivals: her in-laws trudging up the stairs to Dennis and her new home. Sigmund was in his dungarees, creases as sharp as corners. Tatti was so quiet. She barely said a word. Dennis stood behind them, waiting impatiently at each step. Just picturing her mother-in-law enter the hallway was heartbreaking. Oh, Tatti, she thought now. Dear sweet Tatti chomping on a hot dog from a street cart; it always looked so big, so obscene, so *American,* clasped in her thin, white Russian fingers.

"No," Sharon said when Dennis came out of the bathroom.

"No what?"

"I'm not coming with you."

He bowed his head and placed his toiletry kit in the corner of the bag.

Sharon watched her husband pack as she had watched him for their entire marriage. Who cares that it was dramatic: can't a city be like a lover? Dennis had been leaving her for Moscow for over a decade. She thought of that perilous city as she had as a child; the incarnation of all things threatening, as if the country itself would bring its infamous fist down and execute them all, that this was what they'd practiced escaping in those air-raid shelters, beneath the tables at school, the drills rehearsed each morning just after the Pledge of Allegiance. She saw the mushroom cloud in the sky. There was no other way to describe it because that's what it was. That was the A-bomb; it was no other thing. She felt fatigued by the threat of the Soviets, which had bled into her life, now in every aspect.

"I have to get Vanessa, Dennis." As she said it, she felt a pang of remorse for last night's selfish thought. Because their children had provided them with untold joys. The sinews that had connected her to Dennis for all these years could so easily have snapped without Ben and Vanessa, just gone brittle and cracked in two. Their children had not come between them; if anything, they had kept their marriage elastic and fit and sutured and worthy.

He nodded.

"And say good-bye to Benjamin too."

"Okay," Dennis said. "You should order room service. Something nice." Dennis tried to smile.

Sharon laughed, imagining morning light stealing into the room, shining off the silver tea service, and silver plate cover, a single rose bobbing in a crystal vase, and Dennis already on the highway to D.C.

Dennis zipped up his bag, and though she had become inured to their constant parting, the abrupt sound of departure still caught her by surprise. He went to kiss her on the head, which felt gentle and fatherly in all the best ways.

At the door he didn't hesitate, but just as he turned the knob to leave, Sharon said quickly, "Good luck, Dennis."

She watched his back straighten as he breathed in, his shoulders rising, then she saw his back round, his shoulders fall just as they had at the window in the château when the bat had finally been coaxed out of the room. She had imagined that bat was headed straight to the moon.

"I'll see you at home," Sharon said, just after he'd slipped out of the room.

# CHAPTER 17

# Doughnuts

**March 23, 1980**

A radio alarm went off, and Vanessa woke facing the wall, curled up between two teddy bears, one dressed in a sailor suit, the other as a cowboy. Her first thought was of camp, that it was reveille exploding over the campus speakers, blasting the campers out of sleep. She felt the same cold of those early-July mornings and remembered rising from her metal cot and pulling the sheets up tight before marching to the camp center for flag-raising and breakfast. She thought of the trail to the waterfront, past the gum tree—the trunk of a pine covered with the campers' chewed gum, forbidden during swimming. She felt the burn in her ears from the alcohol drops, hot from the sun, all the campers lined up, heads turned ear to the sky after swimming.

Vanessa soon realized she was not at summer camp, but at her brother's school. The radio blared with a program discussing the usual: the hostages. *Day number one hundred and forty,* the reporter stated. *One hundred and forty,* he said again, carefully pronouncing each syllable.

Swimming. Vanessa remembered her last time at the beach with Bee and Heather and Jessica. She had woken in a car in a hotel lot at the beach, the sun rising—she'd understood only then that it does rise in the east just as she'd been taught—and a darkness had come up from within. She had felt it come from in her, and it had stretched its jellyfish tentacles around her heart, squeezing tight. Bee had come back from the beach with a handful of broken shells and a headache; Heather had run up to the car from the slots, hands cupping a small heap of coins. But Vanessa—lying next to Jessica, who had woken up laughing, *laughing*—had come up without effect. Bee drove them all home that night, debunking myths about how great sex on the beach was. No one tells you about all that *sand*! she'd said, slapping the wheel and cackling. It gets in everywhere. And I mean *everywhere*. They'd sat in traffic for hours on the Bay Bridge, and Vanessa had looked out on the Chesapeake, its surface infused with the gray of twilight, the quiet stirring of a still evening, and she had felt deprived of absolutely everything.

Now Vanessa placed her palm on the wall, and the deep cold of the cinder block felt refreshingly cool. She turned over and saw Ben asleep in the next bed. Ben's dorm, she thought, watching him breathe, unfazed by the radio alarm that must have been set for classes. She remembered a rainy day at camp, campers lazing about in their cabins, sitting Indian-style, braiding each other's hair. Someone played guitar: *I'm leaving on a jet plane, don't know when I'll be back again . . .* When was the last time a song made her feel the way that song had? She remembered the camp songs at Hill Valley, all those little-girl voices rising up so sweetly into the hazy, humid afternoon: *Ri-ise and shi-ine and sing out your glory, glory.* Hard-core music was only about now. Was that because it had no history? *Ri-ise and shi-ine and* [clap] *sing out your glory, glory, children of the Lord.* Last night the altogether different drumming through her body had recalled what she had felt for years, which was like a piece of softening fruit, exploding beneath the sounds of all that music, ripped and split apart from the inside. Once she had listened to music to feel all the things she could not. That morning at camp, rain pouring down outside, while she was dry and secure, she felt she was precisely where she wanted to be.

Ben. He was curled on his side and facing her, his lids fluttering, lashes touching and lifting from the tender skin below his eyes.

*How long,* the radio host continued, *can this hostage crisis continue? Call in and let's talk it out!*

She tried to shake away the image of Schaeffer setting down that red bong and moving over to her. It had not felt bad. It was warmth and color and light for several moments, but then again, so, she'd heard, was a seizure. Ben's friends wore so many accoutrements: long hair and ripped jeans and ratty tie-dyes and LSD tabs in their pockets, stamped with cartoon characters; it was a cliché, about as radical as their father had been with his *Make Love Not War* T-shirts, and his beat-up red Beetle he drove as if it would save him from something, the *Whirled Peas* sticker stuck crookedly on the back bumper. That, my dear, her father had told her when she'd asked why he didn't have a sticker that simply said *World Peace,* means more than you can ever know. Food, he'd said, sends a more powerful message than guns. Food, he'd told her, is running out. But there are always enough guns now, aren't there?

*Okay, we have a caller who thinks the hostages will be freed soon! Tell us what you think, caller.*

"Who set the fucking alarm?" Ben lifted his head from his bed.

Vanessa pushed down the teddy bear with its navy blue sailor's cap, as straight and stiff as the paper planes she and Ben once made, to see her brother without the frame of bear fur.

"Oh. Yeah." He let his head fall heavy onto the pillow.

Vanessa held her breath and tried to zip up the sweatshirt she wore—her brother's, she assumed—but it was already fastened up to her neck. She felt the hems of a soft pair of boxer shorts skimming her thighs. "Hi." She curled into a tight ball and used the soft stuffed animal as a pillow.

She had seen her brother coming toward her out of the morning mist, and seeing his face, also her father's face and her mother's, and her own too, and despite her nakedness, or perhaps precisely because she could not arm herself, she had welcomed his strong hands, hands that, she knew, as they lifted her, had experienced so many women's bodies. As he had sat her upright on the field, she had felt the contrast of her own inexperience; few men had lighted upon her. There was an imbalance, as there always had been with Ben and her; Vanessa would never catch up. Yet as he'd lifted her by her armpits, she'd felt safe, so tremendously secure in his arms in a way she had not felt since those rainy days at camp, since coming back from the beach with her family, her hermit crab nestled beneath a lettuce leaf in her little cage, her father carrying Vanessa up to her bedroom after the long, dark drive. *Wait for me,* she'd thought, as her brother lifted her to her feet on that field, and she had felt the soft, wet grass beneath her, realizing that this—love, she supposed, security—was a terrible thing to go without. Who could have told her she was in between these moments of girlhood and womanhood when there is no one on earth who can carry you? Wait for *me*.

The caller was going on and on about what an idiot Jimmy Carter was, and all Benji could do was imagine his friend mounting his sister. He felt sick to his stomach, which could, he decided, also be because he hadn't eaten since the pizza with his parents. Because maybe Schaeffer had done the kind, right thing and had just taken good care of his sister.

Benji looked at Vanessa. "How are you feeling?"

Just the word *feeling*, and Vanessa thought she would disintegrate. "I'm okay," she said.

Benji sat up and ran his palm and fingernails across his scalp. "I'm really sorry about last night. I don't know what I was thinking. It was just such a stressful day, you know?" He shook his head. It had been a brief and stunning moment, then it was gone. "I really shouldn't have taken drugs in front of you, you're only a kid. I mean"—he cleared his throat—"you're not a kid anymore, but I didn't need to force you into making that kind of a decision, is all."

Vanessa pet the teddy bear. "It's all right," she said.

"You ended up at Schaeffer's, didn't you?"

Vanessa nodded and sat up. "Yeah."

Benji bit the inside of his cheek. "Did you two . . . ?" He pointed a finger from side to side.

Vanessa scrunched her mouth into a crooked bow.

He looked down and shook his head. "God," he hissed. "I can't believe that guy."

She shrugged, picking at the stuffed-animal fur. She removed the sailor cap and sat the bear on her lap.

A new caller was on the line. *The U.S. needs to just go in there and get those poor people!* The woman had a high voice, and she sounded desperate. *Does anyone know what's happening to them? Those poor, poor families.*

"V," Benji said. "Can I just ask? Was that your first time?"

Vanessa knew she would cry if she spoke, so she just shook her head.

"Well, that's good, I guess. Because the first time, it should be nice." Benji thought of little Erin Mackaby, a flesh-colored square, naked but for that strand of winking pearls clasped around her thick neck, waiting for him on her parents' four-poster bed. "Really nice, I mean. You know that, right? It shouldn't be while you're tripping on acid." He tried not to think of his sister as one of the girls he'd had but had not wanted. "So you've been sleeping with Jason, then?"

The radio host urged the caller off the line. *This is a case,* he said, *where no news is just plain bad news. Thanks for calling in, folks, and after the break, more from all of you, the phones are ringin' off the hooks this morning! Stay tuned for a few words from our sponsors . . .*

A manic commercial for Jordan's furniture in Waltham replaced the announcer.

Vanessa shook her head. "We used to." She remembered Jason in the grass in the backyard. Zachary must have just mowed the lawn that day, and the smell of cut grass was all over them. When she'd sat up, the individual blades were plastered to the backs of her thighs and shoulders. "But not really anymore." She regretted the time with Sean now. "I can't really explain it." How she regretted it! Jason was slow and sweet, but he did not want her. She pictured their little red house swathed in bandages, and she hated Sean and his whole stupid punk posse.

Benji remembered his sister's bones. As he'd looked down at her on the field, they had seemed haphazardly placed together; he'd wondered how he would be able to set them back to form a person again. "Well," he started to say to her, but he was interrupted by a knock at the door and the sound of their mother's voice.

The taxi let Sharon out in the parking lot outside Benjamin's quad. She made her way into the courtyard balancing the cardboard box of doughnuts—a special treat, who cared about the evils of sugar and fat at a time like this anyway? It was amazing to her that at nine in the morning the campus was silent but for the sounds of nature waking: a bird shaking on a tree, another singing, the obscuring of the sky from a clear night into a cloudy morning. The pond shimmered before her, and walking over to the edge, she could see the old women's fingers of the rough tree branches in the surface and her reflection superimposed over the clouded sky. Startled by the image of her head, which looked enormous from this distance, she leaned in. A duck lit on the pond surface, and the water rippled toward its edges, Sharon's image growing and receding, bending and folding upon itself.

Sharon marched into the dorm. The corkboard out front said *Arnie and Benji live here!* in green cursive. She hadn't noticed it yesterday, and now she had to laugh a little.

"Good morning," she whispered into the door, her head leaning in, the tips of her fingers holding the box of Dunkin' Donuts like one of her servers holding a tray of canapés before heading out into the party. "Time to get up, sleepyheads!" She remembered her children then, little loaves of bread, so tender and young and also *hers*. She saw their red, wrinkled feet scissoring the air. They were delicious. They just had no idea.

Sharon heard whispering and scuffling and drawers opening and closing, then she saw Ben's big brown eyes and his long nose and his scruffy, just-woke-up curly hair through the crack of the barely opened door.

"Mom?"

Why was this so terribly confusing? "Yes, Ben. It's your mother. I brought doughnuts," she said, but it came out far more grimly than she'd intended.

He opened the door, reluctantly if you asked Sharon, and stepped back from it. When she walked in, she saw Vanessa sitting up in Arnold's bed, rubbing her arms.

"You two spent the night together!" Sharon said, a little bit happy and, she couldn't help it, a little bit jealous. "How nice." She looked over at the desk on Ben's side of the room, and after noting the impossibility of clearing a place for the doughnuts, she just set the box down on top of his papers and books, where it sat crookedly.

"Where's Dad?" Ben asked.

*Bedroom sets, dining room sets, sets for your porch and patio too!* the breathless announcer screamed from the radio.

"That sure is loud, can we turn it down?" Sharon asked, standing in the middle of the room.

Ben walked over to Arnie's clock radio, turned the volume down, then crawled back under the covers. "We just woke up," he said. "Is Dad okay?"

Sharon looked from bed to bed and rubbed her hands together. Something had happened there, she could tell. They were always *good* when something happened.

"He's fine," Sharon said. "He just had to leave unexpectedly is all; something came up at work and he had to go early."

"That's what that call was about?"

Her hands hovered over the box of doughnuts. "Hmm, hmm," she said, not knowing exactly what call Ben meant. Had she mentioned the early-morning phone call? "They're still warm. The glazed ones were just out of the fryer when I got them." She didn't look at Vanessa when she said the word *fryer,* but instead picked up the box again and brought it over to Ben. She leaned down and opened the box, offering them to him.

"Thanks, Mom." He took a glazed one, the wet sugar glistening over the fawn-colored dough.

She set the box down on the table between the two beds. She kicked off her shoes and pushed Vanessa over a bit, pulled back the covers, and slipped in with her jeans on. She put the enormous bear that Vanessa wasn't holding at the end of the bed, and Vanessa put her head on her shoulder. Sharon tried to stay as still as possible, knowing that one sudden movement could make her daughter shift away.

With sedulous care, Sharon brought the doughnut box onto her lap and opened it. There were three more glazed and two chocolate, a cruller, and two with spring-colored sprinkles, which she had pointed to at the shop even though no one ever ate them.

"Want one?" she asked Vanessa, adjusting her neck so as not to jostle her.

Sharon felt her daughter's head nod against her shoulder, and then, without moving her head, Vanessa reached out and took a glazed doughnut from her mother's lap.

And now, Sharon thought, also taking a glazed, now I have chosen to love you. She felt snug and so near to her two children; how had she made such wondrous creatures?

Sharon remembered her father as he'd been when she was little, his head full of chestnut brown hair, eyes twinkling, unaltered by impending fear, as he bent toward her on one of the few nights he had put her to bed. She had curled into the reverse *V* made by his arm and his chest like a humming cat, and he'd told her the story of the Snow Maiden. Sharon looked down at the daughter she had created, her left shoulder wet from Vanessa's quiet tears, and her daughter's youth seemed as ephemeral as a snow angel's, just as hers had been. Her father's low, rumbling voice had vibrated through her: *The Snow Maiden listened to the song and tears rolled down her cheeks. And then her feet began to melt beneath her; she fell onto the earth and then she was gone, a light mist rising from the place she had fallen. The mist rose out of the earth and disappeared slowly into the deep blue sky. . . .* It's okay, Snegurochka, her father had assured her, brushing her hair back when she asked, But, Daddy, what had happened to her? She became part of the whole world, he'd said, poking Sharon's heart.

Sharon kept the box open on her lap as the three of them sat silently chewing the sweet, warm doughnuts in Ben's dorm room, until the commercial was over and the news came back softly on the radio.

# CHAPTER 18

# The Cherry Trees

As Dennis pulled out of the garage, he could hear the phone ringing and ringing, but he didn't go back to answer it. He noticed evidence of spring splashed across the neighborhood; the border around the Farrells' lawn boasted many tender buds pushing their way out of the well-tended soil. Soon there would be her red tulips and hyacinths and lilies of the valley. But Boston had still been cold. It had been a brutal winter, even by Washington standards. Even though all winter Ben had called with stories of snowstorms and blizzards when Maryland skies were clear and blue, surprising to Dennis, who thought of the East Coast as one long tendril of a region, its various states connected by the same stars and skies, its uninspired landscape and identical clime, it had still seemed bitterly cold.

Two houses down, the Ellises had a patch of crocuses already framing the walkway by their front door, and a plot of young, bright daffodils by the ivy near the evergreen at the side of the lawn that gave Dennis a moment of jealousy; he wished he'd asked Zach to plant something more than ground cover last fall. But having some kid create a garden seemed worse than paying someone to cater dinner and pretend you did the cooking. Could money buy everything? Well, yes, it seemed it could these days, but it couldn't buy his appreciation. Dennis knew he wouldn't value the seasonal transformations of a hired-out garden—in fact, he knew he would grow to resent even the most vibrant moments had he not done the choosing and digging and planting and watering himself, just like Roberta Ellis in her massive straw sun hat, kneeling into the soil, her green rubber clogs sticking out behind her ass like little squashed, smiling frogs.

Turning off Thornapple and onto Brookville Road, Dennis noticed a car following close behind. Perhaps Gary hadn't trusted him after all. He wished now that he were the kind of man who knew cars so that he would be able to note the type and the model, and that somehow this would illuminate the driver's intention. It was black and shiny, he observed, which was the best he could do.

He drove the exact speed limit of twenty-five down Brookville, making a full stop at every bloody stop sign, then sped up as he was encouraged around the Circle, and down Connecticut on the other side. Still the car followed him past the Szechuan Palace, where he and Sharon ate sweet spareribs and egg rolls on their second date, past the zoo, which he could never drive by without thinking of Ling-Ling and Hsing-Hsing, gnawing on bamboo—gifts from the Chinese! he'd told Vanessa and Ben, who waited hours to see them tumble into view— then over the Taft Bridge past the little park where they were marching today either for a Free South Africa or for a Free Tibet, he was too distracted and habituated to these protests to tell which. The car still followed closely behind as he ducked under the tunnel at Dupont instead of driving straight, continuing on Connecticut until it turned into Seventeenth Street.

Dennis reasoned that his route was the most central into the District, which must be why the car still trailed him as he passed Common Ground, at the bottom of the Circle. He thought to test his pursuer by getting out and going inside, and he remembered that man who had watched him from the back of the store, then followed so close behind as he'd left it. Or had he followed him into the store? Dennis hadn't been watching then, he thought now, annoyed with himself. How could he not have noticed such a thing? Had this man been targeting him or targeting just anybody? It made all the difference.

Stupid fucking feds, that store wasn't even commie anymore; it was barely progressive. Once Sharon had gone to some women's group meetings there, and even now as he remembered her heading out the door with her cloth bag, he pictured a circle of women looking at their vaginas. Now punk kids hung out there because they skateboarded in lower Dupont and because of what it once was, but all they bought was imported British music magazines and obscure poetry. He had seen Vanessa with a Common Ground paper bag—slim with a magazine— just weeks ago.

Washington: such a drowsy weekend town, and today was no different but for the hordes of tourists pouring out of buses along

Independence and fanning out onto the Mall. Dennis bypassed the buses, the Smithsonian to his right, that deep red house whose color he had tried for several classes to replicate in a painting during his Corcoran phase only to find it was simply burnt sienna, then he pulled up at Agriculture. He scanned his ID card in the little yellow machine and pulled into the garage. The shiny black car behind him idled by the curb, and Dennis watched the driver duck his head, perhaps to change the radio station, as the garage door came down the way it only did on weekends. Was he James Bond, climbing a wall between himself and his enemy? Or was he the bad guy getting away? Either way, he had been chased down. Breathing heavily by the elevators, he looked to his left, then to his right, and he found himself safe at last.

Dennis stepped into the elevator and pressed 5 and thought of lifting Vanessa to reach the same button, just as he thought of Tatti lifting him up and up. Dennis would often sit at a typewriter at one of the old wooden desks in that tiny, chaotic office on the fifty-fourth floor and pretend to type letters. *Dear Misha.* He'd press random keys. He didn't know the letters to spell yet, and it looked like a strange code. What's this? Boris had said, coming up from behind and pulling the paper out of the platen. He had smelled like herring and Old Spice. Are you sending secret documents? Boris, that *fraud,* was too fat, and when he laughed, as he had then, spittle collected at each side of his mouth.

Had Dennis ever reached the top of the Empire State? He didn't think it was until twenty years later, long after CHORD had closed down because, Tatti had said, Boris had decided to try Hollywood instead. That was the last Dennis saw of him. He'd thought to invite Boris to his wedding, but his mother had laughed at him. He is long gone, she'd said. Dennis only got to the top of the Empire State Building when he took his own children, and his mother; and that was not until he was a tourist in the city of his birth. He had walked them around and around the tippy-top, pointing to where he used to live. There, he'd said. Where? His mother had looked over his shoulder. I'm going to be sick, she'd said, folding herself in half.

Or was that his mother now, her arms crossed at her stomach, leaning in? Because she could certainly not be feeling well today. The elevator opened, and as he stepped into the hallway, Dennis thought that perhaps it was wrong to stop here, as it had not been indicated by Gary. He required nothing from his office; he had nothing there to hide. Yet he wanted to conceal everything, his entire person, as if he could bury these effects by taking them, make them unavailable to the men who might come looking.

This was where he kept the Coronation Egg! he remembered now as he reached the office. When Sharon had threatened to throw it out with all the other tchotchkes from their travels—a replica of the Golden Gate, a silver spoon imprinted with the Eiffel Tower, matchbooks from Moscow, a lifetime of crud—he had saved it, cupping it in his palms and laying it down carefully in the passenger seat of his car, cradling it all the way up from the garage and into his office, where, lowering it down ever so carefully, he had set it in the bottom drawer of the file cabinet. It was a schlocky knickknack, Sharon had claimed, yet he'd had a powerful fear of breaking it. From some Russian five-and-dime, Sharon had said dismissively, and he had been amused by the image of this small-town American conceit set against a place that felt more like a strange planet than a country.

No Glinda today, no more wishes, he thought, his heart seizing when he opened his door. Of course. Of course the men, James Bond or no James Bond, had already come. As he took in the complete disorder of the room, the mess of glass and dirt and dust and papers, he thought not of all the officious things he'd done here, but of the time, after a long lunch with Sharon at Dubliner's on St. Patrick's Day, he'd tried to have sex with her on the meeting table. He thought of his children at his desk, their feet not even touching the floor, and of his mother visiting—Sigmund had refused—and the way she scanned every part of the place, running her hands over the cabinets and shelves as if to brush away dust, or to make an impression with her own hands.

It was difficult to make out what had been taken. Soon, though, as he went toward his desk, he could see that the Landsat images he'd been looking at last week had been ransacked, the locked cabinet in the right drawer of his desk thrown open, the useless lock broken. The framed photos that had lined his desk were turned over and several were on the floor. Dennis picked up one of Vanessa in profile, sitting on a decaying log fence at the farm in Skatesville, then one of Ben at Pierce Mill, the wooden wheel a whirl of motion behind him. Beside the desk, facing upward, the glass cracked, split from the center as if from a gunshot, was a photograph of Sharon—tanned and freckled, one hand on her hip and the other forming the *V* of a peace sign held up close to the camera, disproportionately large. He leaned down to pick it up, wiping the glass dust from her face.

The three photographs Dennis had behind his desk on the radiator were missing. There had been an old picture of his father sitting on a ledge at City College eating a sandwich, still gesturing with his hands while his mouth was full, and also a photo of his mother as a little girl, all bundled up for the cold, feet wobbling in ice skates. It was such a modern, candid shot for the era—who had taken it? Dennis had wondered many times when he had picked it up at his desk and looked into the little girl's eyes, amazed that they were the same as his mother's. Also missing was the photo of Tatti and Dennis, an image from over a decade ago, his mother reaching her hands out to her sides, a gesture to embrace the world, the Washington Monument rising behind her as if it were stabbing her in the back, and Dennis in profile beside her, clearly amused by his mother's joy.

All six drawers of the standing metal file cabinet were also flung open, most of its insides taken or tossed about the office, as were the few plants Dennis had set atop his cabinets and bookshelves that Glinda kept alive. The floor had a layer of soil flecked with white granules of fertilizer, and the files were torn open, clearly in haste, while some lay unhinged at the bottom of drawers. Dennis brushed the dirt by the file cabinet with his hands as he knelt down at the bottom drawer and peered in. The egg was not there. That fragile, breakable egg, as vulnerable as his mother, and the delicate carriage placed as if to pull it away. He tried to block out the sound of his mother's voice: To carry the czarina, she told him, wiping the red hair from her face.

The car resumed its place behind his as Dennis turned onto Independence. He checked behind him in the rearview, but instead of confirming his fears, he was instead distracted. The cherry trees were in full bloom! To his left, the banks of the Tidal Basin were filled in with soft clouds of light pink and white blossoms, the supple branches reaching out along the water in a motherly embrace. The round swelling of the Tidal Basin always seemed so warm and welcoming, unlike the rigidly rectangular Reflecting Pool, which stretched out long and lean across the way, regally impervious even when the Mall bulged with people. As impenetrable as Lincoln's pool was, the Tidal Basin always held someone in its soft, forgiving waters, and today many paddle boaters—pretty girls with ribbons in their hair and fat children eating ice creams and old men in sandals looking up to Jefferson in his round house—all weaving in and out of the trees bordering Dennis's view.

Surely there had been nothing of note to report when Dennis had driven by this past Friday. He was sure of it; only two days previously the trees had been bare, stripped, their thin boughs and the filament-like branches extending out from them had held the same brittle sorrow they'd cultivated all winter. But here, unexpectedly early, was a whole new day, bright and beautiful, and Dennis had the sensation he'd been punched in the stomach, so stunning was the sight. It was a splendid, startling image; were he someone else—and today he wished more than anything that he were—he would have called it a miracle. How could he have been this wrong, this brutally incorrect? If the cherry trees bloomed for only one moment and then fell away, they were worth every amount of hysterical propaganda this city—this country—offered up. The brevity was the point. He had been a stupid, immature man to ignore them that day he and Sharon had paddled along just here, on their first date, her feet bare, the nails painted a light pink, which he remembered now had matched the blossoms almost identically. He had pointed out all the buildings to her as if she'd been a tourist; these monuments are testaments to history (he thought he might actually have said this), but never did he tell her, See these trees? Do you see them? A gift from the Japanese. In peace and friendship.

He had placed Vanessa in one of these very trees when she was just four; it was the year they'd bought the house on Thornapple Street, and he had lifted her into the V of a low-to-the-ground trunk. Instinctively she had spread her arms and placed each palm flat to the rough bark on either side of her, balancing herself. The blossoms burst above her, giving the effect of a spectacular headdress; it looked as if she wore a cushiony, pink, and flowing crown of flowers. As Dennis framed her in blooms for the photo, he had thought, My little warrior. He had staggered backward, taking in both the tree in its grand entirety and his glorious daughter. My daughter will be a warrior. She will save us, he'd thought, it is her turn. And I will be the warrior's father.

Something this astonishing, this large and meaningful, of course it can only last a moment. Vanessa's childhood was over. He saw it arch like a rainbow, reaching for its unattainable pot of gold, fading fast. Sharon's popovers: if they weren't eaten quickly enough, they collapsed and turned hard as stones. And, yes, when everyone was done singing and making speeches, the protesters filed out and went home. But some threw marbles, Dennis thought, thinking of Sharon's militant college roommate, Louise. He half expected to turn and see the cherry blossoms disappear, but instead they simply receded with the rest of the Mall as Dennis turned onto Memorial Bridge.

Abruptly the light turned violent, blindingly clear as the early-afternoon sun skimmed off the Potomac in sharp shards of glass. The monuments appeared in order in his rearview mirror, but what lay ahead of him was against history. For the first time since he was awoken this morning, still believing as his wife lay across his chest that it was she who needed to apologize, Dennis lost his composure.

Unable to drive, he pulled the car over to the side of the bridge and stepped out carefully, the black car unwillingly passing him, the driver fixing on Dennis, his head turning in disbelief as he sped by. Dennis knew the man would simply go around the circle at the other end and return, and he didn't much care. He went to the sidewalk and leaned into the granite balustrade with his hips, his forearms reaching up to the smooth ledge. He looked north, toward home. It was nothing like where he grew up, like New York, the island tethered to its boroughs with strings of bridges, tautly stretched stitches in the leather of Manhattan. D.C. was low to the ground and sprawling; it was lighter in all ways and it was not an island; there was no danger of the city unhinging and floating away.

Dennis could see the tip of the Lincoln Memorial, which he had stood facing on so many occasions. There was the Kennedy Center with its golden columns, the western terrace suspended above the parkway he'd headed home along more nights than he cared to count. On winter nights the purple and white lights skidded over the river; the building appeared to glow, humming with the golden light of the inside. It really is a beautiful town, Dennis thought each time he drove beneath that terrace. And he thought this now, though this was usurped by the notion of his wife flung across a man that, no matter how many photographs he imagined, did not wear Dennis's face. The man played guitar; he knew that much.

Cars whizzed by, several honking at his idled Beetle, which was taking up an entire lane. Dennis felt his hips and arms warm against the sun-heated granite. He looked down the river and thought of it in all its parts: in Georgetown, where he'd taken his children along the C&O Canal—*it connects tidewater here on the Potomac River with the headwaters of*

*the Ohio River in western Pennsylvania,* the ranger had once told them—
and deep in Maryland, where they'd canoed in quiet waters; at Great
Falls on the Virginia side where kayakers crashed between massive
boulders. Just like government, everyone in his little bureaucratic
department pushing paper toward the gaping mouth. Working in
government, it was no different from being a garment worker; his
father could have rallied and screamed and spit for his rights. Everyone
just does his part, his little bitty part, and perhaps the whole turns out
as swell as that river. But, the whole, it turns out, was too contaminated
to be of use. The river was a polluted organism; Dennis had dreams of
falling into it and being stuck in its muck, unable to get to the surface
for breath. Yet the river was distinct in each place he'd beheld it; it
hardly seemed correct to call it by a single name.

Dennis looked at the water below, the current swirling beneath
him, and he thought of the wide and open light of Texas cast across
immense rolls of hay and catching the steel of the oil rigs, flashing off
the massive web of telephone lines strung high above. There he was as
he had once been, with Len, eager, committed, a little unsure, half the
country still to travel, the Golden Gate, the most spectacular bridge on
earth, still ahead of them.

Now Dennis leaned over the ledge of the small and simple Memorial
Bridge, not even, he thought, high enough to kill a man. He put his
head in his hands and wept.

The car was waiting on the parkway to follow Dennis into the South
Gate of CIA headquarters, where it maneuvered in front of Dennis,
who then followed as they drove through what felt like a winding forest.
Huge trees surrounded a narrow roadway, then suddenly a clearing
appeared, and the headquarters, a long building with a low-hung
terrace over the entrance—clearly the product of fifties architecture—
came into view. Dennis had never been to these new headquarters; all
his meetings were taken in the D.C. office on E Street, just across from
the State Department, and now he felt as if he were entering a college
campus, so immense were the grounds. The modern architecture
made him think of Brandeis, and as Dennis drove into the enormous
lot after the driver cleared his access, he thought of watching his son
speak at his rally. Only yesterday, he thought, remembering Ben's
surprisingly delicate fingers making a point in the air, then gripping
the podium as he leaned in to emphasize his position. It had been brief

and beautiful, there was no crime in that. He had been cruel to place his own jadedness over his son's hope.

We are all living down or living up to a legacy now, aren't we? Dennis thought as he pulled next to the black car. So what now was his son to inherit? Was his a moral, priggish birthright, or was he the heir to something fearless, if foul? In one moment those two inheritances were split directly down the middle, but the differences were so great they were meaningless. Suddenly he felt he understood Caleb Blonsky, posing with Nixon, a glass of white wine held high in the air, because he had circled around and found there was no distinction. A communist could love her country and a Fabergé egg.

The driver—who turned out to be a man in a blue suit, a bureaucrat just like Dennis—nodded.

"Mr. Goldstein," he said, pointing to the stairs.

Dennis took the few steps and headed through the glass door, which he held for the driver, into the shining lobby of the CIA. In all its grand governmental glory. Because something about a government building, no matter what it looks like from the outside, has, on the inside, the faint whiff of Eastern Europe. Inside is always the endless, slow, dusty colorlessness of bureaucracy. Only the Capitol was different. He wanted to be that young man spinning beneath its spectacular dome again; he wanted just once more to shake the incomparable Hubert Humphrey's hand.

Stepping inside, Dennis stood atop a massive CIA seal, inlaid in granite in the floor, the eagle peeking out from a white shield marked with a red compasslike star, its spokes radiating. *The United States of America* was printed in red on a golden scroll, and above the seal, in generic white lettering, it said *Central Intelligence Agency*. Dennis had seen this seal countless times: on stationery, in offices, stamped on book covers and confidential documents, yet he had never noticed how furious that eagle seemed now, even in profile, and how much the great bird resembled an old man.

Before him stood a wall of white marble engraved with black stars, representing soldiers now perished. And below this rather quiet memorial lay an open book encased in glass, The Book of Honor.

"This way," the man said, guiding him to the stairs, then out at the first floor.

Dennis bowed his head and followed, as instructed. He wondered if his father had arrived yet; Gary had refused to give any details over the phone, and Dennis wondered what his father would do or say, what he'd been doing when they'd called for him. Or perhaps they had come directly to the apartment, just walked in as his father sat hunched over those books at the kitchen table, and taken him then and there.

The walls of the headquarters were painted a deep, rather beautiful midnight blue, and the hallway was lined with portraits of men, a Hall of Great Men, each man standing boldly in military uniform, hands hooked to breast pockets directly below his many medals or seated with a hat in hand, or leaning over the ledge of a massive, spinning globe. As the paintings moved chronologically closer to the present, the poses grew more casual: important papers were strewn on slackened laps; a man relaxed in a chair, the arm of his glasses swinging in his left hand. The men had slipped out of formal uniform and into business suits; the last painting captured George H. W. Bush, seated casually on a table ledge in pinstripes.

Dennis watched the footfalls of the man leading him, and he heard their shoes squeak on the linoleum floors, but they seemed inconceivably separated by time, and he could not feel his own legs, which took him up another flight of stairs and down another shining hallway to an office. For the second time today, Dennis lost control.

The man waited—almost gently—for him to stop shaking. Dennis could not think of a single image that would calm him. The past was burdened; the future was fraught. But in the center of those time frames, just as in the middle of the mob of protesters singing and holding their children and waving peace signs, was the Reflecting Pool, its still, clear waters mirroring the few wisps of clouds passing by in the clear sky, unchanged. Somehow he had reached this image, and after about a minute, he was still, and the man in the blue suit wrapped his fingers around the chipped golden knob and opened the door.

Dennis hadn't realized his eyes were closed, but now they shot open. What had he expected? Because it was just an office, a government office, not so different from his own, though it had no plants or posters or framed photographs, and a table, not a desk, faced the door. Today it was set with five chairs, the three facing the door taken, the two on the opposite side still empty.

She sat at the table straight as a needle, flanked by two men in uniform. Her hair was so red! On the carousel on Coney Island he rode a bobbing horse in many circles to the frightening throng of the organ, always looking during each rotation for the safe spot of her bright hair.

Her long neck was tilted a little to the right, as if she were furtively trying to listen. The cookies had names in them. Written in invisible ink, Gary had said. Dennis had been silent, watching Sharon, her long hair falling over her bare shoulders in the gray light. You didn't know this? In lemon, or vinegar. Maybe even urine. When they were baked, the coded names turned brown. They all went to a Misha Baskov in Moscow. What did you say your mother's maiden name was? Gary had said, just this morning, on the telephone. No, he'd said. Don't tell me.

"Hello, Mother," Dennis said in Russian.

He watched his father enter the room, guided by another driver. Sigmund stood straight, his hands resting on the back of the chair. Then the two men flanking his mother rose and came toward them.

# CHAPTER 19

# Just Call Them Wishes

The Sunday-morning call-in program came back on the radio. *Okay, folks, we're talking about the hostages. It's day one hundred and forty. One hundred and forty, folks! Do you really think President Jimmy Carter is gonna get them out?*

Sharon leaned over and turned off the radio. "Christ," she said.

"Hey!" Benji wiped his sticky hands on his comforter. "That sounded kinda interesting. And they might talk about the boycott soon. They could even mention the rally."

"We can listen in later," Sharon said. "I'm tired."

"You're tired? If you only knew what the past twenty-four hours has been like for *me*!"

"Stop it, Ben."

Benji looked back at Sharon, surprised.

Vanessa lay back in Arnie's bed, and Sharon closed the happy box of doughnuts and perched it precariously on top of the clock radio. "Look, guys." She brought her knees to her chest, the sheets tenting around her legs, which she wrapped her arms around. "People in this country say horrible things about the Soviet Union. Just horrible. And they're not all wrong, but they're not all right either."

"I think I know a little about this, Mom. I mean, more than anyone, I should know about empathizing with the Russians. That's what I'm about."

Sharon closed her eyes and worked her toes into the mattress. "Just *listen*, Benjamin. I am trying to tell you something that is difficult."

Vanessa looked at her mother. She was so close; Vanessa could see the little blond hairs above her mouth, and the delicate web of lines at the corners of her mouth and eyes, as well as the darker, greenish-tinged circles beneath. She could see the bits of flaking skin on her mother's chapped lips, and the bright pinpricks of red in the spots where she had clearly chewed or picked the skin loose too soon.

"You know your father is Russian, right?" Sharon ran a palm over her burned hand. "Of course you know that. Well, we're all obviously very much American, but Grandpa Herbert is Polish—though his village was taken over by the Russians a long time ago, but that's a whole other story. And Nana Helen, she's Hungarian. But Tatti, Nana Tatti, you know, she came over from Russia. From St. Petersburg. When she was older. She has many, many ties there. Unlike my father. Anyway, look, people say horrible things now, but Russia was once a wonderful place."

"Have you ever been?" Benji asked.

Sharon sighed. "No, Ben, I haven't." Was it strange that all she'd wanted to hear from her husband was if he'd known? And he had not known, he'd said. Even in the dark in the hotel, she could tell he was not lying.

"I'm just wondering, is all," Benji said. "How you know it was so wonderful?" He stuffed bits of a sheet into his clenched left hand and pulled it out with his right.

"Let me put it this way," Sharon said. Dennis said he hadn't known, but that it wasn't shocking. "Everything has changed . . ." Imagine. Not being shocked by such news. Sharon could hardly imagine anything more revelatory.

There was a scratch at the door.

"In Russia?" Vanessa asked, ignoring it. "How so?"

"No." Sharon put her hand on Vanessa's knee. "What I meant was, well, your father won't be going back to Moscow anytime soon, that's for sure."

"Hey, Benji?" a tentative voice came from outside the door. *Scratch scratch*. "You in there?"

Benji looked sheepishly at his mother and his sister, then rose from his bed, adjusting himself in his briefs as he padded to the door in his bare feet.

"Why? Where's Dad?" Vanessa looked as if she might cry.

Benji cracked open the door. "Hey," he said, leaning in at his hip. "Hey, you."

"Who's that?" Sharon whispered to Vanessa.

She shrugged. "How should I know?"

"I'm not alone," Benji whispered into the hallway. "I mean, not like that. My mother and sister are here with me."

Sharon hit Vanessa on her leg and whispered, pointing at the door, "It's that Rachel!"

Vanessa ducked her head into her hand, a smile passing over her face. "Where's Dad?"

"Well"—Sharon placed her arm back around her shins—"something came up at work and he had to go to the office."

"If you want to, I guess," Benji said, opening the door and stepping aside.

"Really?" Vanessa said. "On a Sunday?"

Sharon nodded, looking straight ahead. "Yes," she said. "Really."

And then Rachel Feinglass stepped inside.

She stood in the center of the small room, a brown leather bag crossing her chest snugly, and a small backpack with two heavy, black shoulder straps dug in tight just at the outside curve of each breast. Her nipples pressed against the faded white cotton of her shirt, where the felt printing of boardwalk T-shirt shops spelled out *I Need a Miracle!* in blue bubble letters.

Rachel swung her backpack to the ground, letting it sit by her ankles as she dipped her head rather ungracefully through the strap of her purse, extricating herself. "Hi there," she said, shaking out her shiny hair and smiling at Vanessa and Sharon.

Sharon warily wiped the corner of an eye with her third finger. "Well, hello," she said, getting out of bed.

"Don't get up!" Rachel put out both hands abruptly.

Sharon laughed. "It's okay; we can't lie in bed all morning, can we, kids?" She looked at Vanessa, who rolled her eyes, and for a brief moment Sharon felt robbed by this brown, pillowy creature of the tender, quiet moment the three of them had been sharing.

"It's getting warmer." Sharon stood, opening the window.

Outside, the water of the pond looked dark and heavy, as if covered by a black tarp. She could see to the other side of the quad, where kids were making their way into the dining hall, and Sharon felt relieved that the campus was finally beginning to stir. Thank God we are no longer alone, she thought as she wiped her hands on her jeans.

She reached out to take the young woman's hand. "You must be Rachel."

"Hi, Mrs. Goldstein." Rachel shook her hand eagerly in both of hers.

Sharon felt a shock, then the cold hardware of many rings against the bones of her own fingers.

Rachel let out a little gasp. "Oh! Did you feel that?"

"I did." Sharon looked down and shook her hand. "I absolutely did."

"So nice to meet you," Rachel said. She had a gorgeous smile.

"Hi, Rachel." Vanessa, sitting cross-legged on the bed, feebly waved a hand.

"Hey," Rachel said lightly. Then she looked over at Benji. "Hey," she said to him, the letters on her chest rising and falling with each deep breath.

He smiled. "Where are you going?" He pointed to her backpack.

"You mean where are *we* going," she said, clearly unfazed by the presence of his mother.

Sharon watched Benjamin, a bemused look creeping over his face as he looked at this Rachel.

"Okay." He grinned at her, sitting down on his bed. "Where are *we* going, then?"

"Well, the way I see it is like this." Rachel placed her hands on her hips, swiveling around to face Sharon and Vanessa, as if they too would be included in her plan. "Getting the big project done for Schwartz was such a volcanic load off for you. I say we head out a few days early and go to the Baltimore shows before New Jersey."

As Rachel spoke, Sharon continued to stand by the window, her mouth slightly open. She thought of Tatiana, her delicate white wrists circled by cuffs. Rachel seemed so convincing, Sharon thought. Such a solid person. In build, yes, this was true, that sure was some bosom, but she could tell this woman would be difficult to say no to. Benji leaned back on his elbows and picked at the comforter with the tips of his fingers, watching her.

"My bag's in the car. Did you bring my stuff in, Mom?" Vanessa looked over by the door where Sharon had dropped her overnight bag.

"Hold on," Sharon said, dismissing her, waiting to see what Ben would do next. Then she turned slowly to face Vanessa. "Daddy's got the car."

"You're kidding me," Vanessa said, leaning against the wall. "You're fucking kidding me."

"Oh, what's the big deal, Vanessa?" Sharon said, ignoring the language. "We're going home soon anyway, you can just put on what you wore yesterday."

Benji sucked on his lower lip and stretched his eyes wide, blinking them purposefully at Vanessa. He turned to Rachel. "You know what? That sounds great." He got up and went to his desk, where he picked up his jeans from the chair and pulled them on. He started flinging shirts and socks and underwear onto the bed from his bureau, not altering his rhythm in the least as he threw a T-shirt and a pair of sweatpants at Vanessa, who let each one hit her in the face and slide onto the bed.

Rachel clapped her hands. "Yaay! Yippee!" She went to the closet Ben and Arnie shared and knelt down, her white underpants and the crack of her exposed round bottom appearing above the top of her jeans. She fished out a backpack, which Sharon noticed beneath the tears and patches and bleeds of blue ink to be the same red L.L.Bean backpack she'd ordered for him his sophomore year of high school.

"So we're just going to forget school, then?" Sharon crossed her arms. "Is that it?"

"For a week we are," Benji said. "For a week or ten days we are, yes."

"Ummm." Sharon tapped her bare foot on the carpet. "Are you forgetting I'm your mother? That Dad and I are paying for this school, which is not exactly cheap? Oh, and did you forget that I'm *standing right here?*"

Rachel went over to her. "Gosh, I'm so sorry." Rachel reached out to touch Sharon's shoulder. "I thought Benji had told you about our plans. It's only a few days extra. And classes are winding down before spring break anyhow. You must think I'm a terrible influence!"

Sharon let her head drop to one side and raised her eyebrows.

Benji took the clothes from his bed and began shoving them into the backpack. "She's a good influence, Mom. The best!" He laughed. "Actually, she really is." Benji was terribly relieved that she had come. He forgave her, he forgave her, he *forgave* her! And he hoped that her showing up meant that he too was exonerated.

"Okay, Mrs. Goldstein?"

Ecch, she couldn't stand this girl. Okay? What about breakfast! We need breakfast. A good one, that is, with nutritional value. Remember, Ben? She'd wanted to reach out to him and make him remember all those cold mornings she had stood over the stove because he had a game out of county, before Rachel had even been a thought. And what of the time together we haven't yet spent? The weekend had been spectacularly different from what she'd planned, but she knew there was no getting it back. And she also knew that none of that was this rather presumptuous young woman's fault.

"What can I say? My son's an adult." My son, my son, my son, Sharon thought. She remembered holding him above the ocean at Rehoboth, and swinging him high into the air as the waves came in.

"Well, good, because you're never going to believe this, Benji. Gerald and Anthony are in town! Anthony's girlfriend, Penelope, is a senior, and they're coming over from western Mass.—remember how they were doing their own farming?—to get her and then head down to Baltimore. They called to see if we wanted to go! Well, they called Schaeffer, actually."

Benji stopped for a moment, then continued stuffing his backpack.

"We're meeting them in an hour in the Rosenthal lot. They told Schaeff there's plenty of room for us on the bus."

"Wait," Sharon said, the memory of Benjamin flying above the sea, screaming with unadulterated joy, fading. "There's a bus going to Baltimore?" You know what? She would just tell her children later. Or, no, she wouldn't. Let Dennis do it. Why shouldn't Dennis bear the responsibility of such news? Perhaps, she thought fleetingly, this wasn't even real.

"It's not really a bus, Mom." Benji pulled on a bright blue T-shirt with a peace sign emblazoned on the front. "I mean, it's not an actual bus."

"Yes, it is," Rachel said. "It's absolutely an actual bus, only it's free."

"We need to get a ride back too." Sharon shrugged, shaking off the burden of making a plan that would get Vanessa and her home. "Can we come too?"

"On the hippie bus?" Vanessa slammed back against the headboard. "Mom!"

Rachel giggled. "Oh my God, of course! Wait." She turned to Sharon. "Let's all go to the show together!"

Vanessa sliced the air with the side of her hand. "No! No! We're going to Washington." She pressed her hand to her head. "Where we live," she hissed. "Where I have school."

"Yeah," Benji said. "They need to get home. Mom, I can get you to the train station real easy." He looked purposefully at Rachel, even stamping his bare foot a bit.

"What, Benji?" Rachel said. "It'll be cool."

"Yes, it will," Sharon said, warming to this Rachel. "Why shouldn't we just jump on the bus with you guys?" It sounded fun, though she was also pleased to be torturing her children a little.

"Absolutely! Come with us, and then, who knows, you two might change your minds," Rachel teased, leaning toward Vanessa. "You might just catch the bug."

Vanessa pulled on Benji's sweatpants. *CIA,* they said in white at the right hip, a gift from their father. These sweats were coveted—it was apparently difficult for civilians to get genuine CIA gear.

"Where are your clothes?" Sharon asked.

Vanessa shrugged. "I just feel like wearing something comfortable." She pictured a busload of Deadheads, smelling of patchouli or, worse, BO, the seats covered in bong water and general freak grime, and was glad to be wearing her brother's soft, worn sweats, clothing that did not define her.

Sharon looked at Rachel's chest—*I Need a Miracle!*—and felt her shoulders slacken a bit. I do, she thought. We all do. Because a miracle is the only possibility here.

Dennis hadn't known, he'd promised her. She needed to be assured that they were on the same *side.* But, he'd said, and Sharon's heart had stopped, I can see it now. Once Tatiana went with him to the office. Tatiana and Sigmund had been visiting—and she and Dennis and the kids were going ice-skating on the Mall. Sharon remembered it because she'd been so annoyed. She'd been browning beef for stew and Sigmund was reading the paper in the living room, and they'd all sort of trundled downstairs and into their jackets and said they were heading into town.

What about me? Sharon had wondered as they all left her to cook dinner and tend to her father-in-law.

I don't remember why I left the office with the kids, Dennis said, the heel of his hand at his forehead, as if he were really truly stumped by it. They were teenagers by then, but when we came back in, Mother had a little Minox camera in both hands. He had made a square with four fingers. The kids didn't see it. I know because I asked them later and they said they hadn't seen a thing, that they hadn't seen Mother slip the camera into the pocket of her coat when we walked in. You know, that hideous camel-hair coat, the one she always cinched so tight. They hadn't seen this, so I thought I was imagining it. I had thought, I am a terrible son, to think my mother is stealing documents from me. I am falling prey to the notion that the Soviets are out to get us. I thought, This isn't me. I've been working for the U.S. government too long. This was my *mother;* I couldn't even tell you. He had wiped his nose and turned away from Sharon when he said this. But then it turned out to be true, Dennis had said. Didn't it? He turned to face her. So of course this must mean I have a terrible mother.

Sharon knew she should have reached out and touched him, even the lightest graze of his wrist, but she did not. She thought of Ethel Rosenberg—why hadn't that woman spoken up after they'd killed her husband? She had a moment when she could have saved herself. Her husband was already dead; he would hardly have known. Had she no concern for her children? It seemed to Sharon, she'd need only have whispered a word and she would have been released. But what then would her children have thought? Because now they believed she was a hero. Still her children were on the news, fighting for their parents' innocence. Perhaps, Sharon thought, Ethel Rosenberg had also been looking for a miracle. It was the very opposite of a LEAP!ism, but maybe we all have been searching for miracles, Sharon thought, only we've just been calling them wishes. Or prayers.

"I like this expression." Sharon ran her index finger along her own chest. "It's what we all need, you know? Every day."

Rachel looked down at herself, pulling the cotton fabric out from her stomach to reveal a pleasantly round belly. "Oh, this?" She laughed, a little embarrassed. "It's a Dead song. And it just means I need a ticket," she said. "But let me tell you, Mrs. Goldstein, the Grateful Dead is the biggest miracle of all."

# CHAPTER 20

# The Bus

"Wild!" Sharon exclaimed when the bus pulled into the dorm parking lot. "Vanessa, look!"

Vanessa closed her eyes and wished that she could keep them closed until this hateful day was over.

"Isn't it ferocious, Mrs. G?" Schaeffer, who had just come running out of his building, limbs flailing, said.

"Mrs. G?" Benji said. "And good morning to you, Schaeff."

"I think it's great," Sharon responded, breathing in the warming air as she waited for the bus to stop. "You must be Schaeffer."

"In the flesh. And fair morning to you all."

Benji rolled his eyes.

"Absolutely! You guys should join us for the shows," Schaeffer said, looking over at Vanessa.

She looked straight ahead at the bus. "I can't speak for my mother, but I'm going home." Vanessa saw Schaeffer without all his freak accessories—the stupid hat, the rainbow tie-dye, the dirty bare feet—as he was last night, and she felt a pang of affection for him, the smooth skin of his shoulder at her mouth, the way he held on to her so tightly.

It was a small school bus—what as kids they'd referred to as the short bus, Vanessa noted, though the orange of the surface had been completely painted over with all the dirty clichés of hippiedom. It was covered with multicolored rainbows and waterfalls, and naked girls with flowering crowns, their hair streaming out into swirls of colors. Doves carried messages of peace in their brightly colored beaks, and ladybugs and butterflies crawled and flew over a backdrop of tropical trees and bright bursting suns and stars. Yin-and-yang symbols, peace signs, and a psychedelically rendered American flag appeared randomly

throughout the lush portrait, and in huge bubble letters, the word
*LOVE* arced over the windows. A sign hung over the large windshield.
*FARM,* it stated in green print, stalks of corn and sunflowers peeking
out from behind the letters and at the four corners.

Hippie vomit, Vanessa thought, laughing for a moment at how
vicious she felt about it. But Sharon had never seen anything like it. It's
just perfect, she thought as Anthony, the planetary-science MIT-grad-
turned-organic-soybean-farmer, opened the doors from the driver's
seat. Music and the smell of incense and sandalwood and pot spilled
out.

"Climb on!" Anthony said, grinning widely. He wasn't wearing a
shirt, and his stiff hair hung just below his shoulders.

This, Sharon thought, gathering up her bags and following Schaeffer
up the steps, was what I meant all along.

Vanessa took a deep breath—she hated the smell of patchouli; it was
heavy and overly sweet and, worst of all, contagious—and followed
her mother onto the bus.

"Isn't this just fantastic, honey?" Sharon walked toward the back of
the bus. "They have everything they need, right here. A kitchen! On
the bus!" She grinned crazily at Vanessa.

When Vanessa reached the top step, she saw a few kids already on
the bus: a girl with two long, brown braids and a flowing dress who
was wiping down the sink, and three guys, one of whom reached out
behind Vanessa and gave Rachel a huge hug.

"Hey, Rayche, man, how's it hanging?"

"Great. Just great! Hey, so, this is Benji's little sister, Vanessa." Rachel
pulled on Vanessa's sweatshirt a bit. "And that's Sharon, his mom."

"Hello," Sharon and Vanessa both said.

"This is Gerald," Rachel said. "And Roy, right? That's Roy." She
pointed to a young man seated in the front wearing a macramé beret,
who was whittling a small block of wood into a sailboat.

"Welcome!" Gerald said, looking up from his work.

"Hey, where's Sarah?" Benji asked about their companion from the
fall.

"She ended up hitching out West not long after we saw you guys
this fall. She's living in a tepee outside of Santa Fe, with her boyfriend,
Chunta, that Native American guy who was always grilling all that
pre-show corn?"

Sharon thought of Elias hitchhiking out West and camping out with an Indian woman along the banks of the Rio Grande. A long time ago, that could have been she.

"Yeah, I remember him," Benji said. "I'm sure it is amazing out there. Wow."

"This is Penelope," Gerald said, pointing to the girl with the braids, who turned around, revealing a swollen belly. "She and Anthony are going to have a baby!"

"Whoopee!" Anthony said, turning the massive bus wheel and guiding them out of the lot.

"I'd say," Roy said. "A lot of it."

"Don't I know it!" Anthony said, turning up the tape deck strapped to the dashboard. "Off we go!"

Someone hit the tape deck: *I lit out from Reno, I was trailed by twenty hounds. Didn't get to sleep that night till the morning came around.*

"How far along are you?" Sharon asked, grabbing a seat for balance.

Penelope rubbed her belly in a gesture of confirmation. "Early June."

"Ah, a Gemini then. I have one of those." Sharon smiled at the girl, then brushed Vanessa's hair out of her face.

Vanessa reflexively jerked her head away.

"How cool is that! A baby!" Rachel, said and Vanessa turned then to see Schaeffer, the first to board, seated in the last row.

Sharon turned back, nearly knocking into Vanessa. "Don't you get any ideas!" she said to Benji, but it came out more to Rachel. Vanessa noticed a slight mania to her mother's laugh that indicated she might not be quite as comfortable on this bus as she wanted everyone to believe. "Please, God," Sharon said again, sliding into the next seat. "Don't get any ideas."

"Hey, Vanessa!" Schaeffer called out from the last row. "Come sit back here with me!" He patted the seat next to him.

"Hey," he said as she slid in next to him.

"Hi, guys!" Sharon turned to face Vanessa and Schaeffer. "Isn't this wild?" she said, but the cast was softer, tinged with the nearly undetectable note of fear.

Vanessa tilted her head back.

Schaeffer reached out and massaged her neck. "You sore? Sometimes the acid gets me in the spine."

"No. I'm not sore." Vanessa sat up straight and crossed her arms, just as Anthony hit the campus road. They wound around the back of

Ben's dorm and along the quad, where, when Vanessa turned to the left, she could see several girls lying back in a straight row on the stone ledge of the pond. Their shirts were pulled up to reveal their flat white stomachs and their long hair fell over the narrow wall, their closed eyes facing the sun. The bus passed the art museum and the theater, then started down the hill, toward the highway that would bring her home.

As Anthony pulled the bus off campus and onto South Street—thank the Lord, Vanessa thought, an end to the longest weekend ever!—Schaeffer leaned over the empty seat in front of him and tapped Sharon on the shoulder.

"Hey, Mrs. G," he said.

Sharon turned to face him. "Call me Sharon, Schaeffer. Please." She glanced over at Benjamin across the aisle and one seat ahead, his arm intertwined with Rachel's.

"Sharon then," Schaeffer said. "You don't mind if we smoke out a bit, do you, Sharon?"

"Jesus Christ," Vanessa said.

Sharon smiled. "You should really be asking Vanessa. Do you mind if they smoke, honey?"

Benji laughed.

"What?" Sharon asked. "Vanessa is very committed to her Straight Edge movement."

"Oh my God, oh my *God,* make it stop!" Vanessa said. "No, Mom, I don't mind, okay?"

"We got her to loosen up a little bit last night," Schaeffer said, hitting her on the shoulder.

"Did you?" Sharon asked. "How so?"

"Nothing big or anything," he said.

"Nah, nothing big at all, Schaeffer," Benji said, pulling Rachel closer and looking straight ahead.

"I see," Sharon said, turning back around. Who knew what her kids were up to anymore. Who knew. But there were bigger things now. "Well, I don't mind." She sighed. "Go right ahead."

Schaeffer lit a joint and held it out to Vanessa.

"No thanks," she said.

"Sharon?" Schaeffer asked, leaning over again and holding out the joint.

"Thank you," she said, taking it.

"Mom!" Benji and Vanessa said at the same time.

Sharon took a drag off the joint. "What?" she said, inhaling. She took another hit and passed it to Benji. "I've smoked pot before. How old do you think I am?" Then, as if every cell of her body had always held the memory, Sharon thought of smoking with Dennis after dinner on the porch in Skatesville, then making love beneath a swath of a million stars out back. She tried now to recall more than the image—a photograph of the trees swaying gently, silhouetted over the night sky they lay beneath—but she could not feel the two of them holding on to each other in the grass. The only true memories that Sharon held of her sexual life were of the several times she and Dennis had been interrupted—the time they had sneaked into a bathroom at a party at the Pearlsteins' on New Year's Eve 1967; the time Ben wandered in, teary from a nightmare, and Dennis had rushed to cover her with the quilt—it was only through the eyes of someone else that Sharon could see herself making love. With Elias there had been the fear that Dennis might, however unlikely, rush through the door at any moment, so it allowed her now to picture that first time with him from her husband's perspective and so see it for herself.

Telling Dennis had been stupid; it had been for no other reason than her own unburdening. All this talk of compulsive truth telling that had begun with consciousness-raising was a lot of bullshit, Sharon thought. It was far harder to hold on to a lie, a stone in one's shoe one could not dislodge. They'd been walking around for so long with shoes filled with stones.

Benji passed the joint on to Rachel without taking a hit, and she paused momentarily, uncharacteristically unsure what she should do. Then she merely shrugged and took a drag, then brought it over to Roy, up in front, where it got passed among the guys, including Anthony, Sharon noted, displeased that the driver would be smoking. Penelope, she was relieved to see, was not offered the joint.

Sharon leaned back in her seat and felt a swell of goodwill. The campus receded behind them, and Sharon thought of the last time she'd departed Brandeis, with Dennis, when they'd dropped Ben off at school last September. The drive back home then had been loaded with dread, but despite what she was returning to now, she was filled with hope. Because now everything was split open, wasn't it? Or perhaps she could slip into this world as if she were still that girl fleeing her hometown, that nineteen-year-old student swinging her crossed legs in class at George Washington, smack in the middle of this American century. Jesus Christ, she had friends who douched with Pepsi then.

It was 1958; one month after she arrived, Pasternak had refused the
Nobel Prize. Out of fear. He wrote *Doctor Zhivago* and then refused the
Nobel, so worried was he over being stripped of his Soviet citizenship.
Would Tatiana, she wondered, be able to get home?

Out of the dizzy froth, the malt shop of her college years, the fifties
closing around her, was this notion that she would break free. She'd
had her chance, she thought, and she had not totally blown it. There
had once been a war she had stood up against. Really she was a child
of war; she'd been born just before the bombs had started dropping in
Europe; she had come of age during Korea; her young adulthood was
formed by Vietnam. The Cold War? This was nothing. Sharon's heart
was beating quickly now; she thought of Dennis and wondered where
he was right this minute.

"My mother," he'd said, "has been taken in for spying."

"For what?" Sharon had said. Of all the things she thought he might
tell her when he hung up that phone, of all the tragedies he might have
reported, this was not one she'd ever thought of.

"Spying," Dennis had said. "My mother has been stealing
information and giving it to the Soviets."

Now Sharon began to breathe heavily and struggled to sit up straight
in her seat.

Up front the boys played guitar and sang, *Take up your china doll, take
up your china doll, it's only fractured and just a little nervous from the fall.*

Once more Sharon felt a rush of panic.

"Information," Sharon had said. It had not been a question. Only
now did she wonder what that might have meant.

"Names," Dennis had said. "A talent scout, if you will." He'd almost
laughed.

Now Sharon remembered Tatiana holding that little green beauty
case so tightly, in both hands, beneath her chin. What the hell was
in that thing? She had stolen a look once when Tatti had gone into
town with Dennis and the kids, and it was just lipstick and face
cream and vitamins, tablets of two and three set in a long plastic strip,
compartmentalized for each day of the week.

What, Sharon wondered, what had Tatiana given over? Dennis said
it had been names. Just people, he'd said, as if this made it some kind of
human act. She had heard Dennis this morning: that CHORD Tatiana
had worked for, that record company her husband had been so proud
of, the one that published "Chattanooga Choo Choo" when no other

company would accept the ridiculous name, he'd told her, it was a front. It was all a front.

Now Sharon wished she had asked what information and why and to whom she was giving it and also how. How had she sent on these names?

"You thirsty, Mom?" Ben stood over her. "You want some water?"

Penelope called up from the front, "We also have aloe vera juice that I mixed up myself if you would like, Mrs. G."

"That would be great," she said, momentarily happy about the prospect of nutritional healing as she tried to tamp down, to tamp *down,* this fear.

She could just drop out and go upstate with these kids and grow healthful things; she could sell her half of the business to Marlene with her gold watch and her slow hands and fat ass and her rich corporate tool of a husband, and she could channel Richard Olney and reject this unending governmental use of food as a weapon. But would these kids take her in? She, who had gotten a diaphragm in 1958? She, who came East when she should have stayed out West? She, whose mother-in-law was about to go down in infamy?

"Thanks." She smiled crookedly.

The music was so sweet, so hopeful, impossibly so, she thought, remembering Elias, naked on the bed, his calloused fingertips picking at the strings. She imagined Dennis getting out of the Volvo and walking into the house, head bent toward the ground. She looked out the window as the trees went whipping by along the highway.

Her father might have liked it here, Vanessa thought, surveying the scene on the bus. She blushed a little at the thought of him trying to whittle with Roy up front, singing along, or talking about when he headed out West in a *jalopy,* with his college roommate. She wondered what Len had been like then, because he was not now the kind of man she imagined doing any of those things. He wore a suit and a tie and ignored his children. I'm the man in the moon, he'd say when she asked what his job was. And his hair was so short! Where had this other Len, the cool one, gone?

*Take up your china doll, take up your china doll, it's only fractured and just a little nervous from the fall,* they all sang up front.

China doll, Russian doll. Vanessa thought of the hours of her youth spent unscrewing each part, then pushing each one back together again, the squeak and *thwop* of the two ends sealing. Next to Vanessa,

Schaeffer slapped his fingers on his thighs and moved his head around in no particular direction. He was an idiot. And yet, Vanessa thought now, and yet. It had not been a bad experience; he had been sweet and he had held her from behind as she'd had her negative thoughts—thoughts of Sean and Jason, her bloated belly, kids throwing each other at Ian MacKaye at a Teen Idles show, all cast by the acid in a frightening and unforgettable light—Schaeffer had not budged from his hold.

In front of her Benjamin sat intertwined with his girlfriend, and Vanessa watched him tip his head onto Rachel's shoulder. He ran her hand through his tangled hair. Normally this would have caused Vanessa untold annoyance, yet today it seemed sweet to her that her brother was in love. One day it will be me, Vanessa thought, just as she had each time her brother had biked ahead or driven away or swum farther out to sea. The feeling never left her, and just now as she felt that nuanced pain at the tip of her heart that told her, let him go on ahead, it's okay, one day it will be you who gets to the center of the ocean first, she knew that her brother wasn't going back. He would stay on this bus for as long as it, like Rachel, would hold him.

She tapped Schaeffer on the shoulder and he turned to her.

"Hey," he said, tilting his head.

"Hi," she said, smiling at him, her mouth closed. She put her hand on his knee, then, seeing her bitten fingernails and bloody cuticles, she shrank back. "Maybe I will smoke a bit after all."

"Sure. No problem, Sister Goldstein."

She leaned back in her seat. "I mean, it is going to be a fucking long ride."

Sharon could smell her daughter smoking pot. She felt her body tensing, and as she looked out the window, she massaged her left shoulder, thinking how only yesterday she had been climbing steadily north in her powder blue Volvo. What would she have thought to see this bus rambling alongside her? She would have thought it was a bus full of youth.

This is what she'd meant, *this,* this crazy bus, *this* journey was what she'd intended when she'd gone in for LEAP! training. It's why she'd had the prescience to understand that synagogue was not the place for her just then, because what, in the end, had not been written there? It was age-old, like grief, and Sharon wanted everything new: new trails, new politics, a new man. But she'd come out with what? Some discarded mantras as soothing as these songs. Awakened desire. She missed then the slow wail of the shofar blowing, and the thought of a congregation rapt in prayer gripped her.

Still, after over two months, her arm felt like a wound scraped open. But there was comfort in the steady hum of the wheels along the asphalt of the road and in Anthony's occasional yelps of joy. In watching Benjamin nod off in the smooth curve of his girlfriend's neck. She was glad he'd found someone. Someone real. Was it possible for the heart to relax? Because she felt hers let go, the mad thumping easing to a tolerable beat. She ran her tongue over her teeth, her jaw loosening, the muscles in her neck going slack. Opening her hands wide and extending her fingers, she could see the half-moon imprints of her fingernails stamped inside her palms.

She stretched loudly. "Anybody hungry?" she yelled out.

Benji jumped, and Rachel gently pressed his head back down.

Gerald and Anthony screamed "Yes!" at the exact same time.

Sharon slid out of her seat, and touching the backs of the ripped leather seats for balance, she walked to the front of the bus, behind the driver's seat, where several of the seats had been pulled out and a sink and a stove and a few cabinets for storage beneath had been fashioned in their place.

She opened the latched cabinet above the sink, where the dried goods were stored, and, contemplating the plastic jars of dried beans and peanut butter, she took out the jar of whole-wheat spaghetti, placed it on the counter, and held it steady as she knelt down. She touched the containers in the cabinet below: flour, sugar, a large plastic bucket filled with vegetables. These must be from their farm, Sharon thought, examining the zucchini, the skin a beautiful striated light green, not spongy like supermarket squash. The carrots and leeks and turnips and radishes still had dirt in their fine, extensive, delicate roots.

Vanessa watched her mother catch herself with her hands, the plastic pasta jar bouncing on the floor as the bus changed lanes. She reluctantly got out of her seat, slapping Schaeffer on the leg as she moved to help. "You okay, Mom?" she asked as she made her way toward the front of the bus, picking up the jar on her way.

"I'm good!" Sharon said, standing. She began to wash the zucchini and the carrots. "Want to find a big pot, hon?"

Vanessa stood next to her mother.

"It's below," Penelope said, rising from her seat. She hooked her hand to her hip so it fanned out at the small of her back.

"Sit!" Vanessa said, retrieving the pot. "I got it."

Her mother filled the pot with water and placed it on a burner.

"It's all right," Penelope said, joining them at the already crowded sink. "I like to cook."

"Me too," Sharon said.

"She has a catering business," Vanessa told Penelope.

Sharon was caught off guard by the pride in her daughter's tone.

"Really! Cool." Penelope laid out a hand towel for Sharon to place the vegetables on as she finished washing them, then set down a cutting board. "There's another one here." Penelope pointed below again, and Vanessa retrieved it. "I sometimes take this board"—she reached behind the closest seat—"and place it over the seats."

"How do you want these chopped, Mom?" Vanessa asked, taking several zucchini and onions from Penelope. It had been a while since Vanessa had sat on those orange kitchen stools as her mother chopped and hummed. It had been many years.

"Everything diced," Sharon said, violently smashing garlic cloves. "Penelope, onions first for the sauce. Vanessa, the carrots. I'll add the zucchini in a bit."

Benji woke from his nap to the sound of his mother hurling instructions over the drum space of a Dead bootleg and to the smell of sizzling onions.

Benji unstuck himself from Rachel and wiped a bit of spittle from the curve of her neck. "Where are we?" he called up front.

"Just north of New York City," Anthony screamed back.

"Smells yummy," Rachel said, straightening.

Benji imagined himself alone with her in the far reaches of her unknowable body. He leaned over. "I just want to say," he said into her ear, "that nothing happened with Alice." He wiped the hair off his forehead. "It was spiteful, I know, leaving the party that way. I mean, I was angry about you not showing yesterday, but it was cold, and nothing happened. I mean, I stopped myself."

Rachel was smiling disingenuously. "Oh, I know. Otherwise I wouldn't be here with you."

"Oh, really."

"Hm hmmm."

He'd seen Rachel's face as he was leaving the party, and though he had been pleased at the time to have made her feel as badly as she'd made him feel, he wished he could take it back now. "So you totally trusted me the whole time?"

"Sure."

"You are amazing. One of the many reasons I love you." He kissed her on the cheek.

"Sure."

Benji pulled back and cocked his head. "Sure? Sure what?"

"Sure I trust you," she said, still grinning.

"Well, good. You know you really could have come to the rally. It was totally fucked that you didn't come."

"Besides"—she turned away to look at the window, ignoring him—"Alice already told me."

"You talked to Alice?" Benji remembered her giggling at his desk, her ass hitting the play button on the answering machine. He couldn't really say what would have happened had Rachel's voice not been piped into the room.

"Of course I did!" Rachel turned back to face Benji. "Something wrong with that?"

Benji took Rachel's hand on his lap and leaned back in his seat. "Of course not." He braced himself for a lecture on female solidarity. He paused, but thankfully that lecture didn't come.

He would never leave her, would never let her go, and now he pictured her out West somewhere, dancing barefoot in the desert or beneath a forest canopy. She wore a flowing dress, a garland of flowers wrapped around her head, not unlike the woman in the commercial for her shampoo, not unlike, he remembered now, that woman on the Mall so many years ago, wrapped up in leaves and flowers, everything about her a flowing tribute to peace but for her angry red mouth.


Penelope scooped the pasta onto paper plates, and Sharon expertly ladled her sauce and vegetables over each portion. Carefully walking through the aisle, Vanessa passed the plates, and Gerald took a six-pack of Pabst from the minifridge and began throwing cans of beer to waving hands.

"Sharon, this is wonderful!" Penelope said when she'd sat down.

"You're a great cook!" Gerald said, inhaling his food. "You should come on the road with us and do the cooking."

Sharon took a deep breath and felt a satisfying sense of accomplishment as she picked up her own plate of pasta. "That's an idea. But I did have some help today." She balanced her plate in one hand as she moved back to her seat. Indeed, she thought, twirling the spaghetti around her fork and piercing a zucchini, I have had the help of many.

★  ★  ★

Gerald was dead asleep, the dirty soles of his bare feet turned up in
the aisles, Roy held his completed sailboat in the air and mimicked a
ship sailing rough waters, and Vanessa and Schaeffer chatted away in
the back as Benji, who had taken over the wheel, steered them back
onto 95 for the rest of the journey to Baltimore. The monotonous East
Coast highway gave him too much time to think. About last night,
his sister unfastening, a loose shoelace he had not knelt to help tie.
He remembered lying out back in the dark with her a few years back.
Then she was a girl with freckles, and he was a kid who played soccer at
the high school. But he had shed his skin when he'd come to college;
it had felt right, and this now was another layer peeled back, only now
was he discovering that *this* layer was the real layer. I am a person who
believes in following my bliss. I will not judge anyone, and in return I
hope that others will do the same.

As he drove south, through Delaware and into Maryland, a landscape
mired in sameness, Benji imagined being out West, with Rachel,
and the way you know where you are, because nature tells you so.
He imagined Colorado, evergreens jutting out along the highway; he
saw New Mexico's sky hanging low before him; in Utah, he'd heard,
the landscape changed by the moment. Soon—within the hour, he
thought, checking the clock that was strapped to the dashboard like
a ticking bomb—he would drop Vanessa and his mother off at the
bus terminal in Baltimore, then he would pull into the parking lot of
the show, and only then would he be himself. He could already hear
the sound of the band warming up; it was light and flighty; fireflies
blinked to the open tuning. He saw the good, great people dancing in
the stadium, night coming in and blanketing them, everyone together.
In this, Benji thought, picking up speed, I can disappear. There was so
much to choose from, an unbroken chain of goodness and music, and
in this, thought Benji, I will be exactly the person I am meant to be.

"Here we are!" Benji said. Several homeless people were sprawled out
on the benches in front of the grimy depot windows, their faces turned
toward the sun.

He stood. "I'll walk you guys in. Make sure you get your tickets and
everything."

"Okay, honey," Sharon said.

"You don't have to do that. We're big girls." Vanessa watched Ben at the driver's seat. She imagined him dancing, arms thrown akimbo, eyes shut, amid a mass of people.

Sharon turned around. "He wants to, Vanessa," she said.

Vanessa shrugged and followed them, waving to Schaeffer once her mother and Benji had stepped off. He blew her a kiss just as she turned back to look at the ridiculous hippiemobile, which, as she took in a final view of it, actually had its charm. It wasn't terribly original—it just needed an orange soda bottle plastered on it to be transformed into a commercial for Fanta—but it was sweet, and the drawings were good. There was nothing *wrong* with it, per se.

The bus to D.C. was leaving in a little over an hour. Sharon went to the depot entrance where Ben and Vanessa stood, clasping two tickets to Union Station.

"Do you want us to wait?" Benjamin looked at his watch.

"No, that's okay," Sharon said. "Bye, honey." She placed her hands on his cheeks and brought her face close to his. "Have a great time, okay?"

The children didn't know! They could still have fun tonight. How would she tell them what awaited them in tomorrow's papers? *I need a miracle;* she thought of Rachel's T-shirt, the rise of her breasts pressing against the truism. That French bat touching down, lightning on the clearest night, a château on a black hill; these were ghosts, and they were miracles. I will not look at this as how it should have turned out between us. How my marriage should have turned out. I have made the best choices available to me. I have tried to live my life authentically, she thought, and she pictured her mother emerging onstage out of a puff of smoke in a long blue satin dress.

"Bye, Mom," Ben said, his eyes cast downward as she looked so intently into his eyes. He hugged her.

When she let him go, he turned to hug Vanessa. "Bye, Van."

"Fucking hippie," she said into his ear. She loved the smell of him. It was her smell and not her smell at all.

"Yeah, yeah. I can tell how much you hate us." He slapped her cheek lightly. "You can keep the sweats," he said as he turned back to the bus.

He slid into the driver's seat, waved, and pulled the bus doors shut. "Onward!" he shouted, pulling onto the street, toward the highway from where they'd come.

Vanessa and Sharon stood silently, arms at their sides, as they watched the bus drive away.

# CHAPTER 21

# Spring

Tatiana sat between two officers, her hands placed one over the other on the metal desk. No lawyer was with her. This was what Gary had promised: You may see her before we take her to the Department of Justice, he'd said, and even then Dennis had pictured them driving her over the bridge and just leaving her there. And then what? You may see her before we take her, and your father may see her. There will, Gary had said, be officers present.

One such officer took Dennis's arm, the other his father's, and they both lowered themselves gingerly into their seats across from her.

"Where have you been?" Sigmund leaned forward. He wore a navy suit and a green-and-blue-striped tie, and despite the puffiness beneath his eyes and the hanging flesh at his cheeks and neck, he looked like the man Dennis remembered disappearing into a crowd. "Tatiana," he said, "it's been days. I've been looking for you. All over the neighborhood." Sigmund leaned back. "No one has seen you."

Dennis was suddenly furious. How long had his mother been taking from him? Since the day he'd walked into his office to find her slipping a camera into the pocket of that hideous coat? He knew that's what his mother had done. He knew that now. Had he known it then?

She had to have been aware of how damaging this could be for him. Do you know a Herndon Skye? Gary had said. Don't tell me, he'd said, just as Dennis was about to say he had no idea who this person was. This was the name in a batch of cookies. That's what Gary had told him on the phone, and that's when Dennis had remembered that asshole in his blue polyester suit eating a tuna fish sandwich over the Landsat images. Your mother named the wrong guy this time, that's for sure, Gary had said, and Dennis pictured Herndon Skye, the Republican holdover, hardly amenable, wiping watery mayonnaise off the glossy surface, dulling the sheen in the napkin's wake.

Those meringues, his mother's hands gathered together at the tips, dropping cherries into the egg whites, mounds of egg whites, like the view of mountains from a plane. He and his sister had pushed them into white peaks in the bowl. The cookies held all the information, Gary had told him. Dennis remembered looking over at Sharon in the dark of that hotel room, willing Gary to stop speaking. It was the last time she could know nothing. He had not known the moment before the call would be his last to know nothing, and so he watched his wife blinking in her final seconds of ignorance. Those cookies. His mother brought them out on plates, browned at the edges, like burned paper, stacked high on the plate. Invisible ink, Gary said, you gotta hand it to her. Inside each one, a note. I see, Dennis had said. Sharon's head was silhouetted in the dark, her hair swept over one shoulder, and he could sense her moment of innocence ending as fear began to etch its way into her brow. It hovered around her like a magnetic field, but it did not reach out to touch him.

Only after Dennis had hung up the phone and laid this all on Sharon had he remembered why he'd left the office that day with the kids. It was to go to the supply closet for a new typewriter ribbon. They were goofing around on the typewriter, the way he used to at his mother's office. And Ben wanted Wite-Out to take home, but Dennis wouldn't let him take it. Because that's stealing from the government, he'd said. And we don't steal, he'd told his son.

Stupid, insignificant Herndon Skye. Isn't it always this way? He'd heard Jerome Mooney had gotten caught merely on the most microscopic trail of apple juice on the documents returned. Mooney had a place in New York State—he was always bringing bushels of Golden Delicious into the office for the secretaries. Soon as they detected the juice traces they printed him. Dennis imagined his mother photographing the names from the contact list Glinda had typed and clipped to the Landsat folder. It is always the smallest things that do us in; Dennis thought of those green guitar picks falling out of the folded envelope in Sharon's drawer. Had the folder been on his desk? Or had his mother been sent by Misha to search for it?

He had been so stupid about Misha! How would a Jew stay so decidedly safe in the Soviet Union? That was all his mother had said.

Had he simply accepted it because his mother had told him so? He had doubted every single thing his father had told him. But his mother he had never questioned. Gary had said the cookies were going to a Misha Baskov. Do you know him? No, he didn't know him! He had no idea who this man was! But his mother had, it seemed. How long? How did it work exactly, this invisible line of communication, a game of telephone even through the Iron Curtain? Dennis might never know.

How could his mother have let him believe this man was his uncle? She was so resistant to giving him Misha's address! Yet he had pressed and pressed and she had relented; he had gone shopping for his kid with him, a KGB agent, for Christ sake. Pick this one, he'd said, at the store just above the grand GUM fountain where they'd cut in front of the enormous queue. He'd pointed to a box with a troika scene, not the golden rooster Dennis had chosen. He thought of following behind Misha now, through those streets, the Kremlin's towers rising ahead. The Bolsheviks, Dennis had said, and Misha had bent his head. It had looked as if he was laughing. Dennis had been thinking of his father when he'd asked, How many Bolsheviks are buried there? Had Misha been laughing? At him? When Dennis hung up the phone at the Ritz, he remembered that night he'd sensed trouble in Moscow—turned out this Misha would have known exactly what he should have done after his slip at dinner. And Boris? Dear, fat, drooling Boris who lifted him in his arms and skated with him across the rink at Rockefeller Center? Boris was not himself either. None of them were, so what did that make them?

And his mother? She was not the weak woman she had always seemed, hiding her glossy magazines beneath the mattress when Sigmund came home; tentatively ringing doorbells to smile so fucking sweetly for the New Deal, for crippled, privileged, adulterous, pioneering Roosevelt. Or perhaps this was the heart of weakness; perhaps inside that door, she was breaking. Perhaps she was breaking now.

Dennis turned to watch the driver go, knowing he'd be waiting outside when he emerged, for his own questioning, then the briefing. Because of course there would be a briefing—beyond this he couldn't fathom. It was out of his realm of experience, now that it was clear that some of the information had been from Agriculture. He had not been able to talk to his father to tell him, No matter what, you didn't know.

Tell them—and please, God, tell me—you knew nothing. We know nothing. Say it over and over and over so you do not fuck it up. Now is not the time to stand up for anything. Now is nothing. Now is the time to protect your family with nothing.

Dennis looked back to the table. Sometimes his mother used to cry as she separated the eggs. Dennis had thought then, What will she do with all those insides? His sister would torment him by saying each yolk was a dead chicken. His mother filled bowls of them; he remembered her weeping over the mixing bowl, and he had thought, not wrongly perhaps, that she was missing her home.

Again Dennis willed his father's silence. Please, God, and then, as if it had been in every memory he'd held, he thought of praying, the hard pews, someone knowledgeable and good and righteous interpreting the past for him so that the present would have meaning. He wished then that he had given Benjamin the chance to decide for himself if those stories held true. He remembered watching his son singing at the Torah, his voice breaking with adolescence, and he tried to offer this gesture up to God now, not all the petty things Dennis had done that had belittled Him, those acts had been performed less against God than those who always seemed to rally around Him. It was God's organizers whom Dennis had protested with the midday Yom Kippur break fasts and the Hebrew-school car-pool boycotts. Please, God, Dennis thought now, my goodness, please, make sure he says nothing. My father has talked his whole life; today please silence him.

"Well, now you see where I've been." Tatti looked down and rubbed the top of her hand with her thumb.

"Mom, it's highly unusual that they are letting us see you now." Dennis looked from side to side, to make sure his mother acknowledged the presence of the officers. They were in blue suits like his father's and they were waiting. In a matter of moments they would take her. "They have let us see you before they decide what will happen. But I'm not going to ask you"—again Dennis looked at the officers—"if any of what they say is true." He was treating his mother as he always had, as an immigrant who needed help deciphering street signs, who needed assistance reading the back of a can of soup, with ordering the prune hamantaschen from the Jewish bakery. All the other women on the block made their own. But his mother bought her hamantaschen at Purim when huge stacks were piled high in the window of Moishe's Kosher Bake Shop all the way on Second Avenue. He had always thought she was so lost in this world. Had she been acting? Or had she been that woman also? He pictured a Russian doll—like the one he'd picked out with Misha for Vanessa—so many pieces inside to make it whole.

Tatti shrugged. The corners of her mouth turned down to tell him, What do I care now? It was Ethel Rosenberg's face, only it was so much older. This was what happened to a face that had not been caught in time. It was Stalin's face. It was his mother's face, the face she wore when he and his sister banded together to inform her, no, they were not staying inside to study as they had told their father, they were going out instead to the pool, to Pitt Street, where even now he could see those girls in their white swimming suits, preening and reading their movie magazines. Dennis and his sister would walk down Orchard Street with their stiff white towels and their bottles of Coca-Cola, and the promise of that day was as lost to him now as anything he could name.

"Okay, Mom," Dennis said in Russian. "You okay?"

"I don't understand where you've been," Sigmund said, and Dennis could not tell if he was serious. "You went out for eggs and you never came home. The house, it's a disaster. And I don't know how to make the rice! I put in what I thought was the right amount, and I have enough now for an army. It's all gone bad. I've spoiled the rice. Such a waste."

Tatti nodded. The face, his mother's face, said, I have been beaten, but this? This is nothing. You would never have known Ethel Rosenberg had children had they not been dragged in and out of Sing Sing to visit her. They carried signs that said *Don't Kill My Mommy and Daddy*. Had the older one not written a letter to Eisenhower that Dennis had read in the *New York Herald Tribune,* you would not have known she was a mother from her face.

Dennis put his hand over his mouth, but he said nothing. He pictured his father sweating over a stove; he imagined him walling himself in that apartment with his papers and his books and his ill will. How would he dig his way out? Or maybe it was better inside there, inside those books, Dennis thought, inside the closed tenement of his childhood where he'd played the clarinet; he could still feel the reed against the tip of his tongue as he wet it before playing. *Live your life taking chances. Commit yourself in your hopes and your dreams!* Dennis had buckled beneath the weight of that demand, and now he had no idea what would become of him. Everyone will soon know. The president will know. There was Carter at his desk: *an unbreakable chain,* he'd said when he'd announced the embargo in that ridiculous Southern accent, and Dennis had laughed at him. Who knew what would happen? The farmers were ruined. The Soviets were not suffering. But his mother, apparently, was a spy.

Tatiana looked at her husband and smiled. "Sigmund," she said so certainly, so surely. This woman who had been scared to go out into the street alone. She had looked up at the Empire State Building holding her hat like a refugee, every time. And that office was a front! Boris didn't go to Hollywood; Boris *fled*. But today her voice was serene and low, and Dennis remembered her telling him stories before bed: *And then her feet began to melt beneath her.* She'd bent over him, a hard shell surrounding his soft child's body, and she'd whispered in his ear, in Russian, *She fell onto the earth and then the Snow Maiden was gone.* "This is something I've never told you," she said now, looking deliberately at each officer's elbow. "I never said this, but I cannot forget a face, believe me I have tried many times, but I can't. And that day, Sigmund, when we met at the Workers Party meeting, do you remember?"

Sigmund fidgeted in his seat and nodded. "Of course," he said.

"It's okay." Tatiana waved her hand in Dennis's direction. "This is not against the law. So we were at a meeting? Many of us were. We were all young then, and we met at that Workers Party meeting, and I tell you, it was Helen on the stage that night. It was no more Ethel Rosenberg than a black bear singing. How could you not have remembered? Helen was in the front singing, and I tell you, she had a beautiful voice, very low, unusual for a woman, I remember. I remember everything! We were all screaming with happiness! Don't you remember?"

Dennis looked over at his father, who gripped both padded arms of the metal chair—it was impossible not to acknowledge the image— and he nodded slowly.

"You were there!" Tatti said. "You were going to be very big in the party then. You were so excited and everyone wanted to hear what you—you!—had to say. Herbert Weissman was there too."

Dennis watched one of the officers take down the name.

"Did you know this?" Tatti said. "He was there this night too. I can still see him helping Helen down from the little stage when she was done with her singing. They were not married then, and he nodded at me before they left; I can never forget that. I cannot forget that because I almost approached him. I liked his hat very much, and so I

almost went up to him and offered the money like we were trained."
She nodded her head deliberately. "Yes, so what, we were trained.
Greetings from Fanny, we would say to the ones who were expecting
it. Sometimes they came to the music office. At the Empire State.
Remember, Dennis?" She looked at him.

Dennis nodded. Then, without thinking, he asked, "Was Misha a
musician?"

Tatiana smiled at the side of her mouth and looked at the officers.
"He was. He was very good, I heard. And Boris was a wonderful skater
too. We had fun together, didn't we?"

Dennis sat back.

"But this night. I almost approached Herbert this night because he
seemed like he was waiting, and I thought perhaps he would say the
right answer, How is she, how is Fanny? And it would be done and I
would have done my job well that night and I would be praised. He did
something, though, and this I don't remember, but it was a gesture of a
kind that made me realize he was not expecting my approach, though
he did seem like a man who would not refuse money. And yet I didn't
touch his arm. Why not? Why did I instead turn to you, to you, who
already I could tell was a man of ideas? You were living in your head, if
not a little bit your heart. But it was all of us there that night; we were
all there together."

Tatiana cleared her throat and looked up at the ceiling. For a moment
Dennis thought it was to keep the tears from rolling down her face, but
her eyes were dry.

"I said to you, Do you want to share secrets? Just like that, I said this
to you. Only you thought I meant my own, Sigmund, didn't you?"

Dennis looked at his father, still frozen in his bureaucratic,
governmental, piece-of-shit seat. Don't they have a decent *chair* in
here?

Tatti looked at her husband, then at her son. Her face was long and
white. Her hair was still so red, she couldn't really be dyeing it, could
she?

"I'm sorry if I have hurt you. Don't think that I did not love my
family. I did. I do." She was calmer than Dennis had ever seen her; had
he made up her fear? This was not his mother. This had never been she.
That person he had spent his youth translating for did not exist. "I love
my family. It's different now. I'm so much older now. The world has
changed; some things we outgrow. Our own principles, we are always

testing them, no? I woke up one day and found I had not outgrown my beliefs." She stood up, and as she did, so did the agents flanking her. This was it. This was all. "But back then, you thought I meant secrets of the heart," she said to her husband, leaning in before leaving the room. "But, darling, my darling, I was talking about a country."

Dennis stood and looked at his father, who seemed momentarily unable to rise. His mother was leaving. A slip of light came streaming through the window. It seemed so sudden, but perhaps the sunlight had been there since they'd entered the room. His father was still seated. She was going now, then she would be gone. Like winter. What a brutal winter it had been. The few times Dennis had thought it might be nice to do so, the weather had been too cold for skating. But now it was spring. Please, he thought. Get up. It was 1980. Dennis went to help his father out of his chair. Where, Dennis wondered, are we supposed to go from here?

# Acknowledgments

I am indebted to many texts, especially E. L. Doctorow's wonderful novel *The Book of Daniel,* Allen Weinstein and Alexander Vassilicv's *The Haunted Wood,* and Irving Howe's *Socialism and America.* But there are always certain details that a novelist can't get exactly right on her own, despite her research. For these I am grateful to Linda Viertel for sharing her extensive knowledge of cooking and cookbooks in the seventies, and to Gus Schumacher and Chris Goldthwait for describing what it might have been like to work at USDA at that time. Thank you to my family friend in the CIA who I don't think would want to be mentioned by name (that's why it's the CIA . . . ), to Lara Vapnyar for fixing my "little Russian mistakes," and to Laurie Brown and André Bernard for their spy-novel schooling. I am also indebted to Nina Revoyr, always one of my most stalwart first readers, and to Peter Cohen, Emily Chenoweth, Jen Haller, and Adam Langer for help with early drafts. Thank you to Pedro Barbeito, who has always read with patience and encouragement, and who, during the writing of this book, listened to music with earphones and painted very quietly as we shared a workspace, and managed to remain married. I'm grateful to Wendy Sheanin, director of marketing at Simon, who, since the moment I turned this book in, has been such a big supporter. And thank you, thank you to Jenn Joel, my agent, who has championed this novel from its tentative first pages, and to Alexis Gargagliano, my fairy-tale editor come true.

# About the Author

Jennifer Gilmore's first novel, *Golden Country,* was a *New York Times* Notable Book of 2006 and a finalist for the National Jewish Book Award and the *Los Angeles Times* Book Prize. She currently teaches at Eugene Lang College The New School for Liberal Arts and lives in Brooklyn, New York.